"You do look like a pirate, you know," Bess said.

"And you look like a wanton."

Bess felt herself flush with anger. "Perhaps we are neither of us what we seem. It is your sword arm I wish to hire, nothing else."

He grinned wolfishly. "Good. For as well formed as ye may be, I've no interest in any lass who fancies herself a man."

"Are you always so crude?"

"Aye. Ye may as well get used to it, for I step aside for no man, and I take sass from no woman."

If You Enjoyed This Book,
Be Sure to Read These Other
AVON ROMANTIC TREASURES

COMANCHE WIND *by Genell Dellin*
MASTER OF MOONSPELL *by Deborah Camp*
SHADOW DANCE *by Anne Stuart*
THEN CAME YOU *by Lisa Kleypas*
VIRGIN STAR *by Jennifer Horsman*

Coming Soon

FASCINATION *by Stella Cameron*

Avon Books are available at special quantity discounts for bulk purchases for sales promotions, premiums, fund raising or educational use. Special books, or book excerpts, can also be created to fit specific needs.

For details write or telephone the office of the Director of Special Markets, Avon Books, Dept. FP, 1350 Avenue of the Americas, New York, New York 10019, 1-800-238-0658.

FORTUNE'S FLAME

JUDITH E. FRENCH

An Avon Romantic Treasure

AVON BOOKS ◆ NEW YORK

If you purchased this book without a cover, you should be aware that this book is stolen property. It was reported as "unsold and destroyed" to the publisher, and neither the author nor the publisher has received any payment for this "stripped book."

FORTUNE'S FLAME is an original publication of Avon Books. This work has never before appeared in book form. This work is a novel. Any similarity to actual persons or events is purely coincidental.

AVON BOOKS
A division of
The Hearst Corporation
1350 Avenue of the Americas
New York, New York 10019

Copyright © 1993 by Judith E. French
Inside cover author photograph by Theis Photography, Ltd.
Published by arrangement with the author
Library of Congress Catalog Card Number: 93-90328
ISBN: 0-380-76865-8

All rights reserved, which includes the right to reproduce this book or portions thereof in any form whatsoever except as provided by the U.S. Copyright Law. For information address Joyce Flaherty Literary Agency, 816 Lynda Court, St. Louis, Missouri 63122.

First Avon Books Printing: October 1993

AVON TRADEMARK REG. U.S. PAT. OFF. AND IN OTHER COUNTRIES, MARCA REGISTRADA, HECHO EN U.S.A.

Printed in the U.S.A.

RA 10 9 8 7 6 5 4 3 2 1

For our beloved daughter, Debbie,
who taught me so much about determination, courage,
and a mother's love.
Your father and I are so proud of you.

There is nothing more painful than the insult to human dignity, nothing more humiliating than servitude.

Human dignity and freedom are our birthright. Let us defend them or die with dignity.

CICERO

Prologue

Maryland's Eastern Shore
December 1724

"If that murderer crosses my path, I'll see him in hell or Virginia—whichever's closest!"

Bold words, and worthy of the mistress of Fortune's Gift, she thought. But it was one thing to utter them in the warmth of a friend's cabin, and quite another to consider her bravado as she rode home alone. Here, on this dark trail, her rash boast rang hollow.

Bess, Lady Elizabeth Lacy Bennett, shivered in the raw wind and hunched low over her mare's neck, shielding her eyes against the needles of driving sleet. The flintlock pistol tucked inside her coat was cold and hard—a constant reminder of the threat that caused her to carry a lethal weapon on her own land.

The mare flattened her ears against her head and quickened her pace on the icy dirt lane. Bess patted the horse's neck and spoke soothingly to her. "Easy, Ginger. You're as anxious to be out of this weather as I am, aren't you?"

The animal snorted and shied sideways at a tumbling branch. Bess's heart rose in her throat, but she moved instinctively with the horse, keeping her balance despite her fright. Chuckling at her own foolishness, she hugged the mare. "Now I'm starting at shadows," she murmured. "Like as not, that escaped convict is across the bay and moving west as fast as his feet will take him."

Nevertheless, she wished that she'd waited for her overseer, Tom, to return before she'd set out to help with the delivery of Sally Walker's baby. Since Mabel had died of old age, there was no midwife within thirty miles. Sally was past thirty and had nothing to show for fifteen years of marriage but three stillborn infants. The Walkers were good neighbors, and it would have taken a crueler heart than hers to deny Sally a woman's aid.

Bess smiled as she remembered the lusty cry of young Moses Walker. Whatever had taken the lives of Sally's earlier babes, this boy-child was fat and strong. He weighed as much as Alice Horsey's twin girls put together.

"This one will live to cause you gray hairs," Bess had promised Sally. Her friend's joyous expression as she looked down into the round face of a living son had made Bess's journey worthwhile.

Sally's husband, Big Moses, had offered to escort her home. "It's not safe fer a lady to be out at night," he'd said. "Not wit dat wild man on the loose."

She'd not wished Sally to be left alone so soon after childbirth, so she'd refused his company. "I'll be fine," she'd assured him. "These two need your attention more than I do."

Big Moses' brown face would have been a comfort to her now, she thought as she summoned up the image of his muscular shoulders and huge hands that could drive a broadax through oak logs for ten hours at a stretch. Not even an escaped convict would dare to accost her with Big Moses at her side.

The wind shrieked through the trees, and Bess's teeth began to chatter. It was unlike her to be so fearful; she'd ridden the plantation alone since she was a child, both day and night and in all kinds of weather. But tonight . . . She shivered and wiped melting ice off her face with the back of a gloved hand. Tonight she couldn't shake a premonition of impending danger.

"Shades of my grandmother," she murmured to herself. Patting Ginger's neck again, she raised her voice and spoke bravely to the horse. "Not far now, girl. Once we're through this stretch of woods—"

An unholy war cry rent the night.

Ginger reared up on her hind legs and before Bess could react, a heavy weight struck her and knocked her out of the saddle onto the frozen ground. Her chin slammed against the road, and for an instant, she lay there stunned. The weight rolled off her, and a shadow lunged toward the shying horse.

"Whoa!"

Bess's mind cleared. Someone was trying to steal her horse! She reached for her pistol and realized that she'd lost it in the fall. "Take your thieving hands off my mare!" she yelled as she scrambled to her feet and launched herself at the bandit's back.

"What the—" The outlaw's protests were cut off as Bess locked her hands around his neck. She tried to encircle his waist with her legs, but the bulk of her riding skirt made it impossible. He slammed an elbow into her middle, knocking the wind out of her. She gasped and tumbled backward.

The man caught one dangling rein. Ginger reared up again, then whirled and kicked at him. Bess recovered and dove at the backs of his knees. He went down and she hit him as hard as she could with her fists.

He was still holding the mare's rein. Bess jerked the leather from his hand and ran toward her horse. She'd got one foot in the stirrup when he seized her shoulder and yanked her around. He drew back a fist to strike her, then stopped and let out a yelp of laughter.

"A lass, by God!" He locked one arm around her waist and dragged her, kicking and punching, away from the horse.

"Let go of me!" she screamed. He loomed over her, taller by a head than she was, and as strong as an ox. Hitting him was as useless as striking a barn door. She couldn't see his face in the shadows, but a mass of fair, tangled hair hung loose to his shoulders, giving him a savage appearance.

"Aye, lass, I'll let go o' ye, as soon as ye quit knockin' hell out o' me."

His heavy Scots burr penetrated her anger, and Bess's heart sunk to her boots. There was no doubt in her mind that this was the escaped convict whom half the Tidewater had been hunting. A yellow-haired Scotsman, they'd said, standing six feet tall.

She drew in a shuddering breath and stopped struggling.

"That's better," he said. "I mean ye no harm, woman, but I have grave need of your horse."

"You'll hang for this. Do you know who I am?"

"I care not. You're English, and that's all that matters," he said harshly.

He loosened his grip on her waist, and she broke

free and backed away from him. She'd bitten her
lip when she'd fallen from the horse, and she tasted
the salt of blood in her mouth. She was so frightened she could hardly get her breath, but the
thought of this brute stealing Ginger made her forget her fear. "She's mine, and I won't let you have
her," she retorted. "I raised her from a foal."

"It's my neck or your mare." He shrugged and
spread his hands palms up.

Bess swallowed hard and she noticed an iron
manacle fastened around one sinewy wrist. She
took another step backward and the heel of her
boot struck something hard on the trail. Her pistol? Her long riding habit covered the object; tentatively, she nudged it.

"You'll nay hold it against me if I choose my own
life," he continued. His deep voice rumbled up from
a broad chest as arrogantly as though he owned the
ground he stood on and she was the intruder.

She faced him squarely. "Surrender yourself,
sir. If you come peaceably with me, I'll see you
have a fair trial."

He laughed. "Before my hanging?"

"Who are you?" She stalled, playing for time.
Perhaps Big Moses had followed her . . . or maybe
Tom would ride back this way. She listened, hoping against hope that she would hear hoofbeats
on the frozen road.

But the only thing she heard was the mocking
cry of the winter wind, rattling through the
branches overhead.

"I've nay time for games, lass. Ye ken well
enough who I be."

"Kincaid."

"Aye."

She nodded. "Your reputation goes before you, sir. Since it's you, then I suppose I must—" She dropped to one knee and grabbed the pistol. Raising the weapon, she took aim at the center of his chest and squeezed the trigger. The recoil of the flintlock slammed her backward. Before she could recover, Kincaid's fist smashed into her wrist, knocking the pistol from her hand.

She gasped as pain shot up her arm. Her first thought was that he'd broken her hand; her second was that she had missed and now he would kill her.

"Ye shot me," he said.

She realized that he was clutching his shoulder. "I didn't shoot straight enough," she dared.

He grabbed a handful of her hair and yanked her so close that she could feel the heat of his breath on her face. "I choked the life from the last man who took a shot at me," he said.

She was inches from the bullet wound. She could smell the sickly-sweet scent of his blood as it seeped down the front of his filthy shirt. The realization that he wasn't wearing a coat on this bitter night flashed across her numbed mind, and for the barest instant, she felt pity for him.

" 'Tis said that Englishwomen are as hard-hearted as their men," he whispered. "Mayhap 'tis true." He pulled her head back. "I gave my word not to harm ye," he rasped, "but I'll take a toll for the gift you've give me. A kiss, so that ye won't forget our meeting." He leaned down and covered her mouth with his.

She braced herself for a crude assault, but to her surprise, his kiss was as tender as it was provocative. Her eyes widened in shock as his fingers loosened their grip on her hair to caress the back of her neck. She felt a flush of heat wash up to the roots of her scalp, then rush down through her chest and midsection to curl her toes. A dizzy sensation unlike anything she'd ever experienced made the earth tilt beneath her.

Instinctively, she grabbed hold of him to keep herself from falling. He was still kissing her, and she knew that she should be fighting him . . . should resist his unwanted attack. But the warm pressure on her lips was as heady as the smell of new-plowed fields in March. And to her horror, she found that she was no longer a passive participant in his embrace—she was kissing him back.

"Perhaps they were wrong," he said. His low chuckle as he pushed her away brought her crashing back to the reality of what she'd done. "Perhaps not all English lasses are cold-natured. A pity I've not the time to stay and prove them wrong."

Bess wiped her tingling lips with a trembling hand. "Don't take my horse," she warned him. "I'll hunt you down if you do. I swear I will."

He bent and retrieved her pistol and tucked it into his waist. "Tell your menfolk to keep a better watch over ye. Every escaped felon may nay be as forgivin' as I am." He seized Ginger's reins and swung up onto her back.

"Don't do it, Kincaid!" Bess cried. "I'll have the hide from your back, so help me God!"

He yanked the mare's head around and drove his heels into her sides. She leaped forward, and Kincaid's laughter floated back to Bess on the wind.

Chapter 1

Fortune's Gift
Maryland's Eastern Shore
April 1725

"**G**od save us, mistress," Tom Purse said as Bess took the coiled cattle whip from his hands. "Ye can't mean to deliver the punishment yerself."

Bess slid the braided black leather between her gloved fingers and swallowed the rising lump in her throat. "I gave the sentence. If I truly mean to be mistress of this plantation, then I must be woman enough to administer the beating."

The two were standing near the back door of the brick manor house in the early hours of a bright spring dawn. A thin ribbon of smoke curled from the chimney of the summer kitchen, and Bess could smell the cook's freshly baked beaten biscuits cooling on a windowsill. From the barnyard, a cow lowed. The answering bawl of her hungry calf was nearly drowned out by the raucous crowing of a rooster.

"Aaah," the overseer muttered, seemingly oblivious of the morning sounds and smells of the awakening plantation. " 'Tis bad business, this. If yer father was here . . ."

8

Bess's blue eyes met the older man's faded gray ones with stubborn determination. "But Papa's not here, Tom, and that's the problem. It's been three years since he sailed for the China Seas. We have to face the fact that he might not be coming back. And if I can't live up to my responsibilities, he may not have a plantation to come back to. I could well lose Fortune's Gift and everything my family put into this land."

Tom scowled and scuffed his feet on the ground as he rolled the brim of his worn cocked hat between callused hands. "It still ain't fittin', Miss Bess."

She sniffed. "Was it *fittin'* for this convict to attack me on my own property? To steal Ginger—the best horse we ever foaled here?"

Tom shook his head.

"No, it wasn't," Bess said sharply. "And now this . . . *Kincaid* will pay for his crimes."

"Better ye'd let the high sheriff take him to Annapolis and hang him."

"I can't stand waste," she replied. "You know that, Tom. He was sentenced to transportation for forty years. Hang him and he doesn't serve another day's labor." Her lips firmed. "I mean to see Kincaid doesn't get off so easy."

Tom jammed his hat back on his head. "I'd as soon buy a rogue bull as bring a Scot rebel on Fortune's Gift," he protested. "Murderin' savages, the lot of them. Indentured servants is all bad luck. Blacks is the thing. Slaves do what they're told, when they're told. White bondmen are nothin' but trouble."

It was an effort for Bess to keep her voice from revealing her exasperation. "We've gone over this a hundred times," she said. "So long as I'm mistress here, we'll have no slaves on this plantation." Unconsciously, she gripped the whip tighter in her hands. "Free men work harder, regardless of the color of their skin."

"Your father didn't think so."

"My father and I don't always agree on everything. And he's not here. I am." She exhaled softly through clenched teeth. Why this morning? she agonized. Why must they have the same argument over and over?

Well, she thought, it would have to be said. No matter what the consequences, she'd have to make her position plain to Tom. "If you'd remain on Fortune's Gift as my overseer," she said flatly, "you'd best remember that you're not dealing with David Bennett, you're dealing with me."

"Maybe I will, and maybe I won't," he replied. "I ain't too old to find another place. Willem Steele, over to Chestertown, he's made me offers." Tom's small eyes narrowed to slits in his seamed face. "Ye had no right to free them slaves once yer father's back was turned."

"I had the right." Bess's stomach turned over. She'd known Tom disapproved of her, but he'd never been so disrespectful before. "My father gave me the right when he put Fortune's Gift in my name."

"More fool him. He spoiled ye because he had no son. There'll be hell to pay if he does come home. Half the troubles on this plantation come from your flighty female ideas."

For a moment, she almost backed down. Losing Tom as her overseer would be a terrible blow to the plantation. He was an honest man and he'd

served her father well. A few words of apology
would placate him, but when she opened her
mouth to say them, they stuck in her throat.
"Since you feel that way, Tom," she said with
more resolution than she felt, "maybe you'd better consider Mr. Steele's position. There's no better overseer on the Eastern Shore, but I'll not be
gainsaid by my own help."

"Ye mean to go through with this? To whip
Kincaid yerself?"

She stiffened. "I do."

"Then I wash my hands of ye and Fortune's
Gift. I'll pack my gear and be off the place by
Sunday noon."

"If that's your decision. I'll have your wages
ready."

"Hard silver."

"You'll have it."

Without another word, he turned on his heel
and stalked off toward his quarters.

Oh, God, what have I done now? Bess thought
with a sinking heart. How could she possibly
manage Fortune's Gift without Tom? Just paying
him his wages would empty her coin box. Why
couldn't she have held her tongue and let him
scold her without forcing a confrontation?

If she called him back . . .

She sighed deeply. If she called him back now,
he'd be the authority here, not her. And as much
as she needed Tom, she couldn't let that happen.

Trust yourself, her grandmother Lacy had always told her. *You've a mind as good as any man,
and better than most.*

"If only you were here, Mama. You or Papa
James," she murmured under her breath. But her

beloved grandparents were buried in the walled family graveyard, beside her mother and an uncle who had died at birth.

She blinked back the moisture that threatened to weaken her resolve. Her father had left Fortune's Gift in her hands because he'd believed she was capable of running the plantation. And truth be told, if he were here, he wouldn't be much help. Her father was an adventurer and a seaman, not a planter. Whatever practical farming knowledge she possessed had come from her paternal grandmother. And it didn't take much consideration to know what she would do about this Scot.

She had delivered the sentence—she must carry it out, no matter how much it hurt the both of them.

The feeling of being watched came over her, and she glanced over her shoulder at the house. On the second floor a curtain stirred in the nursery window. In the early morning light, it was difficult for Bess to make out the shadowy figure standing there, but she knew instinctively who it was.

"I'm going," she said, and raised a hand in acknowledgment. "I'm going." Turning back to her unpleasant task, she walked briskly toward the dock and the assembled men who awaited her.

Kincaid knotted his fists and strained against the iron manacles that bound him to the oak crossbeam. He dug his heels into the soft earth and threw his weight forward until the sinews on

his back stood out like ropes, but he was held fast
between two posts.

He fixed his gaze on the sparkling river and
tried to control his anger and frustration. It was
futile to fight now and he knew it, but all his life
he'd waged a losing battle against his hot Gaelic
temper. It was easier to struggle against hemp,
and wood, and iron, than to stand meekly by and
wait to be beaten like a stray dog.

It had taken four stout men to get him this far,
and they would well remember the taking. His
right eye was swollen, and his jaw ached, but he
knew he'd given better than he'd received.

Damn the luck that had made his wound
sicken, and damn the worse luck that had forced
him to take shelter with a doxy that couldn't be
trusted. But then, he thought wryly, when had a
woman ever brought him good fortune?

"Kincaid?"

The voice was low and husky, definitely female. Kincaid twisted his head around, but he
couldn't see who it was who had called his name.

The onlookers fell silent.

The woman stepped around the left post and
stood in front of him, a bold piece in a Lincoln
green riding habit and boots. She was tall, lacking
only half a head of his own height, and shapely.
He could see that her curves were ample, even
though she was wearing a coat and waistcoat. Her
uncovered hair was a mane of rich dark auburn,
and she wore it loose down her back, as brazen
as any dockside tavern slut.

"Kincaid?"

Her eyes were large and wide-spaced, framed
by thick, dark lashes that fair took a man's breath

away. Her brows were feathery arches, her forehead high and flawless. Her nose was straight and well formed, her sensuous mouth too full for modesty. She was comely enough, this haughty English wench, but her eyes were what drew him. They were as clear blue as the waters of Loch Lomond and as fierce as an Atlantic squall.

And the glare she directed at him was enough to scorch the skin from a lesser man.

"Kincaid," she repeated in a voice that made him think of soft feather beds and softer flesh pressed against his own. "Do you know who I am?"

Aye, he knew well enough. No wonder those full lips tantalized him. He'd kissed them once, and he'd held this armful close on a cold night last December . . . the night he'd lifted the bay mare with one white foot.

"You stole my horse," she reminded him.

"Borrowed," he corrected. He grinned at her, as cocksure as a peddler in the parlor of a minister's daughter. Her riding habit was lined with silver braid; her buttons were sterling. She was rich, and doubtless some man's darling. Whatever game she meant to play, he'd follow.

A tint of color rose to settle along her high cheekbones. This time her tone bore a trace of uncertainty. "You are a horse thief, a pirate, a convicted murderer, and a runaway bond servant," she proclaimed.

"He's that," a male voice chimed in.

"Aye," cried another.

"Should 'ave hanged him."

"Two years ago you deserted your rightful

master at River Run Plantation on the James in the colony of Virginia," the woman continued.

Had she told him her name when he'd kissed her? Kincaid tried to remember. He'd kissed many a sweet lass, and one name was much like another.

"You were one of the pirates aboard the *Nancy Jane* who boarded the *York Lady* and robbed her of her cargo last October. Do you deny the charge?" she demanded haughtily.

He kept silent, as he had before the judge. By English law, a man could not be made to testify against himself. He was no pirate, by God! At least, no murdering pirate. And the only cargo they'd had from the *York Lady* was a gross of ladies' shoes and twelve pewter chamber pots. Hardly a haul to send a man to the gallows.

"And do you deny that you fled the jail at St. Mary's Courthouse?" Her whole face was flushed now. "And do you deny you assaulted the Widow Horsey on her farm west of Chestertown in late November?"

He smiled at her again. "I do," he answered. "I do deny it. I've never raped a lass. Nay . . ." He deliberately let his voice trail off suggestively. "Never had to."

She shifted her feet nervously, and he noticed that she was wearing black boots of the finest Spanish leather beneath her Lincoln green riding skirt. Aye, Kincaid decided, she was some old man's darling, like as not. No young man would allow her such leeway—to stand before men and speak out so.

He also noticed that she was holding a leather whip in her hands. A bloodthirsty chit, for all her ladylike airs. Some women, he knew, were excited by the sight of blood—someone else's. The thought that the lass in Lincoln green might be such a common jade disappointed him. She'd piqued his interest, and he'd rated her above such unnatural lusts.

"Then you also deny intruding on the property of Joan Pollott of Onancock. Holding her against her will and taking liberties with her person?"

He scoffed. Joan was a trollop. She made her living providing entertainment for the local males. She'd welcomed him into her cabin in return for the bay mare. She'd given him a place to hide out and she'd dug the bullet out of his shoulder. But when the money ran out, she'd given him over to the authorities for the reward on his head.

"Do you deny assaulting Joan Pollott?"

"I took no more from *Mistress* Pollott than she sells for a silver penny on a weekday and three-pence on Saturdays."

The men guffawed at his reply, but she ignored him and went on. "Where is my horse?"

"I presented it to Mistress Pollott as a gift."

"Joan Pollott denies knowledge of the mare."

He shrugged, inasmuch as he was able, due to the awkward position of his arms and shoulders. "When I last saw the horse in question, she was headed south, led by Joan Pollott."

"Nevertheless, you stand guilty of the theft. You have been found guilty of enough crimes to hang you four times over, Kincaid. But as your rightful master—"

"You're nay my master," he interrupted. "I've seen Roger Lee's wife, and she'll never see fifty again. Unless she's died and Roger married again—''

"I am Lady Elizabeth Bennett," she said. "I swore to you that if you took my mare, I'd track you down, and I always keep my promises. I am the lawful owner of your indenture. I purchased it in Annapolis in February of this year from Roger Lee. And as your owner, I have the power to pass judgment on you. Once again, I ask you—where is my bay mare?''

"Damned if I know."

"Twenty lashes." Her eyes darkened to the blue of deep ocean water. "Where is my mare?''

"Ask Joan Pollott.''

"Twenty-five lashes," she said softly.

"God help the man ye find to deliver them," he threatened.

The color drained from her face until the freckles stood out on her fair skin like spatters of paint. "I saved you from the gallows," she said, "but you have earned every stroke of your punishment.''

Chapter 2

The first blow struck Kincaid's back before he was fully prepared for the pain. He sucked in his breath hard and closed his eyes. Damn, but a cattle whip could cut a man's skin to ribbons!

He'd been beaten before, in Edinburgh, during an interrogation by English soldiers. They'd whipped him near to death, but he'd not given a single name. He'd thought it was an experience a man never forgot.

He was wrong.

He hadn't remembered how much it hurt, and how much effort it took to keep from screaming. He braced himself mentally for the second blow. The leather curled up from his waist and sliced a furrow of fire across his back to his left shoulder. The crack of the whip echoed in his ears. He swallowed back the cry of agony.

Son of a bitch, he cursed silently. It was enough to ruin a man's day.

''Three.''

That was the woman's voice. And as the third lash fell on his naked back, he realized that the bitch was wielding the whip.

''Four,'' she called.

He shuddered as the stroke cut across raw flesh opened by the earlier lashes and clenched his fists

18

as a red tide of fury washed across his consciousness. She'll pay for this, he vowed. She'll pay dearly for every stripe, if it's the last thing I do. . . .

"Eight," Bess said. The leather of the cattle whip was slick with Kincaid's blood and his broad back was crisscrossed with ugly swollen welts. Bile rose in her throat and she forced it down as she drew back the lash for another blow.

What kind of woman had she become that she could mutilate a human being in the name of justice? What had happened to the child who'd wept when a kitten was trampled under a horse's hoofs? To the girl who had tended a hawk with a broken wing?

The sentence had been twenty stripes. Twenty was fair punishment for a horse thief and a runaway bond servant. Her grandmother would have given him twenty lashes herself without blinking an eye.

But Bess had let her cursed temper get the better of her. She'd argued with Kincaid in front of her servants—in front of the neighbors. In her pride, she'd added an extra five stripes to his ordeal. She'd done it because he hadn't bowed his head and submitted to her authority.

"Fifteen." Her shoulder ached; her muscles cried out from the exertion. Damn her for a proud fool! Twenty-five lashes could ruin a man for life. And she didn't want to hurt him . . . not like that.

He had behaved better than she had for his arrogance, she thought. Her eyes clouded with tears and she blinked them away. Why had she let him goad her into increasing the penalty?

Finish what ye start, her grandmother had always said. *And never bite off more than ye can chew.*

"Twenty-one." I'm sorry, she thought. I'm so sorry. She was so weary she could hardly lift the whip, but she shook her head when one of her bondmen offered to finish the job. "It's my duty," she declared.

Disbelief showed on the men's faces. Disbelief and fear. She knew what they would say of her later. *She takes after the old missus—the witch.* And maybe it was true.

On number twenty-four, Kincaid slumped forward in a dead faint. She gave a token stroke for the last blow, then threw the bloody whip to the dirt. "Take him to the barn," she ordered. "I want two guards watching him day and night." She fixed the nearest bond servant with a scowl. "I'll have the hide off any man of mine who lets him escape."

"He'll not get away, mistress. Ye can count on that."

There had never been a need for a jail on Fortune's Gift, so she'd instructed her servants to clean out one of the stallion boxes in the big barn. The sides of the stall were solid oak, and the door was secured on the outside with an iron latch. She'd instructed them to cover the floor with fresh straw and make a pallet for Kincaid to lie on.

"Give him water when he comes to," she said. "I'll send someone from the house to tend to his wounds." She watched as they cut him down, and his moans made sweat break out on her forehead. "Let it be a lesson to any man on the Tidewater," she reminded them. "Horse thieves will receive swift justice on Fortune's Gift."

She held back the tears until she reached the privacy of her bedchamber, and then she broke down and sobbed. She'd not cried since the day she'd buried her grandmother, but she cried now.

The household maids hurried about their chores and whispered to each other. "What's wrong with Miss Bess?" And the cook, Deaf Donald, shook his spoon at them and went on with his work in silence.

In time, Bess rose from her bed and rubbed her tearstained eyes. She splashed water on her face from a rose-patterned pitcher and patted her cheeks dry.

It must be near her monthly flow, she thought, to make such a fuss about an unpleasant proceeding. She had done no less than her father would have done. Let one horse thief go unpunished, and no plantation stock would be safe. Not cows, nor swine, nor geese would be spared. Too many men thought Fortune's Gift an easy mark without a master in residence.

Taking her father's place had not been easy. She'd been cheated on the price of tobacco seed and overcharged by the shipowners who would carry her cured tobacco to England. Neighbors and bondmen alike had laughed at her when she had freed all the slaves on the plantation. And they had blamed her when one of her freemen had been killed robbing a lonely farmhouse.

In truth, her father had been a worse business manager than she was. He'd known he had no head for such matters, and he'd not interfered when her grandmother had hired the best tutor on the Eastern Shore to teach her mathematics, philosophy, and other subjects more suitable for men than for women. In the years since her grandmother had passed away, her father had gradually allowed her more and more leeway in making the decisions concerning Fortune's Gift.

There were a thousand decisions to be made: what forests should be cleared for new fields, what crops should be grown, which horses should be bred and which sold. Ships brought supplies from England once or twice a year, and a shopping list must cover the needs of over a hundred people on the plantation for eight to ten months at a time. If she failed to order enough cloth, or shoes, or plowshares, a year could come and go before the error could be set right.

She loved her father dearly, but his decision to risk the family fortune in a voyage to the China Sea was one she hadn't agreed with and had begged him to reconsider. Fortune's Gift was rich land, but every planter lived on the brink of ruin. Storms and drought plagued farmers, and political upheavals made shipping products home to the motherland difficult. Every year taxes became higher, and her father had been determined that his manor house would rival any home on the Eastern Shore. He had added on to the original house twice, and he had built a horse barn so beautiful that people came from miles around just to admire it.

Whatever would he say when he came home and found out that she'd sold most of the furniture he'd had custom-built in France? She hadn't been able to think of a way to strip the hand-painted Chinese wallpaper from the grand entrance hall, but it hadn't been for lack of trying. Sir Robert Miller of Chestertown had offered her a pretty penny for the paper if she could get it down without destroying it. She had sold off a complete set of porcelain and a chest of silver plate.

No, she thought as she hurried down the main staircase, Father had ever been realistic when it came to money. He'd expected to live like a king, and he'd wanted her to play the part of the princess.

Deaf Donald nodded when Bess entered the winter kitchen, which was attached to the house. He'd been taking spices from the locked cupboard to use in the noon meal. Now that the weather had turned warm, all cooking for the manor would be done in the summer kitchen, a brick structure set away from the main dwelling. Fire was an ever-present threat, and keeping the kitchen separate reduced the risk of having the big house destroyed.

Bess greeted the gray-haired man with the respect due his position of head cook and gathered up her medicinal supplies. Since she'd caused the injury to Kincaid's back, she felt it only fair to tend him herself. It wouldn't make up for the pain she'd caused him, but it would ease some of her guilt.

She'd never intended to seriously harm the outlaw. Ever since word of his exploits had filtered in to Fortune's Gift, she'd toyed with an outrageous idea. It was too early to speak of her plan yet, but if anything was to come of it, Kincaid might supply a vital ingredient.

Kincaid's indenture had come high. Even though the man had escaped, Roger Lee had been reluctant to part with the Scot's contract. He'd protested that Kincaid was a valuable worker, a man who knew how to grow tobacco and who was at home on ships and the water. Most bondmen had a seven-year servitude—Kincaid's was forty years. He had cost Bess twenty gold sovereigns, a silver cup that had been in her family since her grandfather had stolen it from the Spanish, and a prize bull.

Her father had imported the bull from Devon when the animal was a calf. The beast—named Rupert—had sired fourteen prime milk cows for Fortune's Gift, and he produced hard cash when other farmers brought their cows to be bred. Bess had a son of Rupert's, but it would be another year before he would be old enough to stand at stud. And what if the bull calf proved sterile or fathered only average calves?

If she'd traded a superior bull for a dead man, she'd be the laughingstock of Maryland. She sighed. It wouldn't do to let the big Scot die of his injuries, and it wouldn't do at all to let him slip through her fingers. She'd had to post a bond with the sheriff, promising to be responsible for any harm he caused. And because she had no cash left, she'd promised payment from last fall's tobacco crop—a crop that could well be at the bottom of the Atlantic.

The ship that had carried her tobacco and the hope of Fortune's Gift had sailed with the fleet for London in early November. Now she must wait as the other colonial tobacco planters waited. Three months there, if the weather was with the fleet and no pirates caught them. Another month or two, or even three, before the captains could set sail again for the Chesapeake. No way to tell

if the price for tobacco was high or low, or if any
of her precious crop was damaged by water on
the journey.

Bess paused in the open doorway and pursed
her lips. Looking toward the river was wasted energy. It would be weeks yet before she would
know if the best crop Fortune's Gift had ever produced had snatched her from the jaws of poverty,
or . . . she shook her head. She wouldn't think *or*.
Brow furrowed in thought, she walked on, out of
the kitchen.

She owed the merchants for the tobacco seed,
and the ship's owners for the cost of passage.
Without the profit from her tobacco, the bond
she'd given the sheriff for the convict would be
worthless. Without hard cash and the supplies
that money would buy, how could she keep her
plantation workers and their families for another
whole year? Where would she get seed for next
year's crop? How would she buy harness, and
axes, and wool for winter coats?

A prickly feeling at the nape of her neck caused
Bess to glance back toward the open doorway. A
ragged black tomcat sat there in a patch of sun,
grooming his glossy fur. His eyes were squinted
shut, and she could see the nub where his left ear
should have been. The light was so bright that
Bess blinked, and when she looked again, the cat
had vanished.

"So you're back, are you, you old rascal," she
murmured. He looked good, considering his age.
She hoped he wouldn't cause too much concern
among the maids. "Try and stay out of trouble,
Harry," she admonished the empty doorway.

Continuing on toward the barn, her mood

lightened. Maybe Kincaid had told the truth, she thought. She'd ask the sheriff to inquire with Joan Pollott about her mare Ginger. If they could locate her, Bess would demand her return. After all, a person shouldn't have to buy back her own stolen property—should she?

A lad leading a red-and-white ox passed her. The boy ducked his head and tugged at his shaggy forelock. "Mornin', Miss Bess," he said shyly.

"Good morning, Vernon," she answered. Vernon was the youngest son of her blacksmith, a steady youth—even if he had no head for letters. One of her ideas that her overseer had objected to had been to open a plantation school for her workers' children.

Vernon had been like most of them. He far preferred running errands for his father or working in the forge to book learning. Of the original twenty-three children she'd assembled for daily lessons, only five had continued with their studies. Now Bess held school two afternoons a week in the library of the manor house. Those who did come were rewarded by a special noon meal topped off with a sweet baked especially for the little ones by Deaf Donald. If the children came because of the treats and learned to read in the process, Bess would be satisfied.

A woman shooing a flock of geese and a man carrying wood greeted her as she neared the barn. This was the busiest time of day, and most of her people were in the fields. Tobacco required daily cultivation to keep out the weeds. It was hard, dirty work when the plants were young, but it was a task that must be adhered to or they'd lose the crop before it matured. The best time to pull weeds was early in the morning, before the sun made the fields too hot to work.

Tobacco was her main cash crop, but not the only one. She grew corn and wheat and hay on Fortune's Gift, as well as vegetables, and flax for weaving into cloth. She kept a full timber crew and an army of carpenters, herdsmen, and hunters. Also, she owned several small fishing boats. They caught fish and crabs and eels to add to the daily diet of her employees. Extra fish were dried and salted by women and packed in barrels for shipment to England. There was a dairy, a sheepfold, a weaving shed, and a brick kiln. Fortune's Gift was as self-sufficient a plantation as Bess could make it. But no matter how hard she tried, there were always things that must be purchased from London at high prices.

Such was a planter's life, she thought, and smiled. It was all she knew, and all she wanted to know. Not for her was her father's life of sailing to strange lands. She was happiest here, her hands covered with good tidewater dirt and her eyes resting on the ripening crops. The land was her legacy, one she meant to pass down to future generations.

"If I can only hang on to it," she said softly as she put her hand on the barn-door latch.

The nearest guard looked up as she entered the shadowy building. He was armed with a flintlock musket and a hunting knife. "We're keepin' a good eye on him, Miss Bess. He ain't moved an inch since we laid him down."

She nodded her approval. "Don't relax your

vigilance, Ben. In England, they say Kincaid killed three soldiers."

"Yes, ma'am." He colored. "I mean, no, ma'am, I won't. If he tries anything with me, he'll be sorry."

She walked past Ben toward the far corner of the barn. Despite her uneasiness at the confrontation ahead, Bess felt the spell of the barn slip over her and she breathed deep of the familiar odors of grain and animals. The air was heady with the scent of sweet clover hay the workers had forked into the loft the week before. She could smell the fresh-raked earth beneath her feet and the bite of vinegar that the grooms had added to the horses' water barrels.

Only one horse remained inside the barn this morning, a roan mare Bess had been treating for a split hoof. As she passed the horse's stall, the animal nickered to her. Bess paused long enough to grab a handful of wheat from a feed bin and offer it to her. The mare took the grain daintily, licking Bess's fingers with a raspy tongue. "Good girl," Bess soothed. "Good Jeanie." She bent and kissed the mare's velvety nose and ran a hand along her fine neck. "We'll have you fit as a fiddle in no time."

Bess had always loved the smell of a clean stable. Horses had always been a passion with her. Her grandfather had taught her to ride when she was three, and after that he always knew where to find her. If she wasn't on horseback, she would be in the stable following the grooms around and begging them to saddle a mount for her. And sometimes, she just sat quietly in the corner of a stall and talked to the horses and other animals.

She patted Jeanie a last time and went down the passageway to the secure box stall where Kincaid lay. She waved aside the second bondman's protest and went inside. "Close the door," she ordered. "I'll call you if I need you, Ned. And don't bring that gun in here around Kincaid."

The Scot lay facedown on a clean blanket atop a pallet, seemingly unconscious. He wore only his breeches and boots. If he'd possessed a shirt, there was no sign of it now.

Bess winced when she saw his back. It looked worse now than it had immediately after the lashing. Black streaks of blood had dried on the lacerated wounds, and the waist of his breeches was stained with dark spots. One place, the whip had cut through his flesh nearly to the bone.

God help me, she thought. I did this.

"Be careful, Miss Bess," Ned called.

His words reminded her of her duty. "Bring me water and clean cloths," she instructed him. "I want salt in the water. You can use horse salt, so long as it's clean. And I'll need some of that salve I used on Jeanie's split hoof."

Kincaid opened his eyes and turned his head to glare at her. "What do ye here?" he rasped. "Come to finish me off?" Again she heard the deep burr of the Highlands in his voice, and again she felt that strange flutter in the pit of her belly.

"No," she answered sternly. "I've come to make sure your wounds don't fester. You're of no use to me if you die or become a cripple."

He made a move to sit up, then gasped and fell back on his pallet. His tanned face paled to tallow gray, and she saw the muscles flex along his jaw.

"Are you in much pain?" she asked, then realized how foolish her question must sound.

"I've been better."

She walked toward him cautiously. His right hand was fastened to the wall by a chain, but his left was free. She took care not to come within his reach. "I'm going to wash your back," she said. "If you lie perfectly still, it will be easier on you."

"Easy for ye to say," he taunted her.

Her chest felt tight, and it was hard for her to breathe. What was it about this convict that disturbed her so? She had tended men and animals since she was a child; her grandmother had said she had the hands for it.

"Where's your husband?" he demanded. "If ye were my wife, ye'd not—"

"'Tis none of your business," she snapped. "And I'd not be wife to the likes of you, so there's naught but nonsense in your talk."

"Only an Englishman would be such a fool as to allow his woman—"

"I have no husband," she declared. "Nor am I like to choose one."

He scoffed, twisting his head so that he could stare at her boldly with nutmeg-brown eyes. "I should have guessed. Not even an Englishman would take such a harridan to wife. Now that I look at ye, I see that ye are long in the tooth—past the age of wedding."

Heat flamed in her face. "Hold your tongue," she said, "or I'll fill your mouth with soap. My age is none of your business." She was but four and twenty. Many a maid didn't wed until later than that. Still, his remark stung and she felt anger coil in her chest. "I've come to give you aid, not listen to your insults."

The stall door opened and Ned entered, carrying a bucket of water and the rags she had asked for. "I kin do thet, Miss Bess," he said in his slow way. "It ain't fittin'—"

"I'll say what's fitting on Fortune's Gift," she reminded him. He nodded respectfully and handed her the can of salve. "That will be all," she said.

Ned tapped the knife at his waist. "Keep them hands to yourself, pirate," he warned Kincaid. "You lay a hand on the mistress, and I'll cut you—"

"That will be all, Ned," she repeated. "Close and lock the door behind you."

"Yes'm."

"Do ye always take such chances with wild animals?" Kincaid asked sarcastically.

"Animals have more sense. They know when someone is trying to help them." She wet a cloth in the salt water. "This will sting," she said.

"Aye," he said, "I thought it might."

"Turn over and lie still."

"Aye, mistress."

It was easier to approach him when he looked away. She knew that, even badly injured, he could be dangerous. He was a big man, and powerful; his sinewy shoulders were wider even than her father's. His waist was narrow, his belly flat. His muscular thighs . . . She shook her head. What had come over her, that she was having lustful thoughts about a servant's body?

She nibbled her lower lip thoughtfully. Could

this be the man whose coming her grandmother had foretold?

A man of war will come in a time of great need, Mama had said so many years ago. *A strong man with fair hair and dark eyes. And when he comes, you'll know him, Bess. You'll know him.*

Bess brushed aside Kincaid's hair. It was dirty and matted with mud, but strands of it caught the light. It's the color of ripe wheat, she thought. When she pushed it away, it sprang back and curled around the back of his neck.

. . . a fair-haired man . . .

For an instant, her fingers touched his skin, and it seemed to Bess as though she'd been jolted by lightning. She drew back her hand in shock as the tingling ran up her arm and made gooseflesh rise.

He's only a man, she thought. Just a runaway bondman . . . an outlaw. But her heart beat faster and her mouth went dry. Could he be the one?

"Get on with it, woman," Kincaid growled.

"Be still!" With trembling hands, she took the wet cloth and wiped gently at the bloody welts. She heard his sharp intake of breath and jumped back.

"Dammit, woman," he said, "do it and be done with."

"Remember your place, convict," she admonished.

"I'll remember," he promised. "And I'll remember who laid the stripes in my flesh."

She rinsed the cloth and the water turned pink. "The salt will keep the wounds from turning bad," she explained to him. His grunt was noncommittal. She repeated the process again, and when she was satisfied that the torn flesh was clean, she stitched the bad spot, rubbed the wounds with an Indian remedy she'd brought from the house, and, finally, coated his entire back with the horse salve.

"You must stay on your stomach," she ordered. "It will heal faster if I don't cover it with cloth." She cleaned her hands as best she could. "Are you hungry?"

As she was turning away, his left hand shot out and grabbed her wrist. She stifled a scream of fear.

"Aye, I'm hungry." He pulled her close to his face. "Will ye prepare a meal for me with your own hands, Englishwoman? And if ye do, will it be poison?"

Bess grabbed the small wooden bucket and raised it over his head. "Let me go," she warned, "or I'll brain you. So help me God, I will."

He laughed and released her.

Shaken, she backed away. Her wrist throbbed and she looked down at it, half expecting the skin to show some sign of bruising. "Take no liberties with me, Scotsman," she said breathlessly. "I'll tolerate none from the likes of you."

"Won't you? I wonder what kind of woman takes pleasure in lifting the skin from a man's back with her own hands?"

"I took no pleasure in it," she replied. "But I guard my own. I warned you when you stole my mare. I'll not be bullied by any man."

"Why did ye do it?"

"I just told you. I—"

"Nay! Not that. Why did you buy my contract? What woman's fancy would make ye risk so much money when none knew if I'd ever be captured?"

" 'Tis my affair," she answered. "And not for you to know. At least . . ." She hesitated. "At least not yet."

"Aye, so ye say," he retorted. "But this much I will tell ye. I will not forget the pleasure we shared, and the day will come when—"

"Enough!" she cried. "Hold your tongue, lest I call my blacksmith and have it cut out. You are my bondman, my property. You will do as I say, when I say. And if you ever have a hope of walking free again, you'd best remember that."

Without giving him time to reply, she whirled around and called loudly for Ned. He threw open the door immediately. "Keep close watch on him," she warned. "For I'll have the neck of any man who lets him escape."

Still trembling inside, she hurried back toward the house. This Kincaid couldn't be the man her grandmother had seen in her vision. He could never be trusted. He was dangerous. If she had the sense of a hound pup, she'd sell him across the bay as soon as his wounds healed.

"I will," she declared. "I'll not add Kincaid to my troubles." But even as she mouthed the words, the image of his craggy face and square chin rose in her mind's eye, and she knew that she wouldn't let go of him so easily.

"Lucifer he may be," she murmured. "But if I attempt what I've dreamed of, it may be that a devil is exactly what I need."

Chapter 3

May 1725

Bess sat at a table in her bedchamber as a late-night thunderstorm rolled over the Eastern Shore. Lightning flashed to the west, and the first patters of rain were beginning to tap against her windows. She wore nothing but a silk dressing gown. Her hair was loose around her shoulders, and her feet were bare. A letter lay on the polished wood before her, and beside it was a small leather-bound journal.

She picked up the letter and read it through one last time, then crumpled it and threw it into the cold fireplace. She didn't need to see the words to remember the message. . . . *We regret to inform you of the loss of our vessel* Cecilia Rose *with all hands and cargo off the coast of* . . .

Bess clasped her hands together and tried to conquer her panic. Her tobacco crop was gone. All the sweat and days of toil had come to nothing. William Myers and Son was demanding payment for the shipping, and she had just learned that her father had taken out a loan with them to assist in outfitting his own trading expedition to China. He had secured the loan with the title to a large section of Fortune's Gift.

"How could you do it, Father?" she whispered huskily. "How could you gamble our land on a voyage to the ends of the earth?"

The candle flame flickered, and a breath of cool air stirred the room. Bess raised her eyes from the table to gaze at the figure standing in the far corner of the room. "Ah." She exhaled softly. "Kutii."

The Indian didn't speak, but somehow, his presence was comforting. Bess moistened her lips and waited.

Thunder rumbled overhead, and the rain beat harder against the glass. Words Bess had never wanted to speak spilled out in the shadowy bed-chamber. "Why isn't Father ever here when I need him?"

She loved him dearly. No girl could have a more loving, indulgent parent. He had carried her on his shoulders when she was little, laughed and played with her, and listened to her childish se-crets. He'd taken her on his ship to Philadelphia, to Boston, and even to Williamsburg. He'd show-ered her with gifts, and he'd never forgotten to bring her something special when he returned from a voyage. Never once had he blamed her for not being the male heir Fortune's Gift needed. And he had encouraged her to use her mind and her talents to do anything a boy could.

But he'd never been with her when something terrible happened. . . .

It had been that way all her life. He'd spend two months at home and ten months at sea. He'd remain on Fortune's Gift for a season at most, and then he would be off to England, or the In-dies, or even the coast of Africa.

She had been just a baby when her mother had taken a fall from a horse and lain four months barely conscious. Her father had been in France that spring, and her grandmother, Mama, and her grandfather, Papa James, had cared for her mother.

Mary Carter Sterling had been the prettiest heiress and the best dancer along the James River when she'd wed Bess's father at nineteen. She could ride any horse with four legs, and she was absolutely fearless on a fox hunt. She had ridden to hounds when she was five months gone with Bess. But after that March morning, when Bess was two, Mary had never walked, or danced, or sat a sidesaddle again. She was a frail invalid when her handsome husband came sailing home to the Chesapeake.

He'd stayed by her side until Christmas, but when the call of the sea had been too strong, he'd kissed them good-bye and sailed again.

Bess's father had been on a voyage on that terrible summer night when pirates had attacked the plantation and murdered eleven men and two women. Bess had been old enough to remember the gunfire and the bearded man who'd rushed into the kitchen and stabbed one of the servants. Her beloved dog, Cedar, had leaped at the marauder and been struck down. It was Mama Lacy, her grandmother, who had saved her from certain death, dropping the villain in his tracks with one shot from her flintlock pistol.

"You know it's true that Father was never here when we needed him most," Bess declared to Kutii. "Remember when the hurricane ruined our tobacco crop and drowned half of our livestock?"

"And he was gone when your grandmother's heart gave out." Kutii's softly accented English echoed her sorrow.

"He was her only son, and he wasn't here to hold her hand when she died." Bess's throat constricted. "He was always off chasing a dream."

The Indian nodded, his heavy-lidded eyes shining with the love and compassion she'd always seen there. "Not only your father, but also your grandfather was a dreamer," he said.

"Papa James might have been the dreamer, but my grandmother was the one who made the dreams come true."

"So." Kutii nodded again in agreement. "That too is a gift."

The rain was falling harder now. Wind whistled around the chimney, and spatters fell on the clean-swept hearth. Bess looked around the master bedchamber that had once been her grandparents'. She had been born in the large curtained bed; her grandmother had insisted Bess's father had been conceived and born in it, as well. Now the bedstead, the cushioned settle, the tall, inlaid case clock, and the beautiful walnut chest of drawers were hers.

Her father had not wanted this room or the furnishings. As the only living son and heir, he should have slept here, but he found his parents' things too dark and old-fashioned for his taste. He preferred the new French styles. It had all come to Bess . . . the house, the plantation, and the responsibility.

And she loved it all fiercely.

"I do love Fortune's Gift," she murmured. "I love it more than I love my own life. I'll not let it slip through my fingers. I swear I won't.'' She reached for the leather-bound book in the center of the table, flipped open the stained cover, and began to read her grandfather's bold script by the flickering light of the candle.

If it weren't for Kutii, she wouldn't have known of the journal's existence. It was Kutii who had pointed out to her the hiding place, forgotten for at least ten years behind a loose brick in the fireplace.

No wonder her grandfather had hidden the diary; there was enough evidence in his own handwriting to convict him of piracy twice over. The most fascinating account to Bess was his description of Henry Morgan's raid on Panama City. Apparently, Papa James had been one of Captain Morgan's infamous privateers.

Since she was a child, Bess had heard whispered stories of Spanish treasure, a fortune linked somehow with the founding of Fortune's Gift. She'd asked her mother about the rumors, but Mother had been extremely reluctant to speak about the subject, other than to say it was nothing but servants' gossip and Bess would be better occupied with practicing her embroidery than with eavesdropping on grown-ups.

But once, her grandmother had told her that it wasn't Spanish gold but Incan treasure that had paid for Fortune's Gift. Bess had run to Papa James and asked him if it was true, but he'd only laughed and told her it was more of her grandmother's outlandish tales. ''I am descended from nobility in England,'' he'd said. ''Our wealth comes from my family.''

It was obvious that both her mother and her grandfather had lied to her.

Here, in Papa James's own words, was the proof that such a treasure existed. For the most part, the book had been a recording of crops and births and deaths on Fortune's Gift. The first entry had been made on her grandparents' wedding day. There was no pattern to the account; sometimes he would skip weeks or even months. But the story of the attack on Panama City was complete in blood-curdling detail that ran for thirty pages.

It began thusly. *Twenty years ago, on this day, I signed a pact with my friend and captain, Matthew Kay, to lay siege to Panama City on the Pacific. . . .*

The story ended with the sinking of Captain Kay's vessel, the *Miranda*, in the Caribbean, and the loss of five chests of treasure. It was all fascinating to Bess, but what most intrigued her was five pages in the middle of the tale which told of the attempts to bring the gold of Panama City through the steaming jungle to the Atlantic. According to Papa James's recollection, at least half of the treasure was left behind, buried when natives attacked and killed most of their pack animals. There was also mention of an Incan slave and his bravery under fire.

Bess closed the journal and went to the fireplace. Carefully, she removed the loose brick and reached inside to retrieve the absolute proof of her grandfather's fantastic tale. Cradling the tiny gold statue in the palm of her hand, Bess returned to the candlelight and stared down at the beautiful work of art.

The miniature jaguar snarled up at her, as

bright and perfect as it had been when an Incan craftsman cast it in a clay mold. The eyes were set with polished turquoise, and she could count the claws on each delicate paw.

Bess took a deep breath and closed her fingers around the statue, giving in to the other gift her grandmother Lacy had left her . . . the legacy of a witch. Instantly, the familiar bedchamber receded, and Bess became aware of a series of vivid images, one after another.

Gray mountain peaks jutting into the sky like the fingers of God! Brown, dusty roads, and strange pyramidlike structures. Black-haired men and women of dusky red hue, and a chanting unlike any she had ever heard.

Blood! Spilling red across the golden jaguar. Women's screams and a mounted Spaniard wearing a crested steel helmet. The weight of iron chains. Musty odors of rotting vegetation. Suddenly, Kutii's face. And then blue-green water, choking, drowning . . .

Bess gasped and sat down on her bed. She opened her hand and stared at the golden image. She swallowed hard as her stomach turned over, and her head began to pound as it always did after she'd used her *sight*.

She had possessed the gift since she was a child. Her grandmother, Mama, had assured her that it was a gift from a gypsy ancestor—not a curse, as ignorant people might say. Bess could take an object—usually something solid, like a coin or a piece of jewelry—in her hand and receive impressions from it. Sometimes the scenes that rose in her mind's eye were clouded and faint. Other times, she could clearly see events and people associated with the object.

Occasionally, she could experience similar images by touching another person. These impressions told her if the subject was truthful or lying, or if the stranger could be trusted. The trick worked best with someone Bess didn't know. Her first instincts usually proved to be correct.

Mama Lacy had once asked her what she saw when she made judgments on a person's character, and Bess had answered that it was very hard to describe. And it was. She *felt* rather than *saw* colors. Blue and gold were good colors. Gray and red were bad. A liar always felt gray and sticky; red indicated someone with a violent temper.

When she had first touched Kincaid, she'd not felt any color, only a lightning bolt of energy exploding within her. She smiled, remembering. A hint of green? Had she received an impression of green?

She shook her head. No, she couldn't be sure of Kincaid. He was beyond the edges of her gift. Kincaid was an unknown entity.

"Do you not remember what she told you years ago?" Kutii asked.

Bess started in surprise. She had forgotten he was in the room. "Oh," she said. "You're still here."

"I've never known you to be frightened of me."

She frowned. "Of course I'm not afraid of you. It's just that you creep around so quietly, like . . ."

"Like a ghost?" He chuckled. "Think, Bess. Your grandmother. What did she tell you? She said that a strong man would come when your need was great. Use him to save what you hold dearest."

"I'd have to be mad even to consider hunting for the lost treasure."

"You bear the blood of those who seek what lies beyond the seas. You cannot change who you are."

"It's ridiculous," Bess protested. "I can't do it."

"You are her granddaughter."

"I'm just a woman, Kutii. If I'd been born the son Fortune's Gift needed . . ."

"All that Lacy was is in you."

"How can I? I'd have to be mad to consider going to Panama."

Kutii laughed softly. "What is madness to one is daring to another."

"If I got there, I wouldn't know where to go—where to dig." She looked away, toward the empty fireplace.

"I know."

"You'll come with me?" When he didn't answer, she glanced up. "Kutii?" The door to the hall stood open. He had gone as quietly as he had come.

The storm swirled around the manor house and bent the white poplar trees, sending leaves and small branches flying over the roof and across the garden. Lightning flashed so close that Bess braced herself for the accompanying thunder. The boom rattled the glass and echoed through the room, making her flinch, but when she ran to the windows, she couldn't see any damage.

She returned to her chair and let her hand rest on the old journal. Kutii was right. If she wanted to save Fortune's Gift, she'd have to take action . . .

not sit and wait helplessly for the land to be confiscated.

Kincaid was her biggest problem. Could she trust him? Or was he the pirate and murderer the authorities believed him to be?

She had tended the bondman's wounds and seen to it that he was given decent clothing and good food every day. She had insisted that he be guarded day and night during the past five weeks since she'd whipped him. But all that time, she'd made no further attempt to talk with him.

Now it was time.

Ignoring the hour and the heavy downpour, she dressed as quickly as she could and threw a hooded wool cloak over her shoulders. She stepped over the one-eared cat lying in the doorway and descended the wide front staircase to the entrance hall.

The house was quiet, the servants all asleep. Bess went down the hall and through a low door into a storage room. Taking a lantern, she carried it into the kitchen, lit it from the coals on the hearth, and went out the back way into the rainy night.

Kincaid heard the barn door open and the murmur of voices. He got to his feet and looked out through the bars of the box stall at the bobbing lantern. A hooded figure came toward his cell, and he smelled the strong oily scent of wet wool.

"Leave us alone." The woman's voice. He'd not seen her since the day she'd tended his injured back.

The stall door opened. She shrugged off the

cape and came inside, closing the door behind
her. "Kincaid."

He'd forgotten how husky her voice was. Low.
Sensual. He liked the way his name sounded
when she said it.

"Kincaid?"

"Ye woke me. Ye must have something to say."

She came closer, stopping just out of arm's
reach. He was still manacled and chained to the
wall. She seemed to know exactly how far she
could come without being in danger. "I have a
proposition for you," she said.

"I don't do stud service."

Her eyes widened at the insult. "Damn you,"
she said softly.

He chuckled. "You're not the first to say so."
He grinned at her. "I doubt not I'll end up in hell,
but if I do, I'll nay be lonely."

"I've no time for games." She stiffened, and
he remembered how tall she was, and how strong
she'd been when they'd struggled on the road the
night he'd stolen her mare.

"I did give Joan your horse," he said. "She
sold her, certain, but a mare like that shouldn't
be hard to trace."

"I need you."

He uttered a low sound of derision. "I already
told ye, I pick my own bedmates. Ye may own
my indenture. Ye dinna own me."

"By the king's arse, can you think of nothing
but futtering?" she snapped. "If you can hold
your tongue for two minutes, I'll tell you a thing
that may make a great deal of difference about
how you spend the next forty years of your life."

''I'll nay spend it hoeing your tobacco. I'll tell ye that for nothin', me fine English lady.''

''Will you listen, or shall I go and find myself a man instead of a boasting fool?''

''Talk on, mistress,'' he answered sarcastically.

''I was told that you know something of the sea and ships.''

He nodded. What was the wench getting to? ''A wee bit.''

''And you know something of fighting?''

''I was a mercenary for nine years. I ken a pistol from a broadsword.'' He arched an eyebrow. ''Have ye a bit of a war in mind?''

''No war,'' she said. ''Just a small expedition into Spanish territory.''

''Say on. You've my interest, woman.''

''I want you to take me south to recover a treasure that my grandfather stole and buried in Panama.''

He laughed. ''A fine joke. Now, what did ye come here disturbing a poor prisoner's sleep for?''

''I'm serious,'' she said. ''I've a map to a fortune and I need the right man to help me get it.''

He stopped laughing and locked his gaze with hers. ''And why would I do such a crazy thing? Take a white woman into Panama under the Spaniards' high noses?''

''For a thing only I can give you.''

''And that is?''

''Your freedom, and the gold to keep it.''

Chapter 4

Kincaid's eyes glittered in the lantern light. "Why should I trust ye, Englishwoman?"

"Why should I trust you?"

Thunder boomed, rattling the barn walls. Even the lightning strike that followed seconds later did nothing to ease the tension that sparked between them. Bess repressed the urge to swallow, and forced herself to hold the lantern steady. She'd not give Kincaid the satisfaction of knowing how hard she was trembling inwardly.

He was a formidable opponent, this unshaved, hard-eyed convict. One blow of his fist could kill her; his scarred, muscular fingers could close around her throat and choke the life out of her before the guards could come to her aid. She'd given him every reason to do so when she'd beaten him like an animal. Shamed him. Stripped him of every ounce of human dignity.

But somehow, she knew he wouldn't harm her. Despite the wildness in his dark eyes and the scent of danger around him, her intuition told her to trust him. "I need you, Kincaid. And if you'll help me recover the treasure, I'll make you a free man of substance."

"Ye can do that? Legally?" The sarcasm was

gone from his voice, and for a fleeting moment his rough-hewn features softened.

"There are precedences. Many Marylanders were once indentured servants . . . most have a past they'd not speak of. England is far away. You could have a new start here, Kincaid." She paused, searching for the right words. "Have you a last name, or is—"

"Just Kincaid," he said harshly. He ran a hand through his tangled blond hair. "What proof do I have that you'll give me my freedom if I take ye to Panama?"

She noticed that he badly needed a shave. His beard was sparse; his stubbly whiskers shone as golden as the sprinkling of fair hair on his chest and arms. A golden man to seek a golden fortune, she thought. As he pushed back his hair, a silver earring gleamed in one ear.

"You do look like a pirate, you know," she said, surprising herself as she voiced her thoughts.

"And ye look like a wanton."

Bess felt herself flush, not with shame, but with anger. "Perhaps we are neither of us what we seem," she said, fighting to hold her temper. "It is your sword arm I wish to hire, nothing else."

He grinned wolfishly. "Good. For as well formed as ye may be, I've no interest in any lass who fancies herself a man."

"Are you always so crude?"

"Aye. Ye may as well get used to it, for I step aside for no man, and I take sass from no woman, highborn or low."

Bess stiffened. "Did you do what they said you

did?'' she demanded. ''Are you a cold-blooded murderer?''

His brown eyes narrowed. ''I've killed men that needed killing. . . .'' His voice dropped to a grating rasp. ''And some that probably didn't. A few were English soldiers.''

''That's not what I asked.''

''I sleep nights.''

''You consider yourself a professional soldier.''

He shrugged. ''No need to hide truth with pretty words. I fight for those who pay me, and I'm very good at what I do.''

''I've told you what I'll pay.''

''Nay, 'tis not enough. If I agree to take ye on this wild-goose hunt, and if we find this treasure—I'll take half.''

Bess tensed. ''I'm not bargaining with you over the price of a suckling pig. I said I'd give you fair wages, enough to set yourself up respectful.''

''And I told ye that I'll have half of what we take, or ye can find another fool to take ye.''

''There are plenty of men who would jump at the chance to make their fortune.''

''Not men who can get ye there and bring ye back alive.''

''My chances of finding another rogue to escort me to Panama are better than your chances of finding another woman who will offer you such an opportunity,'' she retorted.

He laughed. ''Aye, I'll grant ye that much. I've seen all manner of wenches from high country to low, but I've seen few with your gall.''

''Your freedom and a quarter of all the treasure we find.''

"One third," he countered. "And I'll have my promise of freedom in writing."

"Done," Bess agreed. She offered him her hand, and as he clasped hers tightly in an iron grasp, she tried again to summon up her witchy gifts and read his thoughts. She listened, straining with her inner senses for some hint of intuition, but all she could hear was the crunch of straw beneath Kincaid's feet and his mocking chuckle.

"A bargain made in hell," he said. His eyes lit with devilish mirth. "And what makes ye think I won't cut your throat and rob ye of all ye possess, halfway to Panama?"

She forced herself to smile as she withdrew her hand. "Until we find the gold, greed will keep you honest," she replied. "And after—"

"Aye? After?" he taunted. "Why should I not decide to have all this wondrous treasure for myself?"

She stepped back out of his reach. "For the same reason I won't cut your throat when you're sleeping. Panama is Spanish land, and it will take both our efforts to get out alive. And once we reach English territory, there's no need for you to rob me. You'll have more money than you can spend in a lifetime. Honest money. Money that will buy you what you've never had."

Kincaid's face hardened to a mask. Bess knew she was treading on thin ice with him, but she thrust home her point, certain that this was one spot the Scot was vulnerable. "My gold will buy you respectability," she said softly. "Respectability, and land that no man can take away from you. Maryland is a good place for a man to start over, and if I've ever seen a man who needed to walk away from his past, it's you."

"Take off these chains." It was an order, not a request.

She nodded. "You can have the run of Fortune's Gift. But stay on my land unless I'm with you. Too many of my neighbors consider you too dangerous to live."

"I'll want decent clothing and weapons."

"The clothing you can have. The weapons can wait until we depart for Panama. I'd thought to take at least six men with us. You can—"

"Nay. You and me. I'll not attempt to smuggle an army past the Spanish. We'll find the men we need in Panama. Until then, we travel alone. And you tell no one where or why we go. Do ye ken? No one."

"Why?" She knew better than to gossip heedlessly about her mission, but she wanted to keep Kincaid talking. It was important to her to learn more about him—to understand the way he thought. If she was going to trust her life and her fortune to this scoundrel, she had to—

"If ye be too stupid to ken that, ye deserve to end up with your throat cut," he answered harshly. "More missions and lives have been lost by loose tongues than by sharp steel." He held out his manacled wrist. "Free me, I say, and we shall plan out this mad venture."

Bess raised her eyes to meet his. "One more thing, Scot. I want my horse back. I hold her dear, and I'll not start for Panama until she is safe on Fortune's Gift."

He shrugged. "I told ye where the horse was. Ask Mistress Pollott if ye'd ken more."

"No, Kincaid," Bess said firmly. "You stole Ginger from me, and it's up to you to get her back."

His lips tightened into a thin line. "Ah, I see. A test. A feat of skill and daring to prove my worth. And how am I to work this wonder, since you've forbidden me to leave the plantation?"

"I'll go with you."

"And you think I'll have more luck in retrieving your mare than the sheriff?"

"You'd better."

"If the treasure is nay where ye say it is, woman, I'll wring your neck like a plump chicken."

"It's there," she said. She turned to go, then paused and glanced back. "And I'll give you a warning. If you betray me, I'll shoot you down like a rabid dog."

"Hard talk for an Englishwoman."

"Just so you know," she answered. "I wouldn't want you to underestimate me." He took a long time to reply, and Bess was conscious of the rain beating against the cedar-shingled barn roof.

"So kind of you." His burred voice came thick with sarcasm.

"I'll have my men release you tonight. Sleep here, and in the morning proper quarters will be found for you. I'll give you tomorrow to recover from your imprisonment. The next day we'll ride out and fetch my missing mare."

He nodded in mocking salute. "As ye wish, m'lady. Your slightest command . . ."

She dismissed him with a toss of her head. As she walked out of the stall, her faint chuckle drifted back and robbed the pleasure from his bluster.

Damn her, he thought. An English bitch, as cold inside as frost on a hangman's gibbet. The skin on his scarred back prickled as he remembered the lashes she had delivered with her own slender hands. He'd not forget that indignity.

He'd not lived so long without taking justice from those who wronged him. And, wench or not, she'd be no exception. . . . He would have his revenge.

A bargain made in hell, he'd told her. Maybe it was. But whether the gold existed or not, he'd never be a slave again. No man or woman would put whip to his flesh again. He'd walk free and he'd stay that way. No matter what he had to do . . . Next time, the pain would be someone else's.

He didn't speak when they came to unlock his manacles. He'd waste no words on such as these, despite their taunts and bullying talk. When he was unchained, he left the barn, walking out into the cleansing rain.

The guards followed him to the barn door, shouting threats, but he kept walking. Lightning bolts lit up the cloud-strewn sky; thunder echoed in his ears. Leaves scudded across the muddy farmyard, driven by gusts of wind. Kincaid paid no heed to the rain soaking his shirt and breeches. He turned his face to the storm, breathing deeply of the scents of wet grass, evergreens, and salt.

From the pound came the heavy, musty odors of manure and livestock. They filled his head and brought back memories of childhood. He grimaced. Scotland . . . Ireland . . . France . . . the

American colonies . . . In the rain, all barnyards smelled alike. At least here the fire in the sky was lightning, not the flames of a burning house. There were no screams of trapped animals or dying women.

How many children, he wondered, learn their sums by counting stolen cattle . . . or subtracting missing comrades at dawn's first gray light? God rot the bloody pictures flashing over and over in his head! Rain and mud. Wind in his face and icy water running down his back . . .

Mercenaries. Soldiers fighting for whoever paid them. Marching in sun and heat, dying in muddy ditches, leaving their lifeblood in crimson streaks across rock, and marsh, and fallen tree trunks, in battles too obscure to have a name.

His earliest memories were of raids on dark, rainy nights. Of bawling wide-horned cattle and gunshots . . . Of chilblains and frostbitten feet . . . Of being so hungry that he'd eaten half-cooked rats . . . Of fighting off men and other boys to keep the vermin . . .

Somewhere, sometime, he must have had a mother. But whether she was whore or luckless lady, no one could tell. A woman named Fiona had once been good to him. She'd nursed him the winter he'd taken a sword slash to his left thigh and it had swelled with poison. He was six that winter . . . or perhaps five.

It was snowing when Fiona took pity on him and stopped beside the road to see if he was dead or alive. She was a laundress with the army. Past her prime and looks, a woman who'd belonged to too many men and followed troops to too many wars. But Fiona had been the only one to notice a bone-thin lad sprawled in the mud, out of his head with pain and fever. She'd picked him up and carried him to her evening campsite.

Fiona's matted gray hair was streaked with auburn, she was missing teeth, and one eyelid sagged, but she'd looked beautiful to him. She'd fussed over him, and fed him, and called him her darling boy.

It had been a hard winter, with soldier's pay and rations late or nonexistent. Snow had drifted around the tents and ice crusted the muddy stream that was both washtub and the only source of drinking water for men, women, and horses. Aye, Kincaid remembered, it had been a fierce, starving winter . . . but he'd not cared a tinker's damn for the weather or the war. He'd warmed his cracked hands at Fiona's fire, and filled his growing boy's belly with her mutton stew and hot, sweet scones.

And then one morning he'd awakened and found her gone. No words of good-bye, no bedroll, no cooking pot. Fiona had vanished without leaving him a crust of bread or a farewell swat. It had been the end of his childhood and the last time he'd looked to a woman for mothering.

At seven, he had slain his first man. On a night like this . . . He'd been grateful to the soldier who shared his tent and haunch of venison with a wet, hungry boy. Until the dog's vomit had demanded payment in a filthy manner that Kincaid had vowed he'd never give. The soldier had chased him out into the storm and torn at Kincaid's breeches until he'd ended the assault by stabbing the soldier with his own skean.

Kincaid wiped his face and rubbed his aching

eyelids. Do the memories ever fade? he wondered. He could still feel the way the knife felt, sliding between the soldier's ribs. He could hear the man's groan, and smell the sickly-sweet scent of fresh blood.

"On a night like this . . ." Kincaid murmured. "A world and a lifetime away . . ."

Lightning struck a giant oak at the edge of the pasture, snapping a limb as thick as Kincaid's waist and setting the tree ablaze. He shielded his eyes against the flash and turned to stride away from the farm buildings. He needed to think, and he needed to be alone.

As he turned, another flash lit up the sky, and he saw a cloaked figure standing near the house. It was the woman, Elizabeth Bennett, and she was staring in his direction.

"Hellfire and damnation!" he swore softly. What sane wench would stand outside in this storm and risk being hit by lightning? Or catching pneumonia from the downpour? Then he began to chuckle. "None that I ken," he muttered under his breath. "I've seen none as mad as I am."

He waited, ignoring the rain beating on his face, hoping lightning would illuminate her again. But when the next strike came, she had vanished like some ghostly kelpie. Kincaid lowered his head and walked directly into the wind.

By dawn he was miles away from Fortune's Gift heading south along the peninsula on a tall, stocky bay gelding he'd taken from the plantation. There'd be hell to pay when Mistress Bennett discovered he'd stolen another of her horses and ridden off. But if she wanted him to try to get her mare back, he'd have to converse with Joan Pollott in private. Having the high-and-mighty Elizabeth along would guarantee that the trollop would keep the horse's whereabouts to herself.

The temptation to keep riding plagued him like a blister from an ill-fitting shoe. Any mercenary worth his salt would put as much distance between himself and the Maryland Colony as possible in the least amount of time.

But he'd struck a bargain with the mistress of Fortune's Gift. She'd promised him freedom and the opportunity he'd been striving for his whole life. Enough gold to buy land of his own. Not just a few rock-strewn acres, but enough property to be a man of importance.

Every war he'd ever heard of had been fought for land. It was the only thing that lasted. A landowner could look a king square in the eye and feel his equal. It was a prize worth dying for.

Besides . . . he'd never broken his word, not when he was a scabby-kneed bairn, and not since. For so many years he'd possessed nothing but his honor, and he'd come to hold it dear. He'd promised Elizabeth he'd take her hunting Spanish gold, and by Lucifer's shriveled cod, he'd do it.

The village of Onancock lay south, across the Virginia line. He'd traveled this way only once before, but the peninsula narrowed to just a few miles across, and Kincaid was certain he could find the small settlement again.

He kept the gelding moving at a mile-eating trot, taking care not to ride too close to the scattered houses. He knew word of his escape would travel fast, and he wanted to reach Joan Pollott before she was warned of his presence. The first night, he slept in a barn and made his breakfast on a clutch of hen's eggs he found in the loft. The second night, he put his feet under the battered table at the Cock's Comb, a disreputable riverside inn.

Kincaid had joined an ongoing game of hazard in the inn courtyard. Since he didn't have a ha'penny in his pocket, he knew he had to win, so he played it safe, calling seven as his main. His luck held, and he nicked on his first throw. The setter, a dour-faced farmer, demanded his turn as caster, then threw out with a deuce-ace. Kincaid lost a penny, then won six more in the next half hour. He quit when he had enough silver for supper and a round of ale for the farmer and his two companions.

The innkeeper promised a clean bed, but Kincaid had known too many comrades who'd gone to sleep in strange public houses and never lived to see morning. He finished his meat and bread, downed a second mug of sour ale, and rode off in the opposite direction he intended to travel. He doubled back twice and finally rolled up in his blanket for the night in the shelter of a cedar grove.

By midmorning, he had come upon the outskirts of Onancock. A few minutes' ride brought him to Mistress Pollott's isolated dwelling. He tied his horse in the woods out of sight, crept up close to the house, crouched in the tall weeds, and waited.

An hour later, a yawning Joan appeared in the doorway of her ramshackle cabin, dressed only in stays and a stained linen shift. Her curly dark hair was uncombed, her feet were bare, and her eyes were puffy and red-rimmed. She shuffled out to the necessary behind the shed, then returned and drew up a bucket of water from the well near the door. She was splashing water on her comely face when he stood up and walked boldly toward her.

"Good day to ye, lass," he called lazily. "A bit late risin' this morning, aren't ye?"

Joan's eyes widened in surprise. She stepped back, dropped the bucket—splashing water over her bare feet—and set her fists on her ample hips. "Go to hell, Kincaid," she said.

"Now, is that any way to greet me after all we meant to each other?"

Joan started to run back to the house, but he was quicker. He beat her to the door and leaned against it, ankles crossed, arms folded over his chest, and grinning.

"Damn ye," she cried. "Ye brought the sheriff down on me, ye yellow-haired son of a bitch!"

"I did nothin' of the sort, sweet. 'Twas you as turned me in for the reward."

Her reply blistered his ears.

"Now, Joan, none of that," he soothed. "What kind of talk is that for a lady?"

"I thought they'd hanged ye. I *hoped* they'd hanged ye. What are ye doin' here?"

"Ah, so concerned for my safety, are ye? It fair warms the cockles of my heart. I swear it does."

"What do ye want of me?"

He threw an arm around her and pulled her close. "Joan, Joan." He grinned provocatively. "Must ye have a man's desires put into words?"

"Ye're naught but trouble," she said. "Go on wi' ye."

He slipped a hand down the curve of her back

and stroked one rounded cheek. "Ah, lass, ye wound me sorely. Do ye nay remember what fun we had together?"

"I'll ha' no truck with pirates," she said, sulking. "I'm an honest whore, I am."

He caressed her full lower lip with the tip of one finger. "There's a mouth that bears kissin'," he said. "I've missed ye."

"Hmmph." She frowned and glanced over her shoulder to see if anyone was watching. "Come inside," she said grudgingly, "before ye're seen."

He stepped aside and gave a mocking bow. "Is that bacon I smell cooking?"

Joan flounced across the kitchen and proceeded to tie a battered canvas and wire hip-bucket hoop around her waist. Over that, she fastened a soiled petticoat that had once been canary yellow. "Ye might ha' the decency to turn yer head whilst a lady dresses," she admonished.

"I like to look at ye."

Spots of red appeared on her round cheeks, and her brown eyes took on a hint of mischief. "Go on wi' ye," she replied. "Ye ply me wi' sweet talk when ye want somethin'." She frowned. "Like as not, your pockets are empty again, and ye ha' the nerve to come to me, knowin' full well I'm a helpless woman alone wi' her way to make in the world."

"Nay," he protested, flipping her a silver penny.

She caught it in midair, bit down to make certain the coin wasn't dross, and tucked it out of sight in her bosom. "A penny won't buy ye much," she said, but she smiled as she spoke.

"Breakfast," he said. "I'd like some breakfast. I'm famished."

"Men is always hungry for one thing or 'tother." Joan took a faded rose wool skirt from a peg on the wall, pulled it over her head, and topped it off with a large blue-and-white-striped kerchief that she draped over her shoulders, tied in front, and tucked into the skirt. She nudged a calico cat out of the way, thrust her narrow, bare feet into Indian moccasins, and finished her morning toilet by running her fingers through her untidy mass of curls and topping her hair with a beribboned linen mobcap.

Kincaid knelt on the hearth and turned the bacon with a long fork. He lifted the lid of a Dutch oven, saw that the biscuits were nicely browned, and removed the heavy iron pot from the coals. "Ye wouldn't have a bit of ale to wash this down with, would ye?" he asked.

Joan gestured toward a keg on a three-legged stool in the corner of the brick-floored room. "Ye know where I keep it."

"There's no need for ye to go to the trouble of dressin' for me, lass," he teased. "I like ye well enough without—"

"Mind yer tongue," she chided, picking up the cat and stroking her. "Have ye no decency at all? And the sun high as it is?"

Kincaid grinned at her. "Don't play games with me, Joan Pollott. How many weeks was it we bedded up together here last winter before ye turned me in for the reward?" He deliberately kept his tone light.

She put the cat down and wiped her hands on her skirt. "No such thing. I never give ye over to the sheriff. 'Twas the law what come to me, as-kin' questions I had no right answer fer. Didn't I tend yer wound—and ye near to dyin'? Didn't I give ye the hospitality of me house? And ye eatin' fer three men?''

"Aye. But I paid ye with that fine red mare—a horse whose worth would buy this house three times over."

"Well . . ." Joan pursed her full lips. "I sup-pose it wasn't so bad . . . havin' ye here, for all ye near ruined my trade by drivin' my gentlemen friends away." She smiled so that her small, pointed teeth gleamed white. "Ye are a man fer the ladies, certain."

Kincaid chuckled. Joan Pollott was much like her cat. Stroke her properly and she'd purr; ruffle her and she was all claws and bristle. "Nay, lass. 'Tis your charms what bring out the rakehell in me. I was an innocent when I came to seek shelter in your—"

She giggled. "Go on wi' ye, ye lyin' rogue! A man with a percy the size and stamina of yours? Ye'd compromise the morals of a holy nun."

Kincaid carried the Dutch oven full of biscuits to the scarred wooden table. Joan brought the ba-con and a kettle of corn mush, wrapping the hem of her skirt around the kettle handle to protect her hand from the heat. She took tin plates and cups from a Welsh cupboard and set them out along with spoons and eating knives. A crock held honey, and a second, strawberry jam.

"I've no butter," she apologized. "I used the last of it two days ago and haven't walked over to Widow Bell's to fetch more."

"This is fine," Kincaid assured her, spreading

a biscuit with jam and handing it to her. "Your jam and bread would bring a man farther than I've come."

"So it's my sweets ye crave?" she teased.

Kincaid grinned. "Ye are a lass for sweets, and that's God's truth." He covered her hand with his and rubbed her fingers suggestively. "I have missed ye, Joan, and that's more than idle talk. But what I came for was that red mare."

"Ye know they asked me about her." Joan pouted prettily. "I told them all I'd never seen the animal."

"So ye did, and clever it was of ye, lass. But now I need to know where ye sold her."

" 'Twas mine. Ye gave her to me for payment. I came by the horse honest. I'm no thief, and I'll not put my neck in a noose by admitting—"

"Nor do I expect ye to," he said. "Ye were innocent. I stole the mare, and I paid dearly for it." He lifted the tail of his shirt to show the whip marks on his back. "What I must do is find the mare. Mistress Bennett of Fortune's Gift has offered a great reward for the animal," he lied smoothly.

"More than the horse is worth?"

"Enough to keep you in silk petticoats for a long time."

" 'Tis a trick," she answered. "Ye've returned to cause me trouble. I know nothing of the mare ye speak of—I never set eyes on the beast. So I will swear before the court. I'm an ign'rant whore, and I keeps to me own trade."

Kincaid shook his head. "Ye are a shrewd businesswoman, Joan. Too canny to let good silver coin go to another. Sooner or later, the mare will be found. No questions will be asked, but the one who sends word of the horse's whereabouts to Fortune's Gift will earn the reward.''

''If I was to know, the law would hang me fer—''

''Ye kenned nothing. Ye did nothing but take payment for board and lodging from a strange gentleman.''

Joan chuckled. ''And who would believe ye to be a gentleman?''

He pulled her onto his knee and kissed her soundly. ''Why, a lady such as yourself,'' he murmured, tugging at the kerchief that covered her bosom.

''I thought ye was hungry,'' she said, giggling.

''And so I am, bonny Joan,'' he answered, kissing her throat and the rise of her rosy breasts. For all her rough manners, Joan was clean enough about her person, and the smell of her excited him.

''Then ye ha' come to the right place.'' She moistened her lips with the tip of her tongue and laughed provocatively. ''But I give nothin' away for free. 'Twill cost ye dear.''

''So I thought, darling,'' he answered gruffly. ''So I thought.''

Chapter 5

Bess opened her eyes and listened, wondering what had awakened her. It was not yet dawn, and she knew that the light, when it did come, would be faint and distorted by the heavy fog that had moved in at dusk. She rose and went to the window.

The world outside was an impenetrable wall of dampness and muffled sound. She couldn't even see the poplar tree that grew only a few feet from the house. She yawned and raised the window. Silence.

She had no idea of the time. It could be three or four; it was too early to get up, especially since she'd been assisting in the birth of a calf in the barn until midnight.

"Kutii?" she whispered. "Are you here?" She didn't think he was. This feeling was not the same as the one she experienced when the Indian was near. Kutii never made her uneasy; his presence was comforting.

She sniffed. Was this what she had come to? Talking to ghosts in the night? Jumping at the normal creaking of a house in the fog? Spinsters did such things. Didn't everyone say so?

If she'd married at seventeen or eighteen, like most of her friends, she would have had a husband and children to keep her company. Her life would have been so full of responsibilities that she'd have no time for such flights of fancy.

If she'd married . . . She shook her head, banishing such thoughts. She'd never marry. She had a life and she was content with it. Fortune's Gift was all she needed.

She closed the window and turned back toward the bed. A candle and a wooden box containing flint and steel and cedar shavings stood on her night table, but she didn't trouble herself to strike a spark. She knew every inch of the house. Mama had always said she could see better in the dark than most people in broad daylight. A smile played across her lips. What did a witch's hatchling need with a light?

Bess wondered if she'd been dreaming. Lord knew she had enough to be uneasy about. Her creditors were demanding money, she was still without an overseer, and she'd let Kincaid steal a second horse from her and vanish like smoke.

She hadn't thought he would run. She really hadn't. Her own stupidity was harder to take than his betrayal. Three weeks he'd been missing . . . and now the sheriff was threatening to collect on the bond she'd posted to guarantee Kincaid's good behavior.

By now the rogue was probably in Carolina, drunk as a bishop, and laughing at her. She could see him in her mind's eye, chest thrown out, arms akimbo, boasting arrogantly of his escape.

She glanced toward the window, and it seemed to her as though she saw a flash and at the same instant heard a muffled boom. Hurriedly, she threw on an old shirt of her father's and a riding skirt. She didn't take the time to don a corset; instead, she covered the loose shirt with an over-sized vest for modesty's sake. She stepped into low moccasins and took her grandfather's pistols from the mantel. They were always kept loaded, and it was an easy task to load the frizzen pans with fine black powder.

Again the darkness was no obstacle. Mama had insisted that she learn to handle firearms in the pitch black. *The devil rarely lashes his tail and causes mischief in broad daylight,* her grandmother had ad-monished. *Look for trouble in darkness, and you'll seldom be disappointed.*

Bess left the room and went downstairs. As she passed through the kitchen wing, she paused long enough to shake the cook from his sleep. "Wake the servants," she ordered. "Arm yourselves and look sharp. Something's amiss."

"You'll not go out—" the cook began.

"Do as I say," Bess whispered sharply. "It may be nothing, but I want you all ready."

Seeny, the brindle hound bitch, was whining at the kitchen door when Bess threw the iron bar aside. "Tan!" she called to the male dog stretched out before the hearth. "Go get 'em." She opened the door a crack and the female shot out. "Tan!" Bess repeated. The dog followed his mate, ears pricked, tail stiff, keen nose sniffing the air.

Bess was halfway down the outside steps when Seeny struck up a cry. Tan began to bark and van-ished into the thick fog. The bitch's deep, re-sounding bellow brought similar responses from a dozen other dogs. The fog muffled the sound and played tricks on Bess's hearing, but instinct made her turn toward the river landing.

Her heart was in her throat. Her mouth was dry, and she clenched her teeth to keep them from chattering. There was no question of running in the murky gray vapor. She shoved one pistol into her waistband, took a firm grip on the second, and walked with one hand out in front of her to keep from striking something head-on.

Still not knowing if she'd alerted the servants and loosed the hounds for nothing, Bess forced herself to take one step after another. Fear coiled inside her. She was perspiring, despite the clammy, damp mist. She felt like a child wandering through a nightmare, waiting for some creature to leap out at her, almost wishing it would. Nothing could be worse than this nameless dread, or the overwhelming sense that something unclean walked Fortune's Gift tonight.

Suddenly she stopped and felt the space in front of her. She couldn't see her own hand in front of her face. Everything was lost in an enveloping cloud. Her breath came in quick, short gasps; her blood was racing. She wanted to turn and run, but she couldn't. If she gave in to her fears, where would she stop?

She moved her hand back and forth. Nothing. Hesitantly, she took a step and stifled a cry as her foot struck something. Shaking, she dropped to her knees and reached out with trembling fingers. She touched something still warm and fur-covered. Something that no longer held life.

She ran her hand along the animal's belly and up over a front leg, stopping when she came to a wet, sticky ooze. It was a dog, a big one, and his throat was cut. She felt for a collar and found braided rawhide. Lafe Johnson's mastiff. Dead not more than a few minutes, unless she missed her guess.

Bess rose and tried to get her directions. Was the dock straight ahead, she wondered, or was it more to the right? The dead dog had frightened her half out of her wits. But it wasn't just the dog. It was—

Without warning, the night exploded into pandemonium. A volley of shots rang out behind her. She heard a woman scream, followed by the roar of a flintlock pistol. The dogs no longer bayed; their snarls nearly drowned out the sounds of the gunfire.

Bess turned and ran toward the commotion. Just ahead of her, a straw stack went up in flames. In the flickering light, she made out a bulky form struggling with a slighter one.

"Help me!"

She recognized the twang of Yorkshire in the terrified woman's voice, followed by the rip of tearing cloth and the sickening thud of a man's fist striking soft flesh. Mariah Carey, Joe Carey's bride of four months, was newly come from England. Mariah's shriek of pain turned to subdued weeping as her assailant threw her to the ground and pinned her with his body.

"No. No," the girl sobbed.

Bess rushed at the man, put the barrel of her pistol against his side, and pulled the trigger. He jerked backward and fell facedown, clutching at the gaping hole in his rib cage.

Mariah covered her face with her hands and cried hysterically. She was naked from the waist up, and blood trickled from one corner of her mouth.

"Get up!" Bess hissed. "There's no time for this."

Mariah lowered her hands and stared wide-eyed at Bess. "They killed Joe," she moaned. "They cut off his head."

"Who? Who are they?" Bess demanded. She rolled the dying man over and stared into his ugly face. He was a total stranger.

"Pirates, Joe said," Mariah babbled. "Run, he said. It's pirates." She began to weep again. "They murdered him. They murdered my Joe."

"How many of them did you see?" Bess asked. She could smell smoke. Screams of women blended now with the panicked whinnying of trapped horses. Two barns were on fire, and it sounded to her as though skirmishes were going on in at least three different spots. More shots rang out through the fog, and off to her left, beyond the pound, Bess saw two men on horseback driving the cattle toward the river.

"I don't know . . . I don't know," Mariah wailed. "He tried to . . ." She pointed at the dead man. "He said he was goin' to . . ."

"Are you hurt?" Bess asked her.

Mariah began to shake.

"Stop that!" Bess said. "Can you fire a pistol?"

"No. I never held no pistol. I'd be feared of a—"

Bess stuck the empty flintlock into her waistband and retrieved the loaded one. "Run and hide in the woods," she said, pointing away from the fires. "Go that way. No one will see you in the fog."

"I'm feared," Mariah whimpered. "They'll come back and get me."

"Do as I say," Bess commanded. "Run into the woods and hide until morning." She turned away toward the pound.

"Don't leave me," Mariah cried.

"Go! Quick, before someone sees us," Bess replied.

"I'm afraid. I can't."

"Get to the woods, you buffle-headed jade, before I shoot you." Bess raised her pistol menacingly. Mariah gave a muffled shriek and dashed off in the direction of the woods. Bess looked around, heard the brindle bitch's bark, and ran toward the sound.

At the corner of the barn, Clyde, one of her grooms, was using a pitchfork to hold off two men with cutlasses. The hound, hackles raised, was snarling at the intruders. Seeny's mouth was stained dark, and she had sustained a deep gash down one side, but she was gamely trying to assist the boy.

As Bess approached, the man closest to Clyde stepped back, lowered his cutlass, and drew a pistol, taking aim at the groom. Bess raised her own weapon and fired. The light was poor, and he was a moving target. With only one shot, she knew she'd not have a second chance. To her delight, the ball tore into his hip. Emitting a yelp of pain, he dropped the pistol.

The second man, a husky seaman with his hair braided into a single tarred pigtail, whirled toward Bess and slashed at her with his cutlass. She sidestepped the blade. "Seeny, kill!" she ordered.

The hound had never hunted men. The order was one given to attack a bear or a crazed steer, but the bitch never hesitated. She flung herself at the sailor's throat. The man toppled over, and Clyde drove the pitchfork through his chest.

For a moment, the boy stared down in shock at the twitching man; then he blinked and passed his arm in front of his face. "Me mam," he croaked. "Me mam is alone. I got to go to her."

"Arm yourself," Bess said, pointing to the marauder's pistol. Clyde nodded, snatched up the flintlock, and ran back along the side of the burning barn. The pitchfork stood upright in the fallen man's chest.

Bess's stomach turned over and she shut her eyes for a second, trying to regain her nerve. Whining, the dog crept close to her leg and licked her hand. "Good Seeny, good girl," she said. She was tired, so tired. The sickly-sweet smell of blood was thick in the air; cinders and burning hay fell around her.

Her head hurt, and the sight of the man with the pitchfork in his chest made her want to be sick. The urge to give in to her fears—to run and hide—was very strong. But she couldn't. This was her home, her people, and if she must meet violence with violence to protect what she loved, then she must find the courage or at least pretend she possessed it.

A deep baying resounded from across the yard, a sound that brought Seeny instantly alert. She leaped away from Bess and hurled herself into the fog as the baying rose to an agonized yelp. Bess recognized the sound as Seeny's mate, Tan. He was obviously hurt, and judging from the fierce growl that came seconds later, it was clear that the hound bitch had gone to Tan's aid. Seeny's enraged snarling was pierced by a man's high-pitched scream and then a musket shot.

Bess knew that she'd fired both pistols and hadn't had time to reload, but she was afraid that if she didn't act at once, it would be too late to save her dogs. Heedless of her own safety, she rushed toward the confrontation.

She'd not gone a half-dozen steps into the blinding fog when someone grabbed her. Bess struck out wildly at her assailant, but a sinewy hand clamped over her mouth so tightly that she wasn't even able to scream.

Terror-stricken, she kicked and punched, trying to break free. She twisted and attempted to scratch the man's eyes, but he was too strong for her. Despite her struggles, he dragged her off deeper into the all-encompassing fog.

"What have ye there?" a rough voice called from the darkness.

"Find your own slut. This'n's mine."

The faceless outlaw answered with a slash of his cutlass. Bess caught sight of it before she was thrown hard against the ground. She rolled away as a pistol spit fire and lead. There was a muffled thud and then silence.

Bess listened. The fighting still raged around the barns and dependencies. But here, in this circle of gray, there was an unnatural quiet. One man had fallen; one waited for her to move. She knew it. But she also knew that if she didn't move, he'd catch her.

Stealthily, she began to crawl away. She'd lost both pistols and had nothing to defend herself with but her wits. She wasn't even certain where she was. Her sense of direction was confused by the fog and by her fright of being seized by a man she couldn't see. She thought there was a split-rail fence a few hundred feet ahead. If she could just reach that line of—

A heavy weight landed on top of her and bore her to the ground. Before she could cry out, her attacker pressed his lips close to her ear.

"Cease your squirming, woman," he hissed. "It's me. I'll nay do ye harm. I've come to save yer lily-white English neck!"

"Kincaid!"

"Shout it a little louder, why don't ye?" He caught her wrists and pinned them against the grass. "Ye can't win, ye know. You've ten seconds to come to your senses, or I'll knock ye cold and carry ye to safety."

She mumbled something incomprehensible.

"I can't hear ye."

"Let me up."

"Not until ye promise to do as I say. The farm is swarming with pirates. They've come to take slaves and livestock, and anything else they can carry."

"We have no slaves on Fortune's Gift."

"Ye may know that, but they don't."

"What are you doing here?"

"A question I've asked meself more than once this night, I'll tell ye."

"Let me go," she insisted.

"My way, woman. I'll brook no argument from ye on this."

"Coward!" she hissed. "Why aren't you fighting this scum instead of me?"

"I've given ye fair warning. Come or be carried."

Her answer was a hard drive with her knee to his groin. Kincaid's gasp of pain lent her strength. Bess twisted her head and bit his wrist. When he let go, she wiggled out from under him and began to crawl away. He caught her ankle and yanked her back. They rolled over and Kincaid threw his weight against her, knocking the wind out of her.

Her head spun. She heard the rip of cloth and seconds later Kincaid bound a gag around her mouth. Panic surged through her and she struggled wildly, but he held on to her wrists and bound them as well. An icy current of pure fear washed over her and she came close to fainting, but then reason conquered the overwhelming terror. She ceased fighting him and listened with her inner senses. Instantly, the awful dread receded. Her rapid pulse slowed, and her breathing came easier.

Kincaid threw her over his shoulder. "I won't hurt ye," he growled. "Devil take ye, woman. If I meant ye ill, I'd ring your neck instead of risking my own to get ye out of this."

His soothing words came to her from far away. She was concentrating, drawing up the witchy power that had come to her from her grandmother. For the space of a heartbeat, Bess's consciousness was flooded with a sensation of sea-green light, and with it came the fleeting impression of being safeguarded by this rough Scot. But before she could take comfort from her intuition, his broad hand came down sharply across her backside.

''Be still!'' he ordered as he delivered the stinging blow. ''Lest ye—''

Bess's sense of well-being vanished in white-
hot anger. She rained muffled curses on his head
and kicked him so hard in the midriff that her
toes felt as though they were broken.

''Witch,'' he gasped. He began to run through
the fog with her, dodging once to avoid being run
down by a steer and again to avoid a group of
men who loomed up in the murky darkness.

Bess couldn't tell how far he ran. Branches
striking her face and tearing at her clothes told
her that they had entered the woods, and the cries
behind them grew fainter and fainter. At last, he
stopped and lowered her to the damp forest floor.

''Now, I'll take off the gag and untie ye if you'll
thank me properly,'' he said. He was breathing
hard. ''You're no feather bed to tote, ye ken. Most
men would ha' dropped ye at the first fence.''

''You bastardly gullion,'' she said as soon as he
pulled away the cloth. ''Crow-hearted, yellow-
backed—''

''Cease your canting, chuck,'' he replied,
''afore I regret what I've done and give ye over
to those priggers.'' He cut the rope that held her
wrists together and stepped back out of the line
of fire. ''It would serve both ye and them right.
For a more ungrateful, shrewish lass I've never
laid eyes on.''

Bess scrambled to her feet. ''Those are my people,'' she cried. ''My horses, my cattle. Why are
you here? Why aren't you shooting those pirates
instead of carrying me off into the woods? You
beetle-headed—''

''Enough!'' he snapped. '' 'Tis not my war. I've

not been paid to kill those churls, and I dinna waste my time on matters that dinna concern me. Ye should be grateful that I came back to save your slender English neck.''

"Came back? Came back? How did you know they were going to attack Fortune's Gift? You were with them, weren't you?''

"Aye, I was," he admitted. "But only for the last three days. I overheard them planning the raid, and I decided that the faster way to get back here was to sign on as one of the crew.''

"Some of my women have been attacked, my men killed." Her voice dropped to a harsh whisper. "You could have warned us . . . prevented—"

"Nay. I could not. I was south of here, too far to ride back. They had a sloop and—"

"My horse! You stole another one of my horses. Where is it?''

"I couldn't very well bring the gelding on the boat, could I?''

"Horse thief. Coward." She balled her fist tightly and struck him in the center of his chest with all her might. "I trusted you, and you betrayed me." She hit at him again, and he caught her hand.

"Nay, no more o' that, woman," he warned.

"You're supposed to be a soldier," she said. "A fighter. You're nothing but a thieving blackguard!''

"I can fight if I have to," he admitted. "I thought that coming back to keep you from doing something stupid was enough.''

In truth, he didn't know why he'd returned with the pirates. It was one of the strangest things that had ever happened to him. It made no sense, and Kincaid prided himself on always using good judgment.

He'd known Elizabeth Bennett would be in the thick of the trouble, and he'd known she'd come to harm if he didn't interfere. He'd realized it the moment he'd heard the bearded mulatto mention Fortune's Gift.

"A plantation run by a wench," the pirate had boasted to his drunken comrades in the Virginia, Eastern Shore tavern. "Easy pickings for a few stout men."

And Kincaid, who'd never had a flight of fancy in his life, had instantly felt the chill of fog and heard the scream of a woman in his head. Despite the clear, star-filled Virginia night, he'd seen a vision of Bess outlined in the light of a burning building and known her life was in danger.

"I'm a stranger to your people," he told her. "Like as not, they'd have tried to kill me along with the pirates. I'm nay fond of being caught between two sides. A man could die young that way." He released her hand. "No more o' that," he cautioned. "I might hit ye back, and ye'd nay wish to wake up with a head the size of a pumpkin."

"Oh," she said scornfully, "you'd strike me. You're afraid of men your own size, but you think you can bully a woman."

"Do ye never tire of hearing your own voice?" He shook his head. "All my life I've been accused of being too soft with the lasses, but I'm not clodskulled enough to stand here and let ye pound away at me."

"I'm going back."

"Nay."

"Don't try to stop me. Fortune's Gift is mine, and if—"

"Ye will do as I say, woman," he said. "And I say ye will remain here where it's safe. Dawn's coming fast, and that band will be back to their boat soon."

"You'd let them escape? When they've murdered and—"

"They'll not go far. I took the liberty of knocking a hole in the bottom once they'd gone ashore."

"They could take my sloop."

"Nay, I put a hole in that too."

"You damaged my boat?"

"Hellfire and damnation, is there nothing I do that pleases you?"

"Precious little!" She took a deep breath. "If you fight for money, I'll buy your services. Just go back and help my men defeat them."

"Aye, I could do that. If the pay is good enough. I warn ye, I don't come cheap."

"Go, damn it!"

"Not until we agree on a price."

"What do you want?"

"The gelding I rode off on. I'd nay be hung for borrowing—"

"You can have the horse. Now, go back and—"

"They planned to drive off the cattle and horses," he said. "I told them I knew the plantation well. I sent them down the river road."

"But that road goes nowhere. It ends in Reedy Swamp."

"Aye, so I found out last fall. But by the time

they figure that out, they'll be too far along to turn the animals back and go another way. If you've any hounds left, I'd guess ye can hunt them down easy enough.''

''It doesn't make up for my people dead, my barns burned. You could have stopped it if you'd warned us in time,'' she accused.

''I told ye,'' he repeated through clenched teeth. ''There was no time.''

''I still think you're a coward.''

''Think what ye please, Englishwoman,'' he said as he turned to go back to the fighting. But her words stung like salt on an open wound. He knew he was no craven. And if he knew, then what matter what Mistress Bennett thought? ''But if ye stir from this spot until I send for ye,'' he admonished, ''I'll tie ye hand and foot and leave ye here for the buzzards.''

He stalked away, trying to put her insults out of his mind. She was nothing to him, nothing but trouble, and he'd been a fool to make a bargain with her. ''Better that lot than you,'' he muttered. ''Dealing with bay pirates will be safer and a hell of a lot less aggravation.''

Chapter 6

Bess stood in the ruins of her farmyard in the slow morning drizzle and breathed in the acrid scent of charred wood and disaster. The fog had given over to rain, and it seemed to her as though the skies were weeping for the fallen. Everywhere around her was the evidence of last night's raid; the big horse stable and a smaller barn that had held tack and grain were smoldering ruins. Part of the pound fence was destroyed; the smokehouse had been looted and the door hung awry. Blackened walls were the only remains of three tenant houses.

Of deaths, there were aplenty to mourn for: three men, an infant, and two women had died in the night assault. Another woman had been raped. Mariah Carey was missing; even now a search party combed the woods, fields, and shorelines for her.

Fortune's Gift had lost a good bull, four horses, and two milk cows in the fire. Another two horses had broken legs and had to be destroyed. Five sheep had run blindly into the river and drowned, and Bess's hound, Tan, was close to death from three stab wounds.

The kitchen gardens had been trampled. Some vegetables could be salvaged, but for many, they were tattered bits, and it was too late to replant. The plantation workers needed the snap beans, potatoes, carrots, turnips, and greens that the garden would have provided. Bess considered the loss as great as that of the livestock.

Even the house had not been spared. The rear wall was scorched by fire and windows had been smashed. House servants had prevented the spread of flames and the morning rain had put out the fire before the dwelling was lost. Still, the manor house would bear the scars of the attack for a long time.

Two pirates had gained entry, slashing their way into the great hall and destroying paintings and furniture. They had escaped with silver and several bottles of brandy. A third marauder had been struck down on the cellar steps by a thirteen-year-old maid. She'd knocked him down the stairs with a tall candlestand and finished him off with a three-legged iron spider.

As for the pirates, Kincaid had sunk their vessel as he'd said. The sloop had reached mid-river before settling on a sandbar. The bow and part of the deck were visible above water, but the occupants had been picked off by Bess's bondmen as they tried to swim to safety. Of those who had driven the livestock into the swamp, one had drowned, another had escaped, and two more had been captured and hanged on Bess's orders at first light. Only three steers and two horses were unaccounted for; most of the animals had wandered back to the barnyard on their own.

Bess was torn between stringing Kincaid up for a pirate and thanking him for preventing the escape of the attackers and saving most of her

animals. For all his bold talk, he'd slain no out-
laws, and she still wondered which side he was
really on.

She'd followed him back to the scene of the
fighting once he'd released her, keeping far behind him to prevent him from seeing her. But by
the time she'd arrived at the farmyard, the battle
was over and a rainy dawn was breaking. Kincaid
had helped to gather the scattered animals, and
hadn't shirked the dirty work of disposing of the
horses that were too badly injured to save, but he
had made himself absent during the execution of
the captured murderers.

Bess had forgotten none of her fury at Kincaid's
interference and abuse, but in the bitter aftermath
of the raid, she was nearly overwhelmed by the
task of bringing order to the chaos. There were
dead to be laid out and washed, graves to dig,
and hurt people and animals to tend. Him she
could deal with later.

She didn't want to think about the price. Re-
covery of Fortune's Gift would be slow and costly.
Every Tidewater planter lived his life in debt, and
the repairs to her buildings and the replacement
of livestock would beggar her.

"How many times can you go to an empty
well?" Bess murmured, unconsciously echoing
one of her grandmother's sayings. She had been
broke yesterday; today she was desperate.

"You know what you have to do."

Bess glanced around and saw Kutii standing a
few feet away, clad only in his usual loincloth and
sandals. His obsidian-black hair hung loose
around his shoulders, and armbands of solid gold

glistened on his muscular, bronzed arms. ''I didn't know you were here,'' she said.

The Incan's tattooed features creased in a sad smile. His dark, slanting eyes were huge and liquid with compassion. ''Where else would I be?''

''You could have warned me.''

He shrugged, spreading his worn hands in an open-palmed gesture. ''I do what I can for you. I always have.''

''You're as bad as Kincaid,'' she grumbled. ''Did you see what he did?'' Bess lowered her voice to a whisper. ''I can't trust him now. For all I know, he could have led the pirates here.''

''He is the one.''

''He's the one. He's the one,'' she mocked angrily. ''I don't care. I hate him. He's lucky I don't hang him with the rest of the scum.''

''You will not.'' The Indian's eyes narrowed in disapproval. ''You will do what your heart tells you.''

''Look at this.''She waved her arms to encompass the damage around her. ''How can I leave Fortune's Gift now?''

''How can you stay?''

''It's a crazy scheme. It's madness. How can I risk everything by running off to Panama in search of buried treasure?''

''Your grandmother risked everything when she set off across the great salt sea in a tiny boat in search of treasure. And she risked all again when she freed me from the sugar mill.''

''I'm not my grandmother.''

''You carry her blood. Her courage will not fail you.''

''Mistress?''

Bess turned to see her blacksmith's son. Obviously bewildered, the boy tugged at his forelock and stared at her with wide eyes. She tried to keep from smiling. Doubtless they all thought her mad, talking to thin air. "Vernon." She acknowledged him with a nod. "Is there any sign of Mariah?"

" 'Twas what I come to tell ye," he muttered. One bare foot made nervous circles in the warm ashes. "We found her, mistress, but she ain't right. She won't say nothin'. She just rocks and cries, rocks and cries."

"I'll come and see to her," Bess assured him. She nodded to the group of men who were dragging a dead steer away from the barn. "Butcher it," she called to the oldest man. "We can't afford to lose the meat. It will have to be salted and smoked today." She looked back to see if Kutii was still standing there, but he was gone, vanished into the drifting smoke. Just like a man, she thought. Never there when you need him.

She rubbed her aching eyes with her fingertips, wishing that there were some way she could get a few hours' sleep before dealing with all this. She was so tired, and she'd always needed a good night's rest. She was cranky without one.

"Mistress Bess!"

Steeling herself, she turned toward the demanding faces and prepared to make whatever decisions couldn't be put off.

It was late afternoon before Bess found time to bathe and change her clothes. She was too tired to eat, so she drank half a glass of wine and stretched out across her bed for a few moments.

Just as she was drifting off to sleep, Janie, the little maid who'd knocked the pirate down the cellar stairs, burst into her bedchamber.

"Miss Bess!" the girl cried. "I told him he couldn't come up here, but I—"

Bess raised her head. Kincaid's rugged form filled the doorway of her room, and it struck her once more how big he was and how out of place he seemed on Fortune's Gift. As though he belonged in an earlier, more savage time, she thought, taking a deep breath. Her anger at him was still with her, but she pushed it back, knowing that anger made poor reason when you were dealing with men or animals. And Kincaid was certainly one . . . although which one, she wasn't sure. "It's all right, Janie," she said in her most authoritarian voice. "I'll see him."

"Not here, miss. Not here. It ain't fittin'. Want I should call—"

Bess dismissed her with a wave of her hand. "Why not? Pirates go where they please, don't they?" Her words sounded slurred and silly, even to her own ears, but it had been a long day, and from the look of Kincaid's face, it was about to get longer.

"Were you serious about our bargain?" he demanded of Bess when the maid had scurried back down the hall.

"I was." She sat up, curled her stockinged feet under her, and stretched. "But that was before you stole my second horse and helped organize a raiding party against me."

"I went off to hunt for that damned mare you're so fond of. It just took a little longer than I thought." He glanced around the room in the manner of a man who always wanted to know where all the exits were.

She glared at him. "You're lucky I don't take the skin off your back again. I'm not accustomed to being manhandled by my servants."

His eyes narrowed. "Woman. We maun come to an understanding." His big frame tensed and Bess realized what an effort it was for him to hold his temper. "I'll nay be bridled or driven by a skittish mare. I'm a mon who—"

"I've a name," she admonished him, noting that his Highland burr thickened when he became angry. "I'll not be addressed as 'woman.' You may call me Bess. If we're going to travel together, it's best we drop the formalities of my—"

"Nay. If I take ye, I'll nay be callin' ye 'mistress,' nor waitin' on ye hand and foot like ye were a bloody duchess."

"If?" She slid off the bed and came toward him. "What of our bargain? Is your word as useless as your fighting ability?"

He shrugged, letting her insult roll off his back as lightly as a spring shower of scattered raindrops. "I did agree to go with ye," he admitted, "but I'm having second thoughts now that I see how witless ye be. A lass has nay business in the midst of a battle. Any wench with a peck of sense would have stayed far away from the shooting."

"I'm not like any lass you've known."

"I see that now, and it's what troubles me." He scowled fiercely at her. "Ye could get us both killed."

"I can shoot and ride better than most men. I can walk all day and find my direction in the deep

woods without sun or stars to guide me. I was
raised as a son, not a daughter.''

''There's little enough that is womanly about
you,'' he agreed, lying. Damn, but she was a
stone in his shoe that rubbed and rubbed until it
drove a man half out of his mind. Her shape and
form was as lushly female as any he'd ever seen.
The way she walked, the way she tossed that
thick mane of curling red hair . . . He'd seen his
share of beautiful women, but only a handful who
possessed the magic that could lure a man to his
death. The devil's jest was that all that allure was
wrapped around a spiteful shrew's tongue and a
mule-stubborn head. ''I'll risk my life on a chance
for riches, but nay on a foolish whim,'' he said.
''If you've a treasure map, let's see it.''

She raised her gaze to meet his defiantly, and
his throat tightened as it did in the last seconds
before he went into a battle. God in heaven, but
she was one of a kind. Not many men had the
nerve to stand an arm's length away and stare
him down.

''I realize that you think you did me a favor by
carrying me away from the fighting,'' she said
softly, ''but lay hands like that on me again and
I'll kill you—I swear I will.''

''Keep talking. I'm less inclined to go on your
jaunt with every minute that passes. You're not
only a fool, you're an ungrateful one. I save your
skin and ye threaten to murder me.'' He sniffed.
''I warn ye, English Bess, I take more killin' than
you ken.'' He folded his arms across his chest.
''Show me proof that there is a treasure.''

She went to the fireplace and removed a brick.
Reaching inside the hidden compartment, she re-

trieved a water-stained book and a leather bag. "This is my grandfather's journal," she said. "He sailed with Henry Morgan against the Spanish. The treasure is part of the gold they took during Morgan's famous raid on Panama City. They could carry only part of it because they were attacked by hostile Indians in the jungle. The journal gives dates and distances and landmarks, telling exactly where the chests are buried." She thumbed through the pages and read aloud the account of the siege of the Spanish stronghold. "Are those the words of a man who lived that day or not?" she demanded.

"Aye," Kincaid said. "They be." He'd fought step by step through enough such carnage to know the truth from hearsay. Just listening to her read, he could smell the stench of fresh blood and hear the bark of pistols and the clash of steel. "Who did he serve under, this grandsire of yours?"

"Captain Matthew Kay."

Kincaid nodded. "I've heard of the man, but not as a buccaneer. Wasn't he a royal governor of one of the English colonies?"

"I don't know. My grandfather never mentioned him or anything of his own life before he came to Maryland."

"Hmmmp." Kincaid grunted assent. That rang true as well. A man with sense kept quiet about his past if he'd come by his wealth with a sword. "Let me see the section on the location of the treasure."

She laughed and shook her head. "Now you *do* take me for a fool. With that information, you've no need of me."

She handed him the book and he saw that a half-dozen pages had been ripped out of the journal. The last entry broke off with the words "Being in dire straits, with three of our party lost and only six mules left, I have decided to bury half of the treasure. This spot is undoubtedly the best one we will find, being only a hundred yards from the waterfall and directly—" Kincaid looked up at the woman. "Where are the missing pages?"

"I burned them," she said.

A foul oath slipped from his mouth before he could mind his manners. "Ye what?" he demanded.

"I committed them to memory and burned them," she replied. "You need me to find the gold, because the only map of the resting place is in my head."

"God rot your lyin' eyes," he swore, and then could not contain a chuckle. "Well done," he admitted. "As slick as I'd do meself." He laughed aloud. "A rare lass, indeed." He handed her back the book. "You've more proof than half a journal, I suppose."

In answer she dumped the contents of the leather bag into his hand. It was a golden cat with eyes of turquoise. He hefted the object in his hand, testing the weight, then bit it. The soft gold gave under his teeth. "Aye," he agreed with a grin. "That's solid gold."

"Proof enough?" she returned cockily.

"Aye, proof enough for a Scotsman." He gave her back the glittering statue. "Now, have ye money enough to pay for the journey? I can travel cheap, but it will cost to book passage and hire men to—"

"We can sell the jaguar," she said. "I've no coin, but I've personal jewelry and weapons belonging to my father and grandfather."

"I'll want good pistols," he warned, "and a sword."

"For both of us," she said. "I find a sword too heavy, but I'm handy with a knife. Kutii taught me; he was an Incan Indian, a great friend to my grandparents."

"I suppose I could use a musket if you've got a good one, as well as powder and shot. And don't be thinkin' ye can carry trunks of fancies with ye. If we go, we go with what we can carry, no more."

"Agreed," she said.

"And ye will play the part of my leman."

It was her turn to stiffen. "We travel together," she said coldly. "I've hired you to protect me, nothing more."

"I said ye were to play a role. I've no wish to part your cold flesh, Englishwoman." It was a lie and he knew it as he said it. He had every wish to bed her, but she was poison and the cost of such action would be far greater than he intended to pay. He'd put himself in a woman's clutches once. He'd let himself be vulnerable, and he'd carry the result to his grave. Nay, for all her showy looks, this was one wench who would be safe from him. He'd never been a man to let his cock lead his brain, and Bess Bennett would be as safe as a holy nun beside him.

Her face flushed deep scarlet. "I mean it, Kincaid," she whispered. "If you lay hands on me, I'll drive a dagger into your heart. I'm no slut, and I'll not whore for you or any man."

"Leave off with your ranting, chuck. 'Twill be safe for us both if we pretend to be a pair."

"I could be your sister."

"What man believes another travels with his sister, be she over the age of ten?"

"Your wife, then. Why do I have to be your light-skirts?"

"Because I am not the marryin' kind, and any with half a head will know it. There is a *brotherhood of the blade*. We ken one another. A wandering mercenary and his doxy. Few will think it odd, and fewer still will venture to try and take what belongs to me, be it pistol or wench."

"You think highly of yourself."

"I've good reason."

"I don't hold it against you," she said. "I think highly of myself."

"So I've noticed."

She laid the book on the table and took a sheet of paper from the drawer. "I've written out our agreement giving you your freedom on our return from Panama," she said. "I've signed and dated it."

"When did you do that?"

"Weeks ago. The day you stole my second horse."

"You knew I'd be back."

"I wrote it before you ran off." She flashed him a cold blue stare. "I don't trust you, Kincaid. I want you to know that. I'll be watching you every step of the way."

"Fair enough."

"I'll read it to you if you like," she offered.

"Nay."

"Then make your mark, here at the bottom, under mine."

"Think ye I canna read and write?" He scanned the simple contract quickly, then dipped a quill pen in an ink bottle and signed "Kincaid" in large, bold script above her name. "Where I come from," he said, "a man comes first above a woman."

"Then it's obvious you come from a backward part of the world," she chided. "In the Maryland colony, women are more highly valued. Any gentleman would—"

"But I'm no gentleman," he told her. "And I doubt you'd find any gentleman who could—"

"Mistress Bess! Mistress Bess!"

Kincaid stepped toward the doorway to see an older man running up the steps. Bess pushed past him into the upstairs hall. "That's my cook," she said, "Deaf Donald. He can't hear, so you must speak slowly when you talk to him. He reads your lips. What is it, Donald?" she asked as he came to a halt in front of her.

"The high sheriff, mistress. He's at the dock with William Myers's son. They say they've come for payment of a loan. They're coming to the house."

"Thank you, Donald," she answered. "Try and delay them as long as you can. I'm going away for a while, but I'll be back. And when I come, I'll make everything right. Do you understand?"

"Yes, mistress," he said in the stiff, oddly accented tones of a man who had not heard human speech in many years.

"You are in charge of the house until I get back."

"Yes, ma'am."

"Tell Ned that he is responsible for getting the crop in. If he needs help, he is to ask . . ." She sighed. "Tell him to do the best he can until my father returns or I do."

"Your father is alive, miss? Master David is coming home?"

"Yes. You can tell the others that, and you can tell the sheriff. My father is coming home a rich man. I've had a message from him. Go now," she urged, "and try to keep the sheriff out of the house for as long as possible."

"Is your father really coming home?" Kincaid asked as soon as the cook had gone.

She shrugged. "God only knows. I had to tell them something." She ducked past him and ran to the foot of her bed and threw open a blanket chest. "There are weapons in here. Choose what you want." She pulled two saddlebags from under her bed and began to toss personal items into it. "We have to go now. If I see the sheriff, he may—"

"I've nay wish to visit wi' the man myself," Kincaid said. "Shall we leave by the kitchen door or the front?" he asked as he removed a pair of French pistols and a powder horn from the chest. Beneath them, rolled in oilcloth, he found an old-fashioned cutlass with a burnished blade of Damascus steel.

"I've another way." She dug frantically through a smaller chest and came up with scissors, a pack of needles, and a hank of thread.

"We'll have little time for fine sewing," Kincaid said.

She ignored him and continued to stuff the saddlebags with garments and odds and ends. The last thing he saw her tuck into her cache was a small, silver-inlaid pistol. "Hurry," she said, grabbing a woolen cloak and a pair of boy's breeches. "The balls are in the bottom of the chest."

He reached deep into the chest, sliced his finger on something sharp, and swore.

"Oh, there's a skean in there too. It belonged to my grandfather. Watch out, it has a—"

"Thank you for warning me," he said, popping his bleeding finger in his mouth. He removed the knife and slid it into his boot top. The pistols went into his belt, the powder horn over one shoulder.

"You're supposed to be a soldier," she said. "Can't you even handle a knife without cutting yourself?" She slung the bags over her shoulder and started for the door. "Come on if you're coming," she urged, then dashed back to the table for the bag with the golden cat in it.

"I would have remembered that," he said, coming after her.

There was a loud pounding at the front door, but Bess paid no heed to the racket. She led the way down the front stairs and through a small door that opened into the cellar. "Close it behind you," she cautioned. "Watch out, the steps are steep."

"I can find me way down a flight of stairs in the dark," he growled. Either the wench had a rabbit hole out or she'd led them into a blind alley two minutes into their journey. He hoped it was the former.

"Follow me," she said.

"Aye, dinna worry."

She ducked into a small room, then through another doorway to a stack of barrels. "Move these," she ordered.

"Yes, ma'am," he answered sarcastically as he laid aside the cutlass. Behind the barrels was a narrow wooden door, and behind that, a flight of brick steps that led upward.

"There's an iron bar across the outside door," she said. "Lift that, and push."

There seemed to be some resistance beyond the door, but it gave when he threw his shoulder into it. As the door opened, he saw it was a hedge of boxwood.

"Let me go first," she said. "I've done it before." She handed him the cutlass. "Don't forget this," she reminded him.

The spiderwebs made it obvious to Kincaid that she'd not passed this way in some time, but he moved back and let her go ahead. She squirmed her way through the bushes and into an enclosed garden with high walls of greenery.

"It's a boxwood maze," she whispered, signaling to him for silence. "There's a secret opening at the far end, near the orchard. From there we can—"

"You get us out of the maze," Kincaid said. "After that, I'll give the orders. We'll ride south into Virginia. There's a tavern there that—"

"I thought we'd sail down the—"

"Hist," he said sharply. "Ye will do as I say from now on." He took hold of her arm and pulled her around to face him. "I mean it. There can be only one leader of this expedition. Do you understand me?"

She nodded. "Yes."

"Good enough, then." He let her go, trying not to think of the tingling that ran up his hand. Her skin had been soft and her nearness a distraction, even with the law three steps behind them. "Just so ye ken the rules," he repeated sternly.

"Do what I hired you to do, and you'll have no trouble from me," she whispered.

He exhaled softly through clenched teeth. Aye, he thought, you'll give no trouble. I believe that as much as I believe gold coins will fall out of the sky into our hands as soon as we set foot on Spanish territory.

Chapter 7

Kincaid glanced back over his shoulder at the woman riding behind him, to make certain she hadn't fallen asleep and toppled off her horse. It was still several hours before dawn, and they'd been in the saddle since late afternoon the day before. She'd hardly spoken to him since they'd left Fortune's Gift. The only time she'd urged her mare up next to his was when she wanted to point out a change in direction or when he'd gotten off the faint trail in the darkness.

They were headed south down the peninsula. Bess had wanted to cross the bay to Annapolis or try to find passage in Chestertown, but he'd had other ideas. More importantly, he wanted to reinforce his statement to her earlier, that he would be making the decisions. He had no intention of spending the next three months arguing with her at every step of the way.

He ducked his head to avoid a low-hanging branch. They'd not sighted a living soul since they left the boundaries of her plantation. And that suited him just fine. He doubted that the sheriff would set out in hot pursuit of them, but there was always that chance.

Of all the schemes he'd gotten himself into in his lifetime, this was undoubtedly the most bi-

zarre. He'd been to Panama before—at least he'd
spent a few days on an island off the coast—and
it wasn't a spot he'd ever planned to visit again.
The Spaniards had no love for foreigners, and the
natives were less than friendly. He'd heard tales
of men who were slaughtered and eaten by the
Indians, and any prisoner who survived long
enough to be turned over to the Spanish might
wish he'd been killed quickly by a blowgun or a
stone war club.

It didn't matter if England and Spain were for-
mally at war or not. Any English-speaking captive
could expect to be worked to death in a silver
mine in the New World or sent back to Spain to
languish in some dank, airless prison. There were
even rumors that the Spanish castrated English
sailors and sold them to the infidel Turks.

His chances of finding the gold—if the treasure
story was true—would have been better without
this Englishwoman along. Her destruction of the
ledger and her refusal to give him the exact location
of the gold had made her a necessary annoyance.

Not that Gillian hadn't faced her share of hardships in the four years they'd been together. . . .
Kincaid stiffened in the saddle. It had been a long
time since he'd thought of Gillian. He grimaced
in the darkness. Days at least, he mused.

And the familiar pain was right there waiting
to stab through him with exquisite, twisting torture. Pretty, fair-haired Gillian, with her delicate
features and fey sea-green eyes. She was a lithe
fairy of a thing, weighing barely six stone, but she
was all woman, and as sweetly shaped as any soldier's dream of paradise. Soft-spoken and de-

mure, she wasn't the type to argue with a man, and she was always ready and willing for a lusty roll beneath the blankets or under a sheltering hedgerow.

Fool that he'd been, he'd fallen head over heels for her the first moment he'd laid eyes on her selling butter at a village fair, and he'd risked life and limb to court her against her family's will. He'd been determined to have her at any cost, and Gillian's price was a ring on her middle finger and marriage lines in a parson's black book.

He'd believed her an angel, yet they'd not been wed three weeks when she miscarried of another man's babe.

He'd cursed and threatened to leave her, and she'd wept and pleaded rape. She'd sworn to him in Saint Andrew's kirkyard that she'd never imagined she was with child from her brutal assailant's attack. He'd accepted her story because he wanted to . . . because he couldn't look into those misty green eyes and believe her guilty of deceit. He'd put his faith and hope in her because Gillian was the first decent thing he'd ever had that was his . . . the first woman who had ever made him feel like he belonged to someone and something.

Suddenly, he'd been the head of a family, not just a woods' colt without father, or mother, or kin. And for the first time, he began to dream of a future that consisted of something more than selling his sword to the highest bidder.

For four years he'd been blind to the rumors about his pretty little wife; he'd fought duels and put two brave men in early graves for sullying her honor. Then one night when the Highland moon rose as fat and round as a newly minted silver penny, he'd found his best friend, Robbie Munro, in Gillian's bed. And she'd taunted him with the news that the child she was swelling with belonged to another man. . . .

Sweet Mother of God. Kincaid shut his eyes and tried to will away the image of Gillian's blood-streaked face. She was as dead as Robbie Munro had been after he'd driven a broadsword through Robbie's chest, but her screams haunted his dreams on nights when the moon glowed full and shimmering-white.

An owl hooted from a tree nearby and Kincaid's mare tensed and quick-stepped sideways. "Hist, now, hinney," he soothed. He twisted in the saddle to look back at Bess. Her horse lunged forward, eyes white-rimmed, ears back, and muscles tightly bunched. "Whoa," he said. "Be ye all right?" he asked Bess.

She tightened her reins to keep the mare from spooking. "I was asleep," she admitted. Her heartbeat quickened. She knew how close she'd come to losing her seat when her mount had shied. Her face grew hot. "I'm fine," she said brusquely.

"We can stop and rest a bit if ye want."

"I said, I'm fine."

"I thought to ride all night and sleep in daylight."

"What else?"

"What did ye say?"

"Nothing." She settled herself firmly into the saddle, ignoring the mosquito that buzzed around her head. It had been a dry summer, so the mosquitoes hadn't been much of a nuisance this year.

She had a suspicion all that would change when they got to Panama.

The insects drive us to distraction, her grandfather's journal had read. *All manner of biting, boring, stinging creatures abound in this godforsaken jungle, making sleeping, eating, and sometimes even breathing impossible. Men claw at their flesh until they bleed, and one of our mules was tormented to the point of dashing headlong into a river where it was devoured alive by crocodiles.*

Bess shuddered at the thought and hoped Papa James had exaggerated about the appetite of the insects.

"It is true," Kutii said, appearing without warning beside her.

"I thought maybe you'd deserted me," she whispered.

"What?" Kincaid asked.

The Indian matched her mare's pace, striding easily along beside Bess. She noticed he had slung a short, oddly shaped bow and a quiver of feathered arrows over one shoulder. "I will never leave you," he said. "I promised your grandmother, the Star Woman. You are the hope of my ancestors."

Bess nodded. "Umm-hum. Well, right now the hope of your ancestors would give an acre of prime tobacco land for eight hours' sleep."

"The journey is long. You will toughen to it."

The mosquito lit in the center of Bess's forehead and bit. She smacked it. Her mare pricked up her ears, reacting to Kutii's presence. Tossing her head nervously, she arched her neck and danced sideways. Bess could smell the fear radiating from her glossy hide. "Don't scare my horse," she cautioned the Indian. "She nearly dumped me on my bottom back—"

"Who the hell are ye talkin' to?" Kincaid demanded.

"Kutii."

The Scotsman reined his horse up short. "Who the hell is Kutii?" He pulled a pistol from his belt and cocked it. The snap of the steel rang loud in the quiet of the forest.

"Just a ghost," she answered mildly.

"Now I know ye've been too long without sleep," he grumbled. He stared around suspiciously, then dug his heels into his mount again. "Try and contain your jests until we are well away from that sheriff, if ye please. Ye stand to lose a few hundred acres of your precious plantation, but I could lose my neck."

"No sense of humor," Bess whispered to Kutii.

The Indian made no reply, and she sensed his disapproval. Kutii could be doggedly stubborn when he wanted to. He liked the Scot, and he thought she didn't trust Kincaid enough.

Bess sniffed. Kutii was right. She didn't trust the convict, but then Kincaid didn't trust her either. And if he knew that she was relying on a ghost to show her where the treasure was buried, he'd probably drown her in the first sinkhole they came to.

The story she'd told the Scot about burning the pages containing the location of the treasure was a gilded lie. Her grandfather hadn't written down the directions. She supposed he always intended to tell someone where it was, but his death had been quick and clean. Papa James had passed away in his sleep without having had a chance to relay the vital information. Now the only one who knew where the gold was was Kutii, an Indian who had been dead for years.

As if reading her thoughts, Kutii spoke again. "I will not fail you, little Bess. You are bound to me and mine by a bond stronger than blood and older than time. Would I forget the pain of seeing my wife and daughter cut down by the Spanish soldiers? Could a slight thing like death keep me from remembering the wailing of the women and the weight of the chains that sent me to my knees in shame? I, Pacha Kutii, hereditary guardian to the treasure of the Incas and protector of the royal line of women, did not die a warrior's death as a soldier should. Instead, I lived. I was made a slave and forced to carry the treasure I once guarded out of our hidden valley and over the mountains to a Spanish ship."

Bess listened with her heart as tears formed in the corners of her eyes. Some of this she had heard as a child, but she had always believed it was a fairy tale, like Kutii's legend of the Incan soldier and the woman from the stars who could swim with the dolphins. Kutii had always been so much a part of her life that she was nearly ten before she realized that most people didn't see or talk to ghosts, and that speaking about him to adults was dangerous.

"We sailed north on the salt sea your people call the Pacific," Kutii continued, "but I did not see the green water or the blue heavens. I was bound hand and foot in the stinking bowels of the ship, with rats and crawling creatures for companions, and the memory of my dead loved ones to keep me from sleep. My tongue swelled to fill my mouth, but I did not drink the foul bilge water. Others did, and died. When we reached the harbor at Panama City, I alone was still alive."

A tear rolled down Bess's cheek and she wiped it away with the back of her hand.

"Living was crueler than dying, but I knew I carried the burden of my family's souls on my shoulder. My mother was of the royal Incan line, as were my wife and my daughter. The men in our family were never considered royal; we were protectors of the bloodline. We were supposed to keep our women safe from all harm. And now my daughter, the last of that ancient line, was dead. According to our beliefs, my ancestors will have eternal life only as long as they are remembered and only so long as they have descendants. And if the chain were broken, the souls of my precious daughter, my beloved wife, and my mother would blow away like dried chaff. Unworthy as I was, little Bess, I was the only hope of their immortality."

She gazed at Kutii, so solid-looking that it seemed she could reach out and touch him, but she never could. Was he real, or was she truly a madwoman?

"Love is the only thing real and lasting," Kutii said. "And I have loved you since you first drew life. You are all that I have left in your world and the hope—"

"I know, I know," she supplied, "the hope of your ancestors."

"Our ancestors," he corrected her. "When I adopted your grandmother as my daughter, you became my grandchild when you were born."

"Great-grandchild," she said.

"Sweet Mary," Kincaid said, reining in his mare again. "Will nothing still your chatter? Do ye ken how far a voice carries in this woods?" He swung down from the saddle, and Kutii vanished in a shimmering swirl. As Bess halted her horse, Kincaid reached up and lifted her from the saddle.

"I can dismount my—"

She broke off, suddenly shaken by the sensation of his hands on her waist.

"Ye shy like an unbroken horse," he said. "I mean ye no harm. Why did ye agree to go with me if you're afraid—"

"I'm not afraid of you." He set her down lightly on the ground and stepped back. She took a deep breath and lifted her chin. "I'm not," she repeated, sounding for all the world like a boastful child. She moved back until she felt the mare's bulk behind her, turned, and began to fumble with her saddlebag.

"I'll keep watch so ye can sleep."

"And who will keep watch on you?" The words were out of her mouth before she realized how they must sound. As though he was interested in her . . . as though she needed to guard her virtue from him. "I'm sorry," she said quickly. "That was ill put. I've ever had a sharp tongue." She shook her head and turned back toward him. He was a darker shadow against the dark trees. "I've been so long without sleep that I'm half drunk. I didn't mean that at all."

"Nay?" He made a sound of derision, mocking her.

She could still feel the touch of him. A hint of green tinged her mind's eye. It was unnerving.

A woman alone in charge of a great plantation had to guard her reputation. A witchling who received sensations from every touch of a human hand had to be doubly careful. When she was a child, her gift had been nearly overwhelming. Her grandmother had taught her how to hide her power and to control it, turning it off and on so that she read another's thoughts and character only when she willed it. As she matured and grew older, her ability to judge others had grown both stronger and more infrequent. Sometimes the power worked, and sometimes it didn't.

With this cursed Scot, she felt out of control. She couldn't read what he was thinking, and she couldn't turn the power off. Every time he touched her, she became acutely aware of smells, and sounds, and tastes. And him.

Even now, she could taste the bite of cedar on her tongue, and her head spun with the scents of crushed leaves, oiled leather, black powder, wild grapevine, and honeysuckle. The musty smell of the horses mingled with a faint odor of rum and tobacco. She could hear the rustle of small animals in the brush, and the jingle of the bridles and the breathing of the horses sounded overloud. She could even hear the flutter of a night bird's wings.

"Have you been drinking rum?" she asked.

"Nay, not since last night. They broached a keg on the pirate vessel. You've a good nose. I might need a bath, but I hardly think I smell of spirits."

She unsaddled her horse. The ease of having the saddle off would rest her mount, and she could use the blanket to keep from lying on the bare ground.

"I'll hobble the horses," he said. "They need to eat what they can. There's no water near, but they had their fill at the last stream."

Bess spread the blanket and put the saddle at one end. Her knees felt wobbly as she lowered herself onto the blanket and curled into a ball with the saddlebags in her arms. Her eyelids were so heavy that it was impossible for her to keep them open, but she fumbled for and found the pistol in her bag. Her fingers closed around it.

She could hear him running his hands over the horses, whispering to them, and she wondered if they saw colors when he touched them.

"Sleep, woman. I'll keep watch," he murmured. His sleepy burr was hard to understand.

"Kutii," she whispered. There was no answer. She wanted to open her eyes and look for him, but the night breeze through the trees beguiled her. Without realizing it, she drifted into a deep and dreamless sleep.

And was awakened minutes later by Kincaid's weight bearing down upon her, and his hard hand pressing against her mouth.

Instinctively, Bess struck out at him and struggled to break free. Her cry of rage was muffled by his fingers clamping around her nose, cutting off her breath. Grappling with him was as futile as throwing herself against a wall of solid hickory posts; he paid as little attention to her formidable blows as a horse did to greenhead flies.

"Be still!" he hissed in her ear. "Quiet, or I'll knock ye senseless."

She choked back her protest and nodded her head. Immediately, he removed his hand, and she sucked air into her lungs. Every muscle in her body was throbbing, and once again she was struck by the size and strength of the man and her own vulnerability.

"Shhh," he warned. "There's someone out there." He motioned toward the heavy growth of cedars to the left. "Don't move."

Moonlight gleamed off a steel blade clasped in Kincaid's right hand. Her stomach lurched and for a terrible instant she thought he meant to plunge it into her heart. But then he released her, rose with the silence of a deepening shadow, and melted into the woods.

She inhaled sharply, breathing deep to clear the fog from her brain. Rolling onto her belly, she fumbled in her saddlebag for her pistol, and when she cocked the hammer, the click echoed like cannon shot.

The stillness of a snowfall draped over the small clearing. Not a nighthawk called or a mouse rustled in the leaves. No owl's hunting cry broke the spell of utter silence. Even the horses froze to ghostly statues.

Suddenly, a wildcat's snarl ripped through the trees. One of the horses whinnied in fright, and Bess scrambled up and ran to catch hold of the animals' halters.

"For the love of Christ, woman, can ye not obey a simple order?" Kincaid asked as he appeared without warning at her side.

Bess let go of the horses and whirled around, leveling the cocked pistol at his gut. "Give me one reason why I shouldn't send you to your well-deserved reward, you cow-hearted bastard."

"Leave off," he replied gruffly. "And put that

down before ye shoot your foot off. Mother save me from a lass who thinks she's a lad. Your father did ye no favor when he first put a pistol in your hand.''

''It was my grandsire, not my father,'' she flung back. Carefully aiming the flintlock toward the ground, she eased down the hammer.

''I told ye not to move.''

''Another minute and the horses would have spooked. We'd have been afoot. How far do you think we'd have gotten then?''

''There was an Indian spying on us. I got a good look at him, but he lost me in the woods.''

''An Indian?''

''Aye. Ye heard me,'' he said. ''Ye have seen Indians, have ye not? Armed with bows and arrows?''

''You scared me out of my wits because you saw an Indian?''

''Painted for war, he was, and naked to the waist. I saw the slash marks plainly on his face. Have ye been so sheltered that ye've nay heard of hostile savages?''

Shaken, Bess turned away to hide her face. Was it possible? she wondered. Could Kincaid have seen Kutii? Since her grandmother had died, no one had ever verified Kutii's presence. At times, she'd suspected the Incan was a fabrication of her own imagination.

For a fleeting moment she covered her face with her hands as she remembered the terror she'd felt when she awoke beneath Kincaid's coiled weight. ''What manner of man are you,'' she asked, ''that you have no respect for a lady?''

''I have respect enough for your life.'' Kincaid

laid a sinewy hand on her shoulder. "I told ye I'd nay hurt ye, Bess. I couldn't take a chance that ye'd panic. I'm sorry if I frightened ye, but you'll take more than one fright if we go through with this treasure hunt. Ye must trust me."

"Trust you?" Sooner trust the devil's hounds, she thought.

"Aye. Or find another to be your—"

"It's late for that, isn't it?" She twisted away from his grip and glared at him in the stark moonlight, fighting the nearly overwhelming urge to smack his face. She didn't want him to touch her. His nearness confused her and filled her mind with reckless thoughts.

"Aye. Past late, I'd say."

Remembering Fortune's Gift and what she stood to lose, Bess forced her voice to a tone of flat civility. "Then we're stuck with each other." Her flesh tingled where his hand had lain. She could feel the heat of him even now. Please, she prayed silently, don't let this be a mistake. Don't make me regret I ever started on this journey with this man.

"Only if ye realize that ye must obey when I give an order," he continued harshly. "This is no game we play. Your willfulness could cost us both our lives, and I for one value mine."

She nodded. She knew common sense when she heard it. It was just that she was used to command, and it was bitter medicine to take orders from a man like Kincaid.

"Do we have a bargain, woman?"

She sighed. "We have a bargain," she said, but behind her back, she crossed her fingers. Unless you ask something of me that I can't do, she thought, or unless I find out for certain that you can't be trusted.

"Good enough," he said. "Let's saddle up and ride. I've no wish to linger here. That Indian may be gone, or he may decide to come back. And if he does, I'd as soon put distance between us and this spot. I like it not. It raises the hairs on my flesh."

"Afraid of shadows, Kincaid?" she taunted.

"A man who doesn't fear what he can't see doesn't live to make old bones."

"Some would say talk like that makes you a coward."

"Some might, but they'd nay speak it twice."

"Bold talk, Scot, but I've yet to see you do more than bully a woman half your size."

"Saddle your horse, and save your venom for what lies ahead. Ye'll find better targets than me for that shrew's temper. If you've nay forgot, 'twas you hired me. I'm on your side."

Just so you keep that in mind, Kincaid, she thought, then vowed, Because the first you time you don't remember, you'll reap the harvest of your own deceit.

Chapter 8

Bess and Kincaid rode until early morning, then spent most of the day sleeping in an abandoned barn. Before dusk, Kincaid left Bess alone for an hour and returned with nine hen's eggs and a golden-brown pie he'd snatched off a goodwife's windowsill. When Bess protested the thievery, he told her that he'd left two pennies to pay for the crockery dish.

"I've never eaten stolen food," she argued. "I'm not about to start now. Why didn't you just ask to buy something to eat?"

"Would ye nay feed any guest who walked through your door?"

"Of course I would. But this is—"

"The fewer people who see my face, the better. I was only takin' what was mine by right of the laws of hospitality. And I saved the lady the trouble of stoppin' her chores to see to my pleasure." Grinning boyishly, he sliced the cherry pie into quarters and devoured two of them without spilling a drop of juice. "Excellent," he pronounced, offering her the dish. "Sure ye won't have any?"

Bess looked at the flaky crust and her mouth watered. The cherries were fat and red; the pie smelled heavenly. "I'm not a thief."

"Too bad." In less time than she would have

believed, he finished the entire pie and reined in his horse to balance the empty crockery on a stump beside the road. ''Someone's sure to find it.''

''But not necessarily the owner,'' she said. Now that the pastry was gone, she began to have doubts about being so noble. She was starving, and if that wasn't bad enough, judging from the sound of thunder over the bay, they were about to get very wet.

''Care for an egg?'' Kincaid balanced one brown egg between his thumb and forefinger, knocked off a top section of shell with his knife, and proceeded to swallow the contents raw.

Bess shuddered. ''How can you do that?'' Uggh.'' She liked her eggs well cooked. How anyone could eat a raw one was beyond her comprehension.

''You'll eat worse before we're done, my fine lady,'' he teased.

Bess looked away as he began on the second egg. ''You're disgusting.''

''I'm hungry, and so are ye.''

''Can't we stop and catch some fish or shoot a duck?'' Thoughts of juicy roast duck danced in her head. Even fried fish would taste delicious now.

''No fire. Unless ye'd care to eat the fish raw? I've done that when I had to. Ye just—''

''Never mind.''

''Certain ye won't have an egg?''

''I'd have to be starving.''

''Aye. Ye probably would, but that just goes to prove that the English have no sense a'tall.'' He chuckled as he cracked the top off his fourth egg.

"I'm used to paying for what I get in life, but then, I suppose you wouldn't understand that."

"Aye, but I do, lass." He winked at her. "It's been my experience that we all pay for every action, good or bad, and none I've kenned has ever escaped the final judgment."

Suspicious of Kincaid's jovial mood, she reined her mount close to his and sniffed the air. "You've been drinking!" she accused him. "Did you steal spirits as well?"

"In the Highlands, none would ride on without a nip. 'Tis only friendly," he answered, lifting a blue-and-white pint-sized jug that dangled by a leather thong from the far side of his saddle.

"You did. What's in there? Rum?"

"Nay. Only a bit of barley-bree." He grinned. "And while I've drunk better, I maun say in truth, I've been known to drink a far sight worse."

"I warn you, I won't tolerate a drunken sot in my employ. If you get tipsy and fall off your horse into a ditch, I swear I'll let you lie there and drown."

Kincaid laughed long and heartily. "You'll nay see the day I drink enough to fall down drunk, hinney," he boasted. "There isna that much usquebaugh in all the colonies."

She scowled at him in disbelief.

Ignoring her disapproval, he began to hum to himself and then to sing softly in Gaelic. Thunder rumbled again, and the horses picked up their pace. Kincaid's voice was deep and rich, and Bess found her mood growing lighter as the miles fell away beneath their mounts' feet.

Bess knew the peninsula that lay between the

Atlantic Ocean and the Chesapeake Bay was growing narrower as they rode south. Sometime the night before, they had crossed the invisible line between the Maryland Colony and Virginia, and they were riding close to the shore of the bay. She could smell a hint of salt water on the breeze, and to their right, cattails and marsh grass framed a lush pasture. Wildflowers spread across the grass in multicolored waves, and the deepening twilight was sweet with birdsong and the sad, soft cry of the mourning dove.

To the left, just beyond the game trail the horses were following, was forest, much of it old-growth oak that had been mature trees when the first Englishman set foot on Virginia soil.

"This is fine land for planting," Kincaid said, rising in his stirrups and looking around. "Nary a rock in sight." The damp wind ruffled his yellow hair and he brushed a stray lock carelessly off his high forehead. "In the Highlands, you're lucky if the topsoil goes deep enough to grow a decent pasture, let alone raise a crop on it."

Bess glanced at him in surprise. The shadows of coming darkness softened the sharp planes of Kincaid's rugged face and made him seem younger. She'd watched him down a stiff measure of homemade lightning, yet the effects of the strong drink had brought a startling change for the better in his personality.

"I've never been anywhere else, so I'm a poor judge," she answered. "All I know is that I love it here. I was born here and I can't imagine living anywhere else. The earth is deep and fertile; the rivers and the bay teem with fish, and crabs, and clams. The woods are thick with game, and in

autumn the skies blacken with ducks and geese.
Most years we get enough rain and plenty of sunshine to make a good crop. Mother England is far
enough away so as not to trouble us overmuch
with laws and taxes, but close enough to protect
us from the French and Spanish." She smiled up
at him. "Some call this the Eastern Shore of
heaven, and I'd be inclined to agree with them."

" 'Tis nay Scotland," he said. "Not by a long
sight. There are no mountains, and only a few
risings that might be called hills. I've seen no
heather, and few women as lovely as our Scottish
lasses—present company excepted." He grinned
at her. "And I've set my teeth into nary a haggis
or a decent cup of whiskey since I've been here.
But this is a fair land, I'll grant ye that, my fine
English hinney." He sighed. "A man could do
worse than set his dreams on this place."

She laughed. "I suppose he could. But this is
Virginia. Heaven starts back there." She pointed
back the way they had come. "I'm Maryland-
bred, and it's hard for me to see how anyone
would choose to be a Virginian, given a chance."

"And what's the difference, I ask ye? A few
more pine trees here, maybe the ground's a wee
bit flatter."

"It's the Virginia air," she said.

"The air?" He sniffed. "I can smell no difference."

"You're a foreigner," she replied solemnly.
"You can't be expected to understand."

"Try me, said the captain," he quipped, then
grinned wider at his own humor and tried to take
a sip from the already empty jug. "Mother save

us,'' he swore. '' 'Tis empty as last month's pay pouch.''

''I'll put it this way, Kincaid. Are you a Highlander or a Lowlander?''

''Ye cut me to the heart, sweeting. How can ye ask a man such a question?''

Kincaid's burr had thickened to the consistency of old porridge, and she could barely understand him. ''I take it you're a Highlander?'' she said.

''Aye, and aye again.'' He lifted the jug. ''I'll drink to that, fair lassie. Or I would, if I could.'' He laughed again and began to sing. ''Her eyes were as blue as the loch of Mc—''

''If you were born here, instead of Scotland,'' Bess cut in, ''then you would certainly be a Marylander.''

''Her ankle was neat,'' Kincaid continued to sing, picking up the ditty without losing a note. ''And her knees, they were—''

''A Lowlander would be a Virginian,'' Bess said triumphantly.

''Lowlanders are fine fellows,'' Kincaid said, ''but they have no sense of politics. They follow all the wrong leaders, and they can't hold their liquor.''

''Exactly.'' She grinned back at him. ''You've described a Virginian to a T. It's the air. It makes them all a little mad.''

A long growl of thunder rolled across the sky, and Bess could see lightning strikes to the west. The temperature began to drop, and the wind whipped sections of the horses' manes off their necks. ''We're going to get wet,'' she said.

''Maybe.'' Kincaid peered through the failing light. ''There.'' He pointed toward a rotten oak

stump at least six feet wide. "Not far ahead the
trail splits. There's a tavern—"

"The only tavern near here is called the Cock's
Comb," she said. "I've never set foot in the place,
but I've heard it's a den for ruffians and—"

"And what are we? Holy pilgrims?" He
smacked his horse's rump, and the mare broke
into a canter. Bess followed, close behind.

The first sprinkling of rain was falling on their
faces when Kincaid turned onto a dirt lane, rode
a few hundred yards, then followed a wider rut
right through marshy ground to a wooded knoll.
The lightning was closer now, and the echo of
thunder vibrated through the trees.

Voices and the crash of wood against wood
sounded in Bess's ears even before she could see
the light from the tavern windows. They urged
their mounts into a stiff trot and reached the shelter of a ramshackle barn just as the first sheet of
driving rain hit.

The icy needles soaked through Bess's clothes
and hair in seconds. Kincaid dismounted and
flung open a sagging stable door. "Inside," he
yelled. His voice was nearly drowned by the wind
and water, but she needed no urging. Ducking
her head to avoid the beam over the door, Bess
rode her mare into the shadowy building.

There were no individual stalls, but there was
room along one wall where other horses were
tied. Quickly, they removed their saddles and
used their blankets to rub down their mounts.
Bess stumbled over a water bucket in the darkness. She plunged her hand into it, smelled the
contents, then carried the container over to water

her mare. Another animal nickered and stamped its feet. Bess paused and looked around.

"Come on," Kincaid said. "Let's make a dash for the tavern."

"But I thought I heard—" she began.

"This is no village kirk, lass. You'll come with me and stay by my side." He caught her arm. "I'd nay leave ye here alone."

She caught a faint whiff of the whiskey he'd been drinking amid the stronger smells of wet wool and horseflesh, but the scent was not unpleasant. "Our saddlebags?" she asked.

"We'll leave them with the saddles for now. Unless I miss my guess, the guests are all inside." He took her hand, and together they made a dash for the tavern. When Bess would have entered first, he grunted a negative and leaned close to her ear. "Remember the plan, lass. I'm a rough soldier of fortune, and ye are my light-skirts. I warn ye, I'm a jealous man, so unless ye'd see heads broken, mind your manners."

Bess bit back the stinging retort that rose on her tongue and followed him meekly into the Cock's Comb. He stopped just inside the doorway and surveyed the public room, blocking her way with his solid bulk. Then he stepped aside and motioned her in out of the pouring rain. On the far side of the chamber was a brick fireplace with a kettle steaming on the hearth. Bess was drawn by the welcoming heat, and she ignored the murmurs and stares of the men as she hurried over and held out her hands to the flames.

The main room of the Cock's Comb was low-ceilinged and poorly lit; overhead, the beams were blackened by smoke. The floor was made up of wide pine boards that looked as though they hadn't been scrubbed since the tavern was built. She counted eight—no, nine—hard-faced men sitting around three trestle tables. There were no women in sight. The place smelled of stale liquor and unwashed bodies.

She concentrated on the crackling fire, and tried not to think of the watching eyes that made her feel like spiders were walking up her back.

"Mite wet, ain't ye, gal?" a bearded stranger called. "I'd be glad to . . ." His voice trailed off as Kincaid closed the distance between them and seized the loudmouth by the collar.

"If ye've something to say, say it to me," Kincaid said as he dragged the man off the bench and lifted him into the air with one muscular arm.

"Sonofabitch!" Struggling, Redbeard drew back a fist and gasped. "I'll show you a—"

Kincaid slammed him back against the scarred trestle table twice and threw him to the floor. Before he could stagger up, the Scot gave him a brutal kick to his midsection and whirled around to grab Redbeard's companion, who'd smashed a bottle on the bench and rushed Kincaid's back, wielding the jagged glass neck.

Kincaid's sinewy left fist closed around the hand holding the bottle as his right one slammed into his assailant's jaw. Before Bess could blink, the second man had toppled, senseless, onto his friend's groaning body. Kincaid raised his head and surveyed the now silent room. "Anyone else care to speak to my woman?" he asked mildly. Bess noted that he hadn't even worked up a sweat during the violent confrontation.

Six pairs of eyes turned to the drinks on the

tables in front of them. A stout gray-haired man, standing by the stairway, wiped his hands on his apron and cleared his throat. "Ed, Lester," he said, "get that trash out of here." He looked at Kincaid and smiled nervously. "Nasty night out, ain't it? What can I get you? Rum? Nice venison steak?"

Kincaid righted the overturned bench as Ed and Lester dragged the two fallen strangers out into the rain. With one sweep of his arm, the Scot knocked away two tankards and a dirty plate. He glanced at Bess and nodded. The innkeeper hurried over to wipe the table clean as Bess, heart thudding, crossed the room and took a seat on the bench beside Kincaid.

"We'll have whatever you've cooked that's fit to eat," Kincaid said brusquely, "and plenty of it. I'll have whiskey if you've got it, rum if ye don't. The *lady* will have ale."

"The Cock's Comb serves only the best, Mr. . . . Mr. . . ." The host looked at Kincaid expectantly.

"Robert Munro," Kincaid supplied.

Liar, Bess thought. She moved a little away from him, still shaken by his attack on the two men. The bearded man had been rude, but rough talk was no reason to beat him unconscious.

"Mr. Munro. I'm Ira Jackson. I own the Cock's Comb. But you look familiar. Didn't you come through here a few weeks back? It seems to me as if I remember a card game—"

"Nay," Kincaid growled. "Not me." He gazed at the gray-haired man with eyes as hard and lifeless as quartz pebbles.

"My mistake," Jackson apologized. "Sally!" he

shouted toward an open doorway that led into the interior of the tavern. "Two suppers, and make it quick." He hurried away and returned with a brimming tankard of ale and a jug of whiskey. He wiped the rim of a pewter cup and set it in front of Kincaid.

"Leave the jug," Kincaid said.

"Will you be wantin' a bed? I kin give you a bed just for the two of you." He tugged at a greasy apron string. "Three pence for the bed, supper included. The whiskey comes dear, though. I can leave the jug if you want, but—"

Kincaid flipped a silver shilling in the air and the innkeeper caught it. "I said, leave the jug."

"Thank ye, sir. That will do, sir. Yes, it will."

"We'll sleep in the barn, but I'll want some blankets. No bugs in them." Kincaid poured a cup of the amber whiskey. "I hate bugs," he said. "If I find bugs, I'll make you eat them, bedding and all."

"My girl just did the boiling of the wash today. You'll find no bugs in my blankets. I run a clean house, I do."

"Aye, and your father was a saint."

Jackson forced a laugh. "He was that, old Pap, a regular saint. Anyone can tell you that."

The serving wench came from the kitchen carrying two heaped plates of food. Bess hoped she had an appetite left. She was wet and tired, and she knew she looked like something the tide had left on the beach, but worst of all, she had the feeling that she'd joined forces with a man as wild and ornery as a deep woods' bison.

Gamely, she picked up her spoon and took a bite of the Indian pudding. Whatever and whoever Kincaid was, she'd made a bargain with him, and if that bargain was broken by someone, as God was her witness, it wouldn't be she.

"Why did you pick that fight with those men?" Bess demanded when they had finished eating and were alone in the barn loft. "You could have gotten us both killed."

Kincaid shook out a blanket over the hay he'd heaped up for a bed. "Hist now, hinney," he scolded. "Nay more of your nonsense. It's been a long day. I thought ye'd be grateful I found ye a hot meal and a soft bed."

"Where's your bed?" Heavy rain was drumming on the cedar-shake roof above them and running down the outside walls, but the spot Kincaid had chosen seemed to have no leaks.

"Two blankets. One beneath and one above. It makes one bed, the way I see it."

"You certainly don't expect me to sleep in your bed," she said. "I'll take one of those blankets, thank you."

"Nay, lass. I'd have ye beside me where I can keep ye safe. It's a bad lot in the tavern, and I'll not have ye wanderin' outside in the night to be snatched up and used as a common whore." He stretched out on the blanket and patted the space beside him. It was nearly pitch dark in the loft, but a tiny lantern gave enough light for her to see his self-satisfied smile.

"You're drunk," she accused. "I'm going to Panama with you, but I never said anything about sharing a bed with you. Our agreement is strictly business."

"Woman, you'd vex a saint. I've had a few

drops, but I'm far from drunk." He exhaled loudly. "And if I was foxed, your virtue would still be safe with me. I've never been so drunk that I've not chosen who I'd futter with."

"Thank you for the compliment," she snapped.

" 'Tis nothing personal, hinney," he said. "I like my lassies womanly, not all claws and spit. You're good enough to look at, but there's imps in hell would give a man less grief than you." He patted the blanket again. "You'd best sleep while you can. I can't promise when we'll have so snug a bed again."

She sniffed. Imps in hell. She'd not have slept with Kincaid if he was crown prince of England and she an actress on the London stage. The man thought entirely too much of himself, and she certainly knew a drunk when she saw one. He'd downed enough whiskey to drop a horse. "Hmmpt," she grumbled. "We could have had a real bed in the tavern."

"Shared with bedbugs and drunken guests. The Cock's Comb has no private chambers, and if they did, I'd fear 'twas only to murder us. This is better. There are no bugs, and the horses will keep watch for us. If anyone comes into the stable, they'll sound an alarm."

"Provided you're not too intoxicated to hear," she said, reluctantly sitting down on the blanket beside him and taking off her moccasins. "I warn you, I sleep with a knife."

"You'd best take off those wet clothes. You'll catch your death of the ague."

"Not on your life, Kincaid. My clothes stay on."

"Don't whine to me when your nose is running and—"

"Will you be still?" she said, curling up as far away from him as she could without getting off the blanket.

"Here." He spread the top blanket over her, and as he did, his hand brushed hers.

Bess's breath caught in her throat as a tingling sensation ran up her arm. His touch had been accidental, but it set her to shivering as the cold rain had not.

"I'd nay have ye take sick," he said.

"I'm fine," she lied. She wasn't fine. The tingling had rippled down to the pit of her stomach, and it was all she could do to lie still. His nearness was unnerving. If she wasn't used to anyone touching her, she surely wasn't used to sharing her bed with a man.

It had been a long time. And besides, what had happened between her and Richard couldn't be called sharing a bed.

Bess clenched her eyes shut and tried not to think of the man beside her, or the other one . . . the one who had made her decide never to marry . . . never to put herself under a man's control again.

Richard's face formed in her mind and she tried to push the image away. It had been so long ago, she'd thought it was over and done with . . . a lot of fuss over a bit of skin and a few spots of blood.

Her face grew warm in the darkness. If Kincaid thought her a frightened virgin, he was wrong. Richard Carter had taken that trophy when she was only sixteen.

She'd trusted Richard. God in heaven, why not? The families had been neighbors and friends for more years than she'd been alive, and she'd had a crush on him since she was thirteen. She trusted him even though her witchy instinct told her that he would bring her no happiness. Even though she saw him in shades of red and gray . . .

He was older than she was, twenty-one or two, and handsome as the devil's guard when he'd returned that summer from school in England. They'd met for the first time in two years at a horse race in Chestertown, and Richard had begun to court her in earnest. Even then she'd known that as a second son, Richard wouldn't inherit his family's plantation, and that Fortune's Gift was a greater prize than she was. As an heiress, she could expect to be wooed by men who appreciated her fortune.

But she'd liked the attention all the same. She'd liked the fancy balls and the parties. She'd liked being included in the social circles of girls who'd always excluded her before. She even liked Richard. But she wasn't in love with him, and she didn't want to marry or even promise to marry at sixteen.

But one afternoon when they'd been fox hunting, they'd stopped at his family's overseer's cottage to take shelter from an afternoon shower. The door was unlocked and they'd gone inside, even after they'd found that no one was home. That was when Richard had begun kissing her and had touched her breasts.

She'd slapped him, but instead of stopping, he had picked her up and carried her into the over-

seer's bedroom. She'd fought him, but he had
been stronger. He hadn't been brutal, yet he had
forced himself upon her. He'd raped her on top
of a ragged quilt, and when he was done, he'd
apologized and assured her that he'd do the right
thing and make her his wife.

She'd been too shocked to cry, and too
ashamed to tell anyone what had happened.
She'd known that her father would have chal-
lenged Richard to a duel if she'd revealed what
he'd done. And only one of them would have
walked away from the field of honor.

She'd hated Richard then, but she hadn't
wanted him dead. And she couldn't bear to think
of her father lying dead with a bullet hole in his
chest. So she'd kept her secret well and lived with
the guilt.

Kutii had known, of course. Kutii knew all her
secrets. And he knew without her telling him that
she'd ignored her own inner warnings when
she'd gone with Richard. But he'd not con-
demned her.

"Life is a series of lessons," the Incan had said.

Her lesson had been that her life was complete
without a man. She hadn't needed or wanted a
husband after that. She still didn't.

She had never seen Richard again. After a few
weeks of trying to speak with her and being refused, he'd gone to Boston to buy a ship with his
father. There he'd met and courted a judge's
widow ten years his senior. Richard had married
the woman and enjoyed her wealth for nine
months before he'd slipped on an icy step and
broken his neck.

Bess had wept then, not for Richard, but for the

girl she'd been. Then she'd put the incident behind her and gone on to a life in which Fortune's
Gift was what truly mattered.

The sex act was vastly overrated, she thought
with a sigh. She remembered Richard's thrusting
as damp and uncomfortable, but nothing nearly
as painful as the time she'd been thrown from a
bull and broken her arm. It had been the shame
of his betrayal and her own foolishness that had
hurt so badly.

No, she didn't want a husband. And she didn't
suffer the pangs of sexual desire that seemed to
plague the lower classes.

Or she hadn't, until this rough-hewn Scot had
leaped out of a tree into her life . . .

Bess rolled into an ever-tighter ball and listened
to Kincaid's steady breathing and to the rain hitting the roof. And when he turned over in his
sleep and carelessly tossed an arm across her
shoulder, she lay still and let the arm stay, feeling
oddly comforted by his warm, hard touch.

Chapter 9

It was just light enough to see and still raining when Bess opened her eyes. For a moment she couldn't remember where she was. The musty smells of hay and horses were familiar, but she didn't recognize the roof overhead or the piece-meal barn with its missing boards and sagging loft door. She lay there still only half awake, star-ing bleary-eyed up at the cobwebs and listening to the cooing pigeons as they strutted along a beam overhead. Then Kincaid mumbled a wom-an's name in his sleep, and Bess snapped out of her stupor and tried to sit up.

With her first conscious movement, she became instantly cognizant of last night's events. "Oh," she murmured in dismay. Heat scalded her face and washed over her as she realized she was curled intimately against Kincaid, so intimately that she could feel the hard proof of his arousal against her buttocks. Her riding skirt and shift were hiked up around her bare thighs, and her stockings were scandalously low. Both of his arms were around her, and one big hand rested inti-mately on her breast.

For a half-dozen heartbeats, panic seized her. Holding her breath, she lay frozen in place, trying to decide if Kincaid was awake or sleeping.

His face was nestled into her hair, and his long, muscular legs were tangled in hers. Sweet Lord! Had he taken advantage of her in the night without her realizing it?

Cautiously, she tried to wiggle loose from his embrace, but he only groaned and clasped her tighter. She couldn't remember him undressing in the night, but his chest and arms were bare, and the brawny leg over hers was certainly unclothed. She thought perhaps her chances of escaping by sliding down would be better, but she reconsidered once she reasoned that if she attempted that move, she would come in direct contact with his swollen male member.

Gathering her courage, she whispered his name. "Kincaid." Her voice sounded scared and breathy. "Kincaid," she repeated. "Roll over."

He sighed and nestled closer. His lips brushed the back of her neck, sending a shiver of delight through her veins. At the same instant, he began to caress her breast lazily with his fingers. To her horror, that not only felt good, but her nipple swelled to a tight bud beneath her stays and linen bodice. "Kincaid!" she hissed. "What are you doing?"

He sat up so quickly that he yanked her with him. She rolled away into the hay as he came to his feet, pistol in hand, stark naked, in the dim morning light.

Bess knew she should look away for modesty's sake, but she couldn't. Wide-eyed, and with her lips parted in surprise, she gazed at him. Her throat thickened and her angry words died unspoken.

By the sweet eyes of God! He was the most

beautiful man she had ever seen. His nearly hair-less chest was broad and corded with sinew; his thewy arms bulged with muscle, and his stomach was board-flat and brown as old honey. His waist tapered to narrow hips, and a sprinkling of gold-dust hair formed a triangle that led to an upright shaft, thicker around and longer than Bess had ever seen. Unconsciously, she moistened her lips with the tip of her tongue and sighed softly.

Kincaid's thighs were like young trees; the one exposed buttock that was visible was as lean and hard as the rest of him. His bronzed skin bore the scars of many battles, but they only added to his beauty rather than detracted from it. His knees were well formed, his ankles trim, and his feet large and high-arched. Even the nails on his toes were as clean and close-trimmed as his finger-nails.

"Have ye never seen a man before?" he asked boldly. The burr in his deep voice was so thick that she could hardly make out the words, but there was no need for her to try.

"I have," she admitted. It was true. No country girl was ignorant of a man's physique. She'd gone with her grandmother to administer to the sick and wounded since she was a child. Human or beast, when a life hung in the balance, Mama Lacy believed that there was no place for false modesty in herself or in her granddaughter. "I've seen many," Bess continued thickly, "but none to match you."

He laughed. "A compliment?"

She forced herself to look into those penetrat-ing ginger-colored eyes. "It was." Her voice was so low that the patter of rain on the roof nearly drowned her answer.

He lowered the pistol and took a step toward her. "Woman, I—"

Fear lanced through her as she realized what he must think. Air hissed through her clenched teeth. Marry, come up! she cried inwardly. She sounded like a common slattern! What ailed her that such words could come from her mouth? Excitement bubbled up from the pit of her stomach to make her wits giddy and her mouth dry.

"If ye'd like a closer look—"

"Cover yourself," she said sharply. "Have you no manners?"

His mouth tightened. "What is it ye want of me?"

"I want you to act like a gentleman," she said, stepping back from the abyss that had opened before her. "You curled around me so tightly in your sleep that you nearly squeezed the life from me." Unfamiliar sensations were still washing over her, and the heat that had started in her neck and face had settled in her loins, making her as jumpy as an untrained filly.

He spread his broad, scarred hands, palms up. "Bess—" he began.

Her hands knotted into fists at her side. "Did you . . . did we . . . Last night, did we do—"

He stared at her in surprise for a moment, then began to chuckle as he turned away to pull on his breeches. "If we had, woman, ye'd not need to ask. I'm nay a boasting man, but when I make love to a woman, she doesna forget so quickly."

To her shame, she could not tear her eyes away.

Bent over as he was, his bare bottom was comely enough to make a spinster weep.

Bess swallowed hard, trying to dissolve the knot in her throat. I'm a spinster, she realized. No one dares to call me so to my face, but many must think so.

But looking at Kincaid's virile body didn't make her weep. It made her think forbidden thoughts that a lady would die before admitting. She could still feel the weight of his arm over her . . . the heat of his manhood against her—No! She'd not allow herself to imagine such wickedness. "You had no right to take advantage of me," she protested, but he cut her short as he turned back and flashed her a devilish grin.

"Nay," he countered. "Who's being taken advantage of? Was I staring at ye like I wanted to eat ye for breakfast? 'Twas ye, hinney. And many a man would take that as a 'come hither and do what ye will' look."

She backed away from him, trying to smooth down her skirt and pull up her stockings all at the same time. "You were the one with your arms wrapped around me," she accused. "And you as bare as a new-hatched egg. I trusted you. And when I went to sleep, you had clothes on!"

"Hist, now. Keep your voice down. There may be someone in the yard. I admit it's early for that pack of hounds we saw drinkin' in the tavern to be abroad, but ye never can tell. They think you're my woman, and 'twould seem mighty strange did they hear ye canting about my bare ass."

"What happened to your clothes?"

"I got up in the night. I heard someone prowlin' around and I—"

"Like as not, you went outside to relieve your-self, as much whiskey as you slopped down."

"As I said, I heard a noise and I went to see what it was. Another rider arrived in the middle of the night, a farmer from one of the islands in the bay. He's here to meet his brother coming in by boat this morning. He was wetter than a drowned skunk, but chirping merry with drink. I had to help him up to the tavern door. When I came back, I realized I'd scolded ye about sleepin' in wet clothes and here was I doin' the same. So I took them off. Ye canna tell me that it's normal for a man in Maryland to sleep in all his clothes."

"You'll sleep in your clothes when you sleep next to me, or I'll have the blankets and you'll be up a tree," she warned. "I never agreed to whore for you on this trip."

"I told ye, I am no wild boar that ruts with every female he sees. 'Twas you sittin' on my lap when I woke up. Like as not, you got scared of a mouse in the night and crawled into my arms."

"I never did."

He pulled his leather vest on, flexing first one arm and then the other to taunt her. "But ye stared, ye canna deny that, can ye?"

"It was a shock."

"And a shock to me to be peered at so. A man has his principles, ye ken. I like to choose my own women."

"And I'm not your type," she finished for him. "You've said that. But I needn't tell you that you're not my type. I want no man, but if I did, it wouldn't be a mangy Scot without a chamber pot to call his own or an acre of land to empty it on."

The barb drew blood. He blanched beneath his tan, but covered it with a quick retort. "We're in a sweet mood this morning, aren't we?"

"And shouldn't I be, after what I was forced to be part of last night? I'm not accustomed to witnessing tavern brawls."

"Bess." His tone deepened. "If I am to protect ye, ye must let me do it as I see fit."

"There was no need for you to start that fight. The man was rude, no more. You needn't have hit him for—"

"Ye are wrong. I know him."

"You can't know him. You're a stranger here."

"I've known his kind from Edinburgh to Stockholm. He was a fool and a bully, and he would have stirred up more trouble than I could have handled if I hadn't stopped him."

"I don't believe you," she said. "I think you're the bully. You kicked him when he was down. That's dirty—"

"There are two kinds of fighting men," he told her softly, "the live and the dead. If I hadn't beaten him senseless, I could have ended up dead and you . . ." He trailed off. "Ye wishin' you were."

She shook her head, still not willing to believe him. "I hope your head feels the size of a coach wheel. It should."

"My head is my own affair, thank you, lady," he said grimly. He ran his fingers through his long hair, snapped a leather fringe off his vest, and tied his unruly yellow mane behind his neck. "Ye've straw sticking out of yours," he observed.

She brushed at her hair with her fingers and pulled out a broken stalk. "Some farmer you'd make," she said, "if you can't tell hay from straw." Grabbing up her saddlebags, she went to the ladder.

"Best let me go down first in case ye fall," he said.

"I'm perfectly capable of going down a ladder," she answered. She was halfway to the bottom when she let out a muffled yelp. "Ginger!"

"What are ye bleatin' about now, woman?" he said, coming after her.

"Ginger! That's my mare." She ran to the last horse in the row and threw her arms around the animal's shaggy neck. "You're a mess," she murmured. "Look at you." The mare nickered softly and tossed her head as Bess ran her hands over the bright chestnut hide, exploring muscles and tendons for some sign of damage. "Look at you," she repeated. "No one's touched you with a curry comb in months."

Carefully, Bess felt Ginger's legs, lifting each front foot to exclaim over the poor condition of her hooves. Then she felt the mare's belly and hindquarters, inspecting the back legs and hooves, then patting her rump. "Good girl, good Ginger," she crooned. She stroked the mare's back and withers and looked through the close-cropped mane for ticks. Finding one swollen with blood and removing it, she swore under her breath.

Kincaid came to stand beside her. "Are ye certain this is your horse?" he asked. "There are many chestnut mares with one white hind foot."

Bess ignored him. She continued whispering to the mare and rubbing and scratching her behind the ears. "Ginger likes being scratched," she said.

"I'm sorry I don't have a carrot for you, girl." Bess bent her head and kissed the horse's velvety nose. "I thought I'd never see her again," she said, blinking back tears of joy. "I thought she was gone for good." Gently, she fingered the outline of the white diamond on the mare's forehead.

"I asked ye how ye can be sure this is—"

"Do you know nothing about horses that you think they all look the same?" she accused. "I was there when she was foaled. I took care of her every day of her life until you stole her from me." She glared at him. "She's in foal herself. Do you see that? God knows who sired it. A jackass, for all I know."

Without warning, Kincaid grabbed her and kissed her. Startled, she tried to fight him off. He silenced her impending scream by seizing a handful of her hair and plunging his tongue into her mouth. When she twisted her head away, he pinned her between his bulk and that of the mare, pulled her hard against his shoulder, and whispered in her ear, "Hist, woman. It's only an act. We're nay alone."

His words penetrated her fury and she nodded. Cautiously, he released her and she slid sideways along the horse's rump.

A broad, pock-faced farmer stood in the open stable doorway. " 'Ware my horse," he growled. "Do yer tuppin' elsewhere. That's a valuable animal."

Bess wiped her mouth with the back of her hand and cast her gaze down at the floor. "The horse ain't hurt," she said with such a good im-

itation of common folks' speech that Kincaid
chuckled.

"No harm done," he said.

"My brother's boat is docked yonder," the
farmer said grudgingly. "Ye said ye were huntin'
passage south."

"We are. I've heard there's work for a soldier
in the Carolinas."

"Don't know about that, but my brother will
take ye, iffen ye can pay. We ain't running no
charity."

"Where did ye get this horse?" Bess asked, still
affecting a country accent.

Kincaid dropped an arm over her shoulder
carelessly. "Hold your mouth, woman," he said.
"Can't ye tell this gentleman and me are talking
business?" When she would have spoken again,
he squeezed her tightly in warning. "She has a
sharp tongue, but she's handy for other things,"
he said to the farmer. "You've good taste in
horseflesh. Could I interest ye in these two
mares?" He indicated the animals he and Bess
had ridden in on. "I can't be takin' them on the
water, now can I?"

The pock-faced man eyed the horses greedily.
" 'Tis God's truth, ye can't," he said. "Are they
stolen?"

"They're—" Bess started to reply, but Kincaid
squeezed her roughly again.

"There's nobody huntin' for them, if that's
what ye want to know," he said. "Ye might say
they were paid for."

"You've got papers?" the farmer asked.

Kincaid made a sound of derision. "I've never
troubled myself with such," he said. "And I'll

wager you've no title to that chestnut mare, neither."

Bess's temper was near to spilling over. "I'd not thought to sell the horses—"

"I don't keep ye for thinkin'," Kincaid cut in.

The farmer scowled and walked around the animals, running his hands over their legs. Then he raised their heads and examined their teeth.

"Sound as a new guinea," Kincaid said. "You'll find no better in these parts."

"This one might have botts," the man remarked.

"They do not!" Bess said.

The farmer spit on the dirt floor. "The near one is favorin' a front leg."

"Nay," Kincaid rumbled. "They're prime, both of them. Go for a pretty price in Dover."

"Well, this ain't Dover. Saddles go with them?"

"Aye, and bridles."

"Name your price."

"They aren't for sale," Bess said through clenched teeth. She'd meant to leave the horses somewhere safe, with instructions for them to be taken back to Fortune's Gift. Now she'd found Ginger, and Kincaid wasn't going to let her do anything about getting her mare back. And on top of that, he was talking to her as though she were dirt under his feet.

"Close your mouth, woman," Kincaid threatened, "or I'll close it for ye."

Bess threw him a whithering look. I'll get even with you for this, she swore to herself. So help me, I will!

Kincaid mentioned a ridiculously low price, and

the other man shook his head. They began to argue in a friendly sort of way, and after a few offers and counteroffers, they shook hands. Bess was too shocked to speak. The Scot had sold two fine riding horses, saddles, and gear for less than what she'd paid for one of the saddles.

Kincaid started for the door, keeping his arm firmly around Bess's waist and forcing her to walk with him. Ginger nickered and Bess looked back at her mare.

"Ye be takin' the stock back to yer place on the island?" Kincaid asked. "Ye said ye had a place on Deal?"

"Nope." The rest of the farmer's reply was muffled by Ginger's frantic whinny as she tried to follow Bess. The chestnut mare tossed her head and tried to pull free.

I'll find you again, girl. I will. I promise, Bess vowed silently. Salt tears stung her eyes and she stumbled.

Kincaid caught her and pulled her hard against him. The stable yard was a morass of standing water and heaps of old straw and manure. It was still raining, and a raw breeze blew from the west. The sky was an angry gray, and moisture-laden clouds hung low over the horizon.

By daylight, Bess could see that the Cock's Comb stood on the bank of a muddy river. The storm had churned the surface of the dark water to short, choppy waves. At the ramshackle dock, a long, low, black-hulled sloop was moored. The sails were furled and the deck was empty, and with each swell, the sloop slammed against the dock.

"There she be," the farmer said. "She ain't

much to look at, but fer a price, she'll get ye to the Carolina coast and no questions asked."

"Aye," Kincaid said, "that's all I ask."

The pocked man grunted a reply and went ahead of them into the inn.

"She looks seaworthy to me," Kincaid said to Bess.

Bess looked at the dark sloop and suppressed a shiver. When she boarded that boat, there would be no turning back. She knew she was risking everything on a dead man's journal, an illusive ghost, and a mercenary's sword arm.

Almost as though he'd read her mind, Kincaid glanced down at her and gave her a playful squeeze. His brown eyes met hers, and a trace of a smile appeared at the corners of his mouth. "Change of heart?" he asked. "It's not too late to back out."

Not certain she could keep her voice from betraying her fear, she shook her head no.

A roguish grin broke over his face and lit his eyes with specks of gold. "You've got grit for an English lass, I'll give ye that much," he said. "Did ye have a sweeter disposition and a softer tongue, we might even get on."

"Luckily for us both, there's no chance of that, is there?"

"Nay," he answered huskily, "none at all."

William Myers Senior, founder and head of William Myers and Son, transporters, consignment merchants, and investment firm, rose from his desk and crossed the office to close his door, assuring privacy from the ranks of clerks in the larger chamber. Without speaking to his visitor, he returned to the window behind his desk and stared out at the rainy Chestertown street below.

Joel Middleton, Esq., solicitor, scratched at his new horsehair wig and cleared his throat impatiently.

Myers forced himself to control his anger at Middleton's appearance at Myers and Son on a Monday afternoon. When he turned back to face the wraith-thin young man, his features were composed. "You were specifically instructed never to come here," he said. "Our contact was to be at the warehouse at a mutually agreed-upon time."

The buck-toothed solicitor sniffed loudly and dusted an invisible piece of lint off his scarlet waistcoat. "My client gave you specific instructions." He removed a large linen handkerchief and blew his nose. "He will be very disappointed, sir. You assured us that acquiring the plantation was a foregone conclusion."

Myers' knee ached. It always ached in the rain, and the damned wooden peg was cutting into his flesh again. He wanted to sit down, but he'd always found that standing while another man sat gave him the advantage. He didn't like Joel Middleton any better than he liked the man Middleton represented, but anyone who had business in the Caribbean had better be prepared to deal with Falconer.

This whole affair concerning Fortune's Gift was distasteful to Myers. Of course, the Bennetts were rascals. Old James Bennett had been little better than a pirate himself, for all his airs. He'd come out of nowhere with a chestful of Spanish gold, and he'd bought himself into Tidewater society.

With the aid of his wife—a lowborn wench if Myers had ever seen one—Bennett had built Fortune's Gift into one of the finest plantations on the Eastern Shore.

Myers had been a young man then, newly come to the Maryland Colony and still in the employ of Jonathan Williams, but he'd heard the rumors about Fortune's Gift and the Bennetts. Strange stories they were, mostly superstitious nonsense about ghosts and witches, and about James Bennett being some kind of royalty.

Now James and his wife were dead. Hellfire and damnation, their only son, David Bennett, was probably dead too. He'd sailed for China and not been heard of for years. David's daughter, Elizabeth, was the only heir. And the chit was as odd as the rest of them. She'd scandalized the Tidewater by freeing her father's slaves and firing a trusted overseer. And most recently, she'd set tongues to wagging again by buying the indenture of a convicted felon, a Scot who should have been hanged for piracy and horse theft.

"My client wants Fortune's Gift," Middleton said.

"No names!" Myers admonished. By the king's ballocks! If he'd been ten years younger, he'd have picked up this reedy-voiced twit by the seat of his satin breeches and tossed him out the second-story window onto High Street.

"Falconer—"

"No names!" Myers' aching knee quivered, and he dropped heavily into his high-backed desk chair. "Your client would be highly incensed to hear that you were bandying his name about in public."

"This is hardly public." Middleton sniffed again and dabbed at his nose. "Why haven't you started foreclosure on the plantation?"

"There's been a complication."

"And that is?"

"Elizabeth Bennett has disappeared." She and the convict had vanished. Myers left that bit of information unspoken. He rubbed at his aching right arm and wished the room weren't so stuffy. He'd known all along that his debt to Falconer would have to be paid, not in money, but in favors. He'd accepted that as a hard fact of the business world. But he didn't have to like it, and he didn't have to like letting vermin like Middleton into his office.

"You know that Falconer wanted the woman as well. He's offered a substantial reward for her delivery to the islands." The solicitor smirked. "Dead or alive."

"That does it," Myers snapped. "Get your sorry ass out of here. You tell your client that there will be no further action on this matter until he provides a respectable liaison. I won't conduct business with scum like you, Middleton."

The younger man leaped to his feet indignantly. His face was rapidly turning puce, and his mouth opened and closed like a beached fish gasping for air. "You . . . you . . . you can't talk to me like that."

Myers opened a desk drawer and removed a small, pearl-handled derringer. "You have two minutes to get out of this building," he said, "and twenty minutes to get out of Chestertown. If I catch sight of you after that, I'll shoot you as a public menace."

"You can't do that," Middleton sputtered. "Falconer will—"

"Falconer will dispose of you as easily as he disposes of dead slaves who don't survive the voyage from the African coast. Your stupidity and your mouth make you dangerous, Middleton. Dangerous to me and dangerous to him. If I were you, I'd take the first boat to England, or better yet, to Holland. Falconer has a long arm in seagoing circles and a longer memory."

Middleton was already halfway to the door. "He won't forget this insult, I can guarantee that!"

Myers glanced at the tall case clock in the corner of the paneled chamber. "You've already used up one of your minutes," he reminded. He raised the pistol, and the solicitor fled from the room.

It was only a matter of seconds before Middleton appeared on the muddy street below. He twisted around to shake an angry fist at Myers, but his feet kept moving. Myers turned away from the window and settled heavily into his chair again.

So Falconer had offered a reward for Elizabeth Bennett, he thought. Wearily, he put the gun back into the desk drawer and covered his face with his hands. Suddenly he felt old.

Falconer had drawn Myers and Son into his net a little at a time. First it had been information the man wanted, nothing more. Falconer had wanted answers to questions about the Bennett family and the plantation. That had been simple to provide, and it had cost the company nothing. Then he'd asked Myers and Son to loan monies to David

Bennett to finance his foolish trip to the Orient. Now Falconer insisted that Myers and Son take Fortune's Gift and sell it to him. All business, all perfectly legal.

Lots of businessmen cooperated with Falconer. He was an important man, a man who had connections with every major contact in the Caribbean and up and down the coast of the American colonies. Some said Falconer was a smuggler and that he dealt with the Spanish and the Portuguese. Some accused him of having pirates in his employ. But no sensible man spoke disparagingly of Falconer in public.

But now Falconer had gone beyond the boundaries of decency by putting a price on an Englishwoman's head. Myers groaned. He'd gone along with Falconer even after he'd smelled something rotten when the ship bearing Elizabeth Bennett's tobacco cargo had gone down. But he'd never agreed to any killing.

The gnawing pain in his right arm grew sharper, and Myers massaged it without thinking. If Falconer wanted Elizabeth Bennett dead, she was as good as a corpse already—and that made Myers a party to murder.

With trembling hands, he opened the desk drawer again, cradled his pistol, and stared at it with tear-filled eyes.

Chapter 10

The Carolina Coast

A bolt of lightning ripped the twilight ceiling of rolling clouds, nearly blinding Bess with its intensity. Rain was already spattering across the deck of the sloop, and the waves were five feet and whipping higher with every gust of wind.

They had been plagued by bad weather since the smuggling vessel had first ventured into the Chesapeake Bay nine days ago. The captain, "Ants" Taylor, was carrying a cargo of French brandy and muskets as well as an assortment of Dutch scissors, needles, and sewing thread. Bess had lost track of the stops they had made, usually in the dark of night to sell or trade contraband.

The forty-foot sloop with its shallow draft and long, pointed bowsprit was ideal for maneuvering in the rivers and coves of the bay. The *Jessie* carried a crew of three: a free black man named Rudy; an Irish bond servant, Ian; and a mulatto boy. The boy's name was Sam, and as far as Bess could tell, he could neither hear nor speak.

There was a tiny, musty-smelling cabin forward and covered-over cargo holds in the aft. But despite the presence of three narrow bunks in the cabin, Bess had not spent a single night below.

Instead, she and Kincaid had wrapped themselves in oiled canvas and camped out on the
deck. Once, in pouring rain, she had ventured
below, but after an hour of foul odors and fleas,
she had welcomed the feel of clean water on her
face.

Much to her surprise, Kincaid had proved a
cheerful companion. Once they left the tavern's
dock, the Scot had stopped taunting her, and although he was still overly protective where Ants
and the crew were concerned, he treated her with
an easy camaraderie. He remained constantly at
her side and never failed to see that she received
the first portion of whatever meal was being prepared and that she had a dry blanket at night.

There had been no repetition of the intimacy
they had shared in the hayloft. If Kincaid touched
her, it was to steady her balance on the rocking
sloop, and his physical contact was as innocent as
if she were his beloved sister. Bess was at once
relieved and confused by his behavior. The man
she had believed incapable of acting like a gentleman was behaving perfectly, and she wasn't certain if this was what she really wanted or not.

Thunder rumbled ominously overhead and the
rain fell harder. This rising storm was the second
one of the day. In early afternoon, thunderheads
had piled up on the western horizon, and lightning had split a tree on an island a quarter of a
mile away.

Bess felt uneasy as flecks of foaming waves
struck her cheeks. Ants had warned them of the
dangerous passage around Cape Hatteras. Moving sandbars and treacherous currents made the

blue-green waters a graveyard for ships when thunderstorms whipped out of the west to lash the sea into churning fury.

"They's islands that only show at high tide," Ants had said that morning, "and wreckers what will lure ye ashore with lanterns and cut yer throat quicker than ye can say 'scat.' I've run the cape day and night fer twenty year. I've seed hurrycanes and squalls that would raise gooseflesh on the devil hisself. I lost one boat roundin' the cape, and I swum to safety on a whiskey keg when the *Nancy Jane* capsized in a thirty-foot wave. It's a bad place, I tell ye. And I've heard stories . . ." He'd broken off to take a sighting of the nearest island with a rusty spyglass. "Some say," he continued when he was satisfied of his location. "Some say 'twasn't our Lord made the cape, but some Injun demon. These coasts is haunted, that's fer sure. Too many good men went to the bottom here. No place fer God-fearin' white folks.".

"Nor black," Rudy had added. He was a small, muscular man with tribal scars on his chin. "Best not talk about wrecks and squalls, Ants," he'd said sharply. "It's bad luck." He'd scowled at Bess. "We've trouble enough sailin' with a woman."

Lightning flared in the growing darkness, a bolt that struck so close Bess could smell the brimstone in the air. She hunkered down on the deck and wrapped a canvas around her shoulders to keep off the rain.

"Maybe you'd be better off in the cabin," Ants said. He and Rudy were furling the sail to a storm rig. "We'll run before the wind and she may get a bit choppy. We'd not want ye to fall overboard."

"She's good where she is," Kincaid said.

Bess noticed that he'd slung over his shoulder the oilskin bag containing one of his pistols and her silver-inlaid one, her grandfather's skean, extra powder and shot, and their store of coin. Her saddlebags were stuffed into an empty wooden brandy keg at Kincaid's back. He'd taken the precaution as soon as they had sailed out of the mouth of the first river. Bess's jewelry, including the little golden jaguar with the turquoise eyes, was sewn into a pocket she'd fashioned inside her stays.

She was too keyed up to be hungry. She'd never had any trouble with seasickness, not even in rough weather, but she didn't like the lightning. They'd eaten nothing since morning. The meal then had consisted of salt fish and damp cheese with French brandy to wash it down.

They'd anchored the night before off an island and waded ashore to dig clams and hunt up seabird eggs. At Bess's insistence, they'd built a fire long enough to cook the eggs. Ants hadn't wanted to advertise their presence to passing boats or natives of the area.

"A man in my trade," he'd said, "is best to figure every soul his enemy until he learns better. If the Crown don't catch ye and hang ye, pirates will take yer cargo and leave ye for the gulls."

Ants was bound for Charles Town on his own business, and he'd agreed to carry Bess and Kincaid that far. Kincaid had told her that it would be easy for them to find passage for the Caribbean from there. So far, despite the hardships, Bess had enjoyed the rough captain and crew and the voyage. She had to admit to herself that the prospect of seeing new country and being treated as a dangerous mercenary's woman, instead of as the heiress of a great manor, was strangely exciting.

The captain leaned hard on the tiller as the sloop fought wind and water to hold a course. The Irishman had gone below with the boy, and Rudy crouched near the bow and listened for the crash of the surf. Kincaid had explained to Bess that it was too dark to see sandbars, so the crew had to depend on the different sounds of the waves to tell where the bottom turned shallow.

"Some of these sandbars run out a quarter mile," he said to her in his deep burr. "An easy drop makes for small surf, but a steep drop can double the wave height."

A shower of hailstones clattered across the deck, and Bess ducked her head to avoid the stinging bits of ice. Closing her eyes, she wondered if her crops on Fortune's Gift had been hurt by the unseasonable wet weather. If the gardens and fields failed to produce, both men and animals would go hungry come winter.

Would she be home by then? She knew how far Panama was on a map, but actually going there was different. Would it take months? Her grandfather's journal had said that Morgan had crossed Panama in a matter of days. Would she be days in the jungle, or weeks?

And most important, would the gold be there

waiting for them when they reached the spot where it had been buried?

She lifted her head and glanced at Kincaid. He was facing into the storm, seemingly impervious to wind and rain and hail. Another flash of lightning revealed that his eyes were shut, and his mouth was a hard, stubborn slash across his chiseled features.

Could she trust him? Her gut feeling was that she could, but her head said no. Kutii had told her that Kincaid was a good man, but doubts still troubled her. And Kutii had been conspicuously absent since they'd come aboard the sloop.

Sweet Lord in heaven! What would Kincaid do to her if they reached the shores of Panama and she had to tell him that there had never been a map? That she was depending on a specter to tell her where to dig?

She shivered. Kincaid had agreed to come with her for the price of his freedom and a share of the gold. She could still give him his indenture, but if she couldn't produce the treasure . . . She had a terrible feeling that she could end up as fish bait herself.

"Bar ahead!" Rudy shouted above the wind.

Bess didn't know how he could tell. The sail was snapping like a bullwhip, the sloop's ribs and planks were creaking, thunder was booming, and the water was crashing all around them. She felt deafened by the storm.

Strangely, she wasn't afraid anymore. If Kincaid could sit there so calmly, he must have faith in the boat and the captain. And hadn't Ants said he'd sailed these waters for years?

She choked and sputtered on a mouthful of salt water and pulled the canvas tighter around her. Nothing could have made her go below and miss this magnificent war of wind and water. The elemental splendor of the lightning was exhilarating. The sloop rode the swells like a cork, plunging down until she thought they'd strike the ocean floor, then rising gallantly to challenge the next wave.

"Surf ahead!" Rudy cried. "Hard alee!"

The sloop rose and dove, slamming so hard into something solid that the shock knocked Bess flat on her face. The boat heeled and the mast cracked and toppled. Rudy's scream rose above the crash of the waves, then was cut off abruptly.

Stunned by the blow to her head, Bess began to slide across the tilted deck. Water was rolling over the gunnel, and it seemed to her as if sky and sea had suddenly changed places. Then she felt an iron hand close around her arm, and she heard Kincaid calling her name. Before her mind cleared, the shock came again. She looked back toward the stern, where the captain had stood a moment before, but all she could see now was dark, tumbling water.

"We've got to jump!" Kincaid yelled.

But when she tried to rise, she found that her leg was tangled in twisted rope and canvas. "I can't!" she screamed. "I'm caught!" A heavy object rolled over her back and shoulder, but she felt no pain, only numbness. The world had turned to water. It filled her mouth and nose and ears, muffling the claps of thunder and blinding her.

She knew what had happened. She knew the

boat had gone down to the bottom of the sea and she had gone with it. She knew she would never see trees or earth or sky again. Then the impossible happened. The sloop rose again from the depths and she sucked in lungfuls of air. And with the life-giving oxygen, some semblance of reason returned, and Bess realized that she wasn't alone. Kincaid was still there, holding her against him and sawing at the thick line that tangled her with his knife.

The boat shuddered under her, and she heard the snap of timbers. Then she was free and Kincaid was dragging her across the deck. This time when the sloop rolled, they leaped off into the water. And in the midst of that jump, his hand slipped out of hers and she sank into the churning waves alone.

Instinct bade her swim toward the surface, but the tide pulled her down. Her skirts and the weight of her jewelry worked against her. By sheer will, she reached the crest of a wave and took a single breath before water closed over her head again. She rolled over and over; once, her hands touched sand, and she knew she was on the bottom. Her mind was going black; her lungs felt as though they were ready to explode. Her arms and legs ached from struggling against the force of the ocean. Then, without warning, the sea flung her upward again, and as her head broke water, lightning lit up the sky.

Bess's heart leaped. There, not ten feet away, a hatch cover floated in the trough of a wave. In the thrill of hope, her exhaustion was forgotten. Nothing mattered but reaching that small square of planking. Using every ounce of strength she had left, she swam toward it.

The light was gone and she was surrounded by darkness. Foam and water crashed over her head. She swallowed another mouthful of ocean. She forced herself to keep going, to raise one arm after the other, to kick and kick until her legs felt as though they were going to fall off. And when the next bolt split the heavens, the hatch cover had vanished.

Not knowing which way to go, she held her breath, trying to keep above the surface, straining her eyes to find the debris again. Then something solid bobbed up beside her and she reached for it without thinking.

Her hands closed around cloth and human flesh, and she screamed as she realized that what she'd grabbed was a dead body. She flung herself backward and was caught in the next swell, and when she came up weeping and sputtering, she heard a familiar voice in her head.

"Do not fear; this is not your time to cross over."

She blinked, and through the salt and the spray she saw Kutii standing chest-deep in the water with his arms extended. "I can't swim anymore," she said.

"You can."

"I can't. I'm tired."

"You carry the blood of Star Woman. Without you, my people will be lost."

"Let me be," she gasped.

"Come, little one. I will carry you."

She thought how strange it was that he could

walk through seas so deep and rough, and how odd that the lightning should flicker around his shoulders in a blue haze, but his arms were strong and warm. Gratefully, she lay back against his chest and closed her eyes.

When she opened them again, Kutii had vanished, and she was only an arm's length from the hatch cover. Somehow she swam the short distance and locked her arms around the water-soaked planks. And then the blackness that had threatened her for so long became overwhelming, and she sank into a deep and dreamless sleep.

It was daylight when Kincaid rolled over onto his stomach and began to choke up seawater. Painfully, he opened his eyes. They burned with salt and grit. Wiping his face, he sat up and looked around the low barrier island.

As far as he could see, there was nothing but sand and low scrub pines. Foam washed against the beach, but the fierce breakers of last night had gentled to rolling whitecaps. Sea gulls and shore birds skittered along the water's edge and circled lazily overhead, and the telltale bubbling holes showed where sand fleas burrowed under the wet sand. A few fiddler crabs scurried from tidal pools toward the sea, but there was no sign of human life.

Kincaid got to his knees and wiped his eyes, trying to get the sand out of them. He coughed again and cleared his throat, then struggled to his feet and stared up and down the deserted beach. "Bess!" he called, cupping his mouth with his hands. "Bess! Where are ye?"

The only answer was a sea gull's harsh cry.

He stripped off the remains of his shirt and waded barefoot into the sea, dipping the torn cloth in the clean, cold water and using the shirt to bathe his aching face and eyes. The salt stung, but he continued to splash water in his eyes until they were free of sand. Then he straightened his back and ran a hand through his long hair.

Shading his eyes, he stared eastward out to sea. No islands broke the surface of the rolling waves. From where he stood to the place where gray, overcast sky and water met, there was nothing but the occasional splash of a fish. The wind that had lashed the sloop's sail and whipped the ocean to fury was gone. Now only a cooling easterly brushed his face and bare chest.

"Bess!" he shouted again.

A whoosh and a pair of sleek backs sliding through the water just beyond the breakers showed the passing of a pair of dolphins.

A frisson played down Kincaid's spine and his throat tightened. "Bess!" he called. His stomach twisted, not from salt water but from the sickening thought that the red-haired lass was dead. As dead as the sloop that had cracked her ribs on the sandbar in last night's storm.

Shame washed over him. He'd had Bess by the hand when they jumped free of the boat. He'd had her, and he'd let her slip away. For the first time in his life, his strength had failed him.

By the sweet tears of Mary Magdalene! If Bess was lost . . . He inhaled deeply and tried to clear his head as his eyes clouded with tears. He dashed them away and tried to swallow the huge lump in his throat.

What was he coming to, to weep over a woman? Was she the first wench to die before her time? The shock of near drowning must have hurt him worse than he'd thought, if he took her loss so hard, he reasoned. After all, she was nothing to him but a means to gain his freedom and a new start. Cursing his own softheartedness, he turned and splashed back toward the shore.

He held to the lie for nearly two minutes before the truth broke over him with the brilliance of the rising orange-gold sun.

Bess Bennett was more to him than a rich Englishwoman who had hired him to guide her on a treasure hunt. For the first time in many years, he'd allowed a wench to get under his skin. And if he lost her, he'd never find her match in this world or the next.

He cupped his hands once more around his mouth. ''Bess! Bess, can ye hear me?''

It made no sense that he was alive and unhurt and the other four had drowned. Doubtless, he reasoned, they were washed up somewhere else along this island shore. He couldn't have swum far last night, so the wreck had to be close. He looked out to sea again, shading his eyes against the ever-brightening dawn. But, try as he might, he could see no sign of the sloop.

Determined to keep searching for Bess and the others, Kincaid began walking north, up the beach. He was unarmed, having lost his knife and pistol sometime during the night. The only clothing he had left was his breeches and his weapons belt. His breeches had come through the ordeal without a single tear.

Thirst plagued him as he strode along, but he ignored it. There would be plenty of time to dig for fresh water. Utilizing an old soldier's trick, he sucked on a pebble as he walked, and that kept his mouth from drying out.

Ten minutes up the beach, he came upon a section of broken mast and the largest part of the mainsail. He dragged it up out of the water, unrolling the canvas so that it would dry, and continued on.

Not a hundred yards farther, he saw something bobbing on the surface of the waves and waded out to retrieve the wooden cask containing Bess's belongings, weapons, powder and shot, and other necessities that he'd sealed inside. When he broke it open, he found that the keg had leaked, but there was nothing that couldn't be salvaged by careful drying.

He stuck her grandfather's knife in his empty sheath, put the cask on his shoulder, and went on. But after only a few minutes, the island curved to the west. Across a wide channel, he could see land with more low trees. He tried calling Bess's name again, but the only answer he got was the echo of his own voice. Discouraged, he turned south once more and retraced his steps.

When he passed the place where the sail lay, he was tempted to stop, erect a shelter, and seek fresh water, but he didn't. With each passing moment, he knew the chances of finding Bess alive were growing weaker. If she had made it to shore, the increasing heat and lack of water could easily finish her off. She was, for all her bold spirit, only a woman.

A woman who had depended on him . . .

Over and over, the desperate moments after the sloop had struck the bar were replayed in Kincaid's mind. He could smell the scent of her hair as he lay over her, trying to protect her from the force of the waves. He could hear the crash of the water and feel the death throes of the dying boat under him. He could see the flash of lightning across a storm-blackened sea and taste the bite of salt on his tongue.

He'd cut her loose from the tangle of sail and rope, and he'd had her hand when they jumped. Involuntarily, he groaned softly as he remembered the desolate feel of her small hand sliding away.

God's teeth! He'd give his right arm to have her here now, alive and sassy, giving him hell for failing her.

An osprey screamed overhead, and Kincaid looked up. The magnificent bird soared on outspread wings, a fish clutched in the powerful talons.

Kincaid spit out the pebble and started south down the beach at a jog. He'd never been a quitter, and he'd not believe Bess was dead until he saw her cold face. He'd keep on looking, and when he'd covered this island, he'd swim to the next and search until he found her. Until he found—

A splash of Lincoln green against the white sand caught his eye. With an oath, he threw down the wooden keg and ran down the beach. And as his long strides closed the distance, he clearly saw the waves lift and wash through the long chestnut mass of a woman's hair.

"Bess! Bess!" he shouted.

His heart was racing as he splashed into the shallows and lifted her in his arms. Her eyes were closed, her long, thick lashes dark against her unnaturally pale face. Her skin was cold to the touch.

Bess's green riding skirt was torn, her white linen shirt in tatters, and her stays undone, exposing her full, rounded breasts almost to her nipples. Try as he might, Kincaid could detect no rise and fall of her waxen bosom.

In agony, he rocked her tenderly against his chest. "Bess," he whispered hoarsely. "Bess, can ye hear me?"

Her head fell back as though she were asleep, her lovely long hair falling like a curtain of dark red velvet. Her rose lips parted, but she made no sound. One arm slipped downward, to dangle lifelessly.

"Damn ye, woman," he murmured. "Speak to me."

He blinked away the moisture that obscured his vision as he carried her up onto the beach and knelt with her still cradled in his arms. "Bess," he whispered. And without knowing why, he lowered his head and brushed her lips with his own.

She sighed and he flinched. "Bess?" Nothing. "Dinna leave me, lass," he said. His shoulders trembled with emotion. "Dinna . . ."

This time, there was no mistaking the long-drawn-out sigh. Her lashes flickered, and startling blue eyes stared into his. For an instant, he read bewilderment there, and then recognition.

She smiled weakly. "Kincaid?" she whispered faintly. "Where were you?"

He kissed her again, crushing her against him, searing her lips with the incandescent heat of all the hope and pent-up longing he'd denied for so long. And found to his surprise that Bess had put her arms around his neck and was kissing him back with more fervor than he would have thought a dead woman possessed.

Chapter 11

Bess's ashen cheeks suffused with color, and she gazed up at Kincaid with half-closed eyes and sighed. Her mouth opened slightly, and she moistened her lips with the tip of her tongue. "Did anyone ever tell you that you're beautiful?" she whispered.

Kincaid swallowed hard. Bess's normally husky voice was deepened by salt and water, and the provocative timbre sent a sweet rippling sensation spiraling through him. "Bess . . ." For a long moment, he held her, not moving a muscle, acutely aware of the sun, and sand, and wind, and of the feel of her mouth against his. "Bess," he murmured again.

He wasn't sure if he was awake or dreaming. Had he really pulled her from the sea, or was she floating lifeless somewhere in the swirling grass-green tide? "Are ye . . . are ye a ghost?" he rasped. Then his stomach knotted as she closed her eyes, and he felt her muscles slacken. "Bess?" His arms tightened around her.

"Sleepy . . ."

He couldn't keep his eyes from the gentle rise and fall of her full breasts . . . perfectly shaped nipples barely hidden by the wet, straining cloth . . .

or the soft contours of her creamy throat that fairly
begged a man to nibble and taste.

"Ye can't sleep now," he said urgently, re-
minding himself of who he was and who she was.
He had kissed her—yes—and she had certainly
kissed him back, but they'd both been caught up
in the emotion of finding the other alive. He'd
done much to be ashamed of in his life, but he'd
never taken advantage of a half-drowned woman.
He had nothing but contempt for a man who was
ruled by his cock instead of his mind.

She drew in a long, shuddering breath. "Kincaid." With a slight, contented whimper, she
tucked her head into the hollow of his shoulder.

Tremors of pleasure shook him, and he
clenched his teeth together, fighting for control.
He'd had whores aplenty, a wife, and several
mistresses, but no woman had ever said his name
that way before. His mouth went dry, and he felt
as though his knees were turning to water. He
raised his head and looked out to sea, trying to
ignore the growing tightness in his groin and the
heat of her sweet, round bottom permeating his
callused palm.

Sweat beaded on his forehead as his cock
swelled against his damp breeches until the
throbbing ache became real discomfort. Rot his
greedy bowels! He wanted her—here, now. He
wanted to strip away the remains of her bodice
and take one of those rosy nipples in his mouth
and suck it until it became a hard red bud. He
wanted to splay his fingers over her flat belly and
bury them in the soft curls below. He wanted to
part her silken thighs and taste her sweet, wild
honey. He wanted to flick his tongue over her

velvet folds until she was wet and eager for his hard, thrusting rod.

Hot excitement fired his imagination and set his blood to boiling. Damn, but he wanted her. He'd never felt so driven to possess a woman. To make her his . . . utterly and completely . . . not just for a single act of passion, but for all time.

And all he'd done was lift her out of the water and kiss her . . .

Bess snuggled against Kincaid, and her fingers intertwined at the back of his neck. She was tired . . . so tired, all she wanted to do was sleep. But after the terror of the shipwreck and the battle to keep her head above water, she was unwilling to relinquish the first security she'd found in a long time.

Had he kissed her, or had that been a dream? Had she kissed him?

Unconsciously, she licked her lips again. She tasted the bite of salt . . . and something else—some essence that instinct told her must be Kincaid.

She stirred languidly, trying to get closer to him. She could feel the sun's heat on her bare skin and the faint stirring of an ocean breeze through her hair, but it was Kincaid's naked chest pressed against her face that proved to her that she was alive.

He had kissed her. She knew it. A warm glow of happiness bubbled up within her. They both had survived the storm and the sea, and now they hung suspended in an enchanted crystal of white beach and blue sky. A mystical island untouched by human laws and past mistakes. A twinkling of suspended time where there was no yesterday and no tomorrow—only this precious moment.

She was safe in his arms. She was alive. Nothing else mattered. . . .

Somewhere in the corners of her mind, Bess remembered struggling in the water, remembered her knees striking the ocean bottom and crawling toward the beach. Exhausted, without even the strength to go another twenty feet, she had lain in the shallows as night gave way to the first violet rays of morning.

Once, she'd thought she heard someone calling her name, but she didn't know if it was Kincaid or Kutii. She couldn't tell if she was hearing a real man's voice or a voice in her head. So she had lain there, letting the gentle waves wash over her and feeling the grains of sand under her fingertips.

Had Kincaid kissed her? Or was she dead and all this a dream? There was only one way to find out. She lifted her head and looked up at him. "Kincaid?"

"Aye, lass, 'tis me," he answered. She could feel the rumble of his deep voice begin in his chest as he spoke.

"I thought so." He had nice eyes for a pirate, she thought, not dark brown, but cinnamon, penetrating and intelligent. So startling with his yellow hair . . . She released her locked hands and traced the hard line of his jaw. The skin on her fingertips was exquisitely sensitive, and she smiled as a stubble of golden whiskers tickled her.

"Woman," he groaned. "Ye dinna ken what you're about." He let go of her and she slid down into the warm sand, then rose to face him on her knees. "You'll start what ye'd nay care to finish."

She was unwilling to break free from the enchantment. All around her, she could feel the soft green light, pulsating, whirling. She lifted both hands and cupped his face between them. "You kissed me," she said.

"Aye." His features might have been carved of weathered cedar; his mouth was hard and still, his eyes unblinking.

"I want you to kiss me again."

"Do ye, now?" Challenge flamed in his rust-brown gaze. Slowly, deliberately, he lifted his right hand to his mouth and licked the pad of his thumb, then gently brushed her lower lip with it.

A smile turned up the corners of her mouth as a curious tingling spread outward from the spot he had rubbed. Her teeth closed over his thumb and she bit down on his flesh, not hard enough to hurt him, but hard enough to make him groan with pleasure.

"Ye want to play that way, do ye?" he asked. His fingers tangled in the back of her hair and he tilted her face up to meet his kiss.

Kincaid's mouth closed over hers hungrily, and it seemed the most natural thing in the world for her to part her lips and touch tongue to tongue. Her world tilted as shudders of intense longing swept over her.

He was strong—so strong. His chest and shoulders were an iron fortress sheltering her from harm. His arms, his hands, his mouth were music to her soul. She wanted the kiss to go on and on. She wanted him to keep touching her the way he was, and when his big hand cupped her breast, the flame of her desire leaped from her breast to the moist heat between her thighs.

"Ah, hinney," he said, trailing kisses away from her mouth to her ear. "Ye be the most loving woman I've ever known." He pushed her back onto the warm sand and stretched over her.

I should be afraid of him, she thought in a brief heartbeat of rationality. But she wasn't afraid. He could never hurt her; she knew that as she knew the earth beneath her was solid. How could he hurt her when he was part of her . . . when it was so right that they be together like this?

As we have been before . . .

The statement rose unbidden from the secret places of her memory, and she did not question it. Instinct told her that such truth was absolute. She smiled as familiar shadows of what once had been glided across the stage of her conscious thought.

I know the touch of his hands, she admitted to herself. I know the feel of his mouth against mine . . . I cannot remember where or when or what faces we wore then, but I know this man as I know my own hands, or breasts, or eyes. He is part of me and he always will be.

Kincaid kissed her again, and his hot fingertips caressed the hollow of her throat and the rise of her breasts. He leaned closer, kissing her where his touch had blazed a trail. She let her eyes drift shut and concentrated on the fluttering sensations that threatened to overwhelm her.

One of his hands was on her bare leg. She could feel the roughness of his scarred palm sliding higher and higher up her trembling thigh. Then his lips grazed her breast and his long fingers began to tease the damp curls above her woman's folds and she arched against him and moaned with delight.

"Sweeting," he murmured hoarsely. His wet tongue skimmed her bare nipple and she shivered. She tightened her arms around him and pulled him closer. He encircled her swollen areola gently, suckling her nipple into his mouth.

Bess's eyes flew open. "Oh," she said.

He laughed, raised his head, and met her startled gaze. "Do ye like that?" he asked.

"Yes, oh, yes." She felt giddy, almost intoxicated by the rush of sensations that tumbled one over another through her head and body. Even her toes tingled with excitement.

A lock of his wheat-gold hair fell over his forehead, and she touched it, savoring the silken texture as it slid through her fingers. She lifted a few strands to her lips and nibbled at them. They tasted of salt.

"Are ye so hungry that ye need to eat my hair?" he teased.

She licked her top lip. "I think I'd like you to kiss me again," she said softly.

"Here?" he asked, kissing her nose. "Or here?" He planted a quick peck on her left eyebrow. "Or maybe here?" He kissed the right one and then moved to capture her breast again. "Or did ye like this best?" He laved her nipple with his hot tongue until she squirmed with pleasure.

To her surprise, she found herself lifting her other breast free of her garments for his attention. "This one too," she murmured boldly. Kincaid chuckled and closed his teeth over that nipple, tugging with tantalizing playfulness until she dug her nails into his bare back and moaned deep in her throat.

But the wonderful feelings weren't coming just from her breasts. His long fingers had found the source of her femininity. Gently, he probed the soft, wet folds, rubbing and caressing until her sensual exultation took on an urgency beyond anything she had ever experienced.

A sheen of perspiration broke out on her skin, and her breath came in jagged gasps. Kincaid was kissing her again; his hard tongue filled her mouth as his scent filled her brain. She could hear the pounding of her blood through her veins and the hammer of her heart.

He leaned close to her ear. "Will ye?" he asked.

She tried to answer him, but her voice caught in her throat. He pulled away from her and she reached out to him, unwilling to part from him . . . unwilling to stop this marvelous blending.

"I've never taken a woman against her will," he said, standing up and stripping away his skin-tight breeches. " 'Tis for ye to say if ye will, or if ye will not."

Bess stared at his arousal in wonder. He had seemed huge when she'd seen him in the barn. Now . . . She swallowed the lump in her throat.

"Bess . . ." He took a step toward her. " 'Tis your last chance to turn me away. I know ye are no virgin, but still—"

In that instant, Bess heard a voice in her head. "Go to him. He is the one. He is your mate, the man of strength your grandmother said would come." And suddenly, her trance was shattered. She looked first at Kincaid, standing naked and proud, his tumescent male member throbbing and thrust out before him, and then at her own disheveled clothing.

What have I done? she cried inwardly. "No!" She rolled away and closed her eyes. "I'm sorry, but I can't." Tears welled up and she dashed them away. "This is wrong," she said.

Kincaid swore a foul oath.

Bess opened her eyes and got to her feet. She was trembling so hard that her teeth were chattering. "I'm sorry," she said. "The fault is mine. I never should have—"

He turned away from her without another word, waded into the sea until the green water washed over his hard, naked buttocks, then dove under the waves and swam out beyond the breakers.

Bess felt as though she was going to be sick. A vise gripped her head, the pain so intense that it was almost blinding. "What have I done?" she repeated. She sank to the sand and covered her face with her hands.

She had gone to him as willingly as any mare in heat. She had let him touch her in places so intimate that she'd never touched them herself. She'd offered her breasts to be kissed and sucked, and she had fair climbed down his throat. Why? Why? What had come over her?

She glanced out at the ocean and saw his yellow head bobbing in the waves. What must he think of her? She had escaped near drowning and come up out of the sea as lustful as . . . She searched her brain for any comparison. "A Babylon whore," she muttered.

Angrily, she pounded the sand with her fist. She had asked to be swived. The only reason she wasn't lying under him now was that he had more sense of honor than she had morals.

It was the same as the first time.

"No!" Bess leaped to her feet and began running down the beach. No, it wasn't the same. The first time with Richard had been rape—she hadn't asked for it. She had willingly gone with a trusted friend. She had kissed him and taken pleasure in his embrace. She'd never given her consent to be used sexually.

Bess's head was thrown back, her disheveled hair flying behind her. Her bare feet pounded against the sand. She sucked in lungfuls of cool, clean ocean air until her chest ached, but she kept running faster and faster. Salt tears blinded her, but still she ran, wondering if she had finally, irrevocably, lost her mind.

At last, her legs cramped and the stitch in her side became too much to ignore, and she slowed to a lurching trot, then sank to her knees at the edge of the water. She was far down the beach from where she'd left Kincaid, out of reach of his accusations. Here, the only sounds were those of sea and wind and birds.

And a ghost . . .

As she watched, the Indian's bronzed figure flickered in the sunlight, his specter image fading in and out before becoming solid. First his face appeared, eyes as black as onyx and hair the blue-black gleam of a crow's wing. Despite the heat, she shivered. No matter how many times she saw him materialize from thin air, it made gooseflesh rise on the back of her neck.

Kutii's nose jutted from an angular face; his eyes slanted beneath raven brows and a high forehead. His cheekbones were granite ridges above cheeks tattooed in barbaric splendor.

He was not a big man, but his chest was deep above a slender, almost girlish waist and sleek, sinewy thighs. His arms were steel cords covered with amber satin. For all the waist-length mane of shining hair, the rest of his scarred body was hairless.

Today he was garbed in pagan grandeur. Bess sniffed. As a child, she had not realized that Kutii was as vain as any London jack-o'-dandy and that he had a flair for the dramatic, taking care to adorn himself according to the occasion.

Woven sandals decorated with precious stones covered his feet, and around his waist was wrapped what could only be called a short skirt of multicolored feathers, secured with a golden pin. A mantle of blue and green and red plumes hung around his shoulders, falling to his waist. A torque of gold, inlaid with a design of silver llamas, graced his powerful neck, and below that, most of his chest was covered with a breastplate of silver-and-gold disks that flashed in the sun like mirrors.

Miniature golden jaguars dangled from his ears, and around each upper arm, Kutii wore a silver band set with deep green emeralds. In one hand he carried a silver jaguar-headed battle-ax on a haft of beaten gold, his staff of office, and on his other wrist perched a green-and-yellow parrot.

"I'm not in the mood for this now," she shouted at him. When he took the trouble to deck himself out like a prize turkey, she knew that he was about to try to talk her into something she didn't want to do.

He waited, not speaking, a half smile playing over his thin lips. Kutii had the patience of an Indian, she thought, wanting to smile back at him but still so upset that she refused to be comforted by the sight of her old friend.

"It won't work. Whatever you want, I'm not going to do it. You're not even there. You're a product of my overactive imagination. I'm as mad as Parson Ebright's daughter, and . . ."

A wave broke around her knees, and she leaned down and splashed water over her face. "I've nearly drowned," she said, keeping her eyes clenched shut. "I'm marooned on an island with a Scottish brigand, and instead of running for my life, I nearly raped him. I've got enough trouble without ghosts. Go away!"

She took another breath and began to count to ten. When she opened her eyes, he would be gone. He wasn't really there. He couldn't be. He was something she'd dreamed up as a child, a will-o'-the-wisp that she'd created because of the wild tales her grandmother had told her.

On ten, she opened her eyes and looked back. The bit of sand where Kutii had stood was empty except for a clump of sea grass swaying in the wind.

Bess sighed with relief. It was true. All she had to do was will the Incan's image away and he'd be gone for good. Maybe she wasn't crazy after all. Maybe—

"Bess."

She scrambled to her feet and whirled around. He was standing behind her, not really in the water, but on what looked like air above the rolling foam.

"Damn it, Kutii."

He held out the hand with the parrot resting on it and motioned toward the beach. "Come out of the water, child of Star Woman. You are wet enough."

Dumbly, Bess followed him up the slight rise to the shade of a scrub pine and slumped down again.

"When did you begin to doubt yourself and your powers?" he asked sternly.

"You don't understand," she began. "I—"

"No, little one, it is you who do not understand. Why did you run from him? He is the one for whom I have waited. He is the man you must marry and the father of your children."

"I have no children," she flared, "and I'll have no husband. Fortune's Gift is mine, and I'll not share it with a . . . with a fortune hunter!"

"And what are you? Do you not seek the gold of my ancestors?"

"It's not the same thing," she protested. "It was you who told me to hunt for the treasure. You said it was mine."

"I did," he admitted, driving the butt of the heavy ax deep into the sandy soil and transferring the bird to the jaguar head of the weapon. The parrot squawked and bit his finger. Kutii popped his finger in his mouth and sucked at the bite.

Bess couldn't help wondering why he carried the dumb bird around when it always bit him.

Kutii laid a hand on her shoulder. It was as warm and alive as her own hands. She rubbed her eyes with her hands. "Why is everything so complicated?" she said. "No one else is haunted by ghosts. Why does it have to be me?"

Kutii laughed, a low rustle, like autumn leaves tumbling in the breeze. "You have the power. You see what others have forgotten to look for. You listen to words too low for the foolish to hear."

"I've done something terrible," she admitted. "You know I've never been a light-skirts, but I let Kincaid . . ." Her mouth was dry and her throat thick. She looked up at the Indian with bloodshot eyes. "Kutii, I—"

"Do not blame yourself. It was my doing."

"You?" She rose to her feet and glared at him. "You made me—"

He shook his head. "It was not so difficult to make you do what your heart wished."

"A spell? You put a spell on me?" she cried.

He shook his head again and made a sign against evil with the fingers of his right hand. "What talk is this?" he demanded. "After all your grandmother and I have taught you—to speak of spells like an ignorant Englishwoman. My belly is full of sorrow."

"Your head will be full of worse than sorrow if you ever do anything like that to me again. I acted like the worse sort of common tavern slut. I let him do things—"

"Things that a man and wife do without shame," he said.

"He is not my husband. Kincaid is a criminal—a common mercenary. I'd not have him for husband if he was—"

"He will be your husband."

"He will not!"

"He is the guardian. He has always been."

"No! Not this time, Kutii. This time I win. You

won't talk me into this. He's arrogant and crude and . . . and—"

"He saved your life when the boat sank."

"Yes," she admitted. "He did. I never said he wasn't brave, but—"

"You must marry, little Bess. You are the child of my heart, but I will not be swayed in this. You must have a child to continue my line. Blood to blood. So long as the family of Star Woman lives, my people live. If the chain is broken, the souls of those I love are as dead as the shards of a shattered clay bowl."

"I'll not be forced into marriage and a man's control. I love Fortune's Gift. I love the dirt and the grass and the trees. I love every inch of shoreline, and the way the house looks when the moon rises over the bay. I'll not hand it over to a stranger. It's mine, and, by God, I'll hold it fast!"

"And a child, little Bess. Will you have a child alone?"

"My father is young enough to have other children."

"You are the carrier of the flame. The line of Star Woman runs through you."

"I will not marry Kincaid. Not now. Not ever."

Kutii's lips thinned and his devil eyes narrowed to dark slits. "Do not say words you will live to regret."

"I'll not have him, I tell you," she repeated.

"Woman!"

Bess's eyes widened in surprise as she heard Kincaid's voice behind her. Shocked, she turned toward him. He stood feet apart, arms akimbo, brown eyes seething with ire. His face was a hard mask, his sensual mouth an angry slash.

"Are ye bewitched, that ye talk to trees?" he demanded sarcastically. "And whether ye be mad or not, no word of marriage has passed between us. Nor ever will."

"Kincaid." Hesitantly, she let her gaze fall to his midsection. To her great relief, he was once more wearing his water-stained breeches.

"Aye, 'tis me." His words cracked like a black-snake whip. "And who were ye expecting, my lady, Peter the Great?"

"I—I'm sorry," she stammered. "I was just . . . just . . ."

"Cantin' to yourself like a bedlamite," he snapped. "I'll have an explanation from ye, woman, and I'll have it now."

Chapter 12

I n desperation, Bess glanced back to Kutii for help. He was gone. I knew it, she cried inwardly. I knew you'd leave me to face him alone. For an instant, she closed her eyes and summoned up all her courage. She straightened her shoulders and lifted her chin, willing herself to appear composed as she gave her attention to the angry bondman once more.

"The fault was mine," she said, ignoring Kincaid's question about talking to herself. "What I did was inexcusable. I can only say in my own defense that nearly drowning must have made me temporarily out of my mind. I'm sorry, Kincaid. I know how you must feel, but—"

"Nay." He shook his head. "Ye dinna ken how I feel. There is a word for women who lead a man to the brink and then run." His expression of disgust made her twist with shame.

"I am no harlot," she said brokenly. "I've never done such a—"

" 'Tis plain ye are no virgin," he scoffed.

Bess felt as though she'd been dashed with icy water. "How did you know?" she asked.

He shrugged. "How could I not?" He eyed her suspiciously. Either the wench was the best actress he'd ever seen, or she really didn't know that he'd found proof of her previous experience with his own fingers. Bess's face flushed a deep crimson, and he thought she was about to burst into tears. Her obvious distress touched a protective chord within him. "We will say no more of it," he replied. "But if ye ever tempt me again . . .''

She stared into his eyes with all the vulnerability of an abandoned pup. "I am truly sorry," she said. "I don't know what came over me."

"I said we'd speak nay more of it," he answered gruffly. "My own control was less than I'd like." It was true. He hadn't been himself. Bess Bennett was not a woman for the likes of him, and if he'd been thinking clearly, he'd not have kissed her in the first place. She'd been half drowned, for the love of Christ! Perhaps he had taken advantage of her when she was too confused and frightened to ken gratitude from desire.

"You're right," she murmured. "I am no maid, but I swear to you that the losing of my virginity was not of my own choosing." A single tear rolled down her cheek. "I . . . I was raped by a man I trusted."

"There's no need for ye to spill your guts to me," he began.

"Yes, but there is a need," she said quickly. Another tear followed the first. "I was only sixteen and foolish. I let myself be put into a situation where he could take advantage of me." Her stubborn jaw firmed. "It won't happen again."

"Then ye have never made love to a man."

She shook her head. "What happened between you and me . . ." Her taut features drained of blood until her freckles stood out stark against her pale skin. "I would be lying to you if I said I didn't enjoy it."

He nodded. The proud British wench was speaking truth. She had nerve—he'd give her that. "Why, then, did ye run away? What use to lock the barn door after the—"

"I am a woman alone with the responsibility of a great plantation," she said, regaining some of her composure. "I refuse to trade my independence to become a husband's play toy. Marriage to a rich woman is a good arrangement for the bridegroom and a poor one for the bride. Once I sign a marriage contract, all that I have I place under my husband's control. He can sell off my land, dismiss my faithful servants, gamble away my money, beat me—even separate me from my children, should I produce any. At his whim, I may be locked in a madhouse, or sent across the ocean to rot."

"It is unnatural for a woman to remain unmarried."

"No. It would be unnatural for me to give up all that I have been educated for and taught to love, for the physical pleasures of the marriage bed."

"Then ye dinna deny that ye have the same wants as any normal woman?"

She nibbled at her lower lip.

"Do ye not?" he demanded.

"I have them," she said breathily.

Her low, husky tone cut through him like a knife, sending his stomach plummeting. "You were meant to be loved," he said, feeling his own growing tightness in his loins. "I've never held a woman with more joy in her."

Abruptly, her mood shifted, and he felt the softness draining away from her spirit.

"I shall never marry," she said. "Never. If my father wants more heirs, he can have them himself."

"If he lives, he can."

"He's alive. I know he is."

"Knowing and wishin' are two different things, lass."

"My father is alive," she said, "and he will be coming home."

"He may be, but we won't if we don't do something about finding fresh water and food." He looked toward the west, where dark thunderheads were building again. "And unless I miss my guess, we may be having more rain soon."

Bess nodded. "I'm so thirsty I could drink pickle juice." She glanced back toward the beach. "I don't suppose anything was salvaged from the sloop."

"Aye. I found the keg with your saddlebags."

She smiled. "And I still have this." She turned away from him and reached down inside her bodice to assure herself that the gold and coin were still inside her stays where she'd sewn them. "No wonder I had so much trouble swimming."

"This island's barren. I can tell by the stunted trees that we'll find no freshwater ponds here." He pointed. "But if we cross that narrow gut, there's another bit of land."

"An island or the mainland?"

He shrugged. "I dinna know, but the trees look

taller over there. We should be able to rig some shelter from the rain.''

Bess looked dubious. ''More swimming?''

''I can't say how deep the water is, but ye can use the wooden keg to keep yourself afloat.'' He allowed himself a hint of a smile. ''I'll nay let ye drown in such a quiet stretch of water.''

''I'll wager I can swim better than you can,'' she retorted. ''It was the gold that weighed me down.''

He chuckled. '' 'Tis no insult I meant ye. You survived a storm that drowned two men and a lad.''

Bess looked stricken. ''Are they all dead, do you suppose?''

''Likely, unless they made another beach. It's been my experience that few sailors know how to swim. They put their trust in boats and God. Sometimes, both fail a man.''

''My grandfather taught me to swim. H said it was something every girl needed to know. He used to throw me in the river fully dressed. Once, he did it in November. I always managed to save myself, but if I hadn't, I know he'd have pulled me out.''

''A wise man,'' Kincaid conceded. ''I taught myself when I was but a wee scrap of a lad. A cart I was riding in overturned at a crossing in the Hebrides. 'Twas sink or swim.''

She gave him a pensive look. ''I'd say you've always been a man with a talent for survival.''

''So far,'' he answered. ''I'll fetch the keg, and we'll see about getting safe to the other side.'' He left her standing there and walked away down the beach. Part of him was still angry with her for

promising something she wouldn't give, but to
give the devil his due, he'd asked her yea or nay
at a time when any man with a lick of sense in
his head would have pressed his suit. And if the
wench had spoken the truth—if she had been
raped when she was little more than a lassie—
then he could see why she'd be skittish.

He scanned the water's edge as he strode south,
looking for anything else that might have washed
up from the wreck. They were lucky to have the
keg with a pistol and powder and shot, not to
mention the flint and steel for making a fire. He
didn't want to think what the chances had been
that they'd recover the supplies. Bess Bennett was
one lucky woman, that was certain. And maybe,
just maybe, some of her luck would rub off on
him. It was past time he had some in his life.

They reached the western shore without incident, and after a few hours' search, Kincaid came
upon a low spot. An hour's digging produced
fresh water, a little sandy, but neither of them
was complaining.

By dusk, Bess had a fire going and she'd dug a
few dozen clams in the shallows to steam for dinner. It was too early in the year for beach plums
or berries to be ripe, so theirs was a one-course
meal. Kincaid had busied himself making a rough
hut with the sloop's sail for a covering. By the
time the first drops of rain hit the canvas, he and
Bess were snug inside, toasting themselves at the
fire and stuffing themselves with clams.

The hut was just big enough for the two of them
to stretch out and not high enough to stand in.
Bess was nervous in such close quarters; she took

care not to brush against him. It was almost
laughable in a way, considering what she'd let
him do to her that morning.

"Ye needn't be afraid," he said. "I'll not bite
ye."

"I'm not afraid of you," she answered.

"Nay? Ye give a good imitation of it."

She ducked her head and concentrated on passing a hot clam from hand to hand and blowing
on it. "No, I'm not. I just think it's better, under
the circumstances, if we don't get too familiar."

He laughed. "Is that what ye call it?"

"Don't think I'll roll over for you," she
snapped. "What happened was a mistake. It
won't happen again."

"It's a long journey to Panama. There'll be a lot
of nights like this, with just you and me and—"

"I said, it won't happen again. I'll never let a
man take advantage of me—"

"Is that what ye think I was doin'?" he asked
softly.

"No. I know better than that. Your behavior
was more honorable than mine."

"So ye admit that I'm not always a monster."
He reached for her hand. It was cold and trembling, but she didn't pull away from him. "Bess,
I'm nay your enemy," he said. "For better or
worse, we're in this together." He turned her
palm over and looked at it in the firelight. To his
surprise, her skin wasn't soft and white like that
of most gentlewomen, but hard and lined like a
man's. "You've spent many hours on horseback," he said. "And I'll wager you've done your
share of planting."

"And harvesting," she said. She lifted her gaze

to meet his. "I like the way you make me feel, but there can be nothing between us."

"Nothing permanent," he agreed. "I've been married once, and I don't care to try it again. A man doesn't always get the best of a bargain either."

"Where is your wife now?" she asked.

"In Hell, I hope."

"She's dead?"

"She'd better be. I buried her." He shook his head, trying to rid himself of Gillian's memory. "I'd nay speak of it. She betrayed me with my best friend, and I killed him for it."

"Did you kill her?"

"I wanted to." He toyed with Bess's hand, rubbing his thumb in lazy circles around the center of her palm. "Because a man and woman have no intention of marrying doesn't mean they canna give each other comfort," he suggested. Bess's dark auburn hair was spread out around her shoulders invitingly, and the firelight played off her face in a way that made his chest tight. The woman scent of her was strong in his nostrils. He'd not take her against her will; that went against his grain. But, as God was his witness, he still wanted her, and he would use all his wiles to turn her to his way of thinking.

The pressure of Kincaid's fingers on her palm made shivers run up and down her back. How easy it would be to respond to him, to forget everything but the nearness of this virile rogue. Bess had wanted him to make love to her—she still wanted it. But if she gave in, it would mean falling into Kutii's trap.

Deny it all he would, Bess was certain that Kutii

had done something to cloud her reason on the beach. For all she knew, the wily Indian had put Kincaid under an enchantment as well. Kutii wanted them matched, and he would stop at nothing to have his way. He was stubborn for a ghost, and when he set his mind on a goal, it was impossible to change him.

Almost impossible . . . She had defied him when she'd let Richard court her, and she had ignored his advice when she'd gone with her grandmother to tend the sick during an outbreak of smallpox. That was the last time she'd seen Kutii in full-dress regalia. He'd been so angry with her that he hadn't appeared again for six months.

She hoped he didn't intend to repeat that disappearing act, not when she needed him to show her where to go in Panama and where to dig for the treasure.

Kincaid leaned close and brushed her lips with his own. What was he saying?

". . . are ways to prevent a lass from conceiving a child. I'd protect ye, Bess. Trust me."

His lips were warm and sweet against hers. The food and the fire made her drowsy. She wanted to curl up in those powerful arms and let him go on kissing her.

Instead, she pulled back and shook her head. "No," she said. "Not now, not tonight, and maybe never. It's not an act I'd make lightly. I'm tired, and I want to sleep, and if you're the man I hope you are, you'll let me."

"You're a hard woman, Bess Bennett," he said with genuine regret. "Whatever memories that blackguard left ye with . . . I could wipe them away with better ones."

She folded her arms over her chest and hugged herself. "Perhaps," she murmured, "perhaps someday I'll let you try. But it will be on my terms, not on yours, and . . ." She stared into the darkness meaningfully. "And not on anyone else's."

"As ye wish, woman." He leaned down and threw another piece of driftwood on the fire. The sparks flared up in an array of blue and orange and green. "But I warn ye that you'll live to regret it."

I regret it now, she mused as she lay down and curled up on her side and listened to the raindrops thudding against the canvas roof. And I fear I'll regret it more when I'm very old and very respectable. The thought made her smile. Every woman should have a scoundrel like Kincaid to remember in her dotage, she decided. And with that in mind, she drifted off to sleep as soundly as if she were in her own feather tick at home.

The smell of broiling rabbit woke her. The sun was already up when she opened her eyes. Every bone in her body ached, but she was starving. She stretched and got up, brushing the sand off her clothes and skin and shaking it out of her hair.

Kincaid had extinguished the fire at the front of their shelter and built a new one a few yards away. He was crouched beside a spit of green branches, turning a fat, well-browned rabbit. He glanced up at her. "About time ye rose, my lady. There are duck eggs and rabbit for breakfast, unless you'd rather have fish. I caught one of those too."

''Cook it,'' she said. ''The way you eat, I'll be lucky if I get two bites.''

''Snappy in the morning, aren't you?''

His hair was wet and slicked back, tied into a club at the back of his neck. His breeches were dry, so Bess knew he'd been swimming naked.

''Did you catch the fish with your teeth?'' she asked.

''Aye, and the rabbit as well,'' he answered solemnly.

She didn't miss the mischievous twinkle in his eyes. ''If you'll give me time to—''

''Use those bushes over there,'' he said. ''If ye wish to bathe—''

''I had enough swimming yesterday, thank you.''

''Well, you'll soon have more. This is an island too. The mainland is west of here. I think I can rig up the sail and a few branches to get our stuff to shore. Then we'll walk south until we come to a farm. If ye still mean to go to Panama, that is.''

''I do, and I will,'' she replied.

''It's a long piece, lass. What we've been through is just a promise of what's ahead. There are pirates and Indians who would as soon cut off your head as look at ye. And the Spanish—''

''Lost your nerve, Kincaid?''

''Nay. Just wonderin' about yours.''

She turned away, toward the privacy of the bushes. She'd gotten up glad to be alive, and she'd be damned if she'd let him ruin her morning.

The horror of the shipwreck and the crew's drowning had left her shaken and subdued, but today in the bright sunshine she was ready to turn ahead to the future. Fortune's Gift and all her people waited, and if she was successful in finding her grandfather's buried treasure, she could still snatch victory from defeat.

Kincaid would be an ongoing problem. She could see that now. He'd not be as easy to manage as she'd thought when she first broached the idea to him at the plantation.

On the positive side, she was now certain that her instincts were right. Under that rough exterior beat the heart of, if not a gentleman, an honorable savage. He had saved her life on the boat at the risk of his own, and he'd not taken advantage of her last night when she was at his mercy.

To the negative was the bold fact that they were both young and healthy, with all the normal appetites a man and a woman might have for each other. If Kincaid were not who he was—a criminal with a life of brutal killing and thievery behind him—and if she hadn't pledged her life to remaining single and independent, then they might have formed a partnership that would extend into marriage. But they were too different.

She was the daughter of a gentleman and the granddaughter of nobility. She had devoted all her life to the responsibilities of her station. She loved the soil and watching things grow. She had been taught to put the needs and wants of her land and dependents ahead of her own.

Kincaid was a marauder, a man who made his living by the sword both honestly and dishonestly. He was without morals—with the exception of sexual matters—and he was bound to end his life at the end of a rope.

What if his shoulders were as brawny as a

blacksmith's and his arms were coiled bands of sinew under skin as bronzed and weathered as an Indian's? What if his buttocks were taut and comely and his belly was flat and hard? What if he did have eyes of cinnamon brown that seemed to stare into the depths of her soul when he looked at her? And what if he had hands that created marvelous sensations when he touched her?

Bess finished her private needs and went to the water's edge to wash her hands and face. Her tangled hair fell forward and she pushed it impatiently away from her face. Kincaid was attractive—there was no doubt about it—but that kind of thinking would get her in deep water fast. What she had to hold foremost in her mind was that Kincaid was an arrogant bastard who must be kept in his place. She'd have to keep her wits about her and him at arm's length if she was to stay out of serious trouble.

She arranged her torn clothes with as much propriety as possible and tried to comb the knots out of her hair with her fingers. Whole sections were hopelessly snarled, and it was all sticky from the salt water. She gave up after a few moments, tore a strip off her tattered shift, and tied her hair at the back of her neck.

"Are ye comin' to breakfast or not?" Kincaid called.

"Coming," she answered. She rejoined him in a dignified manner and accepted the pieces of rabbit he'd heaped on a clam shell.

"The duck eggs aren't bad if ye sprinkle a little salt water on them," he said. "We'll move on as soon as we've eaten. No tellin' how far we'll have to walk to find civilization. And this can be bad country. Lots of folks make their living by robbing travelers.''

The harried look he'd worn yesterday was gone. Bess could tell that the night's rest had done him as much good as it had her.

"You should know all about that,'' she said.

"Aye.'' He grinned. "I ken a wee bit about gentlemen of the road.''

"At home it would be considered stupid to set a fox to guard the henhouse,'' she parried.

"Only if ye consider yourself a hen.''

She threw a rabbit bone at him and he laughed. She was tempted to throw the clam shell as well, but she was still hungry, and the fish smelled good. It was best to save her energy for a real fight, she decided as she reached for a second piece of rabbit. As Kincaid had said, it would be a long journey to the jungles of Panama.

They reached the mainland without incident and picked up a wagon rut running south between marsh and woodland. They camped beside a pond that night and Bess was able to bathe and change into clean clothes from her saddlebags. Her hair still refused to cooperate even after being washed, so in a fit of temper, she took her grandfather's knife and cut six inches off the length, so that the remainder fell just below her shoulders.

"Aye, makes the most sense of anything you've done,'' Kincaid said when he saw the result. "The farther south we go, the hotter it will get.''

And when he shaved, he began to hack off sections of his own yellow hair.

"Don't," Bess said. "You'll make a mess of it. Let me."

He shrugged and handed over the knife. "Just leave the ears," he warned. "I've gotten fond of them."

Carefully, she used the razor-sharp skean to cut around Kincaid's ears and then lower around the back, so that his hair came just above the line of his shoulders. Freed of the weight, the wheat-gold locks curled slightly around his tanned face, making Bess's heartbeat quicken.

"Well?" he asked.

"Just a little more off this side," she said. Touching him made her feel giddy. She didn't sense any of the colors associated with her witchy powers, but her face and throat grew warm and she had to force her hands to hold steady.

He reached up and closed his hand over her wrist. "Best leave well enough alone," he said huskily, "afore ye put out an eye."

She nodded, waiting for him to release her hand, feeling the heat of his hard fingers against her skin. "Let me go," she said, more frightened of herself than of him.

He smiled, a lazy grin that reached to his eyes. "Aye, lass, I will that," he said. "I'm beholden to ye for the hair trim, and I'd not take more than I'm offered."

She pulled free and put the fire between them.

"No need to shy," he said in that same deep tone. "I'll nay steal a kiss unless ye ask for it. Ye have my word."

"And what is that worth?" she asked softly.

"As much as ye wish it to be."

And then Bess heard the rumble of wagon

wheels on the trail, and Kincaid tensed and went for the remaining pistol and tucked it into his waist. "Sit yonder," he ordered, indicating a spot in the shadows. "And keep your mouth shut. No matter what I say or do, you go along with it. Do ye ken, woman?"

She started to protest, but the look he threw her was enough to make her nod agreement. It was clear, she thought as she took her seat on a fallen log and stared down the road, that their truce was over.

Chapter 13

Kingston, Jamaica
June 1725

Peregrine Kay ignored the rising wind outside and concentrated on the charcoal sketch, attempting once more to capture the elusive expression of the red-haired woman in the portrait that dominated one wall of the parlor. A pile of crumpled papers littered the floor beside the table.

Peregrine's wig was slightly askew and his forehead bore a light sheen of perspiration. Annemie knew when she entered the room and saw his taut mouth and rumpled clothing that her master was in danger of another bout of falling sickness.

"Sir?" She kept her voice soft and serene. "Sir," she repeated. "Your supper."

He didn't look up, but she noted a smear of charcoal on his upper lip. His hand over the drawing paper was unsteady.

Annemie set her tray down gently on the table and went to close the tall louvered shutters. "The light is gone," she said. "The hurricane will miss us, I think, but the wind will be very bad and we will have heavy rain."

The sound of her voice seemed to calm him, and his features lost some of their tormented look. Annemie knew that she had been blessed with a gift for calming the afflicted. Her speech was pure liquid, bubbling and throaty, as free of her father's Dutch accent as she could make it. Other than her fair, freckled skin and light brown, straight hair, it was her best feature.

Annemie had never been a beautiful woman, not even in the full bloom of her youth. She was too tall and sturdy, her mouth too wide, her forehead too high, and her nose too long. And now, at two score and one, tiny lines were beginning to appear at the corners of her eyes and mouth. But she had always prided herself on her intelligence and her loyalty to her employer. . . .

She smiled, knowing that her teeth were still white and even, a reward for avoiding sugarcane and other sweet confections for her entire life. "Sir, you must eat something. You've been at this since midmorning, and Sisi tells me you refused to eat anything at noon."

"I have a headache," he said. "You know I never eat when I have a headache."

"Ah." Genuine sympathy for Peregrine Kay rose in her breast. "You work too hard," she murmured. "All the more reason to take nourishment." She stopped just short of laying a hand on his shoulder.

He glanced up at her, and she felt a rush of the old familiar longing.

Peregrine was no longer young either. He'd had a full head of dark hair when she'd come to work for him years ago. His long English face had not been so weathered by the hot island sun, and his

198 JUDITH E. FRENCH

waistline had definitely been less . . . round, she thought delicately.

But if his middle years sat heavy on his broad shoulders, Peregrine was still a striking man. His eyes missed nothing, and his intellect was barely short of genius.

He was far too hard on himself, she mused, looking over his shoulder at the unfinished sketches scattered across the teakwood table. If he had not been born a rich gentleman and the only son of a royal governor, he could have made his living as an itinerant artist, painting the portraits of the wealthy.

As it was, her master's art was only a hobby, or . . . She wrinkled her nose slightly. Or an obsession. Because he limited his talent to one subject—a woman long dead whom his father had painted from memory many years ago.

Annemie had never liked the painting. It was the likeness of a flame-haired woman standing on a cliff, looking out over the sea. She was obviously not a lady of quality or style, despite her puffed-sleeved, blue silk gown. The haunting expression on her strong-willed face made Annemie feel as though someone had walked over her grave. A witch. A witch whose enchantment had not only flawed a great man's life, but had leaped into the next generation to shadow his son's.

The old master, Governor Kay, was already dead when Annemie had come into Peregrine's household, but the other servants whispered tales of his madness. He had died raving, and they said he still walked the island on moonlit nights, calling, "La-cee."

"Sir, you must have a little of the conch soup,"

she coaxed. "I had Sisi prepare it especially for you."

"I can't get it right," Peregrine said. "I've tried and I've tried, but I can't get the . . . the . . ."

"Tomorrow, sir. Tomorrow it will come." She gathered up the discarded attempts and whisked away his charcoal.

He covered his face with his hands and leaned forward on the table. "She destroyed my father, you know. Deceived him with a common pirate and stole a treasure from him."

"Long ago, sir," Annemie murmured. "A long time ago." With graceful precision, she lifted the covered porcelain bowl and set it down on the gold-washed plate. She held a silver soup spoon up to the light and inspected it critically, then placed it to the right of the plate. "I've a special treat for you, sir," she said. "A lime sherbet. I made it myself, just minutes ago."

She sighed, wondering at the cost of the small dish. Ice was a precious commodity in Jamaica, and even Peregrine with his fleets of ships and vast network of connections along the North American coast couldn't always satisfy his taste for the shaved ice confections he loved.

"It drove him mad in his last years," he continued. "After a brilliant career. My father was one of the finest governors Jamaica ever saw. But he never really recovered from the blow she dealt him."

Annemie removed the blue-and-white cover from the soup bowl. "Lots of pepper," she said. "Hot enough to make your eyes water."

"Father never did find them, you know, but he said I must consider it a duty to locate the family and take our revenge. She wasn't punished, you see. She was his betrothed and she broke his heart.''

"The soup, sir.''

Obediently, Peregrine lifted the spoon to his mouth and sipped.

He wasn't normally like this. Weeks could go by, sometimes even months, without this obsession surfacing. And when it did, he usually sank into depression and, after that, suffered an attack of his illness.

The rest of the time Peregrine was tireless in directing his many shipping operations. He was invaluable to the English Crown in his dealings with the Portuguese and even the Spanish. It was said that his information network in the New World was better than that of the French. Peregrine Kay was a powerful figure of almost legendary wealth; he owned vast lands in the islands as well as merchant vessels and investment houses. Using the name Falconer to protect his own name, he was active in the slave trade, and in other business concerns that some would consider outside the law.

Annemie didn't care. She wouldn't have cared if he were a penniless fisherman. She loved him with a deep, abiding passion, an unrequited affection that could never be resolved because of her black Yoruba grandmother, brought from Africa in chains. Annemie was the daughter of a white Dutch merchant and his mulatto slave mistress. Although Annemie had been freed at birth and educated beyond her class, she was still and forever marked as a woman of color.

"I have her now," Peregrine said, pausing in

the middle of his frugal meal. "I've located the family, and I've set certain events into motion. Father will be revenged."

"Of course," she said gently.

"He didn't think I could do it." He shook his head and tugged at his lace stock. "Father was always disappointed in me. I wasn't born afflicted, you know. It was a fall from a horse when I was eight. I was unconscious for days. After that, the spells came. Not often, but often enough. Father should have had other sons."

Annemie made a soothing sound. Governor Kay's wife had been like many Englishwomen, according to Sisi. The lady had never adjusted to the hot island sun after her cold, rainy homeland. She'd sickened and become a semi-invalid, not dying until the governor himself was old and ill, but never strong enough to bear more than one living child. Governor Kay had nearly given up hope of an heir when Peregrine was born. And when that son suffered an accident and showed a weakness, the governor had never forgiven him for it.

"I could have destroyed them with one fell swoop," Peregrine continued, rambling. "It was in my power." He pursed his lips. "But that would have been too easy. No, I wanted to destroy them as they destroyed my father . . . slowly . . . painfully."

Annemie removed the soup dish and substituted a plate of fried plantains and suitable silverware. Peregrine had a fondness for plantains.

He toyed with his fork. "My people captured the ship carrying their tobacco crop. First-quality leaf. It brought top price in Bermuda."

She had heard all this before. Talk of pirates and revenge always made her uneasy. She poured a tankard of ale for her master. "Eat your plantains, sir, do."

"I sent men to burn the house and barns as well," he said, becoming more agitated. The sterling fork fell from his fingers, unheeded. "But that's not enough. I'll have her here to face me. I'll have her in that chair. Do you see, Annemie? In that chair. And then we'll see what alibi she gives . . . what excuse for her treachery."

His left hand began to tremble, and Annemie knew what was coming next. Deftly, she cleared away the dishes and hovered behind his chair. And when the seizure came over him, she took his shoulders and lowered him to the floor as gently as possible.

Peregrine's shoes thudded against the wide-planked floor, his body convulsed, and spittle spewed from his pale lips. Annemie pushed a fold of her skirt between his teeth and cradled his head in her lap. The violence of Peregrine's attacks never repulsed or frightened her as it did the rest of the staff.

She removed his wig and stroked his thinning hair, murmuring softly to him. "I'm here, Peregrine. I'm here, and you're safe."

He wouldn't remember the spell when it was over. He never did—a blessing, really. Such weakness was hard for a man of dignity to live with. But she would remember and savor the feel of his body next to hers when he was only her master again.

She held him tightly against her as the force of the seizure began to abate. "Sleep, my Pere-

grine," she said, "Sleep. Annemie's here. Annemie's here and she'll take care of you." And as
he lost consciousness, she leaned down and
kissed the crown of his head. "My poor dear,"
she whispered, "my poor, poor love."

Hundreds of miles to the north, Bess and Kincaid walked through a market-day fair a half day's
journey from the thriving port of Charles Town.
At a crossroads near a tavern, local inhabitants
had gathered to trade and sell livestock, poultry,
indentures, vegetables, household goods, and
farm products. Bess could see three women offering baked goods, cheese, butter, and eggs from
the backs of farm wagons. Families were coming
on horseback, by cart and wagons, and on foot,
all eager for a day of fun and gossip after long
weeks of labor on their isolated farms.

Children of all sizes and colors ran and
screamed and dodged amidst the tents, and wagons, and tables. They ran in and out of the knots
of adults, raced ponies around the encampment,
and splashed in the muddy stream at the edge of
the fairgrounds. Dogs barked and fought with one
another. Cows bellowed, pigs squealed, and babies cried. Stray chickens strutted around scratching for bugs and snatching fallen crumbs.

Bess could smell the delicious scent of fresh
gingerbread among the mingled odors of manure,
animals, tobacco, rum, and unwashed human
bodies. From every corner of the assembly came
good-natured bickering, shouts of welcome, and
hearty laughter.

"Keep close beside me," Kincaid instructed

her, "and try not to talk. Your gentlewoman's speech would stand out here like a pig in a kirk."

The first wagon that had come along the track where they'd been camped two days ago belonged to a farmer named Will Gist. He was carrying raw whiskey for sale at the gathering, and he'd cheerfully offered them a ride this far. Gist had told them that his wife was ailing, his hogs had run off, and his cow had gone dry, but the profit from his still would see him through another winter.

"I've got three boys," Gist had explained. "Two are still two young to plow, and the little'n is still on his mammy's tit. But when they get big enough to work alongside me, we'll clear enough land to make a decent farm. Until then, what Injun corn we don't need for meal has to go into whiskey."

Once again, Kincaid had insisted that he and Bess play the role of a wandering mercenary soldier and his companion. He'd also told her that he was concerned about buying passage to the islands with the coin they had left.

"But what about the jaguar?" she asked quietly. They were standing apart from the crowd, watching Will Gist inspect a shaggy black gelding that a horse dealer was putting through his paces. It was clear to Bess by his obvious fright that the black was only half broken. He squealed and kicked at the dealer when the man stepped too close to the animal's hindquarters, bared his teeth at another horse, and reared back against the lead rope.

"What would a common soldier be doin' with a gold statue like that?" Kincaid chided her. "If I

go into Charles Town proper and go down to the
dock, it's possible I can find someone who will
give me the name of a man who will buy such
fancy goods, no questions asked. But if the authorities catch wind of it, ye can be certain that
the gold will go to a bigwig and we'll go into the
stocks.''

Bess's eyes narrowed. ''But that's not fair. The
gold is mine. I've only to explain who I am and—''

''Aye. And you've as much chance of being believed as of flyin'. Ye could stand in the stocks a
long time before word gets back here from Maryland. And what if it's the sheriff who comes to
fetch ye?''

''So what do we do?'' she whispered. Will Gist
had taken the lead line from the horse dealer and
was putting the black gelding through his paces
by himself. The animal was still skittish, tossing
his head and shying at every movement in the
crowd.

''I take some of our coin and look for a card
game,'' Kincaid said.

''Bet our last money? Like hell!'' she hissed at
him.

He scowled at her. ''Will ye be quiet, woman?
Why not get up on Gist's wagon and tell the
whole fair you're carryin' gold in your stays?''

''Well, I'm not about to let you lose what
money we have left by gambling,'' she insisted.

''This is serious, Bess,'' he said. ''When I play
for serious, I don't lose.''

Her eyes widened. ''You mean you cheat at
cards?'' she asked scornfully.

''Will ye hold that infernal tongue of yours?''

He yanked her around, so that they appeared to be embracing, and whispered in her ear. "Do ye want me to be tarred and feathered before they string me up to the nearest tree?"

Bess grinned and put her arms around his neck, giving the illusion of enjoying his rough play. Then she pinched him hard.

"Ouch." His exclamation of pain came from between clenched teeth. Bess's chuckle was cut off short as he delivered a sharp smack to her bottom with the flat of his hand. "Two can play that game, lass," he said.

She glared up at him. "A card cheat is lower than a snake," she said. "No gentleman would ever cheat at—"

"I told ye, I'm no gentleman," he reminded her, then lowered his head and kissed her soundly.

She pulled away, cheeks burning, to see a stout woman laughing at her.

"Trouble with yer husband, dearie?" the matron called.

"Not my wife and not likely to be," Kincaid answered, "and I thank God for that every sunrise." A round of laughter came from those within earshot.

Despite her embarrassment, Bess couldn't help staring at him. His Scots burr had nearly disappeared beneath a Carolina lowland drawl. He caught her glance and winked mischievously.

I'll get you for this, she mouthed silently.

A cockfight was beginning in a ring a few wagons over. A tall, rawboned farmer was holding a red-and-white rooster above his head to display the bird's wicked spurs. "All comers!" he yelled. "Two-to-one odds!"

Kincaid turned toward the action, and Bess shook her head. She wanted no part of the barbaric sport. "Stay close, then," he advised.

Will Gist was leading the black gelding away from the dealer, who was already proclaiming the merits of a stocky gray mule. "I traded fer him," Gist said to Bess. "He's green, but he's got grit. What do ye think?"

Bess turned her attention to the small horse. He had a powerful chest and an undersized head. His mane and tail were tangled with burrs, and his rump bore a freshly healed gash. The animal was pure black except for the dried mud on his fetlocks and a white ring around his left eye. "What's his name?" she asked.

"Dandy." The gelding flared his nostrils at Bess and rolled his eyes until the whites showed. "Stay clear," Gist warned. "He's a handful. Just three years old, and needs a lot of gentling." Will Gist's accent was so thick that Bess could hardly understand him.

"Whoa, Dandy," she said, approaching the animal from the left. "Easy, boy." She offered the back of her hand for the young horse to sniff. The animal pricked up his ears and stared suspiciously at her. "Good Dandy," she crooned. "Good boy."

She touched the velvety black nose, then ran her hand up his head and scratched behind his ears. Dandy huffed and grumbled, but he stood still and let her fondle him. "Yes, you're a good boy," she murmured. The warmth of the horse felt comforting to Bess and she concentrated on the swirling sensations that formed in her mind. Red for power and vitality, orange for strength. She ran her hand down the animal's front legs and up across his back.

"What do you think?" Gist asked. "Prime, ain't he?"

Bess nodded and gave the gelding a final pat on the withers. "He's got heart," she said, "but he's been handled roughly. Treat him right and he'll serve you well."

"I'll take him back to my wagon and tie him up," Gist said. "No sense in taking the chance he'll kick somebody's head off."

Kincaid waved to Bess and she went over to him. "I thought I told ye not to talk," he said.

"It was just Will."

Kincaid gave her a disapproving look. "Ye canna take orders to save your life, can ye?" He shrugged. "I smell fried chicken. Let's see if we can buy something to—"

"Do you think of nothing besides your stomach?" she asked. "That's a fine horse Will bought. He can run like the wind."

"That black? He's no more than fifteen hands."

"He can run, I tell you."

"How do ye know? Have you seen him before?"

"No, but he can run. I'm telling you, Kincaid. I know horses, and that little gelding will run the ears off anything else here."

"You're certain?"

She nodded. "Certain."

They walked toward the table where a woman and her two daughters were selling whole chickens roasted over an open fire. Buying bread and cheese from another stand, and ale from a blind man, they found a spot to sit in the shade of Will Gist's wagon and watch the passersby.

After they had eaten, Kincaid instructed Bess to wait by the wagon while he and Gist talked privately. The warm sun on her face and the food in her belly made Bess sleepy. A single bee droned on and on, and before she knew it, she had drifted off.

When she woke, it was to the sound of Kincaid's voice loudly boasting of his knowledge of horseflesh and racing. Several men had gathered by the back of the wagon, and Will Gist was passing around an open jug, obviously handing out samples of his homemade whiskey. Kincaid sounded as though he'd drunk his share and then some.

". . . damned so-called *gentlemen* think they got the only decent mounts in the colony," he said loudly. Bess noted that his Carolina accent was as thick as white gravy dripping off a cold biscuit. ". . . so high in the stomach," Kincaid continued, "that some of 'em wouldn't know a real racehorse from a milk cow."

Word of the free drinks spread and more men joined the group. Shortly, Kincaid and a total stranger were arguing the merits of a Charles Town champion racehorse that Bess was certain the Scot had never heard of until this instant. Puzzled as to what Kincaid was up to, but not wanting to miss any of it, she climbed up onto the rough board that served as a wagon seat.

A few women and still more farmers wandered over as the conversation grew heated. Then a young man in a cream-colored satin coat and waistcoat rode his sleek blooded sorrel up to the edge of the circle. ''And what would you say about this mare, you backwoods buckeen?''

''That's Thomas Ridgeway,'' a gray-haired woman said to Bess. ''His father, Sir James Ridgeway, owns Hopewell Manor and half of Charles Town. And that mare of his won him twenty pounds sterling in a race last Christmas Day. You'd best tell your man to mind his tongue. Sir James ain't a man to be trifled with.''

Bess shrugged. ''Ain't no holdin' him back when he's in his cups,'' she said, trying hard to imitate the woman's speech.

''You folks ain't from around here, are ya?''

''North a ways,'' Bess said.

''Figures.''

''. . . crow bait,'' Kincaid was saying in a grating manner. ''This mare couldn't outrun my mother. She's got legs like a damned mule.''

''The mare or your mother?'' cried a heckler.

''Both of 'em!'' Kincaid guffawed. He slapped his thigh in amusement and reached for the jug. ''Why, anything could outrun that long-legged heron, and I'll wager my woman could outride you.''

''Put your money where your mouth is!'' Ridgeway retorted. ''What have you got to run against me?''

Bess's heart sank as Kincaid's mouth dropped open. For a long minute he looked stunned, exactly like a man caught in his own trap. ''Well . . . well . . .'' he stuttered. ''I reckon . . .''

''You *reckon* what, bumpkin?''

The tide of humor turned against Kincaid as he appeared to wither before the young gentleman's

challenge. Men laughed and muttered among
themselves.

"He's drunk," one elderly farmer said.

"A pig's bladderful of hot air," muttered another.

"By God, I'll show you who's full of hot air,"
Kincaid sputtered. "Sal! Sal, get down here." He
stabbed a finger at Bess.

"Me?" she asked.

"God save me from a stupid woman," Kincaid
exclaimed to the crowd. A general titter spread
through the group. "Get down here," he repeated, "afore I come up there and git ya."

Bewildered, but not knowing what else to do,
Bess complied. Kincaid wiped his mouth with the
back of his hand and grabbed hold of her arm.
"Why, my little Sally here," he said to Thomas
Ridgeway, "she could whip you flat out in a mile
race."

Ridgeway laughed. "Riding what?"

Kincaid looked around, blinked, and pointed to
the black gelding Will Gist had purchased that
morning from the horse dealer. "On that there
little black."

"You're crazy," Ridgeway said.

"She could too." Kincaid nodded to the onlookers. "You scared to ride against a woman?"

Ridgeway's face darkened with anger. "Show
me your money."

Kincaid's eyes widened and he looked doubt-
ful. "Ought to have odds," he grumbled out
loud. "A big fancy horse like that and this little
workhorse. You got so much money, you oughta
give me odds."

"Three to one Ridgeway beats the woman!" the horse dealer yelled from the edge of the crowd.

A swarthy farmer snickered. "You must think we're as dumb as the towhead, Giles."

"All right," the dealer answered. "Four to one. Who'll give me four to one?"

"Ten to one, maybe," a man in a coonskin cap called. "I've got threepence at ten to one."

"Six to one?" Giles offered. "Six to one." When he got no takers, he raised the bid. "Ten to one it is, then. Ten to one against the little black."

Hands were up as men crowded toward the horse dealer. Kincaid put his arm around Bess's waist and pulled her through the shoving mass to where the black gelding was tied. "You said he could run, now ye'd best prove it," he said in a low, coldly sober voice.

"This is some kind of deceitful scheme, isn't it?" she demanded. "Like the cards? You want me to—"

Kincaid held up his hands. "Do ye want to get to Panama or not?"

"Yes, but—"

"Can ye ride the black or nay, Bess?"

"I suppose so, but—"

"Can he run like the hounds of hell are after him?"

She nodded. "I think so."

"Then . . ." He grinned as he threw a saddle on the shaggy gelding's back and cinched it tight. "Then, lass, it's what they call horse racing. And the devil take the hindmost."

Chapter 14

Ridgeway's sorrel mare leaped away at the starting gunshot, showering Bess and the little black in dust. A woman screamed and the crowd backed away as Bess's gelding shied sideways and reared before breaking into a run. Once the horse stopped fighting the bit, Bess loosened the reins, letting him find his own pace.

She leaned low over his neck and spoke soothingly to the animal as she felt him gather his energy and really begin to gallop full out. Kincaid's shouts and the cheering of farmers and their families faded on the wind. Now all Bess could hear was the rhythmic thud of the black horse's hooves striking the hard-packed dirt road.

Bess had always loved riding fast. Since she was a tiny child, her greatest joy was clinging to a horse's mane and seeing the ground float beneath her. The Carolina sun beating down on her was tempered by the feel of wind in her hair and the sense of power she experienced.

She moved with the horse, not demanding more than he wanted to give, letting her body blend with his, absorbing the animal's fear and giving back love. "Good boy," she cried. "Good Dandy." The words didn't matter. What was important was that the gelding feel her kinship with him and the steady pressure of confident hands on the reins.

When she sensed the horse's fear being replaced with the pure joy of running, Bess dared to think of her opponent. She glanced briefly over the gelding's head at the cloud of dust ahead of them and tried to figure the distance between the two horses. The race hadn't been her idea, and she was furious with Kincaid for getting her into the contest, but now that she was here, she meant to do her best.

"Go! Go!" she urged the black. A barking dog dashed out at them, but the little horse didn't hesitate. Without missing a step, he soared over the confused dog and continued after the sorrel. Bess looked up again at Ridgeway, and to her surprise, somehow the distance was much less than it had been. She looked again, certain that her imagination was getting the better of her, but it was true. They were gaining ground fast.

"Good boy!" she cried, and the last of her doubts drained away as the black's hooves flew over the rough ground. His gait was hard—this was no blooded ladies' horse—but he had the gallant heart of a lion and even more speed than she'd suspected.

As they rounded a curve, the black thrust his neck forward and laid back his ears. He seemed suddenly to realize this was a race and there was another horse in front of him. Bess laughed aloud as he leaped over a mud puddle, found solid ground with a bound, and took the bit in his teeth. There was no stopping him now. He'd accepted her as a rider, then ignored her as if she didn't exist.

The track cut through a grove of oak trees and Bess saw Ridgeway veer his mare around a low-hanging branch. Bess didn't even try to rein the black aside. Instead, she kicked one stirrup free, threw herself to one side of the saddle, and clung like a burr to his mane. Leaves brushed her head and shoulders, tearing her single braid loose so that her hair fanned out behind her.

Just ahead of Ridgeway, a covey of startled quail flew up nearly under the mare's feet. Bess tensed her muscles for the black's panic, but he paid no more heed to the flapping birds than he did to the flying dust. He just ran faster.

The course led downhill through softer ground and narrowed as it crossed a marshy stream. There was a shallow wagon crossing through the water, and beside it, a log footbridge without rails. Knowing that the path through the water would lose precious time, Bess reined the little gelding onto the footbridge. The animal didn't hesitate. His hard hooves slammed against the wooden bridge, jarring Bess's teeth, but he never lost his footing.

Then the gelding slackened his pace a little as they climbed a slight rise. When the stretch of road leveled out and widened again, Bess dug her heels into his side and urged him to pick up his stride. To her delight, Dandy leaped forward, thundering down the hard-packed road.

The horse dealer had mapped out a course twice around the fairgrounds, and Bess was shocked to find that they'd come once around already. When she galloped past the starting point, Ridgeway was still in the lead, but the black gelding was two lengths behind and gaining fast. For an instant as they flashed by, Bess caught sight of Kincaid's towering figure and shock of golden hair gleaming in the sun. He was leaping up and down, waving his warms, and shouting.

Bess's excitement rose to fever pitch as they dashed into the final lap. Dandy was still running flat out. His strong legs seemed tireless.

As Bess and the gelding shortened the gap between the horses to a single length, Ridgeway glanced over his shoulder at them. He'd lost his fine wool planter's hat, and his face was purple with exertion. He had a leather quirt in his right hand, and he brought it down again and again on the sorrel's sweat-darkened rump.

Bess squinted against the dust and sand. She was eating the mare's dirt now as they galloped over a particularly rough spot of road. "Go!" she cried to the black. "Go!" She held the reins in her right hand, and her left was tangled in the gelding's mane. The smell of dust and horse sweat filled her head, and she could hardly see the track ahead of them.

Suddenly she realized that Ridgeway's mare was close enough for her to touch. Foam flew from the animal's mouth, and Bess could hear the rasp of her labored breathing. The strain of the race was showing on the big red animal, while the outlaw black was still running for the sheer joy of it.

When they reached the tree-lined spot, Bess guided the black to the left, away from the overhanging branches, and it was Ridgeway who had to duck to avoid losing his head. He looked at her again. For an instant their eyes met, and she read sheer desperation in his gaze.

She looked up at the road ahead and saw they were closing fast on the log bridge. They galloped on, side by side, neither horse able to gain an advantage. Gradually, Ridgeway began to edge the mare over, crowding the black. Bess realized that if they reached the narrow crossing together, one animal would be forced off the road into the water. Closing her eyes, she willed the black to give every last reserve of strength and speed.

Flattening herself against the flying mane, she dug her heels into the gelding's side and let out one of Kutii's Incan war cries. The little black didn't let her down. He shot ahead of the mare, taking the bridge in two bounds, charged up the hill, and raced onto the level stretch. By the time they crossed the finish line, they were three full lengths ahead of Ridgeway and his long-legged sorrel.

It took Bess another quarter turn of the road to slow the gelding to a hard trot. He was still all fire and steel when she reined him back to where Kincaid waited for her.

"Ye did it!" he shouted. "Damn if ye didn't!" He seized her around the waist and lifted her down as Will Gist stepped up to take hold of the black's bridle.

Everyone was shouting, and people were slapping her on the back. Kincaid pulled her hard against him and kissed her. When she caught her breath, Ridgeway was beside them, sitting on his badly winded mare.

"You beat me fair," he said stiffly. "It's plain the black is a fine racing animal." He dismounted and looked at his own mare with distaste. "She's in foal to John Tyler's stud, Shanghai. I'll trade the sorrel and twenty pounds for the gelding.''

Kincaid shook his head. "The black's not mine to sell or trade. Talk to Will Gist here.''

Gist snatched off his hat. "The animal's mine, Mr. Ridgeway. And I'd be glad to trade with ye.''

"You'll give Gist a bill of sale, won't you?'' Bess asked. "Just so there'll be no confusion later.''

"The mare's mine. I can do what I want with her,'' Ridgeway said.

Bess nodded. "Then you won't mind stepping into the tavern over there and writing out the bill of sale. I'm sure the innkeep can find paper and ink.'' She patted the black's neck and hugged him. "I wish I could buy you myself,'' she whispered into the animal's ragged hair.

"The horse will be well cared for, you can be certain of that,'' Ridgeway said. "My father's stables are the finest in Charles Town.''

"I'm sure,'' Bess murmured. "I'll just walk him out for you while you gentlemen settle the deal.'' Strangely sad, she led the animal across the field to cool him off. They'd won the bet, so why did she have such a feeling of loss? And why was she fighting back tears? It made no sense. Gist would have put the black to pulling a plow. Now Dandy would be the pampered darling of a rich man's son, and Gist would go home to his family with silver in his pockets and the beginning of a stable of blooded horses. Everyone, it seemed, had won. So why did she feel so bad?

Kincaid was grinning when he caught up with her. "Ye can't have them all,'' he said. " 'Twas never your horse, ye know. You were just borrowing him.''

"He's special . . . like my mare Ginger." She scowled at Kincaid. "You promised me you'd get her back. Then when I found her, I lost her again."

"Aye, but I know where she's at," he said.

"So you say. I'll believe it when she's back safe and sound at Fortune's Gift."

Kincaid took the black's reins from her. "Time to turn him over to his new master. And there's no need for ye to look so glum. We won a hatful of money."

"How?"

"I bet against Ridgeway, then I found a dozen or so farmers who couldn't wait to give me their money." He chuckled. "To celebrate, I'll get you a room at the tavern tonight. Once we get on the water again, there's no tellin' when you'll sleep in a bed again. But tonight, my lady, ye'll live like a queen. Good wine, clean sheets, and a hot supper."

"You wouldn't let me stay at the last inn," she reminded him.

"Aye, 'tis true, but this one is run by a woman. Will Gist tells me she's clean and she serves good food. And best of all, there are no rumors of her doing in her guests."

Bess looked down at her arms and bare ankles. Her skirt and bodice were streaked with dirt and her hands were filthy. She could imagine what her face must look like. "Could I have a bath? A real one with hot water and soap?"

He nodded and wiped a smudge off her chin. "For you, sweet Bess, I'd even carry up the water myself."

* * *

As Kincaid made the rounds of farmers and the horse dealer to collect his winnings, he wondered what had let him risk their remaining silver on the black gelding. Common sense should have told him that Ridgeway's blooded sorrel would leave the smaller horse in the dust. Bess had said that the animal could run, but that was only a woman's fancy, and it had been a long time since he'd paid much attention to what a woman wanted. He'd always been a man who heeded no instincts but his own, and it was those survival instincts that had kept him alive when men all around him had died.

What was it that had suddenly changed everything and made him go against reason? Why was he experiencing emotions he'd long thought burned away?

There was only one answer—this red-haired woman. Bess Bennett had hooked her claws into him deep. He watched her by day and dreamed of her by night. He hadn't had a full night's rest since Will Gist had picked them up in his wagon three days ago.

The trouble was, as much as he hated to admit it, Bess had ruined him for other women. This past time with Joan Pollott, before the raid on Fortune's Gift, had been something of a disappointment. Joan had used all her ample wiles on him and his flesh had responded, but something vital was missing. For the first time in many years— since he'd learned that his wife didn't love him— the physical act of sex wasn't enough.

He wanted Bess. He wanted her hot and ready for him. He wanted her willing. And not having her was about to drive him mad.

She was right about their having no chance of
making a permanent bond. She was a genuine
English lady, and he was a soldier's by-blow. He
couldn't even say that for certain, and there was
no way he'd ever know who he really was or what
name he should have borne. He'd killed too many
men in too many battles to ever think he could
wash his soul clean and start life over with someone like Bess.

But he still wanted her.

And if they took pleasure in each other on this
journey, who would be the wiser? So long as he
didn't get her with child, what difference would
it make? Any honorable man who offered for her
hand in marriage wouldn't expect a virgin bride,
not from a woman who'd traveled thousands of
miles with a criminal.

Bess Bennett was a rare woman. Watching her
come down the finish on that little black horse
had made him near burst out of his breeches with
pride.

He wanted Bess, and she wanted him. The
problem was how to make her see things his way.

The first stars were twinkling in the black velvet
sky when Bess sank into her bath of hot water.
Nothing had ever felt this good in her life. Well,
almost nothing, she thought with a chuckle as delicious memories of being in Kincaid's arms on a
lonely beach danced in the shadowy corners of
her mind.

Bess moaned with pure delight. The bathwater
was hot and clean, and from somewhere the innkeeper had produced a tin of soft French soap.

She hummed as she scrubbed her knees and feet, then sank deeper into the tin tub.

She was alone in a neat upstairs bedchamber of the inn, and although it was summer, the serving girl had laid a small fire on the hearth to keep off the chill as Bess bathed. A few feet away stood an oversized bed with a high carved headboard of heavy, dark wood and faded blue velvet hangings. The style was so old-fashioned that Bess decided someone had dismantled the bed and carried it by ship to Carolina in her grandmother's time. The sheets and pillow coverings had been washed and pressed so many times that the fabric had worn thin, but the linen smelled of sunshine and fresh clover. A clean cotton shift was laid out on the bed for Bess to put on after her bath.

She had assured her privacy by sliding the latch on the door before undressing and climbing into the tub. The serving wench had carried away her other clothes, the ones she'd saved in her saddle-bags. The maid had insisted she could wash, dry, and press the things by morning.

Bess sighed. Bathing in a freshwater pond was nothing like this. Carefully, she put a dab of soap into her hair and worked it into a lather. She leaned forward and was beginning to pour clean water from a wooden bucket over her head when hard male fingers closed over hers.

"I'll do that for ye, lass," Kincaid said.

Bess was so startled she nearly leaped out of the water. Her eyes flew open, then shut as soap ran into them. "What are you doing here?" she sputtered. She grabbed frantically for a towel, and

he put it into her hands. She rubbed at her stinging eyes.

"I said, I could do that for ye," he repeated.
"I meant to help, not to drown ye in your own
tub."

A mischievous nuance in his voice told her that
he'd been drinking again. And in spite of her in-
dignation at his invasion of her bath, she couldn't
completely hide a hint of a smile as she hastily
covered her exposed bosom with a towel. "How
did you get in here?" she demanded.

"The open window."

"But that window is twenty feet from the ground.
I know—I looked when I opened the shutters."

He grinned. "Aye, 'tis, but I came over the
roof."

"Why in God's name did you do that?"

"I had to," he replied, resting his hands on his
narrow hips. "Ye locked the door."

"Did it occur to you that I bolted the door because I wanted privacy?"

"Aye, but I didna think ye meant to lock me
out." He wiped a dot of soapsuds off her nose.
"Your hair's all soap, hinney. Ye look a fright."

"You've no business coming here like this,"
she said sharply. "I didn't ask you to."

His tanned features creased in another crooked
grin. "I'm sorry ye feel that way."

She pulled the towel higher around her neck
and tried to be firm. "Just go right back out that
window."

"Ye want me to jump twenty feet? Suppose I
break a leg?"

She couldn't believe she was sitting in a tub
without a stitch on, having this conversation with

him. "Go away," she repeated with more conviction than she felt.

"Ye really don't want me here."

He looked so wounded that she relented a little. "So long as you are here, you might as well help me rinse the soap out of my hair."

Kincaid was no more than a hired servant, she told herself glibly. Respectable ladies in London allowed footmen into their bedchambers every day. "This bucket." She pointed to the container holding the warm water. A tin dipper stood upright in the bucket. Beyond that stood another bucket of cold water. "But you must promise to be a gentleman," she insisted. "On your honor."

"Aye," he agreed meekly.

"You're not to lay a finger on me," she said.

"Ye ha' my solemn word as a gentleman."

Bess closed her eyes as Kincaid poured the first dipper of water over her hair. The water was cooling, but it seemed to her as though the room was growing warmer by the moment. "That feels good," she murmured as he repeated the action. She shook her head and ran her fingers through her thick tresses as he continued to stream water over her. "That's enough," she said finally, beginning to twist her clean, rinsed hair.

His lips brushed her bare shoulder and she shivered. "Don't do that," she protested.

"Ye dinna wish me to kiss ye?"

"No. Of course not," she lied.

"Then do ye want another towel?" He picked up a thick one from a stool by the fireplace and folded it over his arm.

"No, I don't want another towel. I won't need

it until I get out of the tub, and I'm not getting out so long as you're in this room."

"Ah, Bess, you're a heartless lass. Ye cut me deep. Have I ever given ye cause to mistrust me yet?"

"You certainly have." She swallowed against the tightness in her throat. He shouldn't be here. She knew she was playing with fire, but the temptation to see how close she could get without being burned was irresistible.

"When did I ever give ye reason to doubt me?" he demanded, returning to stand behind her.

"When you stole my horse. Twice."

"That was before," he said. "I mean since we left the Tidewater. Haven't I been a perfect gentleman?" His burr was thick and lazy. It was difficult for her to remember that Kincaid was a convicted murderer and a dangerous man.

A hard hand rested on her shoulder where his lips had caressed her earlier. "I'll just rub the knots from your neck, then," he said. "I'm an expert at it."

"No. I don't want you to . . ." Her voice trailed off as his strong fingers kneaded her tense muscles. The feeling was wonderful. Against her will, delicious relaxation flowed through her. "You really do know what you're doing," she murmured.

A deluge of cold well water hit her. She leaped up, gasping, and landed right in Kincaid's embrace. "You devil!" she accused him, just before he kissed her.

His mouth tasted of wild mint and rum, and his touch scalded her bare, wet skin. Of their own volition, her arms went around his neck and she found herself kissing him back.

The heat from Kincaid's fingers could not compare with the scorching brand of his mouth. His kiss deepened, fanning the glowing embers in her loins to flames of desire. His hands slid down her naked back to the curve of her bottom, and she molded against him like bark to a tree. Water streamed down them and pooled in puddles on the floor at their feet, but neither of them cared. All that mattered was that the kiss go on and on.

The bed was only a few feet away, but they never made it that far. He was touching her and kissing her, and she was whimpering and tearing at his clothes. Then he went down on one knee, taking her with him. His hot, wet mouth was on her breast, and he was stripping off his clothes faster than a blue crab shedding its old shell.

"Bess, Bess," he groaned against her breast. He tongued her nipple, then drew it into his mouth and sucked it until her knees went weak. "Ah, my sweet lass," he murmured. "My wild, sweet lass."

The sound of his rich, deep voice made her giddy with longing and added fuel to the inferno raging within her. His lips and tongue teased her nipple to aching torment as his fingers slid over her belly and found the source of her pleasure below her damp triangle of curls.

Her breathing quickened and she squirmed closer, running her hands over him, touching and stroking him, not wanting the warm, rippling tremors to stop. She was beyond reason, beyond doubt, as he probed her soft folds with his long, scarred fingers. He found first one breast and then the other, lingering at each nipple, kissing, and suckling until she could take no more. . . . Over and over he brought her to the brink of release, then pulled back at the last second to begin the exquisite torture all over again with consummate expertise.

This time Bess felt no hesitation and no doubts. Nothing mattered but the heat of Kincaid's fevered body entwined with hers and the fulfillment of this inevitable act of uninhibited passion.

With a groan, he rolled her onto her back and lowered his head between her legs. She closed her eyes and arched against the hot, sweet excitement of his probing tongue.

She tangled her fingers in his hair and moaned, letting the conflagration sweep her up in its fury, shutting out everything but the here and now and the fire that threatened to engulf them both.

"Please . . . " she whispered hoarsely. She wanted something more. "Kincaid . . . please," she said, not certain what it was she was asking for. He stroked the inside of her thigh and she cried out with pleasure as he trailed damp kisses to her knee.

He crouched over her and parted her legs. His turgid manhood stood out full and erect, so huge that it frightened and excited her at the same time. She gasped as his member nudged against her throbbing folds, but she strained toward him, eager for his love.

"Bess, hinney," he whispered. "Dinna worry, I'll take care of ye."

With a deep, powerful thrust, he entered her, filling her with a sense of wonder. Her eyes opened wide as she received him, marveling at the sense of fullness. This is what poets allude to, she thought in an instant of clarity. It took a few seconds for her to adjust to Kincaid's size, but there was no pain, only a satisfying knowledge that all lovemaking wasn't the foolish act Richard had shown her.

He kissed her again, and the urgency came rushing back, flowing over her like a river of fire. He withdrew, then plunged into her again. "Oh," she gasped. The feeling was like nothing she had ever imagined. She raised her hips eagerly, thrusting to meet his straining ardor. Was this how it was supposed to be?

Laughter mingled with tears of joy as she clung to him, digging her nails into his back. Again and again he plunged into her, and then, when she was certain she would burn to a cinder in the incandescent heat of their blazing union, another wonder occurred. Without warning, a fiery crescendo exploded within her and she tumbled from the brink of the precipice, down and down through a swirling mist of clouds, falling through a timeless void until she came to rest in Kincaid's arms.

"Bess, my wee Bess," he murmured hoarsely. "Hold me tight, woman, while I ease my own hunger." Slowly, he withdrew and thrust deeply. He groaned and crushed her against him. "Ahhh." He sighed deeply. He plunged into her one more time, then withdrew and pulled her hard against him.

Satiated by this intense experience, Bess buried her face in his shoulder. She felt the hot surge of liquid across her belly, but was beyond questioning him. "Is it always like that?" she whispered.

"By all the saints, I hope so," he answered. He tipped up her chin and covered her mouth with his own in a tender, caring kiss. "Ye are more woman than I have ever known," he said.

She snuggled against him. "This floor is hard," she said.

"Then we must go to the bed." Laughing, he got to his knees and pulled her after him.

"Aren't you supposed to carry me to the bed?" she teased.

"After a bout with ye, lass, you're lucky ye dinna have to carry me." He caught her around the waist and lifted her onto the high feather bed, then threw himself on top of her and rained kisses on her face. "And how do ye like that?" he asked.

"I liked it fine," she replied. "Can we do it again?"

He groaned loudly in mock agony. "Again? Give me a week or two to recover. Perhaps a month . . ."

She laughed, and he cupped her breast in his hand and kissed a rosy nipple. "Kincaid," she whispered, wanting to say his name. "You promised me you would be a gentleman. On your word of honor, you said."

"I lied."

"Aren't you ashamed of breaking your word?"

"Mmmm." He kissed her other breast and brushed the nipple with his tongue. "Nice," he said. "Maybe in an hour we could try."

She giggled and took his face between her hands. "You are insatiable."

"Not me, woman, you. Ye are the one askin' for more when the sweat's not dry on my body and my breath's still comin' in ragged gulps."

"I didn't mean now," she said softly. "I meant, could we *ever* do it again? I . . ." Her cheeks grew warm. "I didn't know if I did it right."

"Hmmm." He rolled over and rested on one elbow. Bess ran her fingers lightly over the bulging muscles of his upper arm, then drew imaginary circles on his broad, sinewy chest. He pretended to ignore her as he considered her last statement. "Nay," he said finally. "I dinna think ye did get it right. 'Twas not bad for a first effort, but 'tis clear to me that ye must have practice."

"And I suppose you will offer yourself as my teacher?"

He grinned. "Who better?"

"I may be a slow learner," she teased provocatively as her fingertips found the hard nub of his male nipple.

He laughed. "I think, lass, that it will be a more interesting journey to Panama than I expected."

Chapter 15

A shifting of shadows in the far corner of the inn chamber brought Kincaid out of bed stark naked, knife in hand, charging at the intruder. Awakened from a deep sleep, Bess sat up and stared dumbly at the Scot as he stopped short, facing a solid paneled wall. "What are you doing?" she asked, rubbing her eyes. "Have you taken leave of your senses?"

For seconds, Kincaid stood motionless and tried to make sense of what he knew he'd seen. Something . . . no, *someone* had been in the room with them only a minute before. He shook his head, still unable to speak, considering and discarding possibilities. He'd had plenty to drink the night before, but he'd never drunk enough to suffer delusions. And he sure as hell wasn't drunk this morning.

His mouth was as dry as it had been the time he'd lain wounded on a battlefield, pinned under a horse for six hours. The hairs on his neck were prickling and every survival instinct he'd developed in thirty-some years of living was raging.

Blood pounded in his temples. How did a man turn to a woman he'd spent half the night making love to and tell her he was seeing ghosts?

"Kincaid?" Concern edged her voice. "What's wrong?"

He straightened from a knife fighter's crouch, deliberately grinned, and went back to the bed. "Rat," he lied. "Big enough to throw a saddle on and ride." he shrugged. "Guess I wasn't quick enough. He outsmarted me."

Bess gave a small sigh of relief and pulled the sheet modestly up around her neck. "I thought this inn was too clean for rats."

He climbed in beside her and put an arm around her shoulders. "The stables are close. As much food as they prepare here every day, I guess it's hard to keep the inn free of vermin." He kissed her mouth tenderly. "A good day to ye, lass. Sorry I am to disturb your ladyship's sleep with mundane matters."

She chuckled and laid her head on his bare shoulder. She felt warm and alive next to him. Memories of what they'd done brought a genuine smile to her face.

"This complicates things, doesn't it?" she said.

"What? A rat?" The incident troubled him and he wondered if his brain was playing tricks on him. He'd lived all his life by his wits. If they deserted him, he might as well go down to the marsh and drown himself, because his days were numbered.

"You know what I mean." She stared up into his eyes, and he noted the flecks of gold that sparkled amid the sea of brilliant blue. "Us."

"Aye, lass, it does complicate things." He drew a callused finger along her cheek to the corner of her mouth. She touched his finger with the tip of her damp tongue and a shiver went through him.

She's only a woman, he reminded himself. She's curled up like a kitten in your bed now, all soft and purring, but she's the same English bitch who took a cattle whip to your bare back.

Her red-gold hair was spread out all around her on the pillow, and he could see the sweet curves of her breasts beneath the sheets. He wanted her as much this morning as he had last night.

"Kincaid?"

"Aye?" He wanted to kiss the hollow of her throat and feel her long legs wrapped around him again. His chest grew tight as he remembered her eager cries of pleasure and the heat of her mouth against him.

"I didn't know it could be like that . . . between a man and a woman. When Richard . . ." A pink flush spread over her cheeks. "When he forced me, I felt nothing but discomfort and . . ." She left the rest unspoken.

"The shame was his," he finished for her, wondering at the rush of possessiveness that came over him. If Richard were in this room, he'd kill him with his bare hands. " 'Twas not your fault."

"It was stupid of me to be alone with him."

"Perhaps, but that does not take away his guilt." He stroked her hair. "Shall I find him and kill him for you?" He made the offer lightly, as if in jest.

"He's already dead."

Kincaid smiled. "Good."

Her thick lashes fluttered, then her blue eyes opened wide. "I wish you had been the first," she said, her expression serious.

"Ye did not take pleasure in what he did to ye."

"No." She moistened her lips. "I felt foolish."

"Ye said before that ye were a young lass when it happened. You're a woman now, and ye wanted what we shared. This was your first time. And . . ." He grinned. "It wasn't the first for me, Bess, but it was . . ." He chuckled, realizing that there were no words for what he'd felt making love to her. "If you get any better at this, woman, you'll kill me."

She laughed softly. "Then you don't mean to give me any more lessons?"

"Maybe ye should give them to me." He laid a hand on her breast. She sighed and closed her eyes, raising her head to be kissed. He didn't disappoint her. And the heat of their fierce embrace silenced his inner voice as they gave themselves over to another act of joyous union.

Much later, when the inn floors creaked with the footsteps of guests and serving maids, Kincaid kissed her gently, got up, and began to dress. She watched him, sleepy contentment on her rosy face, as he lifted a heavy money pouch, fastened it to a leather thong, and dropped it out of sight beneath his shirt.

The sun was well up. He knew he should have been out of bed long ago. He could hear the clatter of pans in the tavern kitchen and the whinny of horses outside in the yard. It was past time he was on the road to Charles Town. "We have much bitterness between us, ye and me," he said to Bess, "and now it seems we have much sweetness as well."

She sat up in bed, covering her nakedness.

"This doesn't change anything between us," she said. "We are both adults. Neither of us has made any promises to—"

A lump rose in his throat. "Promises? We've made promises aplenty, I'd say." He hesitated, then blurted it out. "I'd send ye home, woman, where you'll be safe."

"Send me home?" Her voice tightened. "I'm not your wife, Kincaid. You can't give me orders."

"Nay, not my wife and not like to be."

"Well, we're agreed on something, then." Bess drew her knees up under her. "And what of the treasure?"

"Draw me a map. If it can be found, I'll find it, and I'll bring it back to Fortune's Gift."

"Riding on a unicorn," she scoffed. Her blue eyes narrowed. "Do you think I'm stupid? Do you think that just because I let you bed me, I'd let you go after the gold without me? I'd never see you or an ounce of that treasure again."

"Ye think I'd cheat ye of your share?"

"I do."

Anger welled up in him. "Ye know me little, then," he said through clenched teeth. He picked up the pistol and shoved it into his belt. "Wait for me here at the inn. I'm going to find us passage south."

"I'll come with you."

"I'm going to Charles Town, to the docks. It's no place for a woman." He yanked the money bag over his neck and threw it to her. "This should prove to ye that I'm coming back for you."

She caught the sack of coins. "Will this be enough, do you think?"

"Let me worry about that. You stay here and out of trouble."

He was still seething as he went down the narrow inn stairs. Damn, but she infuriated him! If he'd wanted to abandon her, he'd had a hundred chances.

As he entered the public room, he saw that it was empty except for a family eating breakfast and the horse dealer sitting alone at a table near the door. He was about to take a seat at an empty table when the horse dealer noticed him and waved him over.

"Good day to you," the man said, rising and offering his hand. "I'm Giles Hartly."

"Hartly," Kincaid acknowledged. He was surprised that the horse dealer was in such a jovial mood this morning, considering how much money he'd lost on Bess's race yesterday.

"Join me," Hartly said, motioning to a chair. "You're a stranger to these parts, ain't you? Don't believe I caught your name."

"Robert Munro," Kincaid answered, taking a seat. "Ye wouldn't be headin' back toward Charles Town this mornin', would ye?"

"As a matter of fact, I'm doin' just that," Hartly said.

"I've business there," Kincaid said. "I'd be obliged if ye'd let me ride along. I can pay for the—"

"Keep your money, son. I've bought a string of horses and I can use the help." He motioned to a serving wench. "May! Ham and eggs for Munro." He grinned at Kincaid. "They make a decent breakfast here. Traveling up and down the coast like I do, I appreciate good food. What did you say your business was?''

''I didn't say.''

Hartly laughed heartily. ''Damn, but you didn't. My brother says I always ask too many questions. I like to talk to folks and that's a fact. A man who deals in horses has to like people. Maybe I could interest you in two good mounts. I always say . . .'' Hartly rattled on as the wench brought a huge plate of ham, eggs, grits, and biscuits to the table.

Kincaid nodded as she set it down in front of him, and he began to eat. Hartly was not a man he normally would have wanted to socialize with, but a horse dealer usually knew everything that was going on in the area. When the time was right, he'd ask Hartly a few careful questions of his own.

His immediate problem was finding a ship to take the two of them south to the Caribbean. Jamaica, maybe, or the Bahamas. After that . . . After that, he'd have to buy or steal a boat. Panama was enemy territory, and they could hardly buy passage to Porto Bello.

What had happened between him and Bess had changed things, no matter what she said. He wished he'd never agreed to come on this treasure hunt. Worrying about keeping her alive could make him lose the edge that a fighting man had to have to survive. Bess had touched his soul in a way that no woman—not even Gillian—had ever done. And he felt as though she was drawing him deeper and deeper into a game of chance in which he had no hope of winning . . . even if he drew all the right cards.

* * *

The day passed slowly for Bess alone in the bedchamber. In midmorning, Davie, the serving girl, brought back the remainder of Bess's clothing. Examining what belongings she had left, folding and packing them into her saddlebags, took nearly half an hour. At noon, Bess went down and shared rabbit stew and fry bread with a single guest, an elderly peddler.

She spent another hour looking through the peddler's goods and purchasing a pair of sturdy boy's shoes, darned stockings, breeches, and a white lawn man's shirt with full sleeves and lace at the cuffs. The only women's garments he had were whalebone stays, and Bess couldn't see the need for an additional set of stays where she was bound for.

Afterward, she returned to her chamber and waited impatiently until the heat of the day passed and the sun became an orange globe on the western horizon. She paced the floor and lingered at the diamond-paned casement window, watching the road for some sign of Kincaid.

And she struggled with her own doubts and fears.

What had happened between them in this room had been inevitable—she didn't regret a moment of it. No matter what happened, she would always cherish the joy of their coming together. In one night, Kincaid had wiped away the unpleasant memories of lovemaking Richard had given her and left only good ones in their place.

After Richard had raped her, she'd spent weeks terrified that she carried his child. This time, she found to her amazement, it didn't matter to her.

Becoming pregnant would be awkward at best with Panama looming ahead of them, but the thought of having Kincaid's child didn't frighten her.

If she returned to the Tidewater in the family way, she would simply invent a husband who'd met an untimely death. Neighbors would whisper behind her back—but who could say for certain that she wasn't an honest widow? And if she returned with her grandfather's treasure, she would be wealthy enough to laugh at their gossip. And the child, male or female, would be the heir that Fortune's Gift needed from her body.

She was too wise in the way of the world to expect any more from Kincaid than a brief interlude of passion. There could be no future for them once the treasure was found and Kincaid had his freedom. He didn't belong in her world, and she'd not descend into his. He was what he was—a brutal soldier.

Bess smiled. No . . . not brutal. Kincaid definitely had a tender side. Still, he was hardly a man she would choose as a husband. He was too unpredictable . . . too dangerous. Such a man would never be managed by a wife. Besides, she thought, the last thing in the world she wanted was a husband. No, she'd have this time together with Kincaid and savor it. And when she returned to Fortune's Gift, she'd take up her own life again, a life dedicated to her land and her people.

The night passed, hour by hour. She slept off and on, and the waiting was heavy on her mind. What if Kincaid had run off and left her? What if he'd been arrested? What if he'd gotten into a fight and been killed? In the bright light of day such worries seemed foolish—but in the humid darkness of a Carolina night they plagued her like an onset of fleas.

The second day was worse than the first. She wanted to follow Kincaid to Charles Town, but she was afraid she'd miss him on the road. The innkeeper demanded payment and stared at her with hostile eyes. The threat didn't need to be spoken aloud. ''This is a decent establishment. We'll have no abandoned sluts here.''

''My husband will be back for me when he finishes his business in Charles Town,'' Bess said, trying to keep her gentlewoman's speech from betraying her.

''Husband? Hmmph!'' the proprietor scowled. ''I saw ye ridin' that black horse with your skirts up and your legs bare as an egg. Don't put on airs with me, girl.''

Bess spent the afternoon in her room again. At dusk, she could no longer take the heat and the lazy drone of flies. She went down to the yard and walked across the road to the place where the fair had been held.

She had been walking for the sake of stretching her legs when she saw a black man on horseback riding down the road, leading a mule behind him. She waved, and to her surprise, he reined his mount in her direction.

''Bess?'' he called. ''Be that you?''

She stared and began to run toward him. ''Rudy? Rudy? Is that you?'' Her heart began to hammer against her chest. ''Rudy? God's breath, man! I thought you'd drowned!'' She knew that the black seaman had been on the sloop's bow when it struck the sandbar. "You're alive!" she said.

"I am." For the first time since she'd known him, he smiled. "I swum a far piece and got picked up by a snow headed for Charles Town. Got there ahead of you, I reckon." His dark brown eyes glowed with a deep sadness. "Reckon Ants Taylor has bought it, along with the boy. Ants was a good man. I served with him nigh on to ten year. You won't see many knows the sea like Ants, or many can treat a man like me the way he did."

"Ian?"

"The Irishman?" Rudy shrugged. "Drowned, I guess. But he wasn't much. Ain't seen an Irishman yet could find his way in the dark."

"I'm glad you're alive, Rudy." She waited. He seemed to have exhausted his supply of talk for the day. "Where are you going?" she asked him finally.

"Come for you."

"For me?"

"Kincaid sent me."

"You found Kincaid?"

"Best fetch your stuff, if you got any. We got a piece to ride afore dark."

"Where are we going?" she asked.

"You wouldn't know iffen I tole you." His wide mouth firmed. "You 'fraid to go with a blackamoor?"

"No, Rudy. I'm not afraid of you."

He nodded. "Best get your stuff, then."

In ten minutes, Bess had retrieved her saddlebags, slipped the serving wench a silver penny in thanks for her kindness, and was riding the mule bareback down the road toward Charles Town with Rudy. They left the main track after a few miles and set off on a narrow path through the woods.

Bess endured silence for an hour, then spoke. "When do we meet Kincaid? Has he found a boat?"

"After dark."

"Did he find us a boat?"

"Reckon so."

Another hour passed. Her arms ached from balancing the saddlebags over the mule's neck, and the animal's back was as hard and sharp as a fence rail. Mosquitoes and horseflies buzzed around their heads and bit any inch of exposed flesh. The mule plodded on, seemingly impervious to the annoying insects.

As they neared the coast, the hardwoods gave way to scrub pines and they crossed one stream after another. They passed no farms or signs of human habitation until they came to a lonely cabin just before dark. Smoke puffed from the mud-and-stick chimney, and a few chickens scratched in the yard.

"We leave the animals here," Rudy said. They dismounted and he turned them into a log enclosure.

Bess thought she heard a baby crying, but no one came out of the house. "Could we buy something to eat?" she asked Rudy. "I'm hungry."

He motioned for her to stay where she was and went to the door. Someone opened it and Rudy went inside. In a short time, he was back with two wooden bowls of spicy fish stew and a round of corn bread. Bess took it eagerly.

"I can pay," she said.

He shook his head. "Sara don't like no truck with white folks. I paid her for use of the horse and mule. She says eat and welcome to it. She don't take money for feeding travelers."

"Please give her my thanks, and tell her that I meant no disrespect," Bess said. "I'm grateful."

Rudy smiled. "I tole her what Kincaid say. You got no slaves on your plantation. You freed your slaves. Sara says that's the only reason she willin' to feed you. Sara don't care for white folks. She's a real Africa woman. She's Mandingo."

Bess looked around at the poor cabin with the small, neat garden. "You tell Sara that her fish stew is the best I've ever eaten and I'm much obliged."

When they had finished, Rudy returned the bowls to the cabin, came back and slung Bess's saddlebags over his shoulder, and headed into the woods. Bess glanced back at the house, then followed him down an overgrown path. A short distance from the dwelling, they came to a river. A log dugout canoe was pulled up on the bank. A half-grown black boy stood beside it, leaning on a long pole.

"Get in," Rudy said. Bess obeyed. He and the boy pushed the boat off the shore and stepped into the wide canoe. Using a pole to maneuver along the shallows, the silent boy guided the heavy craft along a narrow waterway. Trees and vines hung over the river on both sides and grew so close together overhead that it was like traveling through a dark tunnel.

More mosquitoes circled Bess's head as she stared into the gloom of the gathering night. They passed islands and glided from one channel into another until she had lost all sense of direction. Then the moon began to rise, and she saw that they had entered a broader stretch of water. Not long after that, Bess saw the flicker of lantern light.

Kincaid's voice echoed over the still water. "Rudy?"

"It's us."

Bess's sigh of relief was audible. As they grew closer, she made out the shape of a longboat with at least six men in it. "Kincaid?" she called.

"Aye, 'tis me. And who did ye think it was? Louis of France?"

The dugout nudged the side of the longboat and Kincaid's strong hand reached out to clasp hers. Her pulse quickened as he assisted her into the boat and pointed out a seat. Rudy handed her saddlebags over and Bess settled them across her lap. He stepped into the longboat, and the boy pushed away with his pole and vanished into the darkness.

"What are we—" Bess started to ask.

Kincaid cut her off. "You'll find out soon enough." He looked past her to the men at the oars. "Well, what are ye waiting for? Put your backs into it!"

The moon rose higher as the sailors rowed the longboat around a point of land. As soon as they cleared the marshy tip, Bess saw a two-masted schooner lying at anchor only a few hundred yards away. She looked around. There were no lights on the ship or on the land. There were no sounds but the wind and the rhythmic creak of oars and the splash of water.

Kincaid leaned close to her. "There she is, Bess.

There's the ship that will take us where we want to go and back again."

"How? Why?" They had money for passage certainly, but not enough to buy a boat. Who would take them to Panama and back? "I don't understand," she said.

"She's mine," he said.

"Yours? But you don't own a ship."

One of the sailors behind her laughed.

"Mind your own affairs," Kincaid snapped. "And remember what I've told you. Lay a finger on my woman—speak to her unless you're obeying a direct order from me—and I'll hang ye by your balls from the yardarm, and feed what's left of ye to the sharks."

"Kincaid, where did you get a ship?" she insisted. "Did you steal it?" God in heaven! What had she gotten herself into? Stealing a ship was worse than horse thieving.

"After a fashion," he answered. She caught a whiff of rum on his breath. He wasn't drunk, but he had been drinking. She knew it by his cocky humor.

"Captain Bartholomew Kennedy had the bad luck to run aground on a sandbar last week with a Royal Navy snow breathing down his neck. He and his crew—what's left of them—have been sentenced to hang in Charles Town tomorrow morning. And since he had little use for his schooner anymore, I hired my own crew and lifted it out from under the Navy's high noses." His amused burr was so thick she could have cut it with a knife.

"You stole a ship from the Royal Navy?" she cried.

"Kennedy's own *Scarlet Tanager*, complete with six cannon, four swivel guns, and a hold full of fresh water and supplies."

It went beyond all belief. Bess shook her head, certain this must be Kincaid's idea of a bad joke. "A pirate ship?"

Figures appeared at the rail of the schooner. Someone tossed a rope ladder over the side.

"You're serious, aren't you?" she said to Kincaid. "You've actually stolen a ship?"

"Aye, woman, if ye care to look at it that way. But as I said before, Captain Kennedy will have no use for the *Tanager* in Hell, and ye did hire me to take ye to Panama."

Chapter 16

Jamaica

The *Scarlet Tanager* glided into the Kingston harbor on an overcast afternoon in late July, and the young captain, Evan Davis, gave the orders to furl the sails and drop anchor. Bess and Kincaid stood near the rail at the stern of the ship and gazed at the bustling port town amid a brilliant sea of green foliage.

Evan strode down the deck toward them. "It's a tame place compared to Port Royal," he said, pointing across the harbor to the far shore opposite Kingston. " 'Twas said the devil hisself thought twice before sailing into Port Royal. A bigger nest of pirates and cutthroats you never saw. A hurricane three years ago destroyed most of it. Twenty-six ships sank and over four hundred people drowned in that single storm."

"It's hard to believe," Bess replied, looking at the jewel of an island nestled in a bowl of blue water. The sweet smell of orchids, lilies, and citrus was nearly overpowering, and the air was so soft it felt like velvet against her skin.

"Aye, miss, but true. Some think Port Royal was cursed. The town was swallowed up by an earthquake around the turn of the century."

"We have fierce storms on the Chesapeake," Bess said, "but nothing like that. I can't imagine what it would be like to have the earth open up under your feet."

Evan nodded and glanced at Kincaid. "We'll have to let the men go ashore, sir. And they'll be wanting—"

"To be paid," Kincaid finished. "Every man will have his fair leave and enough coin to satisfy his hungers. But I want you on this deck when I'm not aboard, and I want them ashore in parties of no more than six. I'll not leave the *Tanager* undefended."

"As she was when we found her?" Evan grinned. "I'll keep her safe for you, Munro, be sure of that." His mood sobered. "The men deserve their recreation, sir. They've worked well together, for all that we were shorthanded."

"You've my permission to take on four more hands here, if you can find experienced men. Their share will be two-thirds of what was promised to those who left Charles Town with us."

"Aye, aye, sir." Evan touched his forehead in respect to Bess and returned to his duties.

"He's a good master," Kincaid said, "for all this is his first command. He knows these waters, and I think we can trust him."

Bess nodded. Of all the men Kincaid had hired, she liked Evan Davis the best. Rudy was as taciturn as always, and the rest of the crew seemed to her no better than pirates. She particularly disliked Floyd Hartly, ship's cook, carpenter, and surgeon. He was the brother of the horse dealer they'd met in Charles Town, and also was one of

the first men Kincaid had signed on. It had been
Floyd who'd led Kincaid to Rudy and Evan Davis.

"Would ye expect church deacons to help me
lift a ship from the Royal Navy?" Kincaid had
teased the first time she'd complained about his
choice of crew. "Floyd's rough, but he's a good
man. He never complains and he's always ready
with a joke or a story to keep the men's spirits
up. I'll grant ye, he's no beauty, but then ye can
appreciate my fine looks all the more."

It was true that Floyd was an ugly man, short
and squat, with an oversized nose that had been
broken so many times that it had lost all shape
and sat on his poxed face like a lumpy potato. His
eyes were pale blue and bulging, and he wore his
sparse graying hair in a tarred knot at the back of
his head. But it wasn't his looks that alarmed
Bess; it was her own inner voice.

She'd come in personal contact with Floyd only
once, when his hand had accidentally brushed
hers as he set a bowl of stew on the table in the
captain's cabin. Her immediate reaction had been
a sickening lurch in the pit of her stomach, and
she'd seen a flash of mud-brown in her mind's
eye. Since then she'd watched him, and had tried
without much success to warn Kincaid against
trusting him.

The voyage south to the islands had been uneventful, and Bess had found out why her father
loved the sea. She never tired of standing at the
rail and watching the ocean's changeable moods.
She thrilled to the magnificent sunrises and the
feel of clean salt wind blowing through her hair.
The sight of dolphins swimming beside the *Tanager* and of great whales rising out of the depths

moved her to tears. If she had been a man and not a woman, and if her heart wasn't already pledged to Fortune's Gift and the Tidewater, she knew she would have been content to spend her life on a spray-kissed deck with the promise of adventure waiting just over the horizon.

She and Kincaid had spent many days and nights together, not just sharing the joys of the bedroom, but also talking and laughing. As they'd left the mainland behind them, Kincaid seemed to shed years from his shoulders and become more lighthearted. He'd shown her great passion as well as respect and tenderness.

And despite her disagreement with him over the *Tanager*, Bess found that the coals of her own desire lay waiting to burst into flame at any moment. When they were alone in the privacy of the small cabin, Kincaid couldn't keep his hands off her, and his slightest touch sent her eagerly into his arms. She had given up thinking of the future; she took each day as it came and savored the sweet, wild rapture of his embrace.

Bess had assumed when she came aboard that Kincaid meant to captain the *Scarlet Tanager* himself, but he'd said he knew his own limitations. Evan Davis had served fifteen years at sea on merchant vessels as junior officer, navigator, and finally second-in-command of a hundred-and-fifty-ton brigantine that carried goods from the Caribbean to the North American mainland and back again.

Bess suspected that Davis had had some experience aboard the *Tanager* under suspicious circumstances, but she couldn't prove it; and neither Kincaid nor Evan would give her any further clues

to the Welshman's past and why he was willing
to risk his life and career on this illegal venture.

Kincaid took her hand and led her back to the
cabin. "I don't want to go below," she protested.
"I want to see the harbor. I want to go ashore
and see what's carried in the local shops. I want
to taste fresh sugarcane and have a hot bath in
something besides salt water."

"And so ye shall, ye greedy wench," he teased.
He closed the cabin door behind them and drew
her into his arms. His mouth was warm and
tender against hers, and she sighed with pleasure. He made her feel loved and secure, safer
than she'd felt in many years.

"I want to eat a meal that Floyd hasn't handled
with his dirty hands," she said.

"His hands aren't dirty," Kincaid said. "At
least not for a sea cook. When I sailed aboard the
Revenge, the cook . . ." He trailed off and grinned.
"Never mind, ye'd nay appreciate the tale."

"You never mentioned a ship named *Revenge*,"
she said. "When did you—"

"Shhh." He put a lean finger over her lips.
"'Tis past, lass, past and best forgotten. I've
done much that belongs to another time and
place." He smiled at her with a hint of mischief,
a smile that made her heart lurch. "I need that
bag around your neck, Bess. 'Tis time ye parted
with that little gold cat and your other valuables.
I ken how much they mean to ye, but the hands
must be paid if we dinna wish a mutiny."

"You said it wouldn't be safe to try and sell the
jaguar in Carolina. Why here?"

"Floyd says—"

"Floyd again!" Bess pulled away from Kincaid.

"Why must it always be Floyd? I don't trust him. There's something—"

"Floyd says that he knows a man to see on this island if ye have fine goods to sell. And I've heard enough about him to—"

"Floyd is not to be trusted, I tell you," she said. "And who will he guide you to? Some crusty old pirate?"

"A businessman, Bess. A shrewd merchant who trades in rum and slaves, and in anything that brings a profit. He uses the name Falconer, but keeps his real identity a secret. Some say the Caribbean is Falconer's own duck pond. I know for a fact that he deals with the Portuguese down in Brazil, and he's reputed to have Spanish—"

"I've listened to my father talk ships and shipping all my life. I've never heard of this *Falconer.*"

"He's not the sort of man your respectable family would know. This Falconer is too canny to allow his connections to be bandied about indiscriminately through the colonies."

"But you say you know of him."

"Aye." Kincaid grinned. "But then, I've never been accused of being respectable, have I? I keep rough company, Bess. It's natural that I'd hear things a tobacco planter wouldn't."

"If Falconer breaks the law, why hasn't he been arrested?" she demanded.

"He's an extremely private man, almost a hermit. They say he lives like a king and keeps his own private army—he's supposed to be wealthy beyond belief. I'm certain he has ties to government officials. There's even a rumor that Falconer might be the royal governor himself."

"You say he deals in the slave trade?"

"Aye. 'Tis a dirty business, I'll give ye that. Ye can smell most slave ships half a league away on the open sea. They pack men and women into cramped, dark holds like kegs of salt pork. But not on Falconer's ships. He pampers his blacka-moors, they say. He deals in only the healthiest slaves and he provides fresh water, good food, and exercise on deck every day regardless of the weather. His vessels transport only half the num-ber other merchants do, but most of those they bring back survive, and he takes the cost of his losses from his masters' pay."

A shiver ran down Bess's spine. "Only an an-imal would profit from the misery of other hu-mans," she said. "I hate slavery, and I hate slavers."

"If there were more like ye in the world, sweet Bess, and less like Falconer . . ." Kincaid shook his head. "Well, we must deal with him if we're to have what we need."

"Why? Why must we?"

"You're an innocent, Bess. When you're in strange waters, ye deal with the biggest shark in the harbor. If we find the treasure, ye can salve your conscience by buying a few more slaves and setting them free."

"You think I'm a fool," she said softly.

"Nay, lass, I never said that. But ye canna change a way of life single-handedly. There has been slavery from China to Africa since the time of our Lord. Ye canna change men's greed."

"Is it right that good men like Rudy should be beasts of burden, whipped like—"

"I was a slave," Kincaid cut in. "I was

whipped, and we both ken who wielded the lash.''

"Not because you were a bond servant," she flung back angrily. "I whipped you for stealing my horse . . . and to keep you from being hanged."

"Aye," he said bitterly. "I'll keep that in mind when my back aches on a cold winter morn." He held out his hand. "I'll have the gold, mistress, if ye please."

Tears welled up in her eyes. "Kincaid . . . I'm sorry. I'm sorry I hurt you."

Fierce brown eyes met hers. "But ye'd do it again."

She was shocked at the intensity of his bitterness. "Not—not now," she stammered. "Not—"

"Under the same circumstances," he insisted. "If ye had it to do again, ye would, wouldn't ye?"

Bess's mouth went dry. "Yes."

"Then ye've no right to question me when I do what needs doing."

With trembling hands she untied the cord at her neck and handed over the bag containing the golden jaguar and the rest of her money and jewelry. "Kincaid . . ." His features were hard; the brown eyes that gazed back at her seemed those of a stranger, not of the man she'd made love to in this cabin only a few hours ago.

"Wait for me here," he commanded. "I'll come back for ye when I've finished my business with Falconer."

"Kincaid, I didn't mean to—"

"We'll talk later," he said gruffly.

"Can't I come with you?"

"Why? Do ye still think I'll cheat ye out of what's yours?"

"You know better than that," she said.

He threw her an angry glare. "We are like flint and steel, woman. We canna be together for long without making sparks. 'Tis nay your fault, nor mine." He grimaced. "If we'd met five years ago, perhaps things might have worked out differently, but I am too old to change my ways—and I suspect ye are the same."

She stared after him as he left the cabin, wondering why they had argued. For weeks they had not exchanged a cross word, and now Kincaid had gone off like a Chinese rocket. "Men," she muttered. "They are the most perverse animals God ever created."

Three hours later, the man known as Falconer balanced Bess's golden jaguar in the palm of his soft white hand. "Exquisite," he murmured, turning the piece carefully. "As fine as I've seen." He smiled at Kincaid disarmingly. "Where did you say you came by this?"

"I didn't," Kincaid replied.

The older man lifted a magnifying glass to his eye and inspected the detail of the figure. "Perhaps you will enlighten me as to how you came to be aboard the *Scarlet Tanager*. It is my understanding that Captain Kennedy has had some difficulty in Charles Town."

"Ye might say that." Falconer's intelligence was good, Kincaid thought; better than good, it was uncanny. When he'd left Charles Town, Kennedy and his crew were counting the hours until their hanging. The *Scarlet Tanager* had never carried her own name on her hull. Kennedy had wisely used dozens of ships' names, painting one overtop the other in bold gold lettering. When Kincaid had seized the *Tanager*, the name on her side had been *Charlotte* and he'd had the men paint over that, leaving the boat nameless. Only a man familiar with Kennedy and his practices would have recognized the schooner.

Falconer reluctantly added the jaguar to the other objects on top of a wooden barrel and gave Kincaid his full attention. "A pity about Kennedy," he said. "Damned luck to go aground as he did."

"Aye," Kincaid agreed. He wondered if Falconer's interest in Kennedy and the *Tanager* was more than curiosity.

"The jaguar is Peruvian. Did you know that?" Falconer asked. "Quite possibly came across Panama on a Spanish mule train. Incan grave goods, I should imagine. But the piece is beautifully preserved."

"And the other jewelry?"

"Genuine, all of it." He mentioned a figure much higher than Kincaid had expected, an amount that would more than cover their immediate expenses.

Kincaid shook his head. "I see I've come to the wrong man," he said softly. He reached for the goods.

Falconer lifted a hand, palm up. "You can't expect London prices, you know," he said. "There are risks involved."

"I thought ye were serious," Kincaid said. "I have a buyer in Barbados who will—"

"John Nicholls?" Falconer scoffed. "He'll pay

half what I offered and then turn you in to the authorities for pirating. Take my silver, Scot. I'm not an amateur. And if you come into possession of anything similar, we can always do business again."

"It's a long way to Barbados."

"Indeed it is."

"Give me a better reason to sell to you and not . . ." Kincaid met Falconer's eyes and smiled. "Not someone else," he finished.

"I'm afraid you don't understand," Falconer said quietly. "My offer stands. I'm not a horse trader. If you wish to sell your merchandise for a fair profit, you will accept my proposition. If not, we have nothing more to say to each other, today or . . ." He opened a silver snuff box and put a pinch in each nostril, then covered his nose with an Irish lace handkerchief and gave a genteel sneeze. "Or ever."

Kincaid nodded. "I believe we have a deal."

Falconer smiled condescendingly. "I thought we might." The elegantly attired gentleman extended his beringed hand to shake on the deal; Kincaid clasped the warm fingers and was surprised at how much strength the older man possessed. "You need not fear for your safety in Jamaica," Falconer assured him. "I keep my bargains, and I never wrong my friends."

"An admirable policy," Kincaid agreed as Falconer counted out the silver coins that completed their business.

"Will you be staying with us long?"

"Nay."

Falconer wiped a drop of perspiration from the corner of his mouth. "Wise. There are others here who will know the *Scarlet Tanager*, friends of Ken-

nedy,'' he said pointedly. ''And they may not realize that you came by her honestly.''

Kincaid left the boarded-up tavern as he had come
in, by a back way, through an alley and then a baker's shop. It was the flour-dusted baker's wife who
had arranged the meeting with Falconer. Floyd had
suggested that he take Kincaid to him, but Kincaid
had made certain Floyd remained on the *Tanager*.
He'd given explicit orders to Evan Davis that no one
leave the ship in his absence.

Kincaid had been certain he could find Falconer
himself, and he'd been right. He'd gone into a
wharfside inn and asked the wench pouring ale.
She'd sent a lad to ask someone for permission
to answer Kincaid's question. In half an hour, a
grizzled seaman had come in and seated himself
at Kincaid's table, asking the Scot to buy him a
mug of rum. After they'd shared a few drinks and
mentioned a few mutual acquaintances, the old
salt had advised Kincaid to go to the bakery and
ask the baker's wife for a mincemeat pie. The
goodwife had provided the time and location of
the rendezvous with Falconer.

On his way back to the ship, Kincaid noted that
the baker's wife was of a size and shape of Bess.
He asked her if she had a decent lightweight
gown and petticoats that she would be willing to
sell. His sister, he explained with a sly wink, had
nothing suitable to wear. The baker's wife nodded and in ten minutes' time, he was out of the
shop with a bundle of women's garments and she
was pocketing a silver English crown.

Kincaid regretted the hard words he'd thrown
at Bess, and since apologies never came easy to
him, he hoped the blue linen dress would help to

ease the sting. He was hardly conscious of the amused glances passersby were giving him as he walked down to the dock.

He'd promised Bess and the crew time ashore, but he'd feel better once they were out of Kingston Harbor and on the open sea. Falconer's promises of friendship rang false, and despite his arguments to the contrary, Bess's doubts about Floyd were beginning to make an impression.

Deep in thought, Kincaid almost missed the black man in green livery who was trailing him at a discreet distance. Deliberately, Kincaid stopped to look idly into a shop window, and saw in the reflection of the glass that the suspicious servant had stopped as well. Falconer, Kincaid thought, and his lips tightened into a thin line. Certain that it was the merchant and not the authorities who had ordered him to be watched, Kincaid continued toward the end of the dock. He put his forefinger in his mouth and lifted it, gauging the wind, and wondered just how peeved Bess would be when he ordered Davis to weigh anchor and sail out of Kingston immediately. Not half as upset as Falconer would be, he guessed. He smiled. Then again, he mused, when a man came between a woman and her shopping . . . His smile widened. Bess might be even more angry than Falconer.

Falconer struck Floyd Hartly a blow that sent him staggering back against the wall. "You knew Elizabeth Bennett was aboard the *Scarlet Tanager* and you didn't tell me in time to keep them from sailing?" He whirled on a burly mulatto standing stiffly with a musket in his hands, yanked a pistol from the guard's waist, and aimed it at Floyd's head.

"You maggot-ridden bastard. I ought to blow your brains all over that wall," he threatened.

Floyd's face was ashen except for the rising red imprint of Falconer's ring. "For God's sake, don't shoot!" he cried. "My brother didn't know it was her for sure. He just thought it might be the woman you was lookin' for, her travelin' with a Scot and speakin' all fancy-like."

"They sailed out of the harbor an hour ago," Falconer said, advancing on Floyd with the flint-lock pistol. He cocked the weapon. "You sailed with him from Carolina to tell me they were in my waters and then you let them get away?"

Annemie watched from the doorway, certain that this excitement would be too much for Peregrine. She had known there would be trouble from the moment he'd come home with that golden cat. He'd put it on the table and sent her to fetch the box containing his most valuable possessions.

The jaguar stood there now, along with three other similar golden figures: a beautiful bird, a glittering llama, and a tiny Indian paddling a reed boat. Each piece was a work of art, precise to the smallest detail. The boat was so perfect that Annemie could count the individual bundles of reeds and make out the tattooing design on the paddler's face. The golden cat had turquoise eyes, and the llama and the bird were made in the same manner. A blind woman could have touched them and realized they were created by the same artist.

Gooseflesh stood up on the back of Annemie's neck, and she felt a sense of impending doom. She was afraid—not for herself, but for Peregrine Kay.

Her employer had long since given up hiding his Falconer activities from her, so she knew she was in no danger when she entered the parlor. "Sir," she soothed. "You don't want to shoot him. Not here, at least. You might spoil the floors."

"You invade my private home," Kay accused Floyd. "You come here when I have given orders that no business will be done from my house. You come here and tell me you've been waiting on the deck of the *Tanager* while I was—" He broke off, too furious to continue.

"I couldn't get off the ship," Floyd protested. "The Scot was suspicious of me. He left orders with the captain that anyone leaving without permission would be shot. He calls himself Robert Munro, but the woman calls him Kincaid." He stood up slowly and backed up until he felt the wall behind him. "My brother heard that you wanted the woman, and he thought this might be her." He glanced up at the painting on the wall. "That's her fer certain, sir. She's on the boat. I swear it."

Annemie laid a hand on Kay's arm. "Whatever the problem is, sir," she said, "I'm sure you'll find a way to remedy it. This gentleman meant no harm. After all, he did come from the mainland to bring you news."

Peregrine Kay lowered the pistol and thrust it into Annemie's hands. Then he advanced on Floyd and seized him by the front of his shirt. "You say the woman in the painting is on the *Tanager*?"

"On my soul, sir," the cook gasped.

Annemie's chest tightened and the hairs on her arms prickled. Lord, save us from the witch's spell, she prayed silently. "It can't be so, sir," she murmured. "She's long dead, sir. Long dead and in her grave."

"No," Floyd insisted. "She's as alive as you are.

I seed her not two hours ago. It's her, all right. Not many ladies with red hair and blue eyes.''

''Blue eyes?'' Kay said. ''Blue?''

''Yes, sir.''

''You see, sir,'' Annemie said, ''it can't be her.'' She pointed at the woman in the painting. ''Her eyes are brown. They can't be the same person.'' She chuckled. ''If that one—'' She glanced at the painting again. ''If that one was alive, she'd have to be close to eighty. Her hair would be snow-white.''

''Do you take me for a madman?'' Peregrine Kay asked, turning on Annemie. ''I know Lacy Bennett is dead. This is her granddaughter, Elizabeth.''

''Yes, sir,'' Floyd insisted. ''That's her. I heard Kincaid calling her Bess.''

''Where are they bound for?'' Peregrine asked.

Floyd cleared his throat. ''Panama, sir.''

''Why?''

''I don't know. Nobody does but Kincaid, and maybe the woman.''

''If they're here in the Caribbean, they won't get away,'' Annemie said. ''You'll have them, sir. You know you will.''

''Yes.'' Peregrine smiled a cold smile. ''Yes. At last. I will have her.'' He motioned to the mulatto. ''Take Hartly to the kitchen and see that he's given supper.''

''I'm not hungry,'' Floyd said. ''But I should have something for my time. I came all this way.''

''Of course you did. And we've treated you badly.'' He released Floyd's shirt and waved his hand toward the table. ''Take those in payment. They're solid gold.''

Floyd hesitated.

''Go on, man,'' Peregrine said. ''They're yours.''

Floyd rushed toward the table and Peregrine nodded to the mulatto. The guard crossed the room in one fluid motion and drove a knife into the cook's back. Annemie covered her face and turned away as Floyd screamed once and struggled weakly before sinking onto the table, hands outstretched toward the golden figurines.

Peregrine motioned to the mulatto to remove Floyd's still twitching body. "Hurry, before he bleeds on the rug," he ordered.

Annemie felt sick. She closed her eyes and took deep breaths, trying to find some excuse for her employer's behavior.

"I'm sorry you had to see that," Peregrine said, picking up the jaguar and holding it up to the candlelight. "Regrettable. But he did come to my home. We can't have anyone linking Falconer to the son of a royal governor, can we? Very untidy. Whoever sent him to the house will have to be disposed of as well."

"You know how I hate this sort of thing," she said. It was as strong a criticism as she permitted herself to make of Peregrine's business affairs.

"You have my deepest apologies, Annemie. It will never happen again, I assure you." He smiled at her. "The jaguar belongs with the others, don't you think?"

"Yes, sir, it does."

"It belongs to me . . . just like Elizabeth Bennett." He turned and gazed at the painting. "And I'll have what's mine," he swore softly, "if I have to storm the gates of Hell to take her."

Chapter 17

On the third day out of Kingston Harbor, Kincaid spotted the square sails of a brigantine on the horizon, and shortly after, he saw that another ship, a single-masted sloop, followed closely in her wake. As he ran up the ladder to the quarterdeck, he noted that Evan Davis was watching the two ships through his spyglass.

"Company, I see," Kincaid said.

Evan grinned. "Nothing to worry about. Likely they're merchant ships."

Kincaid held out his hand for the glass. The two ships were too far away to be identified, but he decided that they were probably English because of the lines and the way they were rigged.

The *Scarlet Tanager* was a schooner; her fore-and-aft sails and narrow hull gave her the advantage of speed and maneuverability that larger craft lacked. She could navigate in less than six feet of water, an attribute that Kincaid knew would come in handy when he tried to land in some nameless waterway along the Panama coast.

The brigantine and the sloop were obviously traveling together, perhaps for protection against pirates. Otherwise, the much faster sloop would have left the heavier two-masted ship behind.

"The Spanish are the ones we need to keep a

sharp eye for, Mr. Munro," Evan said as Bess joined them on the quarterdeck.

"May I see?" she asked. Kincaid, alias Robert Munro to Evan and the crew of the *Tanager*, passed the spyglass to her and she gazed through it.

"A brigantine and a sloop," Kincaid said. "Traveling together for some reason, and following the same course we are."

"Not necessarily," Evan said. "This is a crossroads for shipping. Lots of—"

"I count three masts," Bess said.

"You're wrong, miss," Evan told her. "The lead ship is a brigantine. Two masts."

Bess handed the glass back to Kincaid. "I may not know the sea, Captain," she said, "but I can count."

Kincaid looked and swore softly. "Aye, I see it too," he said. "Not two ships, but three. The sloop, the brigantine, and a larger vessel." He turned a steel-edged gaze on the Welshman. "Lift her skirts, Evan. I'd leave this company behind."

Evan shrugged. "Whatever you say, but I'm certain they're just harmless—"

"Full sail. We've enough wind for ten knots," Kincaid said, "and I want to see it." He handed the glass back to Bess and turned toward the ladder. "I want the men at their stations and cannon and swivel guns ready to be fired."

Bess hurried after him, then remembered Evan's glass. "Oh," she said. "Here is your—" As she gave him the instrument, their fingers brushed. Bess froze.

"Come along, woman," Kincaid said, glancing back at her. She was wearing the baker's wife's blue linen gown this morning. The dress was worn, the material thin in spots, but the blue matched Bess's eyes and the modest scooped neckline gave him a pretty view of the top of her rosy breasts.

Annoyed with himself for letting his thoughts wander to Bess and her obvious attractions, he spoke again, sharply. "Bess."

She murmured something and followed him down the ladder. When they were amidships, she caught his arm. "Kincaid." Her voice was huskier than normal, and her eyes showed concern.

"There's no need for ye to become alarmed yet," he said. "I'll take no chances that—"

"Kincaid, I've got to talk to you," she said. "Now."

"It can wait." His thoughts were already racing ahead to gauge which of his men would be useful in a fight. Floyd Hartly's desertion in Jamaica had disappointed him badly. Bess had said Floyd couldn't be trusted, and he hated to admit she had been right. By the time he'd gotten back to the *Tanager*, Floyd was gone. Evan Davis had said that the cook must have slipped over the side of the ship and swum to shore. Lots of sailors deserted their ships, but very few did so just before getting paid. Why Floyd had done so still troubled Kincaid's sleep.

"No," Bess insisted. "It can't wait."

"What is it?" he asked impatiently.

"Not here," she said. "Below, in our cabin."

Reluctantly, he followed her belowdecks to the captain's quarters, which they shared. Bess looked around the empty cabin, then motioned him to close the door. "It's Evan," she said. "We can't trust him."

Kincaid felt a headache coming on. "We've no time for woman's fancies, Bess. Aye, ye were right about Floyd, I'll give ye that, but Evan . . ." He shook his head. "Evan's loyal."

"He's not," she insisted.

"You're the one who's been singing his praises all the way from Charles Town. What's changed your mind this morning?"

"He touched me."

A red wave of anger rose in Kincaid's brain. "Touched ye? How? When? I'll throttle him with my bare—"

"No, it's not like that," she said, her words tumbling over one another in a rush. "I'm a witch. I read people's hearts by touch. Evan's planning on killing you. I know it."

He stared at her as though she had taken leave of her senses. "Ye be a witch? Likely ye fly about the ship at night on your broom."

"Damn you!" she cried. "You've got to believe me. I knew you wouldn't hurt me. It's why I ran off with you. I knew Floyd would betray us, and now I know Evan wants you dead. I saw red when he touched me. Don't you see? Red for blood—your blood!"

At that instant knuckles pounded against the cabin door. "Mr. Munro, Master Davis wants you on the quarterdeck at once." Kincaid recognized the voice as belonging to a sailor named Albright, a close friend of Floyd Hartly. Motioning Bess to a spot between the door and the bunk, he swung open the cabin door.

"Captain wants ye—" Albright began.

He raised his right hand and Kincaid caught the gleam of a pistol barrel in the sailor's hand. Directly behind the sailor was a bearded man in a striped shirt. Kincaid lunged sideways and delivered a bone-breaking blow to Albright's knee. As the mutineer cried out in pain and fell forward, Kincaid drove the knife edge of his hand against the side of Albright's neck.

The second sailor swung a cutlass at the spot where Kincaid had been standing only a heartbeat before. He charged into the cabin and stumbled over Albright's body. Kincaid hit the man with all his weight and the two of them slammed against the doorjamb. Kincaid's right hand closed over the hilt of the cutlass as the base of his left hand struck his assassin's nose, smashing it and killing him instantly. As Kincaid leaped up, cutlass poised to defend against another attacker, he found that he and Bess were the only ones still breathing in the cabin.

Bess's face was the color of whey, but she held Albright's pistol in her hand. "I would have shot him for you if you'd waited a moment," she said. Her hand was steady on the weapon, but her voice was trembling.

"We'll be all right, lass," he said with more conviction than he thought. The killing fever was passing easier than it usually did, but he didn't trust himself to lay hands on her yet.

"How many are against us?" she asked.

He shrugged, keeping his eyes on the shadowy passageway. "You're the witch, not me."

"Yes, I am. But I don't know what to do now."

He glanced back at her. She lowered the flintlock, but kept her finger on the trigger. Kincaid could see that her bosom was heaving, her breath coming in ragged gasps as though she'd been running. She looked small and frightened.

"I'll keep ye safe, Bess," he promised thickly.

She glanced down at the sprawled bodies. "You killed them with your bare hands," she whispered.

"Aye." He could feel his blood cooling, the battle frenzy draining away, leaving him with an intense desire to protect this woman at any cost.

"If we had Evan, could we force the others to do what we want?"

"Maybe." Kincaid shook his head to clear away the last of the single-mindedness that took over his brain when he was faced with imminent violence. "Can ye play a part, Bess? Evan sent them down to kill me, but he doesn't know yet if they succeeded. Go to the passageway ladder and scream for him. If he comes, we'll take him."

Bess nodded. She waited, not speaking as he dragged Albright and the second sailor out of sight of the door; then she wiped up the few drops of blood with a blanket. "So he doesn't see it," she said, handing him the pistol.

"Ready?" he asked. He stood behind the partially closed door as she went to the bottom of the steps and let out a terrified scream. "Evan! Evan!" she cried. "Oh, my God, Evan! Help me!"

The first man down the ladder was the bosun. Kincaid barely had time to hit him over the head with the barrel of the pistol and move him out of the way before Evan came running.

"What is it?" he called to Bess. "What's happened?"

"They've killed him!" she shrieked hysterically. "They've killed him!" She pointed at the open cabin door. Evan Davis ran in, and Kincaid grabbed him from behind and put a knife at his throat. Bess stepped into the cabin and closed the door and locked it.

"What is this?" Evan said.

Kincaid put just enough pressure on the knife to strain the captain's skin without breaking it. "Who do ye work for, Evan?" he demanded softly. "If ye answer wrong, I'll show ye less pity than I did them." He glanced down at the two dead men at Evan's feet.

The third man, the one Kincaid had only knocked out, was stirring groggily. Bess knelt by his side and held the cutlass over him. "I'd lie there, if I were you," she warned. He moaned and sank back to the floor, eyes wide with fear.

"Myself," Evan said. "I work for myself."

"Wrong answer," Kincaid replied, digging the blade in a little deeper. A single drop of blood ran down Evan's neck.

"Falconer wants the lady," Evan croaked. Kincaid eased the pressure and the captain went on. "He's put out a reward for her, dead or alive."

"Why?" Bess demanded. "I don't know him. Why would he want me?"

"I don't know," Evan said. "I swear I don't. He's offered silver in every port from the Bahamas to Boston."

"And you were going to oblige him," Kincaid said softly.

"I was going to have you killed," Evan said, "but I was going to turn her over to Falconer."

"Those ships following us?" Kincaid prompted.

"Falconer's. The brigantine is the *Charlotte Rose*. I don't know the names of the other two, but they're his."

"Can we outrun them?" Bess asked.

"With me at the wheel, you can," Evan dared to reply.

Kincaid pulled his head back farther. "Give me another reason why I shouldn't cut your throat here and now," he said.

"Because . . ." Evan swallowed hard. "Because I'm the only one who can get you to Panama."

"Why should we trust you?" Bess asked.

"Evan is a practical man, aren't ye?" Kincaid said. "This wasn't personal, it was business, wasn't it?" Evan's frightened face whitened to the color of tallow. "What did ye want, Evan? Not just money. Ye wanted the *Tanager*, didn't ye?"

"Yes."

"Ye can have it if ye lose Falconer's ships and take us to Panama and home to Maryland," Kincaid said. "That, and a share of the Spanish treasure we're going to dig up."

"What?" Bess cried. "You're not giving him a share of my—"

"Aye." Kincaid said. "Him and every hand on this ship. There's enough gold to make every man a king." He looked down at the man Bess was holding prisoner. "Silver and precious jewels," he continued. "A fortune . . . gold rings and nose plates, necklaces, crowns, and strings of pearls."

"Pearls?" Bess said. "There's no—"

"No end to the riches," Kincaid said. "We're going for Henry Morgan's treasure that he stole from Panama City and buried in the jungle. Bess

has a map, left to her by her grandfather who
served under Morgan. We know where the gold's
hidden. With the right crew, we'll be in and out
before the Spanish know we've set foot on the
coast.''

"God's truth?" Evan said. "You have such a
map?"

"Why else would a man like Falconer go to such
lengths to capture a lady he's never laid eyes on?"
Kincaid lied smoothly. "Falconer knows about the
treasure, but he doesn't know where it is." He
released the captain. "Well, Evan, do ye still want
to turn Bess over to Falconer?"

"I'm not sharing the gold with him and his
crew of pirates," Bess protested hotly.

"I'm your man," the Welshman said. "Let me
return to the wheel and we'll leave Falconer's
ships behind so fast that they'll think we vanished."

"No," Bess said. "You're both out of your
minds. I'm not going to—"

"Woman, cease your clatter," Kincaid said
roughly. "Pay no attention to her, Evan. She'll
do as I tell her."

Bess's blue eyes flashed angrily. "Oh, I will,
will I, you bloated bag of haggis!"

Bess was still protesting weeks later when the
Scarlet Tanager anchored in the shelter of the San
Blas Islands off the mainland of Panama. "Was it
necessary to promise a share of the treasure to
every living soul south of Charles Town?" she
demanded of Kincaid as they sat in a longboat
being rowed toward shore.

"Aye, and I'll promise part to the devil if need be," he replied.

Evan Davis was in the boat with them, along with eight members of the crew. Kincaid had left Rudy in charge of the *Scarlet Tanager*, because he was the only man they could trust in their absence.

It had rained earlier that morning; now the air was thick with a heavy, hot mist. Bess felt as though she was standing in the heat of the washhouse at home with steam rising off the boiling kettles of soapy water. It was so warm that the perspiration on her face and arms didn't evaporate; it just gathered into trickles and rolled down her body, soaking her thin linen shirt and breeches as thoroughly as if she had put them on still wet from laundering.

Her attention was riveted on the swaying coconut palms and the thick wall of trees, shrubs, and interlaced vines that ran down to the island shore. The air was so filled with the earthy scents of decaying plants and wood that it was difficult for her to breathe.

For months Bess had thought of nothing but this journey into the jungle, and now that she was here, it still seemed a dream. Nothing she had ever known had prepared her for the multicolored birds calling and flitting through the hundred shades of green. This tropical forest reverberated with unfamiliar cries, snaps, rustles, and howls. Monkeys peered from the treetops and soared from branch to branch, chattering and squawking. Insects buzzed around her head and swarmed over every inch of bare skin, crawling and biting; and somewhere in the dripping verdant mass she could hear the loud, piercing *de-de-de-de* of a cicada.

Kincaid pointed to the nearest bank where a huge moss-backed turtle reared his ancient head to stare at them. "Keep your hands away from the water," he warned.

Bess didn't need to be told. Not five feet from the longboat, the snout and glassy eyes of a bumpy-backed alligator bobbed just above the surface of the dark green water. As she watched, an unfamiliar diving bird plunged into the river and came up with a fish. Before the creature could rise with its prey, the alligator's hideous jaws gaped open, closed around the bird, and dragged it under.

The crewmen muttered among themselves and one man crossed himself. "You needn't be afraid," Evan said. "When we go into the jungle, we'll take Cuna guides. They know this country like you know the pimples on your own backside."

Bess glanced back at the young captain. He'd given them no reason to doubt him since the day the *Tanager* had been followed by Falconer's three ships. Once Kincaid had allowed him to take control of the vessel again, Evan had directed the men to raise every sail, and they had lost sight of the trailing ships within an hour.

Now Evan had brought them to a village of Cuna Indians, people whom he knew and had had experience dealing with. "The Cuna have good reason to hate the Spanish," he'd said. "They murder the men, feed their infants to their hounds, and rape and enslave their women and children. But the brotherhood has always had a working relationship with these people. I once spent a month in this village during the dry season.''

This, Evan had explained, was the rainy season. They could expect downpours daily. Their clothes, shoes, and supplies would rot; their pistols and muskets would rust within days. They could travel inland by boat, something that was impossible in the dry season, but the constant rain made survival difficult. ''Without the Cuna, we wouldn't last a week in the jungle. There are trees that give off deadly poison to the touch, snakes and scorpions and blood-sucking bats, crocodiles and jaguars, and colonies of flesh-eating ants. Swamps and thorny thickets bar the way, some so thick and impenetrable that the jungle floor is as dark as night. The slightest scratch can fester into a mortal wound, and a white man can go for days without finding anything to eat. I've seen strong men lose their wits and devour human flesh.''

Bess hoped the Cuna Indians were as peaceful as Evan said. Two dugout canoes sliced through the water ahead of the longboat. Naked but for odd cones of bark and leaves covering their genitals, the husky, dark-skinned warriors with waist-length, flowing black hair manned the paddles of the native crafts.

When Bess had climbed down the ladder from the *Tanager* to the longboat, the Indians had stared at her with round black eyes, and she had stared back, unable to contain her curiosity. Every Cuna male, young and old, seemed cut from the same bolt of cloth: their sleek bodies were oiled and their wide, thin lips were nearly covered by silver, saucer-sized plates that dangled from their identical, rounded noses.

The Cuna had not seemed hostile. They laughed and called to Evan as though he was an old friend, but Bess didn't miss the razor-sharp steel machetes they carried, or the short bows and bundles of arrows resting in the bottoms of the dugouts.

The river narrowed and turned to the left. Ahead, in a clearing, Bess saw dozens of Indian women and children standing on the bank, waving and chattering in their native tongue. The females were as striking as the males—round-faced, pleasant-featured, and completely innocent of their near-naked condition. The small boys and girls wore nothing but flashing smiles; mature women had only a twist of leafy vine across their loins. Babies bounced in woven slings around their mothers' necks, and toddlers clung to their bare ankles.

Other dugouts were drawn up on the shore, and beyond that, on a small rise, stood the village. Most of the huts seemed like leaf-covered porches without walls to Bess. But she could see one huge building stretching windowless nearly the length of the town, taller and broader than any other, with sides of stout poles and woven vines. Smoke came from a hole in the roof of the longhouse, as it did from most of the other dwellings, and through the doorway she saw woven hammocks hanging from the framework.

A piglike animal nearly as big as a heifer sizzled on a spit over glowing coals under one roofed area. An old woman with a monkey on her shoulder turned the roasting meat and kept a pack of

skinny dogs at bay with a palm frond. As the first
canoe grated against the shore, the curs abandoned the pursuit of dinner and rushed down in
a frenzy of barking to greet the men.

As the second boat touched, the crowd parted
to make way for a tall, dignified man of obvious
importance. His thinning gray hair framed a lined,
round face adorned with a glittering gold nose
plate. His broad chest boasted an ivory cross, and
beneath that, his codpiece was a thin, beaten cone
of silver suspended from his waist by a length of
silver chain.

"That's Pablo, the village chief," Evan whispered. "He's very influential, related by blood to
all the other major Cuna tribes."

"Pablo?" Bess questioned. "But that's Spanish. I thought you said the Cuna hated the
Spaniards."

The captain shrugged. "They do, but all the important men in the villages have taken Spanish
names. Actually, it's rare for anyone to tell you
their native name. They're very superstitious.
They think if you know their name, it gives you
power over them."

"How will you talk to them?" she asked. "Do
you speak Cuna?"

"No," Evan answered. "But Pablo knows
enough English and Dutch for us to get by. He's
been trading with buccaneers for years."

"That's why we brought cane knives and trade
goods from Charles Town," Kincaid said. "We'll
smoke a few cigars, hand out gifts all around, and
see if we can't convince some of the Cuna to guide
us to the treasure site."

"And what about the Spanish?" Bess asked. "I know we're not far from Porto Bello."

"If they find us, they'll shoot us on sight," Evan said. "But the Cuna know something about avoiding the Spanish. With their help, we should be all right."

"Stay close to me," Kincaid cautioned Bess. "Don't speak until you're spoken to, and eat anything they offer ye—snake, alligator, bugs, or dog. If you insult their hospitality, they'll turn their backs on us."

"The women are subservient to the men," Evan added. "They won't expect you to do anything but smile and do what Munro tells you."

"Wonderful," Bess said.

Kincaid grinned at her. " 'Tis a practice we could well adopt in the Maryland Colony. The women there have forgotten their place."

Bess shot him a withering glance.

Then the bow of the longboat struck solid ground, and Kincaid stepped out into ankle-deep water. Evan followed close behind, open hands outstretched so that the Cuna chief could see they came in peace. Bess climbed over the side and waded ashore as women and children surrounded her, picking at her hair and clothes and chattering like birds in their soft, lisping speech. They rubbed her arms and face, crying excitedly to each other and making obvious jokes about her appearance.

A stout woman thrust a coconut into Bess's hands and motioned for her to drink. Tentatively, she raised it to her lips and sipped the sweet liquid, then smiled and nodded her thanks. That action brought a round of approving twitters, and the women began touching and patting her all over again.

Kincaid paused in greeting the chief and glanced back at her. "Come here, Bess," he said. The Cuna women scattered like leaves, leaving a pathway open. Gratefully, Bess hurried to his side.

Without smiling, Kincaid motioned to a place behind him and she didn't argue. She stood there woodenly, trying to look harmless as dozens more Cuna men filed silently out of the forest carrying bows and machetes.

After many exchanged compliments and elaborate greetings, Kincaid nodded to Evan, and he ordered the sailors to bring the bundles of gifts from the longboat. Kincaid stood proudly as rolls of red and blue linen were spread out, and the knives, machetes, needles, scissors, tobacco, hand mirrors, and hawkbells were arranged on top.

"These poor things I give to you and your people, Pablo," Kincaid said.

Bess noticed the gleam of anticipation in the dark Cuna eyes, but no one made a run for the presents. Each man waited his turn until an elder called him forward to choose something from the gifts. The chief took nothing for himself. When the last length of cloth had been handed out, Kincaid turned to Pablo and removed the gold earring from his own ear and gave it to the Indian.

A slow smile spread across the older man's face, and he clasped Kincaid by the shoulders and embraced him, rubbing his nose against the Scot's cheek vigorously. "You give Pablo honor," he rasped.

"No," Kincaid said. "It is the great Cuna chief, Pablo, who honors me."

A general cheer went up and the old woman at the spit began to slice off hunks of the roast meat. The men, including Kincaid, Evan, and the sailors, squatted down in a large circle. Kincaid's warning glance told Bess not to attempt to join them, so she retreated to the shelter of the porch where the pig had been cooked.

The Cuna women and girls ran to fetch baskets of smoked fish, coconut, bananalike fruit, nuts, berries, pineapples, avocados, and squash to pass out to the men. They served the meat on palm leaves woven into crude plates. One woman carried a huge wooden bowl full of gray liquid on her shoulder. She lowered the drink to the damp earth and offered the chief a clamshell brimming over. He waved to Kincaid, and the woman giggled and extended the offering to him. Kincaid motioned back to the chief, bringing another round of pleased murmurs from the gathered warriors.

Pablo took the shell this time and drank with loud sips. Next Kincaid and then Evan were served, before the woman took refreshment to every man in the circle.

Suddenly, it began to rain again. With much confusion and shouting, the men rose and dashed toward the longhouse. When Bess rose to follow, a woman stepped in front of her and took hold of her arm. She said something that sounded like "Noh-noh." She pointed toward the ground. When Bess sat down again, the woman smiled and handed her a plate heaped high with fruit and meat. To Bess's great relief, none of the women seemed to be drinking the gray liquid. However, all of them were entranced by the strange white woman. They gathered around her again, urging the children to touch her, pointing at Bess's hair and laughing behind their hands.

Hours passed. Laughter and talk floated through the arrow slits and smoke hole of the longhouse. Night fell, and hearth fires glowed in the sudden darkness. The mosquitoes made Bess miserable until a young woman shyly appeared at her shoulder and offered her a handful of paste. When Bess raised it to her lips, the woman giggled and shook her head, making motions to rub the stuff on her skin instead of eating it. Bess did as she was told and found immediate relief from the biting insects.

Finally, one by one, the women and children drifted away. The sleepy whines of children and the wail of babies faded, and the eerie jungle sounds reigned once more. Deep coughs, screeches, and an occasional roar made the hairs on Bess's neck rise, but she remained where she was and waited for Kincaid.

She had nearly drifted off to sleep when someone tugged at her hand. Her eyes flew open, but she couldn't make out the woman's face in the shadows.

"You come," the voice in heavily accented English insisted. "You come."

Obediently, Bess stood up and let the woman lead her through the village to a hut on the forest's edge. A smoky fire had been lit, and there was a stack of wood beside it.

"No fire go out," the Indian woman said. "Fire good." She pointed to the looming jungle. "Fire good.'' A single hammock swung from the corner posts. Bess could see no other furnishings or implements in the hut. The woman pointed to the hammock. ''You,'' she said. ''You.''

''You want me to sleep here,'' Bess said. The woman smiled and hurried away without another word. With a sigh, Bess climbed into the swaying hammock and closed her eyes.

If I'm going to be eaten, at least I don't have to see what's eating me, she thought as she tried to find a comfortable position in the strange bed. Something with wings brushed against her face and she batted at it. She opened her eyes and nearly screamed.

A man's figure loomed over her.

Before she could gather her wits, he leaned down and kissed her. ''Kincaid,'' she gasped when he came up for air.

''Aye, and who did ye think it might be?'' he teased in his husky burr. ''The Prince of Wales?'' He touched her cheek with his rough hand and she went all quivery inside.

''You scared me half to death,'' she whispered.

''I said I'd keep ye safe.''

''Yes, but—'' He cut off her protest with another kiss, and before she knew what he was doing, he was in the hammock with her.

''Kincaid!''

''Aye, lass.''

''What are you doing?'' He didn't smell like rum, but she knew by his amorous tone that he'd been drinking again. His shirt was open, so that his bare chest was pressed against her thin linen shirt, and his long legs were tangled in hers.

''What do ye think?'' he murmured.

His hand cupped her breast, and her knees turned to water. "We can't, not here," she said.

"Why can't we, Bess? Pablo offered me his youngest wife for the night, but I told him I'd brought my own." He trailed warm kisses down her neck. "The Cuna say hammocks are . . ." Kincaid whispered into her ear and she felt her face grow hot.

"Kincaid!"

"Shall I tell the chief I've changed my mind about his youngest wife?"

"Just try it," she taunted him. "Just you try it."

Chapter 18

The heat of the throbbing tropical night enveloped them like a velvet cloak. Kincaid's sensuous kisses grew more and more demanding as Bess's own passion flared. Suddenly, she couldn't get enough of him . . .

Ribbons of flickering light from the fire illuminated his face and upper body. A sheen of glistening perspiration covered his chest and arms as Bess ran exploring hands over the tightly coiled muscles in his shoulders and nipped lightly at his bare skin.

Kincaid groaned and wrapped his fingers in her hair, arching her neck back to kiss her throat and breasts. Her linen shirt was damp; it clung to her like a second skin, and under it she wore only a cutoff cotton shift. She wore no stays and no skirts or petticoats, only breeches and stockings below the shirt.

Now even those few garments were too much. She could feel her breasts swelling to his touch, her acutely sensitive nipples straining against the thin cotton shift. She wanted him to take off her shirt and shift. She wanted his mouth on her flesh—she wanted him to lick and suck her throbbing breasts. She wanted him inside her, hard and

full . . . She wanted to feel the hot rush of his
seed filling her.

A silken ribbon of fear floated across her consciousness, but she closed her eyes tightly and
willed it away. All her doubts about Kincaid were
nothing compared with the feel of his arms
around her and the heady scent of his aroused
male body.

The threat of danger surrounded them. She
knew that neither of them might live to see the
sunrise, but this wild moment was theirs alone
and no one could take it from them. She opened
her eyes and stared into his face, then deliberately
cast away a lifetime of reason and caution to follow her heart's whim.

"Love me, Kincaid," she whispered. "Love me
tonight . . ."

"Aye, darlin' Bess, I will . . ."

His demanding mouth scalded her. His fierce
embrace was as overpowering as the jungle
around them. She savored the feel of his tongue
against hers, and her heartbeat quickened as she
dared to think of what it would feel like if he
kissed her all over.

"Bess, Bess, let me take off your shirt," he
murmured. "I want to suck your beautiful
breasts. I want to lick them and suck them until
you're wet and ready for me."

Inhaling deep gasps of the thick, damp air, Bess
let him do what he asked without protest. His big
hands were gentle on her taut body and his
mouth drove her wild with wanting him. She uttered little cries of intense pleasure as he laved
each areola with his wet, hot tongue and then

drew her aching nipples between his lips to tug and tease until she writhed with desire.

In turn, she tasted his nipples, nipping at them with her teeth, and tonguing them until they formed tight nubs.

"Woman," he moaned. "What are ye doin' to me?"

She laughed softly and wiggled down, nestling her face against his belly and feeling with her lips the whirled line of hair that ran down to the spring of short curls below. Still laughing, she eased his breeches down over his hips, set his tumescent shaft free, and dared to stroke the throbbing length with light, teasing fingertips.

Kincaid groaned deep in his chest, and she felt tremors of pleasure shake his body. His fingers tightened in her hair and his breath quickened. "Bess, Bess," he whispered hoarsely. Tentatively, she touched the smooth surface with the tip of her tongue, marveling at the sleek texture and the hint of salt.

"Dinna stop," he begged her. Brazenly, she ran her tongue around the head of his shaft and took him into her mouth, sucking gently. He groaned again, then pulled her back up to kiss his mouth. "Now me," he said. "Now it's my turn to pleasure you." His mouth found her breast again and she sighed with delight.

And when he slid searching fingers down beneath the waistband of her boy's breeches, she felt no shame, only a yearning to have him thrust his long fingers through her damp triangle of curls and then deeper still into the source of her flaring hunger. She squirmed against his touch, whimpering at the carnal bliss of his intimacy . . .

shamelessly giving herself body and soul to the enchantment of his lovemaking.

"Bess . . ." he murmured.

The deep chords of his whispered endearments sent chills of delight from her head to the soles of her feet. She buried her face in his chest and sighed with joy.

"Do ye like that?" he asked huskily.

"Yes, oh, yes," she answered. Her own hands were not still; they slid over his heavily muscled arms and down his waist to stroke and rub the hard curve of his thigh. She cupped his heavy stones in her hand and clasped his tightly muscled buttocks.

The hammock swayed precariously as they pulled away the remainder of each other's clothing and lay, limbs entwined, thudding heart against thudding heart, as naked as they were born.

From the forest, Bess heard the blood-chilling cough of a puma and the screams of fleeing monkeys. Strange birds shrieked, and heavy, swollen drops began striking the leaf canopy over her head. She heard all those things, and she smelled the earthy, pungent scent of rain on damp grass, but she sensed all those things vaguely, as though from a great distance or as a faded memory.

All that mattered was the man she held in her arms, the man who rolled her on top of him in the gently swinging hammock. "Ride me," he ordered. "Ride me, Bess, as hard and fast as ye rode that black horse."

Provocatively, she moved over his turgid manhood, reveling in the sweet sensations that flowed through her . . . enjoying the novel power of being in control.

Groaning, he caught her by the hips and lifted her onto him. She settled onto his hard, prodding shaft, opening to him, and sliding down until his enormous erection was buried deep inside. Then he bucked against her and she felt a bolt of lightning explode within her.

"Kincaid," she whispered.

The rain became a torrent, pounding against the leaf roof, drowning out the world, deafening Bess to every voice but that of her own desire.

Kincaid arched his back and she met his thrust with blazing ardor, loosing her own primitive flame, letting the incandescent heat of the jungle night sweep over them, adding to the unforgettable feeling of joyous rapture.

This time Kincaid didn't withdraw at the moment of ultimate release, and she felt the warm flood of his passion fill her just before she soared to her own earth-shattering climax. He murmured her name and crushed her tightly against him, and they tumbled from the high place into infinity together.

His voice was deep and burred as he whispered to her in the black velvet night. "I wish it was true, Bess," he confided. "I told the chief ye were my wife. I wish it was so." He cradled her in his arms and gave her a lingering kiss of such tenderness that tears welled up in her eyes.

"I wish it was true too," she said.

"Nay, ye dinna. Ye do not know the things I've done in my life—the man I am."

"I know enough to never want another," she

said softly. "Enough to know that a man like you comes into a woman's life only once."

He pulled her closer against him and gave a muffled groan. "I'd not hurt ye, Bess, but I'm not a marryin' man. I was married once, and it brought only pain for us both."

She caressed his chest with her fingertips and moved her head to lie against his heart. The beat was fast and strong, and it gave her courage to press him further. "I'm not that woman, Kincaid. I'm—"

"I know what ye are," he replied. "Damn it, Bess, can't ye be satisfied with this? I've never felt so with another lass, never."

"Nor I with a man."

"Then let's enjoy it and make the most of it without talking of marriage."

"Why, Kincaid? Why shouldn't we be married?"

He kissed the crown on her head and wound a lock of her damp hair around his index finger. "I'm no planter, Bess. I'm a hired killer. I fight for whoever pays me. I've nothing to bring a highborn wife, not even a name. And . . ." He lifted her chin and stared into her eyes. "I don't think I could trust a woman again."

She pushed herself up on one elbow. "I trusted a man and he raped me. Is that any reason for me to give up on all men?"

"What happened between me and Gillian is different. I loved her. I never slept with another woman while I was married to her. I was such a fool over her that I closed my eyes to what was going on. She was no better than a whore. Worse than a whore. A whore is honest about what she

does, and she gives good measure for good coin.''
His voice cracked. ''I wanted a son, Bess. A son
who could be more than I was. And when she
swelled with child, I was so damned happy. I
would have cut off my sword arm for her if she
asked for it.''

A tear rolled down Bess's cheek and she dashed
it away. ''Kincaid . . .'' she murmured. ''I'm so
sorry.''

''Dinna feel pity for me. Save your pity for Robbie Munro. He was my best friend. We saved each
other's skins more times than you can count. He
was like a brother to me. But when I caught him
in Gillian's bed, I called him out, and I put a
sword through him.''

''She wasn't worth it,'' Bess said.

''The babe wasn't even mine. She laughed
when she told me that. She taunted me with it.
'Another little bastard,' she said. What difference
did one more little bastard make to a man like
me?''

''Did you kill her too?''

''Gillian?'' Kincaid shook his head. ''God
knows I wanted to.'' His voice grated with pain,
and the eyes that looked into Bess's were desolate. ''Nay, I didn't lay a hand on her. I was afraid
to. I wanted to stop her mouth. I wanted to stop
her from sayin' those hurtin' things.''

''What happened to her?'' Bess asked.

''She died in childbirth, her and the bairn both.
It was stillborn and too small to survive. But it
wasn't mine.''

''Maybe she lied to hurt you, because of Munro.
Maybe it was yours, Kincaid.''

''Nay. The poor wee lad had an extra finger, ye

see, six fingers on one hand. Like Robbie Munro. 'Tis the curse of the Munros. The devil's mark, they say.'' He laughed wryly. ''Robbie Munro could fight like one of Lucifer's fiends. He was hell with a broadsword.''

''But all that's past,'' she said. ''Robbie Munro and Gillian and their son are long dead and buried. You didn't go in that grave with them. You still have a chance to make something of your life . . . to have the son you wanted.''

''Ah, Bess, Bess.'' He kissed her. ''I do love ye,'' he admitted. ''Devil take me, but I do.''

''And I love you.''

''But it's nay enough. I'd bring ye only unhappiness, woman. Ye need a gentleman, someone of your own kind.''

''You are my kind, Kincaid. You are the man I want for a husband. What do you say? Will you marry a landed woman and try a planter's life?''

''Ye'd wed with me?''

''I would.''

''After all that canting about wanting no man to rule you and your precious Fortune's Gift?''

''Not any man, Kincaid, just you.''

''Ye must be sufferin' from a jungle fever. I do believe you've lost your senses.''

She swallowed hard. ''Then the answer is no? You don't want me?''

''Want ye? Hellfire and damnation! Of course I want ye. It's the marryin' that sticks in my craw. You're the finest wench it's been my fortune to know. You're brave and bold and wily as a Campbell. There's none I'd rather have at my back in a fight or beside me like we are now. There's none in all the world I'd rather have as the mother of my child, but it's too late for all that now.''

''Too late?''

''I'm afraid, Bess . . . afraid of lettin' myself dream again.''

''And this treasure hunt? What is that but a dream?''

''Aye, but one I can deal with.''

''And when we find it?''

''I'll take ye safe home to Maryland.''

''And then you'll leave me?''

''It's better for us both, I tell ye. Here we can be together. I'm Munro the mercenary, with no loyalty to anyone or anything. You're my woman. No questions, no problems other than us stayin' alive. But on the Tidewater, it's different. No one expects a woman like you to be with a—''

''To hell with what anyone else thinks. It's what *we* think that matters,'' Bess said hotly.

''Ye say that now, but in time, as ye grow older, you'll see my faults. I'm a rough, plain man and I belong in a place where there's few laws. I'll take my share of the gold and go west to Indian country. I'll build my own farm, lass, and if the nights are lonely, I'll find a woman of my own kind to warm my bed.''

''So you won't marry me.''

''It's what I've been sayin'.''

''You love me.''

''Aye.'' He sighed heavily. ''I can see it was a great mistake to admit it. You'll never let it rest.''

''You love me, but you won't marry me, because you think I'm some great lady and you're a bondsman.''

He scowled at her. "Ye have a way of twistin' a man's words."

"What's not true? That you love me, or that you don't think you're good enough for me?"

"Enough. I won't marry ye, and that's that. We're better as we are, Bess. You're innocent of the world. What ye think ye feel for me here and now—"

"Forget it," she said, turning her back on him. "Forget I asked you. I'll raise your babe alone."

"What babe? You're not wi' child; there's no way ye could be with—"

"Tonight," she whispered. "In this hammock. Tonight we made a baby."

"You are sufferin' from the fever."

"You admit that I'm a witch, yet you refuse to believe me when I tell you that I'm going to have your child."

"Woman, ye are as mad as a shipwrecked sailor."

"If I am pregnant, will you marry me then?"

His forehead creased with exasperation. "Where is your pride that ye'd force a man to wed ye against his will?"

Bess laughed. "No one ever forced you to do anything you didn't want to do in your entire life, Kincaid. If you do marry me, it will be for love and forever."

"Enough of this talk." He sat up in the hammock and walked to the edge of the shelter. Rain was pouring down so heavily that it made a shimmering wall of silver and black in the firelight. "Out there somewhere is what we came for, Bess. It's time to tell me what was on the pages of your grandsire's journal. If we make a misstep, we could wander out there in the jungle until we rot. I need to know numbers. How many days? What landmarks do we follow? How deep is the treasure buried?''

Bess's heartbeat quickened. She'd been afraid of this. She hadn't seen Kutii since they'd been shipwrecked on the island off Carolina. He'd promised to lead her to the gold, and now she was left without a clue to which way to go.

She reached for her shirt and pulled it over her head. It was damp and had something crawling on it. She brushed away the insect and pulled the long shirttail down over her bottom. Sliding out of the hammock, she knelt by the fire and added wood, one piece at a time.

''Damn it, woman, do ye never do what you're told?'' Kincaid asked. His words were hard, but his voice still showed his vulnerability.

She opened her mouth to answer, but nothing came out. Her throat felt like it was being squeezed by an invisible hand. Kutii! she screamed inwardly. Kutii, where are you?

''Has the fever stopped your ears?'' he demanded. ''I want ye to draw me a map. I've a larger one of the land from the Darien swamps to the Azuelo Peninsula. The Chagres River runs roughly west and south from the San Blas Islands. God help ye if you've forgotten anything.''

I can't tell him, she thought desperately. If she told him the truth . . . Merciful heaven, what had she gotten herself into? Please, God, she prayed, if the power I've always had is good and not evil, please send me a sign. Help me out of this.

''Bess?''

She stirred the coals of the campfire with a

charred stick and tried to picture Kutii in her mind. All she could visualize was confusion, doubt, and fear. "I'm trying to remember the exact words," she lied.

Kincaid stood there stark naked with his fists braced against his hips and his brows set in a straight, scowling line. He held himself so rigidly that Bess could barely make out the rise and fall of his chest as he drew breath in the hot, humid air. "If ye've tricked me . . ." he said softly. The unspoken threat sent shivers down her spine.

" 'Morgan sent us another way,' " she said, repeating the lines that had been set down by her grandfather so long ago. " 'He'd had word of a heavily guarded mule train carrying a load of treasure to Porto Bello. He was following the Chagres River with his main body of men while we traversed the overland route . . .' " Bess's mouth was dry; she had to will the hand that held the stick not to tremble.

Swirls of smoke rose from the fire, spreading out under the roof of the hut and seeping into the flood of falling water outside. At least the smoke keeps away the mosquitoes, she thought.

Even the scent of the burning wood was unfamiliar; it smelled like nothing she had ever known. And when she looked down at her hands, she saw that they were stained with blood-red sap.

Kincaid came closer and squatted across the fire pit from her. The drumming rain on the roof and soaked earth seemed to chill her to the bone, not with an earthly cold, but with a freezing of the soul.

Why did I do it? she thought. Why did I leave

the blue of Chesapeake skies to come to this green hell? I should have let them take part of the land. In time I could have cleared more forest and planted a larger crop. I could have fed my people on fish and game. It would have been hard, but no harder than . . .

She inhaled deeply of the spicy, rain-drenched air. No, she said firmly to herself. I chose this path. I made a decision, and I'll stick by it so long as I have breath in my body. Right or wrong, we're here, and we'll finish this treasure hunt, one way or another.

And then, in the distant shadows of her mind, Bess heard a faint whisper. "All that Lacy was is in you. You bear the blood of those who seek what lies beyond . . ." She held her breath and waited, but there was only silence.

"All that she was," Bess murmured.

"What did ye say?" Kincaid asked.

She had the God-given power, Bess thought. "My grandmother was a good woman, not an evil one. She never let a child go hungry or failed to speak up when she thought someone was being wronged."

"Your grandmother? What does your grandmother have to do with anything? 'Tis your grandfather's journal that's important."

"No." Bess smiled and shook her head. "No, it's not." My Grandmama Lacy had the power, she thought. And I have it too. "I have it," she said triumphantly. "I do."

"Well, then? Show me," he insisted. Quickly he removed a folded map from an oilskin wrapping. "Show me where the treasure is."

Bess looked down at the map. For long seconds, she held her index finger over the damp parchment, then—guided purely by intuition—she closed her eyes and touched a spot. "Here," she said. "The gold is buried here."

Kincaid looked up at her. "You're certain?"

"Would I lie to you? After all we've been through?" she asked as she slipped her left hand behind her back and crossed her fingers.

It had been Bess who'd convinced the Cuna to guide them through the jungle to the place where the treasure was buried. All of Evan Davis's promises and bribery had been in vain. Pablo had insisted that he'd not risk his warriors' lives for steel machetes and bolts of cloth, at least that was what he'd said until an old woman had whispered in his ear and he'd summoned Bess before him.

"*Quién* you?" the Cuna chief had asked her in a mixture of broken English and Spanish. Evan had translated Pablo's words.

"Bess," she'd replied, knowing that her full name would only be confusing to this wise, primitive man.

He had stared at her with eyes as dark and fathomless as Kutii's. Then the old woman, the same one who'd been in charge of cutting up the meat the day before, had whispered something more to Pablo. Abruptly, the chief's demeanor had changed from wary to genuinely warm. "We are honored to have you among us," he'd said. Again, a puzzled Evan explained the meaning to Bess and Kincaid.

Pablo waved his hand and gave an order in his own language. Immediately, a woman ran to a hut and returned with a beautiful multicolored cloak of tightly woven feathers. *"Esta es para la mujer estrella."*

Evan shook his head. "I don't understand."

"I know enough Spanish to get that," Kincaid said. "He said the cloak was for the star woman."

"That's what's crazy," Evan said. He looked at the chief questioningly. *"Mujer estrella?"*

"Yes," Pablo answered firmly. "Wom-man *de* star."

Bess had not known why the Cuna had called her that either, but for her he said he would send four canoes of warriors. Only for her, he insisted, and he refused all payment.

And Bess's reply had been a wide smile of thanks, and the most gracious curtsy she could manage in breeches and boy's shoes.

Now, after three days of paddling down some godforsaken river in the rain, she wondered if Pablo had done them a favor or not.

Actually, there were interludes during the rainfall. But whenever the downpour stopped, the earth began to steam. Clouds of fog and mist rose from the surface of the water and the land. Insects swarmed around their exposed bodies, buzzing and crawling, finding their way into noses and mouths and ears. They were saved from being devoured by the biting creatures by more of the potion the woman had given Bess back in the village. The mixture kept most insects from stinging, but did nothing to keep them from driving Bess frantic. And any spot of flesh that she'd missed when she applied the herbal potion was quickly discovered by the mosquitoes and attacked in full force.

Not that Bess didn't find a strange beauty in the land. She watched the riverbanks and surrounding jungle with a sense of wonder. There were huge crabs and toads, alligators, slender red deer, black-bearded monkeys, and tree sloths that hung like petrified fruit from the branches. Iguanas and wild hogs, birds of every size and color, and once, a snake so long and thick that it could have devoured a man whole.

Huge bats drifted like ghostly shadows over the river at night, and the sound of the rain was often pierced by the hunting cry of the big cats and the scream of dying animals. Bess napped from time to time in the darkness, wrapped in her feathered cloak, but the paddlers never slept. They drove the canoes on and on, carrying the Englishmen deeper and deeper into the interior until Bess thought they must surely have crossed the isthmus and be close to the Pacific coast.

And finally, when she'd given up hope of ever setting foot on dry land again, the Cuna beached their dugout canoes and the headman pointed into the jungle.

Evan spoke to him briefly, then turned to Kincaid. "This is as far as they can take us by boat," he said. "From here on, they will give us one guide. The other Cuna will remain here. They call this place 'El Tigre's hunt.' They say there is great danger in this place."

"From wild beasts?" Kincaid asked.

"No." The headman spoke again rapidly, and Evan exchanged words with him. "He says there is another tribe here. This is their hunting grounds. They are not Cuna or Choco or Guaymis." He glanced at Bess. "This man says they

call them the Tiger People, and that they steal
Cuna babies and eat them."

"Superstitious nonsense," Kincaid said gruffly.

Bess regarded the frightened faces of the Cuna
warriors and felt a sudden draft of icy wind.
"No," she said. "It's true. Look at them."

"So we go on alone," Kincaid said. "Bess?"

She nodded. She didn't want to walk into the
jungle any more than the Cuna did, but she knew
they were near the end of their search. She could
feel the pull of something elusive and indescrib-
able. "We have to go on," she said. "We're close
to the spot."

Kincaid, Evan, and the eight sailors they'd
brought with them from the ship took machetes
and weapons, and loaded packs on their backs.
Kincaid thrust an oilskin bag into Bess's hands.

"The map is in there," he said, "along with a
pistol. Keep it dry, if you value your life."

Two Cuna warriors stepped forward.

"Can we trust them?" Kincaid asked Evan. He
shrugged, and Kincaid glanced at Bess. "Touch
them," he ordered. "Touch their hands and tell
me if they'll betray us."

Bess's eyes widened. "But you said you didn't
believe me," she protested. "You said—"

"Damn it, woman, do as I say."

Hesitantly, she walked forward and held out
her hand to the nearest of the two guides. He
stood motionless. "May I?" she asked. He raised
his hands, palms outward, and she pressed her
hands against his.

"What is this?" Evan said. Several of the sailors began to grumble among themselves.

Bess smiled as she saw a welcome tint of blue.

"This man will be faithful," she said. The second man turned and darted off into the jungle. Before anyone could move to stop him, he was hidden by the dense foliage.

"Now what?" Evan asked.

Kincaid's gaze met Bess's. "Lass?"

She nodded. "We go," she said, moving into place behind him. One way or another, she thought. "If we don't, it's all over."

As if by signal, rain began to fall again. Kincaid nodded to the waiting Cuna guide and he led the way along a twisting game trail into the forest. Her heart in her throat, Bess fell into step behind Kincaid and just in front of Evan and the other Englishmen.

Minutes later, when she looked over her shoulder, she saw no sign of the river, only sheets of water against a curtain of green. Whispering a silent prayer, and fixing her gaze on Kincaid's broad back, she trudged on through the mud and tangled mass of vegetation.

Chapter 19

Bess's confidence seeped away drop by drop as she trudged through the wet, clinging ferns and trailing vines. Ahead of her, the men took turns hacking a path with their machetes. The rain had stopped as quickly as it had begun, but now the heat and humidity made walking an effort. Her shirt and breeches were soaked through from her own sweat; thorns had ripped her stockings to threads and embedded themselves in her flesh. Ants and spiders crawled up her legs and fell onto her face and hair from the greenery above. Her leather shoes were so soggy that blisters had formed on her heels and broken into raw, open sores that burned with every step.

The shadowy forest was strangely empty, the primeval silence broken only by the slash of machetes and the occasional roar of a howler monkey. From time to time a strange bird would shriek, or underbrush would rustle, but most of the time Bess could hear her own heavy breathing.

Gradually, the palms and giant ferns gave way to ancient groves of cotton trees, cedar, mammee, calabash, and nameless hardwoods. Huge trees with trunks as wide as London streets formed a leafy green canopy overhead, shutting out even what feeble sunlight filtered through the overcast sky. Here the walking was easier; the all-enveloping verdant ceiling made the mossy forest floor as open as a plantation lawn.

But it was still hot . . . and sticky. And something was biting her elbow. Again.

Bess kept walking, glad for once that she wasn't a man and wasn't expected to take her turn at the front of the column . . . glad to have Kincaid's solid bulk ahead of her. There was something unnerving about the jungle, something forbidding. In Maryland, Bess had always loved the woods. The trees there seemed protective rather than sinister like these. August on the tidewater could be much hotter than this rain forest, but it had never been as wet.

The Cuna guide answered to the name Hah-kobo, but whether it was the Spanish form of Jacob or some Cuna word, Bess didn't know. Hah-kobo's entire English vocabulary seemed to consist of "We go" and "No," with a few hand gestures thrown in for clarity.

The second guide, Che, the one who had run away before she could touch his hand at the landing site, seemed to have vanished. She had seen or heard nothing of him since.

Presumably, they were trekking toward the spot on the map that she had pointed out to Kincaid in the village. The concept of a map was foreign to the Cuna, but Kincaid had showed the place to Evan, and he knew enough of the territory to tell the chief where Bess wanted to go.

Now that she was actually in the jungle, where one tree looked much like another and every hard-gained mile took them deeper and deeper into a tangle of green hell, Bess doubted if she would ever see the coast again, let alone find a treasure buried more than half a century ago.

"Kutii, where the hell are you?" she whispered. She had looked for him so hard that she'd almost given up hope. Never before in her life had he gone so long without appearing beside her. "You promised me," she murmured urgently. "You said you knew the way and you'd come with me."

Kincaid stopped so quickly that Bess almost ran into him. "What?" he asked.

"Nothing," she mumbled, putting her head down so that he couldn't see her eyes.

What would Kincaid do if she couldn't point out the exact spot where the gold was hidden? What if they just kept walking until they were swallowed up by the rain and the jungle? Would anyone know or care if they simply disappeared?

At nightfall, Hah-kobo found a hollow tree large enough for all of them to crouch inside. Efficiently, he drove two lizards and a snake out of the recesses and chopped off their heads, then cut bark from a cedar tree to reach the dry inner layers so that he could build a fire just inside the shelter. Without speaking, Hah-kobo went out into the darkening forest and returned a few minutes later with palm shoots and nuts, two over-ripe wild pineapples, and a palm leaf full of what could only be tree sap sprinkled with fat white grubs. Bess contented herself with a raw palm shoot and a section of pineapple. She was certain that she'd never sleep, but no sooner did she rest her head on Kincaid's chest than she fell into a deep, dreamless slumber.

Dawn came in a rush of pelting rain and high-pitched squeals. A black peccary sow with three offspring in tow had wandered near the camp. Kincaid and Evan managed to kill two of the young pigs while Hah-kobo kept the mother at bay. The peccaries joined the two lizards and the snake on a makeshift spit over the morning fire. Bess thought the taste of the scorched peccary a little strong, but a definite first choice over the lizards.

When they had devoured all the food and kicked the remains of the fire out into the rain, the grumbling men picked up their packs and began to fall in for the day's march. Hah-kobo, who had not looked once at Bess or spoken to her, glanced expectantly at her now.

Bess met his sloe-eyed stare. For a long minute, nothing happened; then she felt a frizzen of excitement run through her. Without knowing why, she lifted her right hand and pointed. *"Catarata,"* she said. Waterfall. She hadn't known that she knew the Spanish word or that she would utter it. Her grandfather had mentioned a waterfall in his journal, but she wasn't certain whether or not it had been in reference to the place where the ambush had occurred and the gold had been buried.

"Catarata," Hah-kobo repeated. He looked up at the trees overhead, and Bess wondered if he was trying to see the sky. Then he cupped his hands over his mouth and gave a loud, hacking call. Immediately, the sound was answered by a similar cry from the forest. Hah-kobo nodded and set off, the soles of his bare brown feet padding catlike against the thick carpet of the jungle floor.

They passed from the tall trees into a morass of
scrub palms, fallen logs, and thorn trees. Fungus
grew thickly on every branch and tree trunk.
Frogs of all sizes hopped and climbed amid the
lush creepers and rotting leaves. Bess felt them
squish beneath her feet, and jump against her legs
as she walked. Here and there orchids grew. The
air was heavy with the scent of decay and wet
undergrowth. With every breath, she drew in the
smell and taste of an alien world.

Then, suddenly, Hah-kobo stopped in his
tracks. He raised a hand, and one by one, the
seamen fell silent. Bess stared. Ahead, in the
shadows of a fallen log taller than she, something
moved.

Sunlight. Black against gilt . . . flowing liquid
gold. Gleaming eyes and teeth like shining ivory
blades.

Bess's breath caught in her throat as the creature—a huge jaguar—materialized from the dark
into the relative light. He faced them unafraid,
fierce cat eyes glowing with the fire of twin green
emeralds.

Bess could see the beads of sweat running down
the back of Hah-kobo's neck. She waited, motionless, knowing that if the jaguar leaped, he could
rip out the Cuna's throat before any of them could
lift a weapon to stop him.

Kincaid didn't flex a muscle, but she could feel
his sinews tighten; she could sense his readiness
to attack the big cat, and she could smell the mixture of fear and courage that emanated from his
taut skin. His unspoken shout of warning came
loud and clear in her mind, a command as real as

any she had ever heard with her ears. *Stay still, Bess! Don't move!*

The jaguar opened his mouth and uttered a mixture of bone-chilling cough and roar. Bess stood riveted, but the sailor directly in line behind her broke and ran.

The black-and-gold animal became a blur as he leaped through the air. Then the sailor screamed as the weight of the jaguar bore him to the ground. Evan raised his pistol and tried to fire, but the hammer fell harmlessly, the gunpowder soaked beyond use. The victim screamed again, a hideous high-pitched wail of agony.

With a Highland war cry, Kincaid threw himself at the jaguar. Bess's heart missed a beat as the Scot's machete descended on empty air. The cat snarled, leaped straight over Kincaid's head onto an overhanging branch, and was gone before anyone else could shoot.

Bess ran to the dying man and tried to stanch the blood bubbling from the great gash in his throat. The sailor's face and chest had been sliced to the bone. He gasped and tried to rise, but his eyes were already glazing over. Blood trickled from his mouth. He groaned once more and lay still.

"Holy Jesus," one seaman muttered.

Another prayed in Gaelic.

"Enough of this," still another cried. "This is no place for us. Back to the ship, I say. Back to the ship before we're all dead."

Kincaid went to Bess, pulled her to her feet, and wrapped his arms around her. "He's gone," he said.

She closed her eyes and soaked up the security

of those strong arms. She'd been afraid, but not
for herself. It had all happened too fast for that.
But when Kincaid had charged the jaguar, her
blood had turned to ice water. "You could have
been killed," she whispered. That could have
been him lying there with his lifeblood draining
away into the wet leaves. "Kincaid," she murmured thickly.

"I couldna do anything," he said.

Her knees were weak; her head felt light. Take
me home, she wanted to beg him. Take me out
of here. Forget the gold, forget everything but us.
Just take me home.

Kincaid's hands tightened on her shoulders,
and he pushed her to an arm's length away and
looked into her eyes. "You're all right," he said.
"You're safe, Bess."

Shame made her cheeks hot. He thought she
was frightened for her own safety. "I'm fine,"
she muttered. "You'd best see to them." She motioned toward the knot of angry crewmen.
"They'll desert us if you don't stop them."

"I say we go back," the bosun argued. "There's
no gold here—only death."

Evan grabbed the front of the bosun's shirt and
yanked him out of the group. "You'll go where
you're told," he said harshly. "So long as I'm
captain, I have no—"

"We're not on the ship now," a tall, one-eyed
sailor shouted. "Ye can't—"

Kincaid moved so fast that Bess wasn't sure
what was happening. Suddenly the one-eyed man
was lying face-up on the ground and the Scot was
leaning over him with one knee on his chest and
a knife at his throat. "Ye heard your captain,"

Kincaid said softly. "We'll have no mutiny. Either ye hold your tongue or I'll cut it off with the rest of your head."

"Don't kill me! Don't kill me!" the sailor begged.

Kincaid glanced at Evan and the captain nodded. Kincaid stood back to let the sailor up. "Same goes for any of ye," the Scot said. "Mr. Davis is your captain, and he works for me. Any man who wants to shirk his duty better just go."

Bess's eyes widened in surprise, but she refrained from saying anything.

"Remember," Kincaid continued, "that jaguar is still out there. And he's still hungry."

The crew's faces remained sullen and angry, but they obeyed Evan's orders to make a stretcher for the dead man. They wrapped him in palm leaves and carried him with them as they continued the march.

About an hour later, they crossed a narrow river by wading hip-deep through the brown, muddy water. As they gained the bank on the far side, the bosun slipped and grabbed at a tree root. A large snake struck at him, sinking its fangs into his wrist. The man's screams brought two of his companions, who chopped the huge reptile into pieces with their machetes. But despite all Bess's efforts to help him, the bosun died in less time than it took a kettle of water to boil.

A tree had toppled near the river, and the ground beneath the exposed roots was still soft. Kincaid ordered a single grave to be dug in the black earth, and both dead men were buried there with only a brief prayer and two simple twig crosses to mark the spot.

They had gone only a few hundred yards from the grave site when Che appeared from behind a bibby-tree and began to speak rapidly to Hah-kobo. The Cuna scout, Che, had a dead monkey and a dead opossum slung over his shoulder. Those he gave to Hah-kobo, but before Evan could question him, he dashed off again.

"What is he afraid of?" Kincaid asked Hah-kobo. The dark-skinned guide merely shrugged, picked up the animals, and continued walking.

It rained again for a short time, and when the rain tapered off, Bess could hear a new sound nearby, the rush of water. A few hundred yards more, and Hah-kobo led them into an area of giant mammee trees. The underbrush grew sparser and was replaced by ferns that grew taller than a man's head. The ground beneath the ferns was covered with moss and tiny yellow flowers. Hah-kobo stopped, pushed aside a curtain of ferns, and Bess gasped.

Just ahead of them was a waterfall, perhaps thirty feet high, with a wide, still pool at the bottom. Hah-kobo went to the water's edge, knelt down, and drank from his cupped hands.

Bess stood speechless. Her heart thudded against her chest, and she had the strongest feeling that her grandfather had once stood on this very spot. Grandpapa James. She hadn't felt so close to him in years. Her throat tightened, and her eyes began to tear.

"Well, lass?" Kincaid's deep voice yanked her from her reverie. "Are we any closer to this treasure of yours?"

She nodded, still unable to speak. It was here. She knew it. Gooseflesh rose on her arms and she struggled to breathe. Her eyelids fluttered. She took a step toward the pool. The water was so dark that it looked black. A narrow stream trickled away on the far side, but the flow coming over the falls seemed far too great in volume to be contained in this small, still tarn.

As she drew nearer, the sound of the cascade filled her ears; she was mesmerized by the music of the frothy, tumbling water. She could almost swear she heard voices coming from the falls . . . voices long stilled by time and circumstance. Her grandfather's voice. His laughter.

And more. Suddenly, Bess stiffened as she heard the sound of musket fire. Men screamed and horses snorted. A flaming arrow arced across her consciousness and—

"Bess! Get down!" Kincaid slammed into her, knocking her facedown on the mossy ground.

She blinked, trying to clear the cobwebs from her mind, realizing that the screams and shots were real. They were here and now, not coming from the past.

She raised her head and stared across the glade to see dozens of naked Indians running toward her. An explosion went off just above her head, and she smelled the acrid scent of black powder. Kincaid was shooting at the attackers. She fumbled for her own pistol, but realized that it was gone. She looked frantically around, saw the weapon lying close to her, seized it, and took aim at one of the hostile Indians. She squeezed the trigger, but the gun wouldn't fire.

"Caribs!" Hah-kobo yelled.

An icy current of fear seized her as the meaning of the Cuna's words sank into her consciousness.

Caribs! The cannibals of the Caribbean. The stuff of late-night horror stories and sailors' warnings. Not phantom ghosts, but real. Their eerie, trilled war cries turned her blood to ice.

Time slowed to a stop. Etched against the vivid green of the forest wall were howling barbaric figures, brandishing bows and arrows and stone-headed war clubs. One fierce apparition, his bright copper skin painted with stripes of yellow and black, leaped high into the air. His face was contorted with an expression of sheer savagery, and in his outstretched right hand he bore the ravaged, dripping head of Evan Davis.

Kincaid fired again, and the Carib fell, his chest blossoming a bright red flower. But the tide of carnage flowed on toward them. Vaguely, Bess realized that Kincaid had jerked her to her feet and shoved her behind him. But even his raw courage could not protect her this time. The battle waged hand to hand throughout the clearing, and three more painted devils stood beyond the pool, firing short, feathered arrows so tiny and delicate that she knew the tips must carry instant death.

We're going to die here, she thought as an arrow struck the moss only inches from Kincaid's boot. I'll never see the sun go down over the Chesapeake again, and I'll never live to hear my baby's first cry.

Her child. Kincaid's son. The black chasm of hopelessness yawned before her. The tiny scrap of life that she carried under her heart would perish with them, the flame snuffed out before it had kindled.

"No!" she screamed. "No!" She summoned

all her strength and will for one last chance. "Kutii!"

A single bolt of lightning rocked the clearing, followed by a blinding downfall of rain. Bess shut her eyes against the onslaught, and when she opened them, Kutii was standing there, larger than life, in full Incan battle array.

Bess felt for Kincaid's hand. It tightened on hers, and she heard his sharp intake of breath.

The rain stopped abruptly and a shaft of sunlight broke through the interlaced foliage overhead. The clearing was so quiet that Bess could hear the drip of raindrops off the leaves.

Kutii's war club glittered gold in the sunlight, blinding the eyes of the Caribs. His golden breastplate, his jeweled diadem, his silver armbands incised with the emblems of his rank and ancestry, awed them into silence, and one by one, their war cries died in their throats.

A ripple of fear went through the Carib warriors. The line wavered; then one brave screamed a challenge and lunged forward. Kutii swung his razor-edged war club. The terrible weapon didn't touch him, but the Carib fell as though he'd been struck by lightning.

Kutii turned, his fierce black eyes lingering on first one Carib and then another. "She is the Star Woman," he said in a terrible voice. "You have dared to attack one who comes from the stars."

A painted warrior dropped his bow and fled into the trees. Another followed. Suddenly Kutii spun around and pointed his war club at a brave who stood on the far side of the pool. Bess whirled to see that man fall dead in his tracks. The remaining Caribs dropped their weapons and ran. In seconds, Kincaid, Bess, Hah-kobo, and four sailors were the only living creatures in the clearing. Kutii's specter image flared bright, then faded until the spot where he had stood was empty.

Hah-kobo spoke in rapid-fire bursts in his own language. He pointed to the place where Kutii had been, and then at the Caribs the ghost had slain; then he moved closer to Bess, touched the center of his forehead, and extended his open, weaponless hand toward her in a graceful but obvious gesture of reverence.

Kincaid shook his head and turned to Bess, his eyes glazed with shock. "Did ye see—" he began, then broke off and looked back at the empty glade. The sunlight still formed a golden pool, but the Incan was no longer there. "Where in hell did he come from?" Kincaid rasped.

"Not Hell," Bess murmured. "I don't know where he does come from, but I know it's not Hell."

"Ye saw it too?"

She nodded and went into his arms. He crushed her against him. She could hear the pounding of his heart and feel the tremor of his muscles.

Kincaid released her and drew the back of his hand across his eyes. "A ghost."

She nodded.

"I saw him before . . ." he said. "In the woods that night. Just after we left Fortune's Gift."

She nodded again and laid a hand on his arm.

"I must be losing my mind."

"If you are, we're losing it together," she assured him.

"Ye saw it."

She smiled at him. "I've been seeing Kutii all my life."

"Kutii?"

She nodded.

"A futterin' ghost."

The sailors rushed forward, crowding close around them. "What happened?" a man clutching a bleeding arm asked. Bess recognized him as a troublemaker named Tick Warder.

"Why did they break off the attack?" another demanded. "Will they be back?"

A bearded seaman tried to reload his pistol with shaking hands. "There must have been two dozen of 'em! Howlin' little bastards!"

"They got the cap'n," the last man, John Brown, said. "Cut 'is 'ead clean off."

Kincaid glanced at Bess warily. She shrugged.

"Get us out o' 'ere!" Brown urged. "Get us out o' 'ere before we all ends up like Cap'n Davis."

Kincaid looked at the Cuna guide. "Will they be back?"

Hah-kobo smiled. "Carib no." He laid one brown hand on top of the other and separated them in a sharp, sweeping motion that said "Finished" as clearly as words.

"He saw him," Kincaid said to Bess.

"All three of us did," she replied, "but they didn't."

"Saw who?" the bearded sailor asked.

"This is all his fault," Tick Warder cried, giving Hah-kobo a shove. "If he'd done his job, they wouldn't've—"

Kincaid seized the man's good arm and spun him around. "Touch Hah-kobo again and I'll kill ye my-

self, ye worthless salt,'' he said. ''This Cuna's all
that's kept ye alive so far. He stood by us during the
attack, and maybe he'll lead us safely back to the
Scarlet Tanager so long as ye don't make him mad.''

Bess went to the nearest fallen man to see if he
was still breathing. He was dead, his eyes open and
staring. She rolled him onto his back and closed his
eyelids. She found Davis's headless body at the edge
of the clearing, but she couldn't bring herself to touch
it. It was the Cuna who retrieved the captain's head
and replaced it on his severed neck.

They gathered the English dead and laid them
in a row and covered them with giant ferns. The
Caribs they left as they lay. When Bess and Kincaid had finished the onerous task, they washed
the blood from their hands in the pool.

The Scot's face still bore the traces of shock. His
lips were pale, his features tightly drawn. ''What
happened here?'' he whispered to Bess.

''I'm not sure.''

''We saw a ghost.''

''You could call him that.''

''What is all this about ye being from the stars?''

She shrugged. ''Kutii's an Indian. I don't
know, and he won't tell me.''

''Ye talk to this *thing*?'' Kincaid's burr thickened.

''He was a dear friend of my grandparents. He's
buried in the family plot at Fortune's Gift. He's not
a thing; he's a man.''

''Nay. No man, but a spirit. Either that, or the
lizard we ate had been samplin' funny mush-
rooms.''

''I didn't eat any lizard, Kincaid,'' she whispered urgently. ''Kutii is real. At least, I see him

and hear him as though he's real. He fancies himself my protector.''

Kincaid arched a heavy eyebrow. ''And was this *protector* of yours with us when I thought the two of us were alone and . . .'' He searched for a word. ''Intimate?''

''No. It isn't like that. I have to ask him to come—at least, I think I do. He never comes . . .'' She sighed. ''How can I explain it to you? I told you I was a witch, but you didn't believe me.''

''What I want to know is how a ghost can slay a man. I've heard of plenty of spirits, but I—''

''The Caribs saw him too,'' Bess said. ''I don't know how they died, but I'll wager they died of fright.''

Kincaid splashed water on his face. ''What of the treasure, Bess? Can ye find it, or shall we turn back while we still can?''

She paused, kneeling by the bank of the pool, her hands in the water. As Kincaid asked the question, she had the strangest sensation of falling. She swayed and he caught her.

''Bess, are ye all right? Ye weren't struck by a poison arrow, were ye?''

''No . . . no.'' Her chest felt tight. She closed her eyes and saw a vision of brown mud. And in the mud, a single gleaming bowl rested. ''The pool,'' she cried. ''It's here, in the pool.'' She pointed down into the black water. ''Here, Kincaid, at the bottom of the pool. Grandfather didn't bury the treasure. He sank it. Right here, by the waterfall. No wonder he was certain he could find it again! It was right here, all the time.''

Chapter 20

T he waiting was unbearable as Bess watched the surface of the pool for Kincaid to come up. Her hands were clenched so tightly that her nails cut into her palms; her knees were shaking, and sensations of numbness had spread to her hands and feet.

Surely, he'd been down for more than a minute. How long could he possibly hold his breath? she wondered for the third time.

They had no idea how deep the pool was—or, if the treasure was there, if it could be recovered. Kincaid had insisted on diving down himself to explore the bottom. He'd insisted he was a good swimmer, but what if the water contained poison snakes or alligators? What if the pool was bottomless? What if he went down and never came up?

Unable to stand the strain of waiting any longer, Bess began to strip off her shoes and stockings. But as she prepared to dive in after him, Kincaid's blond head broke the surface.

He gasped for air, blinked to clear the water from his eyes, and gave her a slow, satisfied grin. Then he raised one hand over his head in triumph. In that hand he clutched a golden disk inlaid with crescent moons of beaten silver.

"It's there!" she cried.

"Aye, lassie." He laughed. "Twenty feet down, in mud as thick and black as hell's ashes!" He tossed her the shimmering object. It spun through the air like a golden bird and she caught it with both hands.

Instantly, the sailors crowded close around, each man stretching out his hands to touch and heft the weight of the Incan nose plate. "Here, there! Let me see!" Tick Warder insisted. He snatched the massive piece of jewelry from the man called Long Tom and tested the gold with his teeth.

"Is it real?" Brown asked.

"Real as the nose on your face," Warder replied. He stared gape-mouthed at the golden disk as though he expected it to vanish at any second.

Bess ignored the seamen. Her eyes were on Kincaid as he took another deep breath and dove down again. This time the seconds passed like minutes instead of hours, and when he resurfaced, he brought up a hammered gold vessel in the shape of a llama's head and a crumpled golden glove covered with strange designs. Three more dives brought a mace head of silver, a life-size ear of corn with gold-and-silver kernels and a silver husk, a single golden earring the size of Bess's hand, a silver figurine in the form of a man with shell eyes and jeweled sandals, and a reed boat five inches long and worked in exquisite detail down to the last knot, carved of solid gold.

The sight of so much gold turned the seamen to raving fools. They danced and shouted and laughed as though they were drunk. Each man clutched a portion of the treasure as he cavorted and rambled on, repeating to whoever would lis-

ten just what he would do with his share when
he got back to English territory.

Bess was strangely unaffected by the discovery.
The treasure they'd come so far to find suddenly
seemed unimportant. Her overwhelming concern
was Kincaid's safety as he continued to plunge
down into the swirling black water.

"I'll take a turn," she offered. "You're tired. I
can swim."

"Nay." Kincaid wiped the water from his face
and rested against the bank between dives. "The
bottom is treacherous. It's a tangle of logs and
grass. The chests that held the treasure are long
gone, if it ever rested in chests at all. It's no place
down there for a woman."

"No place for you either," she said, gripping
his hand tightly. "We've enough already. Quit
before something happens to you." She couldn't
keep the quaver from her voice. "You've brought
up a fortune already. There's no need to be
greedy."

Kincaid's eyes narrowed and he shook his
head. "The men must have their share, not just
these with us, but Rudy and the others who remained on the *Tanager*. It costs money to maintain
a ship and a crew. We need enough to get us back
to Maryland, and then enough to assure us both
security once we get there. I'll bring up what I
can, woman. For we'll not pass this way again."

"The Caribs could come back," she reasoned.
"Let's take what we have and go."

His only answer was to dive again and yet
again, until darkness fell over the glade. Bess
knelt by the bank, heedless of the growing pile of
priceless artifacts, while tears slipped down her

cheeks. So intent was she on Kincaid's condition that she didn't notice when the men's mood shifted from joyful to sinister.

Tick Warder, John Brown, Long Tom, and Murray—the fourth sailor—gathered in a knot on the far side of the clearing while Hah-kobo busied himself with making a fire. The Cuna guide had shown little curiosity about the treasure. Instead, he'd spent most of the afternoon constructing a crude shelter of branches and interwoven ferns and palm leaves. Hah-kobo's back was to the sailors as he crouched by the fire pit and blew patiently on the glowing tinder.

Kincaid heaved himself up on the mossy bank as rain began to fall yet again. "All right," he said wearily to Bess. "That's the last of it. If there's more gold down there, 'twould take the devil himself to dig it out of that mud."

She threw her arms around him and pulled his head close to her breast. It was impossible to miss the exhaustion in his low burr. "There was no need to go down so many times," she murmured, running her hands through his wet hair. "Senseless."

Rain spattered against their bare skin, but Bess continued to hold him tightly until she was as soaked as he was. "Hah-kobo's going to cook something he shot," she said. "I saw it, but I don't know what it is. I guess—"

Without warning, Kincaid shoved her down and threw his body over her. A flintlock roared and a man cried out. Bess looked up to see Tick Warder staggering across the clearing toward the fire, a fired flintlock in his hand and a tiny feathered shaft protruding from his neck. "What?" she gasped. Her insides twisted and she felt a sensation of the earth falling away beneath her. "Caribs," she whispered hoarsely.

"Nay," Kincaid said. "Stay down." He was already rising and crawling toward the place where his pistol lay on top of his shirt and boots.

Bess stared as Warder fell to his knees, then sprawled forward on the deep moss and lay still. She glanced at Hah-kobo, but the Cuna hadn't moved. He was watching the remaining sailors as they grabbed what they could carry of the gold and dashed into the forest. When they were gone, he got up and came over to Bess and Kincaid with his hands open to show that he held no weapons.

Kincaid grabbed his pistol and checked the priming, but Hah-kobo shook his head and made a "finished" motion with his hands. He moved in front of the Scot and pushed the barrel of the gun toward the ground.

Bess glanced warily around the clearing. Nothing moved. The only sounds were those of a cicada trilling shrilly and the hushed patter of rain against the forest floor. "I trust him," she said. "Whoever killed Warder, I don't think he'll hurt us."

Hah-kobo smiled. He cupped his hands to his mouth and uttered a bird call. Seconds later, Che stepped out of the green wall of ferns into the clearing.

"No shoot Che," Che said loudly. In his hands he carried a blowgun and a handful of miniature arrows. "Englesh bad," he said. "Englesh want kill yellow hair. Che stop."

Bess swallowed the lump in her throat and forced a wan smile. "Thank you, Che." She

looked up at Kincaid. "Why?" she demanded.
"Why would they want to kill us? We were going
to give them a share of the gold."

"They wanted it all," Kincaid answered.

"Englesh no kill Star Woman," Che said. "Che
hear Englesh—this fellow . . ." He pointed to the
body of Tick Warder. "This fellow say kill yellow
hair. Take woman. Take gold."

"They wanted you as well, Bess," Kincaid said.
His face hardened in the flickering firelight. "And
now the jungle will take them. They'll not get far
without Hah-kobo to guide them. They'll die of
thirst or snake bite, or maybe the Caribs will find
them first."

"Che watch all time," the little Cuna said, coming to stand beside Hah-kobo. "Carib come, Che
watch. Che kill." He held up two fingers. "Carib
bad. Englesh ship fellow bad. Star Woman no
bad. Yellow hair no bad. Friend Cuna. Yes?"

"Friend Cuna, yes." Kincaid extended both
hands to the Indian. Che shook them vigorously,
then leaned forward and hugged Kincaid.

"Could we get in out of the rain, do you
think?" Bess asked. She was all too aware of the
dead man lying not ten feet away and of the fortune in gold scattered across the clearing, but she
was nearing the breaking point. She had wit-
nessed so much since daybreak that she just
wanted to curl up in Kincaid's arms out of the wet
and not have to think. Her head was pounding,
and her skin felt hot and goosebumpy all at the
same time. "Please?"

Kincaid put his arm around her and led her into
the relative shelter of the open-sided hut. "Take

off your clothes," he said. "You'll catch a fever if you stay in those wet things."

Bess's eyes widened. "Here? In front of all of you?"

"I've seen you without a stick on more than once, and I doubt you'll shock Che and Hah-kobo. Out of them, I say."

"In a pig's eye!" she cried. "I'll dry off by the fire, but I'll be damned if I'll strip stark for a gaggle of wild men."

He chuckled. "Ye put me in that lot, do ye, Bess?"

"First in line," she flung back at him. "Crowned king of barbarians and lunatic savages."

"But ye love me all the same," he teased.

"Aye," she answered softly. "God help me, but I do."

Later, after Bess and Kincaid and the two Cuna had shared a meal of grilled sloth and wild plums, Che and Hah-kobo slipped out into the rainy night. Kincaid stretched out beside the fire, and Bess curled up in the shadow of his arms. "Why did they go?" she asked sleepily.

Kincaid chuckled. "I don't think they feel too comfortable so close to a witch. I think Che's afraid that you'll turn him into a frog."

He was weary unto death, and his eyelids felt as if they were packed with sand, but he knew he couldn't sleep. He trusted the Cuna, but only so far. In the end, Bess's safety depended on him.

What had happened here in the clearing was almost too much to accept. The gold was real enough, but before, when the headhunters had attacked them and the ghost . . . He'd gone over and over it in his mind, trying to make some sense of it. He didn't believe in spirits, or witches, or water sprites. There was no way he could believe this woman in his arms was anything but flesh and blood. But there was no way he could dismiss what he'd seen with his own eyes either. A ghost. An Indian ghost had appeared in a bolt of lightning and slain two of the Caribs by pointing his war club at them. It was crazy, and thinking about it could make a man crazy.

Bess lifted his hand to her lips and kissed his knuckles one by one with caresses as soft as thistledown, causing ripples of excitement to run along his spine. "Am I a witch? Truly?" she asked him.

He stared down into her pale face. In her prone position, her eyes were in shadow, but he felt the heat of her azure gaze and his throat tightened. "Ye have the sight, that's certain," he admitted. "And there's many would name ye witch, but I see no evil in ye, lass. Your soul is as lovin' and pure as mine is black."

He felt her flinch. "Don't say that about yourself," she said. "You're a good man."

His gut wrenched. "I've spent a lifetime killin' men, some a hell of a lot better than me." Robbie Munro's homely grin rose in his mind's eye. "I'm bound for Hell, and I've none to blame but my own actions."

"Soldiers fight."

"I killed my best friend over a whore."

"Yes, and you can't change it. But that's in the past. It doesn't mean you don't deserve some happiness. You can build a new life with me."

He tensed. "That again."

"And again. I do love you, you thickheaded Scot, and I know you love me. Can't you admit it?"

"Admitting that I love ye isn't hard to do, sweeting. 'Tis what I know you'll ask next of me that's difficult."

"To be my husband?" She twisted in his arms to face him. "You're not a poor mercenary any longer. That gold you brought up from the pool today makes you a rich man."

It was true that his share would buy a lot of dreams, but they were still a long way from home free. "Provided we live long enough to spend it."

She touched his bare chest, running her hand lightly over his skin, rubbing and massaging until he sighed with pleasure. "It wasn't all bad," she murmured, "being a soldier's woman."

"Nay," he answered, remembering the days and nights they'd spent together. There was no chance for them together. He knew it, and if she were thinking straight, she'd know it too. Bess deserved better.

He ground his teeth together as she rubbed lazy circles on his chest. Where would he find a woman to match her? Nowhere. She was one of a kind. And he knew he'd miss the feel of her hair through his fingers, and the sound of her husky laughter, so long as he drew breath. "Ah, Bess," he murmured. He lowered his head and kissed her tenderly, and the taste of her lips was as sweet as new-milled cider.

For a few seconds he allowed himself to think of what life would be like for him as her husband, living on Fortune's Gift. Clearing virgin forest

land and planting crops . . . Watching the turn of
the seasons with Bess at his side . . . Raising children together. Seeing her with his child at her
breast . . .

"Nay, Bess," he repeated, more for himself
than for her. "It's too late for us. I'll take ye home
to your grand plantation, and after a time you'll
forget about me and meet a gentleman who's
worthy of ye."

"Don't tell me that," she said. "It's not that
you're not good enough for me, and you're lying
to yourself if you say so."

"And why would I do that?"

"Because you're afraid of letting yourself love
me. You loved your first wife and she betrayed
you. Now it's easier to make excuses than take
the chance of being hurt again."

He let go of her and sat up. "Ye know nothin'
of it, Bess. Leave it be."

"I'm not Gillian, Kincaid. I'm Bess. You can
trust me."

"I got over Gillian a long time ago."

"Did you?"

Resentment flared. Biting back the angry words
he wanted to say, he rose, snatched up his pistol,
and walked out into the rain.

"How far can you run?" Bess called after him.
"You know that what I'm saying is the truth."

He kept walking until the rush of water over
the falls drowned out her words and the pool was
a black void at his feet. Rain beat down on his
face and soaked his breeches, but he paid it no
heed. He knew he was being stupid, laying himself open for a Carib arrow or a jaguar's attack,

but he had to get far enough away from Bess to think.

His bare foot struck something hard, and he stooped and picked up a thin, beaten-gold, footed vessel with a hawk's head. It was too dark to see more than a faint glow of reflected light, but as he ran his fingers over it, there was no mistaking the winged handle or the proud, curved beak on the spout.

He held a fortune between his hands—the price of an earl's ransom. For once in his life, a wild dream had come true. Idly, he stroked the line of embossed feathers that made up the beautiful design.

Once, long ago, when he was no more than sixteen, he'd run from a lost battle. It was a stormy night; he was in unfamiliar territory with the enemy in hot pursuit. All around him, he could hear the clash of steel, the boom of muskets, and the screams of dying men. He'd run a long way. He had a sword slice along his arm and he was losing blood fast. In the darkness he couldn't see much of anything, except when the cannon fire lit up the sky. Suddenly, just ahead of him, the path split. One way would lead him back to his own troops, the other to the opposing army's territory. Trouble was, he didn't know which trail to take.

Kincaid ran a hand through his wet hair. He felt like that tonight. Despite all he had said, he knew if he left Bess he'd never buy land or carve his own farm out of the wilderness. He'd find another war, and then another and another. He'd spend his share of the gold on strong rum and loose women. And when his luck ran out, there'd be no one to mourn his death or even to carve his name on a grave marker.

Calling him a coward was a killing offense, but Bess had done it. And, sweet Jesus, she was right. He was as scared as he'd ever been in his life. He wanted to believe her when she said she loved him. He wanted to trust her, but he didn't know how.

All she had to do was look at him with those sea-blue eyes and he hardened like a steel pike. Brushing her hand with his, seeing the curve of her neck when she bent down to pick something up, watching the proud way she walked—all those things tore his guts apart . . . and made him feel ten feet tall. Bess was the most sensual woman he'd ever known. He thought about her every waking hour, and she danced through his dreams at night. She infuriated him, tested him at every step, and made him want to take her in his arms and keep her safe forever.

Want Bess Bennett as his wife? Hell, yes, he wanted her. But it was the keeping her that worried him. If he took her for his own and she ever left him for another man . . . He wasn't sure what he'd do. God knew he'd never want a repeat of what had happened with Gillian. But the emotions Bess caused him were so much stronger than those he'd felt for his first wife that he was at a loss for direction. If he took Bess, will she nill she, he'd hold her fast, no matter the cost.

Intuition prickled the skin at the back of his neck and he whirled around to see a pair of green eyes staring at him from the jungle. ''Go on, get out of here!'' he yelled. ''Ha!'' He clapped his hands together, and the glowing orbs vanished.

"I might as well be a married man," he muttered. "I've lost all reason if I'm standing in the rain arguing with a jaguar." He turned back to the fire and Bess.

He found her there, huddled by the flickering light. "Can ye forgive a fool?" he asked.

A smile more radiant than the sun spread over her face as she threw herself into his arms. "Kincaid?"

He hugged her against him, thinking how warm she was, how much dearer to him than all the gold that the Spanish had ever stolen from the Indians. He tilted her chin up and kissed her long and passionately. "Damned if I know what they'll call ye," he said gruffly when they parted long enough to take a breath. "I don't even know if Kincaid's my first name or my last."

"I thought of that," she said. "And Robert will serve very well. Mistress Robert Kincaid, if you please."

"You've figured it all out, have ye, ye bold wench?" He kissed her throat, and traced the hollow between her swelling breasts with his lips.

She laughed softly and tightened her arms around his neck. "I've waited long enough for a proper proposal."

"Who said that's what it was? I was only askin' what a man would call ye if I did ask."

"You're not weaseling out of this, Robert Kincaid," she teased between kisses. "I take your words as a declaration that you intend to make an honest woman of me, and I accept."

"Ye do, do ye?" He groaned, trying to maintain his dignity when his heart was turning cartwheels in his chest and he felt like a drowning man who'd just been pulled from the sea.

"I love you," she said softly. "Love you more than I love Fortune's Gift."

He nibbled her bottom lip provocatively. "That's reassuring."

"But you're still an unrepentant horse thief, and I'll not wed you or forgive you until you bring back my Ginger."

"So the knight is set a noble task to win the hand of the fair maiden?"

She laughed. "You hardly qualify as a knight and I'm no maiden. But, yes, bringing home my horse is a noble task, and there'll be no marriage lines until my mare's safe in her own pasture."

"And if the beast is crab bait?"

"She'd better not be."

"You'd reject my suit for the sake of a dead horse?"

"If you know what's good for you, Scot, you'd best pray for Ginger's safety. I raised her from a foal."

"You're a hard woman, Bess."

"Am I?" She took his hand and brought it to her breast. "I love you very much, Kincaid."

"So you've said," he murmured, savoring the soft feel of her breast. He swallowed at the thickening in his throat as he slid his free hand down over her hip and cupped her sweet, rounded bottom. She raised her face for his kiss and parted her lips so that he had access to her silken mouth.

The weariness fell away as his blood grew hot and his loins tightened. He and Bess dropped to their knees together, and he pushed up her shirt

and tasted the perfect buds of her ripe breasts.
"Little Bess," he whispered. "I want ye so bad."

Her hands were all over him, touching, caressing, making him rock-hard and aching for her. He
groaned with pleasure as she arched her hips
against him and uttered little cries of yearning.
He wanted to fill her with his love, to claim her
once and for all as his, to feel her one with him.

She wriggled free and pulled the shirt over her
head. His breath caught in his throat as he surveyed her beautiful naked breasts, the proud arch
of her throat, and the long, slow look she gave
him. Intense desire burned in that steaming
gaze—desire to match his own hunger and an in-
born sensuality that glowed white-hot beneath her
rosy skin.

He reached out slowly and untied the ribbon at
the back of her head, letting her wild auburn hair
fall loose in curling waves around her bare shoulders. She smiled at him and moistened her lips
with the tip of her tongue.

His erection strained against the thin cloth of
his breeches. Breathless, wanting her now, yet not
wanting this moment to end, he stripped away
his single garment. "Come here, woman," he
said to her.

She didn't move, and when he grabbed for her,
she laughed and ducked back to snatch up a wild
plum from the remains of their supper. Deliberately, she sank her white teeth into the ripe fruit,
and the juice ran over her lips and down her chin.
Her eyes dared him as she offered him a bite of
the plum.

"I'd rather have it from your lips," he said,
seizing her and pulling her hard against him. He

knew that the jaguar paced not far from the firelight, but the lure of Bess's tempting body beckoned more urgently than the voice of reason.
Laughing, he kissed her mouth and ran his
tongue over the trail of sweet purple juice.

"That was nice." She sighed and squeezed the
fruit, letting the dripping juice spatter over her
throat and upthrust breasts.

"Aye," he agreed. His swollen cock pressed
hot and throbbing against her leg. He kissed one
breast and then the other, tasting her skin and
licking the sticky plum juice away. Her nearness
and the feel of her warm body were driving him
mad; he knew he was nearing the point of no
return. "You are a witch," he whispered as she
caressed the length of his tumescence with her
teasing fingers. "You've cast an enchantment
over me, and there's only one way to deal with
you."

"Ummm," she murmured, tightening her grip.
"And just what is that?"

"Some things are better shown than told." The
force of his need was gathering like a flood behind a dam. Sweat beaded on his forehead. The
pulse of his blood drummed in his veins. It took
every drop of willpower that he possessed to keep
from throwing her back against the heaped palm
branches and driving his aching manhood deep
inside her sweet, wet folds.

"I want you to love me," she whispered. "I
want you so bad." She moistened the tips of her
fingers and brushed them over his swollen skin.

"You've no need for these," he said, making
short work of her breeches. She was breathing as
hard as he was now, and he could tell by the

tenseness of her muscles that she wanted him as badly as he wanted her. But he was unwilling to let this pleasant game end just yet, no matter how exquisite the torture was for both of them.

The plum fell from her fingers and he caught it. "Not yet," he rasped. Slowly, he drew the remains of the fruit down across her flat belly to the soft curls below. She moaned softly as he continued on, kissing each drop away, letting his tongue linger on her damp, quivering skin until he brushed the entrance to her secret garden.

With a cry, her fingers dug into his arms and she crushed him to her. "Now!" she urged. "Now. Love me now."

Tears clouded his eyes as he granted her wish and his. He crouched over her and drove deep and hard into her loving embrace. She rose to meet him thrust for thrust, until their shared flood of passion broke over the dam with a wild rush of thunderous joy, and he was carried beyond the bounds of physical pleasure to the warm, pure state of utter contentment.

Twice more that night she came into his arms. And it was as if they were drawn together by a power they could not resist, using the act of love and a growing flame of trust to sear away everything in the past that had hurt them, leaving only the shimmering promise of a shared tomorrow.

Dawn came slowly, filtering through the lacy green boughs overhead, slowly silencing the night cries of the jungle, replacing them with the ever-present bark of the monkeys and the chirp of the cicadas.

Kincaid sat up and rubbed his eyes, looking around. Bess was curled up next to him, still sleeping, one arm thrown over her head. The fire had gone out, and ants were marching over the heaped saddlebags. Kincaid stood up and stretched, retrieved his pistol and reloaded it with what he hoped was dry powder, dressed, and walked outside the hut.

The golden treasure still lay strewn beside the pool. As he neared the bank, he drew in his breath sharply. On the muddy rim of the tarn were the clear tracks of a big cat. Sometime in the night, while he and Bess had made love, the jaguar had come to drink.

"Damn," he muttered. The thought that he'd put her in danger by his carelessness grated on his nerves. He washed his face and hands, cleaned his teeth, and drank deeply. It was beginning to rain again as he returned to the shelter.

"Will ye sleep all day, woman?" he called to Bess. She stirred, and he glanced at her face. Was her skin more flushed than normal? "Bess," he said. "Wake up, lass." He bent and touched her arm.

A chill ran down his spine as he felt the unnatural heat of her skin. "Bess?"

Her eyelids fluttered. "Kincaid? " She moistened her lips. "I'm thirsty," she said. "So thirsty."

Pain lanced through his gut as she opened her eyes and he met her feverish gaze. "Bess, are ye all right?" he asked, knowing the answer, but asking all the same.

"I don't feel so good," she said weakly. "My head hurts, and I . . . I don't feel so good."

Chapter 21

❧ ❧❧❧

Jamaica, October 1725

Bess fought to open her eyes, but the struggle was almost too much of an effort. From far away she heard the soothing voice of a woman that had brought her back from the black void again and again. A window casement creaked and a light breeze kissed Bess's hair. Then the bright island sun spilled like hot syrup across her face.

"Missy. Missy, you must eat."

Obediently, Bess parted her lips and allowed the shadowy figure to spoon rich, salty broth into her mouth. A drop escaped and rolled down her bottom lip. Before she could lick it away, a soft cloth brushed her skin, catching the errant liquid.

"Your color is much better today, Missy Bennett. The fever leaves you, I think. I have made you hot tea, a private blend from Java. Would you like some?"

Bess sighed and turned her head away. The plump down pillows beneath her head and the clean smell of fresh sheets gave her a feeling of security. She didn't want to open her eyes and let in the light. So long as she wrapped herself in the mantle of sleep, she didn't have to face reality.

A cool sponge massaged her forehead. "The fever plays with you, Missy," the rich, throaty voice coaxed. "You must fight it. Open your eyes for Annemie. Do."

Stubbornly, Bess refused to listen. She let go of consciousness and fell backward, slipping down and down, until her head was filled with the chirp of cicadas and the harsh shriek of jungle parrots . . . until the roar of howler monkeys drowned out the tinkle of wind chimes and the muted swoosh of surf lapping against a sandy Caribbean shore.

Kincaid's strong face materialized from the wet green curtain. His nutmeg-brown eyes burned into her soul. She could feel his arms around her and hear his urgent pleading. "Don't die, Bess. Live. Live for both of us."

Images rose and faded, some clear, others hazy and indistinct. The pounding in her head reverberated like the tramp of marching soldiers; her skin burned like fire. She blinked, her eyes blinded by the shimmering radiance of a golden mask flashing in the blood-red glory of a setting sun. Green leaves arched overhead and the overwhelming scent of rotting vegetation submerged the smells of immaculate linen and steaming tea.

Blue waves ebbed and flowed through her mind . . . azure swells tipped with white . . . a sapphire sky over a tropical sea. She tasted the sting of salt against her tongue . . . felt the ocean wind in her tangled hair.

Bess moaned softly as she summoned Kincaid's memory from the depths of her heart. Kincaid's deep laughter . . . His muscles rippling beneath the bronzed skin of his broad back as he leaned into the oars of a small, open boat.

Suddenly, Bess's body jerked violently as she heard again the thunder of a cannon's roar. She screamed and sat bolt upright, reliving the terror of the cannonball striking the water close beside the longboat. "Kincaid!"

"Elizabeth. Elizabeth, what's all this?"

A man's arms tightened around Bess and her eyes flew open at the stranger's touch. She stared at the elegantly dressed gentleman who pressed her back against the pillows, and she tried to make sense of where she was and what was happening to her.

"Lie back. Lie back and rest." He stroked her forehead and cupped her chin gently in his hand. "Shhh," he soothed. "Your fever's rising again."

Swirls of red-and-black colors teased the edges of her consciousness as an unfamiliar male scent filled her nostrils. Bay, and rum, and tobacco. No, not the odor of a pipe, but snuff overlaid with French toilet water. Bess fought to orient her senses. Where was she? Who was this middle-aged Englishman in the floral-brocaded banyan and black, curled wig? She caught sight of his slender, ringed fingers as he brushed stray tendrils of hair away from her face.

"Annemie! Come and give her something to lower the fever. Annemie!"

Annemie. That was the woman, Bess reasoned. Who, then, was this man? Her lips formed the question, but no sound came from her throat. She tried again. "Who . . . who are you?" she rasped.

He smiled. "Peregrine Kay, my dear," he murmured. His smile widened. "Falconer. At your service, my lady."

Too weak to fight and too tired to care, Bess closed her eyes and willed herself back into the welcoming arms of fevered dreams and half-remembered pictures.

Steel clashed against steel. All around her, men were fighting with swords and pistols. The *Tanager*'s deck ran red with blood. She stood at Kincaid's back, a flintlock in one hand. A swarthy sailor ran at her, crimson cutlass arcing through the air. She raised the pistol and fired point-blank into his chest. Rudy stumbled through the smoke, his black face twisted with pain, and fell almost at her feet. The handle of a knife protruded from his back. She screamed, but her cry was lost in the blast of a musket.

Hostile faces surrounded them. Flames shot up from the deck. Kincaid shouted something to her, but she couldn't make out his words. Bloody hands grabbed at her. Kincaid cut and slashed, forging a protective circle of bright steel. Then another shot rang out and he shuddered as a musket ball pierced his flesh.

"No!" Bess screamed. "No!"

Kincaid sank to the deck and she flung herself over him, shielding his body with her own. "Bess," he whispered hoarsely. "Leave me. Save yourself, lass."

A swearing seaman ripped her away from Kincaid and drove a rapier into his side. Then merciful blackness ended her agony, and she tumbled down and down into a bottomless abyss.

"Elizabeth."

The commanding tone dragged her back to the

present. She opened her eyes. Kay was still hovering over her, watching with the eyes of a predator. "He's dead," she said. "I saw him die."

Peregrine nodded solemnly. "That was weeks ago. You must put it behind you, my dear, and concentrate on getting well." He took her hand and lifted it to his lips, brushing her knuckles with a light kiss. "I will care for you now, sweet Elizabeth. Nothing or no one will ever harm you again. You have my word as a gentleman on it."

Bess tried to pull her hand free, but he held it tightly. "Bastard."

He smiled, releasing his grip. "You have her spirit. I'm glad of that. You look so much like her, you know, except for the eyes. Your eyes are as blue as—"

"Who? Who do I look like?" she demanded, struggling to a sitting position.

He laughed. "Why, Lacy Bennett, of course. Your grandmother. You're the very image of my father's portrait of her."

Weakness assailed her, and she covered her face with her hands. She wanted to get up and run, to strike out at Kay's smug face, but her body betrayed her. She was so weary, and the bed was so soft. She felt herself sinking back again. "Please," she whispered. "I must know. Please. Is Kincaid really . . . really . . ." Her eyelids closed and she didn't hear Kay's mocking answer.

It was raining when Bess woke again. The shutters were closed and barred; the room was in twilight. Raindrops drummed rhythmically on the low roof and patted at the precious glass windowpanes.

She felt stronger, but when she tried to raise her head off the pillow, the elegantly furnished chamber began to spin.

"Rest," Annemie advised, coming into the room and closing the door behind her. "Rest is what you need, missy."

Bess looked around anxiously. "Where is *he?*" She glanced back at the tall woman, wondering if she was wife or servant.

"He is lying down," Annemie explained. "His own health is fragile. Too much excitement is bad for him." She lifted a painted glass chimney and lit a lamp from the candle she carried.

"Who are you?" Bess asked.

"I am Lord Kay's housekeeper." She extinguished the candle with a silver snuffer and brought the lamp to the table beside Bess's bed. "I have been with his lordship for many years and he allows me great liberties in his household."

"You have been very kind," Bess said. "Thank you."

Annemie nodded and paused beside the bed. Only her twisting hands gave away her desire to speak further.

"Why am I here?" Bess demanded. The events of the past weeks were hazy, but she remembered the expression on Kay's face when he introduced himself, and she remembered that he had identified himself as Falconer. "Why does he hate me?"

The housekeeper's lips thinned to a narrow line and her forehead wrinkled. "He does not hate you," she said softly.

"If he is Falconer, as he said, then he wants to kill me."

Annemie shook her head sadly. "No, lady. No more. You misjudge him."

"He sent the ships after us, didn't he? His men attacked the *Scarlet Tanager* when we came out of the jungle."

Annemie sighed. "There is no need to trouble yourself over what happened in the past. You are in no danger from Lord Kay now."

"And Kincaid?" Pain knifed through Bess as she said his name. Her eyes welled up with tears. "Falconer—Kay—killed the man I loved. He might as well have murdered him with his own hands."

Annemie lifted a finger to her lips. Without speaking, she went to the door, opened it, and looked out into the deserted hallway. Then she closed the door and returned to Bess's side. "In the parlor is a portrait of your grandmother," she began. "My master's father, Governor Matthew Kay, loved her desperately. She betrayed him with another man—the man who later became your grandfather—and together, they stole a fortune in Spanish treasure from him."

"But—" Bess started.

"No." The older woman lifted a palm. "You must listen. I will speak of this once and never again. And if you ever tell that I said anything, I will deny every word."

Bess sank back against the pillow and nodded.

"Your grandmother, Lacy Bennett, haunted Governor Kay's memory. In his later years, after a brilliant career of government service, his mind began to wander. My lord, Peregrine Kay, was the governor's only child. All of his life, my master heard of the evil done to this family by your grand-parents. Revenge against them became an obses-sion, first for the governor, and later for Lord Kay.''

Annemie drew a chair close to the bed and sat down. "I know that none of this is your fault," she said to Bess, "but you must realize the depths of wrong done to the honor of this family. My master suffers from the falling sickness. No." She lifted a work-worn hand again to silence Bess. "Do not speak. Listen, for it pains me to be dis-loyal to Lord Kay."

Bess took Annemie's hand and squeezed it. For a fraction of a second Bess experienced a haze of swirling blue color. I can trust this woman, she thought. Here, in the home of my enemy, I've found one who will tell me the truth. She offered Annemie a weak smile.

Encouraged, Annemie went on. "The governor is long dead, but Lord Kay considered it his duty to continue to search for your grandparents and right the wrong. When informants told him that they were dead, his feud passed from them to the next generation. Your parents."

"My mother died years ago."

"And your father chose to abandon his duties on your plantation and vanish in the Orient. That left you." Annemie exhaled softly. "My lord wished you dead. That much is true. From bits I overheard, I know that he ordered ruffians to attack and burn your plantation, and I know that he has tried—so far unsuccessfully—to seize your land."

"But if he wants me dead, then why—"

"Shhh," the housekeeper warned. "Keep your voice down. I did not say he wants you dead—you are completely safe here, perhaps safer than you have ever been.'' She closed her eyes for a few seconds, and when she opened them, Bess read the anguish written there. "Often love and hate are two sides of the same coin. My master has forgiven you for the sins of your grandmother.''

"And?'' Bess urged, knowing there was more.

"And he has decided that what he had always felt for Lacy Bennett was not hate but admiration.'' She looked Bess square in the eye. "He wants to make you his bride.''

"What?''

"He thinks he loves you.''

"Loves me? After what he did? After he killed the man I—''

"Be still. I endanger myself by confiding in you.''

"He must be insane! Surely he can't expect me to agree to marry—''

"Do not refuse his offer so lightly. My master may not be a royal governor, but he makes and breaks governors. His wealth could not easily be counted. He controls ships, islands—I daresay his opinion weighs heavily in the House of Lords itself.''

"You're suggesting I marry a murderer? A madman? I'd sooner—''

"Don't say that!'' Annemie said sharply. "Never say that. You don't know him. He is a good man, kind and trustworthy. He is the soul of—''

"If you feel that way, you marry him!''

Annemie's face paled to ivory in the twilight room. She turned away and looked toward the shuttered window. "I am the grandchild of a slave,'' she whispered hoarsely. "If only I could wed with my Peregrine. If only I could.''

"You love him?'' Bess asked.

Annemie's strong hands trembled. "I have always loved him."

"I'm sorry," Bess said.

The woman stiffened and looked back at Bess. "Do not feel pity for me. I live in my master's house, I sit and eat at his table, I see to his needs, and I listen to his joys and sorrows. Is that not as much as most wives can expect?"

"And his bed?" Bess asked. "If I became his wife, would you continue to share his bed?"

"You insult me," Annemie said, "and you insult Lord Kay. He isn't like that. He respects me and his own conscience. I have never gone to his bed. Never."

"I apologize. This is all so much," Bess murmured. "I never meant to hurt you. It is just that I expected—"

"You expected Falconer to be a pirate, in his home as well as on the sea."

"Most men in his position—"

"Exactly." Annemie nodded firmly. "Most men would take advantage of the granddaughter and daughter of slaves. But my Peregrine has allowed me my honor. He respects me—even loves me in his own way, I'm certain of it." Her expression softened. "He is not a man for other men either, if you are thinking that. He has all the normal tastes, but he never brings his mistresses here. He keeps them decently hidden away in their own apartments. If you become his wife, be assured he will never shame you with loose women."

"I will never become his bride. I'd rather be dead."

"Dead is a long time, and the grave is dark, they say."

"Let him kill me if he wants. He's already killed Kincaid."

"Kincaid?"

"He was the man I wanted to marry—the father of my unborn child."

Annemie smiled. "Yes, you are telling the truth. I bathed you. I felt the swelling of the little one in your womb. You are not far along, but you are with child."

Bess clutched her belly. "You don't think the fever—"

"It is too soon for you to feel life yet, but only time will tell if your babe has been damaged by your jungle illness. You were out of your head for many days. When they brought you to me, I did not think you would survive."

"Better if I hadn't."

"You speak with the foolishness of the young. Life is always better than death. My Yoruba grandmother clung to that thought in the filthy hold of a slave ship, and later, when they took away her firstborn son and sold him away from her forever. She was a wise woman, my grandmother. She could teach you much."

"This is Kincaid's child I carry. I've got to take him home to the Chesapeake."

"My lord will never let you go."

"I'll go, or one of us will cease to breathe— Falconer or me."

"I would kill you myself, Missy Bennett, to protect my master."

"Then why did you tell me all this?"

Annemie's shoulders slumped forward. "Because I too am a woman, and I could not bear the thought of him marrying you who must hate him, instead of me. You will only bring him unhappiness, and my master has had so much unhappiness. He deserves better.''

''But you don't hate me?''

''I should. When they first brought you here, I wanted to let you die. But as I tended you day after day, I realized that you want this no more than I do. We are only women, after all. We are at the mercy of men as always.''

''I've never considered myself—''

The ringing of a bell broke into their conversation and Annemie rose swiftly and started toward the door. ''My master needs me. I must go. Think on what I have told you, missy. But do not ask me any more questions, for I will not answer. I have told you all that I can. Use what I've given you, but always remember—if you try to hurt him, I will kill you.''

Bess moistened her lips and reached for a glass of water on the bedside table. Annemie was a complex person, one who would make a better friend than an enemy. Bess took small sips of the citrus-flavored, sweetened water, and willed her headache to recede.

She was still as weak as a newborn pup, but she needed her wits about her if she was to find a way to save herself and Kincaid's child from this madman, Peregrine Kay. The overwhelming pain she felt when she thought of the big Scot was too great to bear, so she mentally pushed it away. There would be a lifetime to mourn him. Now she must survive.

''I approve.''

Bess choked, spitting water across the fine cotton coverlet. ''Kutii!''

The Incan leaned casually against the shuttered window, feet apart, arms crossed over his tattooed chest. He was wearing just a simple red loincloth, and his only weapon was a stone knife with a handle of bone, inlaid with a shell pattern. The sheathed knife dangled from a woven cotton belt slung over one muscular shoulder. Today, Kutii looked younger than she had ever seen him, younger than she felt.

He flashed her a rare smile, and she realized that long ago, he must have set many feminine hearts aflutter with his ready charm. "Do not drown yourself."

"Where have you been?" she demanded.

"You forget. My time is not yours. Did I not slay the headhunters for you? Did you see how they fled before me? I am a mighty warrior still, am I not?"

"This is no time for your boasting, Kutii."

His brow creased in a frown. "This one needs not boast. His deeds speak for him. Men speak of Kutii the great—"

"Stop it." She covered her face with her hands. "Not now, Kutii. Not now. I need your help." Hot tears spilled from her closed eyelids. "They killed him. They killed Kincaid. Didn't you see it? Why weren't you there then?"

The Indian made a sound of derision. "Don't do that. You know this one cannot bear to see the child of his heart weep."

She took her hands away and glared at him. "Why shouldn't I? I've reason to cry," she sniffed. "They killed the man I loved right in front of me. And now I'm being held prisoner by—"

"Yes, yes. This one knows of Peregrine Kay. He is much like his father, and this one knows him well. He was a great trial to the Star Woman, your grandmother."

"He wants me to marry him."

"I heard the woman tell you so."

"I won't do it."

"You cannot. Matthew Kay's blood is not fit to mix with that of my people. Not yet."

"What?"

"Your grandmother was my adopted daughter. You carry her blood and that of my people. You must marry the father of your child. He is the chosen one, the strong man your grandmother told you would come in your time of great need."

"You're not making sense, Kutii." She struggled to concentrate on his fading image. "Don't go. Stay with me. I need you." Even his oddly accented English was growing fainter.

"To remain in your time—to make this warrior bright—is hard. Your power to see and hear beyond time is dimmed by fever."

"What must I do, Kutii?" she begged him. "Don't leave me yet. Please."

"You have her strength, little one. All that your grandmother was is in you. Have faith in yourself."

"I can't do it alone."

Only the dark eyes remained, a glowing mask against the white shutters. The rest of his outline was gone. "You are not alone," his voice promised.

"Kutii!"

Her anguished cry broke off, leaving only the sound of the wind and the rain in the still room. Where the Incan had stood were only shadows.

Bess closed her eyes. And from the depths of her heart came a message, one radiant with hope.

He's not dead.

Chapter 22

Three days had passed since Bess had seen
Kutii and become convinced that Kincaid was
still alive. Annemie still cared for her with all the
tender consideration of a friend, but, true to her
word, she had refused to discuss her master or
his affairs again.

Bess reasoned that Peregrine Kay would not
demand that the wedding take place so long as
she remained ill, so she concentrated on regaining her strength without allowing anyone to know
she was getting better. When she was alone at
night, she would get out of bed and walk around
the room. In the daytime, when there was too
much danger of being discovered, she contented
herself sleeping as much as possible, and eating
and drinking everything that Annemie brought to
her bedside.

Lord Kay, the man she now knew to be Falconer, visited her every day at noon, at six, and
again, precisely at nine o'clock in the evening. Always, he was a complete gentleman. He did not
attempt to touch her or threaten her in any way.
He asked after her health, offered to play cards
with her, and chatted politely about the weather
and events currently occurring in Jamaica and the
Caribbean. If Bess questioned him about the fate

of the crew of the *Tanager* and the whereabouts
of the fortune she and Kincaid had brought out of
the jungle, he ignored her completely and went
on chatting about mundane affairs. Although she
saw that Peregrine Kay was an extremely astute
man with a keen intelligence, she found his company disturbing.

She never asked him about Kincaid. Since Kay
had led her to believe that Kincaid was dead, she
didn't expect him to change his story, and she
didn't want him to know that she thought he was
a liar.

Her memories of leaving the camp by the waterfall were still clouded by her sickness. She did
remember that Kincaid had thrown back into the
pool what gold he and the Indian guides couldn't
carry. What remained of the treasure had been in
the longboat with them when she and Kincaid returned to the ship. Once the fighting began, she'd
not given the treasure another thought until she'd
awakened in this house.

Hour after hour she'd lain in bed and tried to
summon Kutii's image again, but he hadn't come.
Her grandmother had possessed the ability to see
into the future or—sometimes—events occurring
in the present in a different place. Bess had always been afraid of the *sight* she had inherited
from her grandmother, but now she wished she
had more of the power, not less. She wanted desperately to know for certain if Kincaid was alive—
and, if he was, whether he was recovering from
his terrible wounds or near death.

On the fourth day, she could wait no longer.
When Annemie came to open the shutters in the
early morning, Bess was standing beside the bed.

"I want to dress," she said. "I must see Lord Kay at once."

Annemie nodded. "I thought you must be feeling better. I will have a bathing tub and suitable clothing brought to you. My master will be available at twelve. He—"

"No," Bess said firmly. "Not noon. This morning." When she had awakened just before light, she'd had the strongest sensation that Kincaid was in even greater danger—that if she didn't act quickly, his life force would be extinguished like a snuffed-out candle. "Please tell Lord Kay that I must see him before breakfast."

Annemie hesitated. For an instant she gave Bess a shrewd gaze of appraisal.

Bess's stomach churned. She had no idea what she would say to Kay when she saw him. She only knew she must do something at once. "Please," she said.

The older woman nodded. "I like you, missy. If my master must take a wife, perhaps you are not the worst one for this household."

Bess shook her head. "Oh, but I am," she answered softly. "My heart is already pledged to another. Nothing can come of this relationship with Lord Kay that will not bring sorrow to all of us."

An hour later, bathed, perfumed, and dressed in an indigo undergown and an old-fashioned azure silk gown with puffed sleeves, Bess was ushered into a bright, richly furnished parlor by Annemie. Lord Kay was seated at one end of a magnificent teakwood table set for a morning meal for two. He rose as Bess entered the room, smiled, and bowed with all the grace of a polished courtier.

"Elizabeth. How lovely you look this morning! I'm so pleased you could join me for breakfast." He waved her to a place beside him. A uniformed footman pulled out the chair, and Bess allowed him to seat her.

Lord Kay smiled warmly at Annemie. "I know you'll not mind breakfasting in the kitchen this morning, my dear. Elizabeth and I have much to discuss."

Bess glanced up at Annemie and read the anguish written on her plain features as clearly as if it had been lettered in gilt script.

"As you wish, sir," Annemie murmured. She curtsied and left the room with the footman.

Lord Kay was dressed in a black, purple, and orange flowered morning gown of quilted satin, and a black silk turban. But despite the fashionable clothing, there was no hint of effeminacy about him. His long face was weathered by the tropical sun and the sea, and the intensity of his gaze as he scrutinized her figure left no doubt as to his romantic interests.

He was freshly shaven. Bess could still smell the bite of shaving soap in the air and see damp spots on his face. His hands were clean, his long fingers heavy with rings, and his nails neatly trimmed.

Her gaze drifted past her host to rest on the large oil portrait that hung on the wall. The painting was that of a striking woman standing on a cliff overlooking the sea. Bess's lips parted in astonishment; she might have been staring into a mirror. The gown she was wearing and the one

in the painting were identical. "My grandmother," she said. "That's my grandmother
when she was my age."

Kay chuckled. "The gown is a nice touch, don't
you think, my dear? I had it made especially for
you. I'd like you to wear it at our wedding—along
with this." He picked up a velvet case from the
table, stood up, and came around behind her.

Bess stiffened as he hung a heavy necklace of
gold disks around her throat, then fastened earrings in her ears. She couldn't see the design on
the earrings, but she caught a gleam of gold reflection in the silver wine goblet in front of her
plate. She raised one of the disks and stared at
the beautiful etchings of strange symbols, mythi-
cal birds, and animals. She didn't recognize the
piece as one she and Kincaid had brought out of
the jungle.

"This is part of my inheritance from my father," Kay explained. "Lovely, isn't it?" He returned to his chair and sat down. "Are you
hungry? Shall I have—"

"We need to talk," Bess said. "Lord Kay, I—"

"Peregrine," he corrected her. "You must call
me by my Christian name. There is no need for
formality between us."

"What do you want of me?" she asked frankly.

His lips curved in a smile, but his eyes hardened. "My dear, you disappoint me. I thought
you knew. We are to be husband and wife."

"Why?"

"Because I want you. I've wanted you for
years." He leaned forward and reached across the
table to take her hand.

She pulled it out of his reach. "I'm not my

grandmother, Peregrine. And I'm not the Elizabeth you imagine. I'm Bess, and I can't marry you."

"You don't have a choice." His voice took on a steely edge.

"But I do. I don't belong to you. I'm not a slave like Annemie."

"She's not a slave," he snapped. "Annemie is a free woman and a devoted friend. She—"

"She is yours to command. I am not. Whatever is behind this scheme of yours—whatever happened in the past between your father and my grandmother is long dead."

"Don't speak of things you know nothing about."

"You cannot control my life. I don't love you. I could never love you. You nearly killed me. You sent men to burn my plantation. And you stole the gold that I risked my life to get. Why in God's name would you ever think I'd wed with you?"

"You owe it to me, Elizabeth. If you become my wife, it will end this feud between our families and wipe away the disgrace committed against the Kay name. My father—"

"Your father is as dead as my grandmother. It's over, Peregrine. It's *been* over. You are an intelligent man. If you know anything about me, you know that I'd sooner kill you or kill myself than marry my enemy—a man I can never love."

Peregrine's face darkened and his breathing quickened. "I will have satisfaction, madam. You have wronged me, and I will redeem my family's name."

"What will satisfy your honor?" she demanded. "What do you want? Really? You don't

want a wife who would make every hour of your
life miserable. A wife you would have to imprison
to keep her from shooting you in the back.''

''If I cannot have your love, in time I will have
your respect. But you will be mine.''

''I carry another man's child. Do you know
that?''

He nodded. ''Annemie told me. But it doesn't
matter. You can keep your little bastard. We will
tell Jamaican society that you are a widow. Do
you think I'm some sort of monster that I'd separate a woman from her babe?''

''I know that Kincaid is alive,'' she said softly.
''I love him. I want you to give him back to me,
give us our gold, and let us go.''

''By God!'' Peregrine slammed his fist down on
the table, sending flatware flying. ''By God, you
do think I'm mad!''

''Not mad,'' she said boldly, rising to her feet.
''Not mad. A man larger than life, perhaps, but
never mad. You've proved that much. Who has
done what Falconer has done in his lifetime? Did
Governor Kay wield so much power for all his
titles? You are a greater man than your father,
Peregrine, and this is beneath you.''

''If I'm not mad, you think I'm a fool, to give
up both you and the gold,'' he scoffed.

''You are no thief, Lord Kay,'' she said, attempting to play on his vanity. He was far worse,
but she knew she'd get nowhere with him by in-
sulting him.

''The gold belongs to me, in payment for what
was stolen by your grandmother.''

''It is mine,'' she insisted. ''Not Lacy's. Not
your father's. Mine. And if you take what is mine,

you become the worst sort of pirate. And from this day forth, when you look in the mirror, you will see the face of a common thief.''

He shrugged. ''The gold was never important—you were what mattered. And I will not be denied my revenge.''

''Revenge. Is that what marriage is? A punishment?'' She took a deep breath and tried to control her trembling. Her instinct told her that Kay was more dangerous than the jaguar that had attacked them in the jungle. She knew she could not afford to make a mistake with him. ''Is it my hand in marriage you want, Peregrine, or is it sex?'' she asked him. ''If you want me to sleep with you, I will. But I want Kincaid alive. And I want your promise that you will set us both free and never trouble us again.''

He sank down in his chair and covered his face with his hands. For long minutes there was no sound in the room but the tick of a tall case clock and the muted whisper of their breathing.

Bess clenched her hands into knotted fists beneath the folds of her skirt. What had she said? How could she have offered to sleep with this man? Had she taken leave of her senses? But the truth was, for Kincaid's life and the life of their unborn child, she'd sleep with the devil himself.

At last, Peregrine raised his head and looked at her. ''My father never knew Lacy in the biblical sense,'' he said. ''She was a prize that always escaped him.''

Bess waited.

''Willingly? You would give yourself to me willingly?''

''One night.''

"A week," he countered.

She shook her head. "No. I couldn't. One night only, and then you must give us our freedom. And the gold," she added as she sat down.

"It is not what I'd planned," he said.

"Things in life rarely are." She moistened her lips. "But this might be better than what you'd planned. You thought you wanted me dead, then you changed your mind. You can change your mind about this too. Wouldn't it take a better man to heal the breach between our families than it would to exact a heartless revenge?"

"My father loved her, you know," Peregrine said. "He loved her and she utterly destroyed him in the end. He lost his mind before he died."

"Lacy didn't destroy him," Bess said. "He destroyed himself. He let the hate eat him up. You don't have to do that. You can prove yourself a wiser man than he ever was."

"You value yourself highly, Elizabeth Bennett, to think a night in your arms would be worth a fortune in gold and a lifetime of enmity."

She forced herself to smile at him, then lowered her lashes seductively. "If I do not, sir, then who will?"

"And what makes you think your Scots barbarian is still alive?"

She tilted her head and looked up at him. "You are a businessman, Peregrine, are you not? You did not reach your position by destroying useful tools. Since you didn't know if Kincaid would be of use to you, I think you kept him alive."

"You are very clever for a woman."

"You reasoned that you could always kill him later." Kincaid is alive, she cried inwardly. He is!

Her insides turned cartwheels. She wanted to cry and weep all at the same time, but she didn't. She concentrated on Peregrine Kay and what he was saying.

He chuckled. "We would have made a good match, Elizabeth. Are you certain you won't reconsider? I could make you a very rich woman."

"I'm already rich."

"I would be good to you."

"I'm sure you would."

"One night, I believe we agreed on. And I would expect your full . . . cooperation."

"Our ship, our gold, Kincaid—alive and breathing—and my own freedom." Bess's heart was pounding so hard that she was afraid Kay would hear it and know how frightened she was. "And . . ." She flashed him a charming smile. ". . . your undying friendship."

"Men have killed for my friendship," he said deliberately.

"I would have your word, sir." She stood and extended her hand to him. He took it, and as he squeezed her fingers, she willed herself to know if he was telling the truth or not. If he meant to keep the bargain, then she could do no less—but if he was lying to her . . . If Kay was lying, she'd have to think of another plan, and the time for schemes was fast running out.

"You have my word, as a gentleman." The left corner of his mouth turned up in a sly smile. "But I give you warning, Elizabeth. If you try to cheat me of my prize, I'll hand Kincaid over to the Spanish. They'll castrate him and sell him to the Turks. He'll spend the rest of his short life as a galley slave."

She hesitated, clinging to his hand as the awful threat sunk in. The first faint flashes of violet that crossed her mind's eye were bewildering until she perceived the thread of silver that laced through the purple color. And when she let go and nodded her assent, she was certain in her heart that she had made the right decision.

Nearly another hour passed before Kay instructed Annemie to take Bess to the place where Kincaid was imprisoned. The housekeeper's manner was cool as she led the way out of the house and through the garden. At any other time, Bess would have marveled at the beautiful trees and flowers, but now her only concern was Kincaid and his well-being. Bees buzzed around her head, bright-colored birds flew overhead, and lizards scampered across the grass in front of her feet, but she didn't stop to look at them.

"Have you seen him?" she asked Annemie. "Are his wounds healing?"

The older woman didn't answer. She just kept walking.

A black gardener doffed his woven hat as the two women swept by. "Morning, Missy Annemie."

"Albert."

At the far end of the garden was a dovecote, and beyond that were the stables. Two grooms, also very dark-skinned, were working with the horses. One was exercising a roan colt; the other was plaiting the mane of a gray mare. Both men called out a greeting and removed their hats.

The housekeeper acknowledged them and walked faster. A hound ran toward her and she sent it scampering away with a sharp command. After passing the carriage house, she made a right turn, walked down a shallow grassy slope, and continued onto a well-worn path.

Bess tried again. "I'm not going to marry him, Annemie. I've made a bargain with him, and when I keep my part, I'll go away—forever. Please tell me, have you seen Kincaid?"

"You will soon see for yourself this man of yours." They followed the trail for about five minutes, then skirted the edge of a sugarcane field and entered a grove of palms. "There," Annemie said, pointing to a stout wooden enclosure. "My master sometimes keeps slaves here if they cannot be trusted."

A light-skinned native carrying a musket stepped out from behind a tree to block their way.

"Let us pass," the housekeeper said. "Lord Kay has given orders that the lady shall see your prisoner."

Two more brutish men stood in front of a locked gate. They stepped back and slid the iron bolt at Annemie's request, and the women entered a small, high-walled courtyard. A huge iron sugar kettle stood at one end of the space. Stocks loomed at the other. Three walls were upright logs; the fourth side was a long, low building lined with doors. Four white men, armed with pistols and cane knives, obviously guards, squatted on the dirty sand, casting dice.

"Each door is a single cell," Annemie explained. "Sometimes more than one man is kept in the stalls. If they are, they are chained."

Bess cringed. The high walls cut off the breeze and made the enclosure an oven under the burning rays of the tropical sun. The fetid air smelled of fear, and sweat, and human waste. This jail was far worse than the stable they had passed. She knew that Kincaid had been badly injured in the fight on the ship, and she wondered how he could possibly survive under these conditions.

Annemie called to one of the men. Reluctantly, he abandoned the game and came to open the door she pointed to. As the sunlight poured into the dark cell, Bess saw Kincaid lying on a mat on the floor and ran to his side.

"Kincaid," she cried. She laid a hand on his forehead. His skin was hot to the touch. "Kincaid," she said, taking hold of his bare shoulders and shaking him. "Can you hear me? It's Bess!"

"He had a physician," Annemie said. "Twice he came to wash and bandage him. Without medicine, your man would have died. The sword cut to his side was minor, but the musket wound was slow to heal. He broke a guard's arm. That is why he is chained."

Bess ran her hands over the bloodstained bandages and down his filthy body. He was naked, his hair snarled and sour-smelling, his skin covered with insect bites. A rusty leg iron encircled one ankle, and a heavy chain bound him to a ring in the wall. There was no water and no food in the cell. "Oh, Kincaid," she whispered. She laid her cheek against his, then kissed his parched lips.

His eyes flickered. "Bess?"

"I'm here," she said. "I'm here, and you're going to be all right. Everything's going to be all right." She turned on the burly guard with the rage of a cornered lioness. "How dare you leave him like this?" she demanded, coming to her feet and jabbing the man squarely in the chest with her fist. "I want clean water for him, and I want it now. I want him washed—no, I'll do that myself. Bring me soap and towels." She hit him again. "Are you deaf?"

The guard swore a foul oath and raised a meaty hand to strike her down.

Bess didn't flinch. "Touch me," she warned, "and Lord Kay will have you boiled alive in that sugar kettle."

Annemie chuckled softly. "That's so," she said. "Lord Kay has bidden me to tell you to follow the lady's orders as you would his own." She moved to stand by Bess's side. "I would do as she asked, if I were you."

Bess glanced at the housekeeper. "You know what I need here. Can you see to it?"

"Yes, missy," Annemie said. "I will be pleased to help you." She followed the guard out of the cell, leaving Bess and Kincaid alone.

Bess turned back to Kincaid and knelt beside him. "It will be all right," she murmured. "I'll have you out of here in no time."

"Falconer?"

"Never mind Falconer. I'll deal with him." Her hands were trembling as she stroked his hair and cradled his head in her lap. "I'll take care of you, Kincaid. I'll take you home to Maryland. You'll see." Her eyes clouded with tears and she blinked them away.

Kincaid's fingers clamped around her wrist. "Get away if you can," he whispered hoarsely. "Don't worry about me. I've survived this long— I'll survive to escape." His eyes looked golden in the shadows; they seemed to glow with a fierce inner light. "I can take care of myself, Bess. It's ye I've failed."

"You don't understand," she said. "Falconer— Peregrine Kay—is going to let us go. He's giving us back the *Tanager* and the treasure. We're going home."

Kincaid's grip tightened. "Why?"

"Trust me. I'm going to get us out of here."

"Why, Bess?" he demanded. "Why would he let us go?"

She didn't mean to tell him, she didn't want to, but it was impossible to look into Kincaid's intense gaze and lie. Before she knew what she was saying, the words tumbled out. "One night," she said. "I've promised him one night. And after that, we're free to go."

"The hell ye say!"

"I had to," she whispered. "It was the only way."

"No. I'll not have it."

"I gave my promise, Kincaid."

He let go of her wrist and turned his face to the wall. "Do as ye will," he whispered, "but if ye sleep wi' him, I'll have no more of ye. We're through. Do ye ken that, woman—we're finished. I'll nay have a woman whore for me—not to save my soul from hell!"

Chapter 23

B ess stood by the open window and stared out into the black Jamaican night. There was no moon, and fog lay thick on the ground. From far off came the haunting sound of African drums, and closer, the lapping of waves against the sandy beach. Bess's hands were clenched around the windowsill so tightly that she could feel numbness creeping up her wrists. And her heart was as heavy as the great slab of limestone that reared out of the garden lawn just beyond her window.

Kincaid's infected wound had been tended by the physician again. The Scot had been washed and fed and properly clothed. Now he lay aboard the *Scarlet Tanager*, which was anchored in the harbor. Bess didn't believe he would die, but he was still very weak. When they had moved him, he'd insisted on walking on his own two feet, but he'd staggered like a drunken man. And he was still fevered.

Lord Kay had told her that a crew and a captain waited for the morning tide to take her back to the Chesapeake, and he'd assured her that her fortune in gold artifacts was safely stowed aboard in her cabin.

She was ready to take her leave of Jamaica and Peregrine Kay—as soon as she had completed her side of the bargain. Tonight she would belong to Falconer; tomorrow she would be free. Bess wondered if the price she had agreed upon had been too great.

The physical coupling between herself and Kay she could bear. There could be no rape when she had given her consent willingly. And even if he was cruel during the sexual act, he could cause her no greater pain than she was already suffering.

Kincaid would never forgive her. Never!

No amount of arguing had convinced him that she had made a sensible decision. What were a few hours in the arms of another man compared with the lifetime they would have together? Kincaid's stubborn ire was irrational.

But now there would be no years of happiness . . . no wedding with Kincaid . . . and no father for her coming child. He'd said that this proved to him, once and for all time, that she was no better than his dead wife, Gillian. By bargaining with Kay, Kincaid felt, she was betraying him and his honor as a man in the worst way.

But for her there could be no other choice. To save Kincaid from butchery and enslavement, she would give herself to a dozen pirates like Peregrine Kay. She would trade her life for Kincaid's life and never regret her decision. So tonight there were no tears and no regrets, only bittersweet longing that things could have been different.

Bess drew in a deep breath, filling her head with the heavy scent of a dozen strange flowers. This island air was deceptively soft, she thought, all sugarcane and salt breeze and wild citrus. It lulled you into a false sense of paradise.

She wished with all her heart that she were home on the Eastern Shore, smelling the rich brown earth, the spicy tang of pine needles, and the musty autumn leaves. The oaks and maples would be a glorious rainbow of gold and green and orange, and overhead, vees of ducks and geese would be winging their way south to winter in the Chesapeake marshes. The air would be crisp and clean. In early morning, the horses would crack a skim of ice on their water troughs, and frost would gleam like scattered diamonds on the fields. The farmers would be grinding tart apples into cider, and their wives would be baking pumpkin and sweet potato pies.

Home . . . She was going home tomorrow with the gold she needed to rebuild all that had been destroyed. And if she couldn't have the man she loved beside her, she could make a future for his son and all the people who depended on her at Fortune's Gift.

The sound of a door opening behind her caught her attention, and she turned to see Annemie coming into the bedchamber carrying a tray. "Is it time?" she asked bleakly.

"Yes, missy. The clock has already struck half past ten. My master awaits you."

Annemie was dressed in a simple white linen night rail tied at the throat with narrow pink ribbons, much like the nightgown Bess was wearing. Annemie's light brown hair hung loose around her shoulders and her slender feet were bare. She looked more attractive tonight than Bess had ever seen her.

"We might be sisters," Bess said, trying to cut through the wall of awkwardness between them.

"Look at us." She laughed. "Oh, am I wearing your—"

"Yes, missy," the housekeeper said. "We are much of a size."

"Too tall for beauty, both of us," Bess agreed.

"You are kind for a witch." Annemie sighed. "My skin freckles like yours, but there the similarity ends. I know that I am plain."

"Strong," Bess corrected her softly. "Not plain, but strong. And you move with a grace I will never have."

Annemie smiled and ducked her head shyly. "A gift from my African grandmother."

The two eyed each other like schoolchildren meeting for the first time, not ready to make peace, but not ready to fight either. Bess picked up a brush and began to brush her already smooth hair. It had grown longer since she'd come to the Caribbean, and the hot tropical sun had brought out red-gold highlights. For once, Bess hated the color of her hair. Perhaps if it were dull and gray, Kay wouldn't have desired her.

"You do not wish to do this thing," Annemie said.

"But I must. I've given my word."

Annemie sighed again. "You talk like a foolish man. We are women—have you forgotten?"

Bess stared at her in puzzlement.

"Will this night make you happy?"

"Of course not," Bess replied.

"Will you make my master happy?"

"Not unless he fancies making love to a wooden ship's figurehead."

"Then he will be greatly disappointed."

Bess's anger flared. "You expect me to care?"

"Then why do it?"

"You know why! If I don't, he'll turn Kincaid over to the Spanish. And he'd keep me a prisoner."

"You wish only to go home with your man?"

"Yes." Bess swallowed hard against the thickening in her throat. "But there's no other way."

"My Yoruba grandmother had a saying, 'There is always more than one way to satisfy a man.' "

"How, Annemie? How can I get out of sleeping with Lord Kay and escape his revenge?"

The older woman beckoned Bess closer. "Tonight, when I brought him his evening brandy, it contained a potion that will cloud his mind."

"He will fall asleep?"

"No. For he is clever. He would know you had tricked him. The ground roots will make our deception easier. You must go to him. Let him embrace you if you must, but do not speak. Say only yes or no. I have told him that you are overcome with shame, and that you had begged that there be no candle in his bedchamber tonight."

"But I still don't understand. If the drug won't put him to sleep, then how can—"

Annemie raised her hand for silence. "In the Bible it speaks of the servant who went to her master in place of her mistress. Once you are with him and he knows it is you, you will offer him wine from this jar. You must take some, but you must only pretend to drink it. This wine contains a sleeping mixture, very powerful, but it will keep him asleep only for a short time. When he has succumbed to it, I will take your place in his bed."

"You would do this for me?" Bess asked.

"Not for you, but for my own self. I have loved

him for many years, and I have kept myself pure. Now that I am no longer young, I do not wish to grow old without knowing what it feels like to be loved by a man. If my master would have a sacrificial maiden, let it be one who goes to him with a heart full of joy—one who will give him only happiness."

"And if we get away with it? What will happen in the morning? He will awaken and know you are not me."

Annemie laughed. "I will give him such a ride that he will sleep the sleep of the dead. At dawn, I will slip from his bed. And you will be free to go to the ship. Who will stop you? While my Peregrine dreams of his night in heaven, you and your Kincaid will ride the morning tide out to the open sea."

"And later? What will you do later?"

The housekeeper shrugged. "I did not know I would do this until tonight. Who knows what I will do tomorrow? But one thing is for certain. I will not go to my grave a bud, but a full-blooming flower." She took Bess's hand. "And my Peregrine will have memories of this night to delight his old age."

"And if he catches us?"

"He will kill us both," Annemie assured her.

"Then we have no choice. We must do it so well that he doesn't catch us."

Her brave words echoed in her head as she followed Annemie through the house to Peregrine's apartments. And with each step, her apprehension grew.

"This is as far as I can go," the housekeeper said, pointing to a wide door. "There. Keep your head about you, missy. And remember, he must drink the wine, and you must keep him at a distance until he grows sleepy.''

Bess shivered as she took the wine tray and knocked twice. ''Don't fail me, Annemie,'' she whispered.

''Come in,'' Peregrine called.

With a nervous final glance at the other woman, Bess pushed open the door.

Peregrine was a shadowy figure in the darkened room. ''Come in, my dear. I've been waiting for you.''

Bess hesitated in the doorway and tried to get her bearings. Without a candle or moonlight, she was at a loss. The bedchamber smelled of orchids. Although she couldn't see them, she knew that there were dozens of them in the room.

''Come to me, Elizabeth.''

She forced herself to take one step and then another across the cool wooden floor. She was so frightened she could hardly hold the tray with the wine and the glasses steady. Tall, curtainless windows stood open to the veranda; she could feel the warm breath of the night air on her bare skin. I can't do this, she cried inwardly. I can't. But she kept walking. ''I brought wine,'' she said. Her voice sounded overloud to her ears.

A hand closed on her arm. ''Give me the tray,'' Peregrine said. ''I've no need for spirits tonight.''

God knows I have, she thought with black humor. Kutii! Where the hell are you when I need you? It took every ounce of her willpower to stand still as Peregrine took the tray, set it down, and cupped her face in his hands. When he bent to kiss her, she felt his stale breath on her lips and turned her head away.

"You're cold," he said. "Come to bed. I'll warm you."

"I'm . . . I'm not ready," she said. "Please, I'd like a glass of wine."

He kissed her throat.

"No!"

"You gave me your word. We had a bargain, Elizabeth. Are you breaking that—"

"No," she murmured, backing away from him. Her hand brushed against a bedpost. "I . . . I feel silly in the dark," she said. "Light a candle."

"As you wish." She heard his footsteps and the door opened. "Bring a lamp," he shouted. A male servant hurried from the adjoining chamber, and a pale circle of light illuminated the master's bedchamber. She had been right about the orchids; there were large porcelain bowls heaped with them on every table. Kay's oversized bed loomed above her, hung with heavy draperies of red flowered silk.

Her gaze lit on Peregrine Kay, and she couldn't contain a gasp when she saw that he was stark naked. He wore not a stitch, not even a nightcap to cover his shaved head. His chest was sunken and covered with black hair, and he had a pronounced paunch. Before she averted her eyes, Bess noted that he was still very well endowed, and he was definitely having a better time than she was.

He returned to the bed carrying the lamp. Bess put the table between them and hastily poured two glasses of wine. Drops splashed onto the tray and over her hand.

"Your modesty is refreshing," he said.

She glanced toward the open windows, wondering how far she could get if she ran. Not far enough, she decided. "Let's drink to our bargain," she said. She kept her eyes fixed on his face as he took the glass she offered. She lifted her own goblet and pretended to drink.

"Into bed, Elizabeth. I tire of this game."

She climbed up onto the high mattress, still clutching her glass, and scooted to the far corner. "Tell me about your empire," she said. "I have heard of Falconer for years, but I never guessed that—"

Peregrine set down his glass and slid into bed. He reached for her, and Bess deliberately spilled her wine down his bare chest. He swore, and at almost the same instant, the chamber door banged open.

"Stop this abomination!" Annemie said.

Kay grabbed Bess's hand and glared at his housekeeper. "How dare you?" he demanded. He paused, and glanced back at Bess. "You're wearing the same gowns. What trickery—"

"Take your hands off my woman!"

"Kincaid!" Bess cried.

Peregrine whirled toward the deep, burred voice at the window, and Bess twisted out of his grasp. "What the hell—" Peregrine said.

"Dinna move," Kincaid ordered. He stepped over the low sill into the bedchamber and raised the double-barreled flintlock pistol until it pointed dead center at Peregrine's chest. "Dinna even breathe." Kincaid's own breaths were deep and ragged, and he was as gray as tallow, but he held the weapon steady as he leaned against the window frame for support.

"No! Don't hurt him," Annemie cried. "Take her and go, but don't shoot him."

"You're mad, all of you," Peregrine said. "How far do you think you can get? I don't know how you got through my guards, but—"

"Cease your blather," Kincaid said. His voice was low and strained, but Bess knew that Kay's life hung by a thread. "Bess."

She moved around the bed to Kincaid's side. Sweat beaded on his forehead and the bandage around his chest was soaked through with fresh blood. She slid her shoulder under his free arm to help him stand. "You shouldn't have come," she murmured. "You're killing yourself."

"You cheated me," Peregrine said. "We made a bargain and—"

"No!" Annemie dashed across the room and put herself between Kincaid and the man she loved. "Let them go. The fault is mine, sir. It was me who drugged your wine. I wanted to take her place in your bed. If someone must die tonight, then let it be me."

"Why, Annemie?" Peregrine demanded. "Why would you betray me after being faithful all these years?"

"Because she loves you," Bess said. "She couldn't bear to see you bed another woman in this house."

"Annemie, is this true?" he asked hoarsely.

The housekeeper looked into Peregrine's eyes. "Forgive me. I know who I am and what I am, but I . . ."

Peregrine shook his head. "We will talk of this

later. For now, stand aside. Do you believe me a coward to need a woman to protect me?''

"Stand aside," Kincaid warned Annemie.

"I will not," Annemie answered in her throaty voice. "If the Scot would kill you, he must kill me first."

"Leave them both and come away," Bess urged Kincaid. "We'll go to the *Tanager* and catch the outgoing tide."

"I believed you, Elizabeth, when . . . when you . . ." Peregrine's speech slurred and he began to tremble. "Annemie . . ." A frightened look came over his face.

"Please," the housekeeper begged. "My master is not well." She put her arms around Peregrine and covered his nakedness. "Go," she said. "He is ill. He cannot harm you now, and when he awakens he will remember nothing." Peregrine's body convulsed, and Annemie pushed him gently back against the heaped pillows.

"Will you give us time to get away?" Bess asked.

"Yes," Annemie replied. "Go now, while you can."

Bess tugged at Kincaid's arm. "He's having a seizure," she said. Kincaid lowered the pistol. Together they stepped back over the windowsill and out onto the veranda. "What of the guards?" she whispered.

"They'll give us no trouble," he answered.

As they moved away from Peregrine's bedchamber into the garden, Bess heard Annemie crooning to her master.

"I'm here, my sweet. Annemie is here, and no one will harm you."

"You shouldn't have come for me," Bess murmured to Kincaid. His skin was hot, and he was hurting terribly; she could tell by the unnatural way he moved.

"Aye, you'd have me stay aboard the *Tanager* and let ye sell yourself to that popinjay."

"I had a plan."

"To hell with your plan."

"You're near dead on your feet."

"I'm nay dead yet, am I?" he snarled.

"Give me that pistol," she insisted. "Damn, you're bleeding all over me."

"Who's the man here, ye or me? I'll keep my weapon."

She staggered under his weight while tears rolled down her cheeks. "Stubborn fool."

"Aye, I am that."

Miraculously, they saw not a soul as they crossed the garden and neared the stables. Bess prayed that the stable hands didn't sleep with the horses. She knew that Kincaid could never walk as far as Kingston Harbor. Her only hope of getting him there was astride a mount.

"Where are ye takin' me?" he demanded. "This isna the right way."

"I'm going to steal us a horse."

"Hellfire and damnation. And who is it that made my life a misery because I borrowed a horse?"

"Be still," she whispered. "You'll wake the dogs. Are you drunk, to ramble so?"

"I've not had a drop."

She eased him down to the ground. "Wait here while I see if I can get a horse."

"I was stealin' horses when ye were—"

"Hush," she said, putting her fingers over his mouth. "Hush, Kincaid." For a few seconds, she leaned against him and held on to him tightly. "I'll get us a horse, darling. I will. We'll go back to the ship and . . ."

She trailed off, suddenly realizing that she had no idea which way to go. "I don't know where the harbor is."

"I do," he said, breathing hard. "But I'm not so sure I can stay on that horse if ye catch one."

She kissed him, one brief kiss, and then she was up and running across the open space to the stables. She reached the building and pressed herself against the wall, then felt her way to the first set of Dutch doors. Each stall opened outward; she remembered that much. The question was, where could she find a saddle and a bridle in the dark? And if she did, would a strange horse let her saddle him and lead him away without making a fuss?

The first stall was empty. The second contained an animal too flighty to try to steal, but at the third she was lucky. The animal was wearing a halter and was tied by a length of stout rope to a ring in the far corner.

Running her hands over the mare, Bess spoke soothingly to her. When she was satisfied that the animal was gentle, she tied the end of the rope into a slipknot, forced the mare's mouth open, and eased the loop over the horse's lower jaw. The rig made a crude bridle, but it was better than none. When the mare didn't protest, Bess led her out of the stable and back to the spot where she'd left Kincaid.

"No saddle," she apologized as she helped him

to his feet. "But you won't have to walk." She led the horse to a mounting block and held her still while Kincaid struggled up onto her back. Then she hiked up her gown, swung up behind him, and dug her heels into the mare's side. "It's going to be all right," she said, as much to convince herself as to convince Kincaid. "We'll get back to the ship and sail out of Kingston Harbor before Peregrine Kay can stop us. We're going home, Kincaid. Home to Maryland. We can be married in the church at Oxford and—"

"We'll not be wed," he rasped.

"What?" She swallowed back the disappointment. "But I thought—"

"I love ye, Bess. I'd die for ye. But I dinna wish to wed with ye."

"Why not?"

"I've had my fill of cheating women. I'll not lay my heart open to be broken again."

"Cheating? You call what I did cheating? I never meant to sleep with Kay. I—"

"Dinna lie to me, woman. Ye did mean to sleep with him. Ye told me so yourself."

"I did, but that was before. Damn it, Kincaid. It was to save us, so that we could get away. And then Annemie and I made this plan—"

"I'll not change my mind. If I'd not come for ye, can ye swear ye'd not have let him have his way with ye?"

"I didn't want to."

"No. But ye would have."

For a long time they rode in silence. And when he finally spoke, it was to say, "I'll take ye back to Fortune's Gift, Bess. I'll see ye safe on your land. But then we'll divide our gold, and we'll each go our own way.''

"But I didn't sleep with him," she protested.

"Ye still dinna listen, do ye?" he said. '' 'Tis your way, Bess. Ye set your mind to a thing, and then ye do it—no matter what I think. I want no wife who will not heed me, and I want no woman who thinks so little of my honor that she'd make herself a whore to save my life.''

"You're a fool, Kincaid," she murmured.

"Maybe."

"I carry your child."

He sighed. "If that's true, then we'll have the ship's captain marry us. I'd not willingly bring another bastard into the world, and I'd not shame ye publicly. I'll give him a name, and I'll send you money for his upbringing. But I won't live under your roof, Bess.''

"You'd abandon your own son?"

He forced a bitter laugh. "If ye like, ye can send him to me and I'll try my hand at being a father. But you've a way with helpless creatures. I've no doubt you'd be a better mother than a wife. And a damn sight better parent than I'd be.''

"I want you to stay with me. I love you."

"And I love *you*, lass. But a house canna have two masters, and we'd be forever fightin' to see who wore the breeches in our marriage.''

"Kincaid!"

"We'll speak no more of it, woman. I'll see ye safe home, and I'll do my duty by ye if we've made a child between us. But I'll nay change my mind about this, and that's the end of it.''

Chapter 24

~~~~~~~~~

Maryland, May 1726

Bess climbed into the high two-wheeled dog cart and took the leathers in one hand. With a flick of the reins and a loud click, she urged the dapple-gray hackney into a swift trot down the curved front lane of Fortune's Gift. The baby kicked Bess hard and she laughed as she caressed her swollen abdomen with her free hand. "Soon, little one," she murmured. "Soon you'll be born, and out in all this big, bright world."

Bess smiled with satisfaction as she looked at the wide field of tobacco spreading down to the river on her right. The fragile plants were green and upright, promising to make the best leaf crop she'd ever had. On the other side of the lane marched tall rows of Indian corn.

The showy gelding's slim legs moved gracefully in long, low strides. The high red wheels spun merrily as the fancy yellow gig fairly flew over the hard-packed road. It was a sparkling late spring day—one which promised a warm afternoon and lengthening sunlight for the burgeoning crops—and Bess was still seeing the beauty of the Eastern Shore with an almost hushed reverence.

The winter voyage home to Maryland from Jamaica had been uneventful and swift. And with the treasure the *Scarlet Tanager* had carried, Bess had been able to clear her debts with Myers and Son, and purchase supplies to rebuild all that had been destroyed by the marauders' attack. Even after she had divided the gold with Kincaid, there was still enough to assure Fortune's Gift's future for a long time to come.

As the road ran down to the water, it split into two paths. One led to her dock, where the *Tanager* and two smaller boats were anchored; the other, to the pastureland and, beyond that, the edge of the virgin forest Kincaid was clearing for new tobacco fields. Bess reined in the dapple-gray just enough to keep from overturning the cart and headed left onto the woods trail.

She glanced at the brownish-green surface of the river, edged by thin strips of buff and, interspaced with clumps of cattails and ferns. A great blue heron tucked in his wings, stretched out his long neck, and drifted down to perch on cranelike yellowish legs in the shallows. Farther out in the current a rusty-headed canvasback bobbed, tail up, then vanished beneath the water. And just to the left of the dirt lane, a red-winged blackbird swayed on a willow branch and scolded the passing horse and cart with a sharp *chek-tee-err*.

Bess smiled and called, "Good morning to you too." Not even Reverend Thomas's unexpected visit just after breakfast had been able to ruin her lighthearted mood. She'd given the disapproving cleric twenty minutes to tell her that her behavior was a disgrace and that people were talking, offered him breakfast, and made her escape in the dog cart.

She had cared not a fig for neighbors' gossip, that she—large with child—was still an unmarried woman. Kincaid had tried to force her to wed him on the ship once it had become evident that she was telling the truth about being in the family way. But she'd refused.

"When I marry, I marry for life," she'd informed him. "Since you have no intention of staying on Fortune's Gift with me, then I have no intention of becoming your wife and making myself subject to a man who will be conspicuous by his absence."

"Ye canna make our babe a bastard!" he'd threatened.

"Why not? It never killed you," she'd replied.

Their relationship had been stormy after that. Kincaid had insisted that he was leaving once she was safely home—but it had been three months, and he was still here. Bess chuckled to herself. First it had been the tobacco seedlings . . .

"I'll nay go until the seeds have sprouted in the woodlots," Kincaid had proclaimed sternly. "If they are not tended carefully, you'll lose them all."

"I'm capable of overseeing the seedlings," she'd retorted. "Who do you think did it last year?"

"Last year ye were nay a woman with a swelling belly."

A rabbit darted across the pathway, but the dapple-gray horse never missed a stride. Bess was glad she'd brought the cart this morning and not dragged herself up into the saddle. Riding astride was definitely more difficult with a great bulge in front of you, and Velvet, the mare she usually rode, had an aversion to rabbits. If she'd ridden Velvet, she might have been rudely dumped on her bottom.

Let's see, she thought, returning to the subject of Kincaid. After the seedlings were safely up and transplanted, then it was the dock that needed rebuilding, and then the barns. After that . . .

"I'll see your corn crop in, and then I'm going. There's nay use to argue with me, Bess. I've made up my mind," he'd said in that deep burr that never failed to make delicious shivers run up and down her spine. "I've my own future to consider, and it's growing late for me to think of spring planting on my own land."

There was no denying that having Kincaid to direct the farm workers and the lumbermen was a great relief. The grumbling from the bond servants had lasted just long enough for Kincaid to knock the first troublemaker head over heels. After that, whatever the inhabitants of Fortune's Gift might think about Kincaid's dubious past, they gained respect for him with every passing day. When Kincaid gave an order, men and women jumped to obey.

And he worked as hard and long as any field hand on the plantation. From early dawn until dusk, he rode the fields, carried fence rails, chopped wood, and hoed tobacco seedlings. Bess usually saw him only at the light meal in the late evening, when they sat down together in the great hall. By then, he'd washed the dust from his body and hair, tied his golden hair back in a damp queue, shaved, and changed into a gentleman's shirt, waistcoat, and breeches.

And for a brief few hours, Bess was able to pretend that they were man and wife. They rarely argued anymore. He was too excited about the day's progress and the plans for expanding the southern fields. They laughed and talked together like old friends, each one eager to share humorous incidents and dreams with the other.

He had taken her advice about his name. His freedom-from-indenture papers, now duly recorded in the courthouse in Annapolis, read Robert Kincaid. She never called him that, of course. For her, he would always be simply Kincaid, and no matter how respectable he became in the future, she knew that he'd remain—in her mind—an adventuresome rogue.

For the past week, Bess had missed their evenings together. Kincaid had informed her that he was going away on business matters and that he would return by Saturday. This was Sunday morning. When Vernon had brought the horse and cart around to the door, he'd assured her that he'd seen Kincaid having breakfast with the timber crew. Bess assumed that he'd returned sometime in the night and had slept in the bachelor quarters rather than come into the manor house and risk waking her.

They slept in separate rooms. It was not by Bess's choice. Married or not, she would have been willing to go on as they had begun. She missed him beside her at night, and she missed his lovemaking terribly. But so long as he remained stubborn, she had been determined not to beg him to return to her bed.

But today, when she'd awakened alone and lay curled around a pillow, feeling Kincaid's child kick within her, she'd decided they'd played the game long enough. She had fretted over his absence and worried herself sleepless that he'd find a plantation for sale and not return to Fortune's Gift at all. Today she would confront him and insist that he realize he'd been behaving like a spoiled child.

He loved her and she loved him. There was no reason that they shouldn't marry and live happily ever after. Actually, she'd wrinkled her nose and laughed aloud over that. Happily, perhaps, but never peacefully . . . They were both too volatile to get by without arguing from time to time . . . and—she had to admit it—locking horns to see which one would get the better of the other.

And since she'd already decided to become a dutiful wife, Reverend Thomas's sermon had been "preaching to the saved." I consider Kincaid my husband anyway, Bess told herself. Hadn't they pledged their love to each other and lived like a married couple? If they weren't *handfasted* in the old custom, then who was? She'd never felt she was sinning in giving and taking Kincaid's love. He was the only man for her, now and forever.

"In this world and the next . . ." she whispered to the dapple-gray horse. The animal flicked his ears, tossed his head, and quickened his trot.

Big trees, mostly oak, maple, and chestnut, stretched eastward from the river as far as Bess could see. A few charred stumps and piles of branches were scattered along the woods line. A team of spotted oxen blocked the road ahead.

From the forest came the ring of steel against green timber.

"Gee-hah!" the driver called. The huge beasts threw their massive shoulders against the thick leather harness and moved an oak log along. "Mornin', Miss Bess!" The workman touched his hat in greeting.

Bess waited until the oxen had dragged the log off the path, then flicked the reins again. The gelding trotted into the shadowy woods, and the sounds of chopping grew louder. A crash and the crack of breaking limbs came from her left. She slowed the dapple-gray to a walk and guided the cart past a pile of fresh-cut logs. Under the direction of a black man, another team of oxen was attempting to pull a fallen tree loose from the tangled underbrush.

"Mornin', Miss Bess," Big Moses said. He pointed with the tip of a bullwhip. "Mr. Kincaid's back that way."

"Thank you." Bess remembered that Kincaid had told her last week that he'd hired Moses Walker and his team of oxen to help out with the lumbering for a few weeks. "How's Sally and that fine boy of yours?"

"Right as rain, both of them. Sally says you call her when your time comes."

Bess nodded her thanks. She halted the gelding, climbed down from the cart, and tied the horse to a tree. Then she picked her way carefully through the chips and branches in the direction Big Moses had pointed. She found a game trail and followed that through a stand of cedar and found Kincaid busy chopping down a tall, straight beech tree. A dark-haired man, his face in shadows, stood next to him with a broadax in his hand.

When Kincaid caught sight of Bess, he said something to his companion, handed over the ax he was using, and hurried toward her. "I didn't look to see ye this early," he said. He was stripped to the waist and grinning like a man who'd just won reprieve from the hangman.

"Good day to you, sir," she said, stopping and waiting for him.

"Ye didn't ride out here, did ye?" he asked.

"No, I did not. I brought the dog cart." She smiled up at him. "Welcome home, Kincaid."

He took her arm gallantly and escorted her, not back toward the woods lane, but off through the forest into a small clearing. Then he stopped, caught her around the waist, and lifted her up onto a broad, flat-cut stump. She sat there, skirts spread around her and legs dangling over the edge. The stump was high enough so that her eyes were on a level with his. "I missed you," she said shyly. Now that she was face-to-face with him, it wasn't so easy to say what she'd practiced in her mind.

"I thought ye might." His features were immobile, giving no hint of what he was thinking. Only his nutmeg-brown eyes twinkled with mischief. "The crews dinna work so well when I'm nay here, do they, lass?"

"No," she admitted, "they don't. But that's not why I missed you." She nibbled at her bottom lip. Suddenly feeling a little dizzy, she steadied her balance with both hands. "This standoff has gone on entirely long enough," she said.

"Reverend Thomas came by this morning to tell me that we were a scandal on the Eastern Shore."

"Fancy that."

"Kincaid," she chided, "I'm serious. You know you love me. And you know you don't want to go away. You've been making excuses for weeks to stay here. We need to be properly married."

"For the sake of our child."

"No. For our sake. I'd never be happy without you."

"Not even here?" he asked wryly. "On the fabled Fortune's Gift?"

"Don't tease me," she said. "I'm serious." She took a deep breath. "I was wrong about Peregrine Kay, and I'm sorry. I didn't listen to you, and I got into trouble I couldn't get myself out of. If you hadn't saved me, I—"

"Is this an apology, woman?"

"In a manner of speaking."

"Is it an apology or not?"

She lowered her head, then looked up at him with teary eyes. "It is, sir. Please," she whispered. "Please, can we not try? I want to be a real wife to you, Kincaid. I want—"

"Aye."

Her lips parted in astonishment. "What did you say?"

"Aye."

"Aye, what? Aye, I was wrong about Peregrine? Aye, this is an apology, or—"

"Do ye never listen, woman?" he demanded.

"I don't know what—"

He stopped her with a kiss. He encircled her with his arms and pulled her against him, kissing her so hard and for so long that she felt all giddy inside.

"Oh, Kincaid," she cried when he let her up for air. "I do love you so."

He laughed and gathered her up in his arms again. "That's why ye make my life such a misery, is it?" He glanced back the way they had come. "David! It's all right! Ye can come out now!"

"What?" Bess said. She squirmed in his arms, trying to see, but Kincaid blocked her line of vision by kissing her again.

"Put me down," she insisted. "What are you—"

He swung her around and set her on her feet, supporting her with a strong arm. "I went to fetch your—"

"Father!" Bess cried in astonishment. She tore away from Kincaid and threw herself into David Bennett's arms, almost—but not quite—failing to see the chestnut mare he was leading. "Father, is it really you?" She was laughing and crying all at the same time. She stepped back to look at him. He was thinner and older than she'd remembered. His Indian-black hair was streaked with gray, and his face more deeply lined, but he looked hale and hearty.

"It's me, girl. I've come home, and my ship with me. But it was a near thing, I can tell you. We were aground on a hellhole off Java for months, and Chinese pirates— Well, there'll be plenty of time for all that later. What's important is that I'm home with a cargo of the finest silk and tea, and I've a contract with Song Lo for all the beaver pelts and tobacco I can carry."

"You're going back to the East again?" she said.

"Not until fall. I want to see this grandchild born. But first—" David Bennett fixed her with a stern gaze. "What's this about not wanting to make the heir to Fortune's Gift legitimate? Robert here says that you've lived with him as his common-law wife, and that now you're dragging your feet about the marriage lines."

Bess threw Kincaid a stabbing glance. "It was an honest difference of opinion, Father." She smiled at her parent. "How did you two meet, and where is your ship?"

"My ship is in Annapolis being unloaded, and we ran into each other there. Your betrothed was fetching home Ginger and her colt, although why your mare was there in the first place, I—"

Bess whirled around and embraced the chestnut mare. "You found her!" she cried. "You brought her back to me." The horse nickered and rubbed against her. "Good girl," Bess crooned. "Good Ginger."

"Aye, 'twas that or listen to your canting for the next forty years," Kincaid remarked. "Do you know what this foolish horse cost me? Twice what she's worth, not to mention the price I had to pay for her colt."

"Colt? She has a colt? And I suppose it was fathered by a dish-footed workhorse," she said, straining to see around the chestnut mare's rump. A tiny red face appeared behind Ginger's tail, all great dark eyes and white blaze beneath twitching ears. "Oh . . . ! He's beautiful!" she said. "Does he have a name?"

"I thought to call him Scot's Folly," Kincaid replied.

"Folly," she repeated, ignoring his sarcasm. "Little Folly." She hugged the mare. "You've done well for yourself if that's a woods colt," she murmured.

"Woods colt, nothing," Kincaid said. "I turned your mare in with a blooded stallion in a Chestertown paddock last spring."

"Why did you do that?" Bess asked.

He shrugged. "I'd had a nip or two, and it seemed the thing to do, at the time." He grinned at her. "Well, woman. Will ye nill ye? I'd say we'd best get to the house and have the reverend read over us from his Good Book."

"Here? Now?"

"The sooner the better, I say," her father put in. "From the looks of you, daughter, time for this wedding is fast running out."

"But . . . but . . ." She looked from Kincaid to her father. "Reverend Thomas may not be there still," she finished lamely.

"And since when has a minister come to Fortune's Gift and not stayed for at least two meals?" David scoffed. "He'll be there, girl. In fact, I sent Big Moses to make certain of it."

"You two! You had this all planned out! You—" She stopped in mid-sentence as Kutii appeared at the edge of the clearing. "You," she said.

"Would I stay away from my daughter's wedding vows?" the Incan asked. He wore a feathered breastplate, gold armbands on each arm, and a kilt of gold disks that hung to his knees. He smiled at her. "I was right about Kincaid. Admit it, little one. I was right, as I am always right where matters of the heart are concerned.''

''You're not always right,'' Bess said.

''No,'' Kincaid agreed. ''I am not, but between us, lass, we are hard to beat.'' He took her hand. ''Come, Bess. I'd make ye mine, before ye go into labor and make our child as much a woods colt as your Folly.''

Bess glanced back at Kutii. ''I'll settle with you later,'' she promised him.

But he merely laughed, fading until only his dark eyes glowed against the velvet shadows of the forest.

''Come, Bess,'' Kincaid repeated, taking her hand in his. Together, they walked out of the forest and into the bright meadow, and into all the days of wonder that lay ahead of them.